ALL FOR ALL

(CAST ADRIFT—BOOK III)

CHRISTOPHER G. NUTTALL

The characters and events portrayed in this book are fictitious. Any similarity to real persons, living or dead, is coincidental and not intended by the author.

Printed in the United States of America.

ISBN: 9798389094246

Independently published

Cover By Tan Ho Sim

https://www.artstation.com/alientan

Book One: Cast Adrift
Book Two: Standing Alone
Book Three: All for All

http://www.chrishanger.net
http://chrishanger.wordpress.com/
http://www.facebook.com/ChristopherGNuttall

Cover By Tan Ho Sim
https://www.artstation.com/alientan
All Comments Welcome!

PROLOGUE I

FROM: *A Short History of Galactic Civilisation V.XXVI.* Alphan History University (Terran Campus). 505PI.

EARTH'S ISOLATION FROM GALACTIC AFFAIRS, as far as anyone knew, came to an end when the Alphans, the *de facto* masters of the known universe, invaded, occupied and subjugated the planet. The human race did its best to fight back, and there were three major and over a hundred minor revolts during the first two hundred years, but against an enemy with massive technological superiority and the willingness to use it ruthlessly the revolts were futile. The Alphan Viceroyalty had plenty of carrots and sticks at its disposal, as the humans noted, and had few qualms about using them. There was no reason to think that humanity would ever see independence, let alone become a great power.

Indeed, by the time of the First and Second Lupine Wars, humanity had become one of the most useful client species in known space. Humans served Alphans as soldiers, spacers and industrial workers, as well as hundreds of roles the Alphans were unwilling or unable to perform themselves. Human starship designers lacked the first-rate tech of their alien masters—some advanced weapons and drive systems were kept solely in Alphan hands—but they put together modular freighters that revolutionized interstellar shipping and, it was later discovered, could be rapidly converted into cheap and surprisingly effective warships. Human traders, free and independent, wandered far from the Alphan Empire and brought back tales of wonders beyond the rim of explored space. Human researchers, even, pushed the limits of the tech assigned to their species, sometimes working on ways to improve it and, at others, figuring out how to duplicate the tech forbidden to them (and not get caught).

The Alphans did not notice. They had other problems. The First Lupine War was a brief set of skirmishes, just another border clash with an up-and-coming junior race that thought it could take on the masters of the known universe; the Second Lupine War was a determined attempt to destroy the Alphan Empire that came alarmingly close to success. The Lupines were technologically inferior, but they had the numbers *and* a willingness to take horrendous losses in order to wear down their enemies. If humanity had not fought beside its masters, adapting tactics and technology to meet their foes on an equal basis, the war might have ended in complete disaster. As it was, the Alphan Empire emerged victorious...but broken, bleeding, and with a whole string of new problems. The worst, they came to realise, was simple. What were they to do with the human race?

There was no way to avoid the problem. The humans had fought well and no longer saw themselves as subordinates. The demand for a greater share of power within the empire was becoming irresistible. Even loyalists thought human service deserved a great reward. The Alphans found themselves caught between two fires. If they accepted humans as equals, their empire would very rapidly become a *human* empire. The economic dislocation alone would be utterly disastrous. But if they refused, they would face another—and perhaps final—rebellion. The days when the human race was confined to a single planet were long gone. Now, humans had starships, modern weapons and a powerful presence right across the empire. The Alphans decided, reluctantly, to cut their losses and grant the human race its independence.

It was a shock. The economic dislocation of being cast adrift on a sea of interstellar troubles was quite bad enough, but the perception of weakness was worse. The Vulteks—a client race of the spider-like Pashtali—invaded human space, intent on crushing the newborn star nation before it could rise any further. But the humans had learnt their lessons well and, in a stunning military campaign, turned the tables on their attackers and defeated them. The Pashtali saved their clients from total defeat, but humanity had clearly won the war. The Galactics ceded control of a sizable chunk of territory to Earth.

This region—known as the Occupied Zone—rapidly turned into a millstone around humanity's collective neck. The countless settlements within the zone had rarely, if ever, bent the knee to the Vulteks. They had no intention of letting the human race take control without a fight, even though humanity had made it clear they had no intention of imposing total control. Worse, it provided an excellent opportunity for the Pashtali to bleed the Solar Navy, and damage humanity's reputation in front of the other powers, without ever quite showing their hand.

And then, the unexpected happened.

Multispace storms are far from uncommon, but the storm that blew up along the threadlines between Earth and the Alphan Empire was unprecedented. *This* storm made it difficult, if not impossible, for ships to move between the two powers, largely isolating the human race from its former patrons. (Indeed, there were suggestions—then and later—that the storm wasn't *natural.*) The Pashtali saw their chance and moved, feinting at the Occupied Zone to draw a chunk of the Solar Navy into a trap and then striking directly at Earth itself. The war seemed on the verge of being lost.

But the human race struck back, adapting its tactics and accepting massive losses to destroy the enemy ships or force them to surrender. The Pashtali broke and ran, saving what they could, but—in the aftermath—it became clear they were far from defeated. They were *still* a Great Power, they *still* badly outnumbered their enemies, their technology was *still* more advanced...

Humanity had won a great victory. But the war was very far from over.

PROLOGUE II

THERE HAD BEEN A TIME, Ambassador Yasuke had read in the history logs, when ambassadors lived so far from their governments that they had the power to sign binding agreements without having to ask permission first. *Those* ambassadors had been trusted to understand what was going on and make the right decisions, before time ran out and their decisions no longer mattered. It had been true, back in the glory days, that military commanders—too—had wide authority to react as they saw fit. In hindsight, after the carnage of the last war, Yasuke suspected that deferring such decisions to the homeworld had been a mistake. Too many commanders, in the opening days, had tried to call home for orders, orders that hadn't arrived until it was far too late.

The humans learnt from our experience, he reflected, as he waited for the secure communications link to be checked and rechecked by operators on both ends of the line. *If their commanders had waited for orders, the war would be over by now.*

It was a chilling thought. The Pashtali had come very close to victory. They'd ignored most of humanity's colonies, few of which had any real industrial base, and driven straight at Earth, using their new crossroads technology to take their enemies in the rear. *That* had been a surprise. The Alphans had known, only a few months ago, that *they* were the only ones who could enter and exit multispace without a crossroads. They hadn't imagined the Pashtali could do it too...Yasuke muttered a human curse, savouring a word that had no direct equivalent in his tongue. Every race that thought itself a great power—and even those who didn't—had been working on the tech, ever since they'd discovered it was possible. His people should have known that, sooner or later, someone else would crack the secret. They had the great advantage of *knowing* it was possible.

The room darkened, the holographic projector displaying the chairman's face. A faint flicker of static crossed the image, a grim reminder that the conversation was heavily encrypted and yet vulnerable to interception. The Pashtali would be doing everything in their power to hack into the network and there was no way to be sure, now, they *weren't* listening to every word. He would have sooner returned home and spoken to his government in person, but there just hadn't been time. Hopefully, the encryption would minimise the risk.

"Ambassador," the chairman said. He was alone. That was generally a good sign. "We have reviewed your proposal."

Yasuke nodded, then waited.

"It is risky," the chairman said. "Do you really think we should take the risk?"

There was a time, Yasuke thought coldly, *that we didn't shy away from risk.*

He kept *that* thought off his face. The chairman—and the government—had too many problems. The mighty fleet of warcruisers had been badly weakened—in the time it took the Alphans to produce a single ship, the Lupines had turned out hundreds—and the empire was in full retreat, granting clients independence and abandoning colony worlds. The empire was still mighty, still capable of defending itself, but the days they could send an entire fleet thousands of light years from home were gone. And they wouldn't be coming back.

"I believe I argued my case quite clearly," he said. "The humans have won a major victory, true, but the war isn't over. The Pashtali will regroup, concentrate their forces and resume the offensive...if they have time. And they will win. The balance of power is firmly in their favour."

"Perhaps," the chairman agreed. "But what does this have to do with us?"

Yasuke wasn't sure if the chairman hadn't read his report, or if he was merely getting the matter on the official record, but he wasn't inclined to waste time worrying about it. If the chairman wanted to play games, that was fine as long as Yasuke got what *he* wanted out of the deal.

"The Pashtali are a Great Power," he said, calmly. "If they succeed in enslaving humanity, or even occupying their worlds and banning them from spaceflight, they will be on our borders, in a position to threaten us. They have already cracked the secret of slipping in and out of multispace without a crossroads. What *else* do they have?"

"I was informed their crossroads tech is inferior to ours," the chairman said.

"Yes," Yasuke agreed. "But that doesn't mean it can't be effective."

He leaned forward. "But if we assist the humans now, we will have a friendly power on our border, the Pashtali will be weakened and we will have fewer problems in the future."

"The humans cannot win," the chairman said.

"The Pashtali have already poured out a vast amount of blood and treasure," Yasuke countered. "Sooner or later, even they will cut their losses."

"They may," the chairman agreed. "But will that be in time to save our former clients?"

"Our allies," Yasuke corrected. "We aren't their masters any longer, but we can be their allies."

"And they will draw us back into the mainstream," the chairman said. "We need time to consolidate."

"Which we can only gain by assisting the human race," Yasuke insisted. "The Pashtali will not rest on their laurels, once they have crushed humanity and occupied their worlds. They will come for us. They must. They want to rule the known universe and the only way to do *that* is to defeat us, before we rebuild and return to the galactic mainstream."

If we ever do, his thoughts added, silently. *We don't want to admit it, even to ourselves, but we may have given up.*

It was hard to keep his face impassive. They'd ruled the known galaxy for centuries. The thought that the Alphans could be defeated, that they could accept *de facto* decline, was unthinkable. And yet, the idea haunted him. The Pashtali wanted to build an empire. They had a vigour Yasuke's ancestors had shared, one their descendants had lost. And they might never find it again.

"The humans must win," he said. "And they cannot do it without our help."

"So you have said," the chairman observed. There was a long, chilling pause. "We have debated the issue. We will assist the humans. But only to a point."

He leaned forward. "Remember that, Ambassador. Only to a point."

Yasuke bowed, hiding his relief. "Yes, Mr. Chairman. I will not forget."

CHAPTER ONE

TROJAN, DEEP SPACE

"SIR?"

Captain Leo Patel looked up from his datapad, keeping his face under tight control. The sensor operator looked too young to be a responsible adult and he kept thinking, at times, that the navy had raided the nurseries and junior schools for recruits. It was going to hurt the Solar Navy badly, in the months and years to come, that far too many military recruits and training officers had been pulled out of the pipeline and sent to the front, but there was no choice. Too many officers and crewmen had died in the Battle of Sol, too many ships destroyed or damaged beyond immediate repair. The human race had never been so close to absolute defeat.

"Yes, Carola?"

The sensor operator glanced at him. Leo sighed inwardly. Sensor operators were meant to keep their eyes on their consoles at all times, just in case something changed so quickly their original report was no longer accurate. Leo had been in the navy long enough to know a situation could go from controlled to absolute chaos in the blink of an eye, then be made worse by an officer responding to the first reports and not realising things had already slipped out of control. He made a mental note to discuss the situation with the academy officers, when they returned home. They could reduce their focus on spit and polish and concentrate, instead, on honing the skills the recruits needed to survive.

"Captain," Carola said. "I picked up a brief flicker of sensor distortion, closing from the rear."

Leo sucked in his breath. They were on a well-travelled shipping line, running through the Occupied Zone—*the former Occupied Zone,* his mind whispered—and leading straight to Terminus. There'd been surprisingly little traffic when they popped out of the last crossroads and set course for the next, something that bothered him. There should have been a *lot* more starships ploughing the spacelanes. And the fact everything was so quiet suggested...what?

Everyone might be keeping their heads down and hoping to remain unnoticed, he thought, rather drolly. The independent shippers tried to remain politically neutral, although—with a handful of wars burning through the galaxy—that wasn't always possible. *Or someone might be deliberately suppressing unwanted trade.*

He studied the display, refusing to allow his concerns to show on his face. The Pashtali had kicked the human race out of the Occupied Zone, before driving on Earth in a desperate bid to win the war before humanity could rally and fight back. They'd come far too close to succeeding before their fleet had been forced to surrender. And now...his eyes narrowed as the sensor flickers grew stronger. The Pashtali had been ominously quiet for the last six months. The intelligence crews hadn't known what to make of it. Leo suspected he knew, now, what the spider-like aliens had been doing.

"Captain?" Carola looked up, again. "Should I do a sensor focus?"

"No." Leo didn't have to think about it. Whoever was coming up behind them didn't know—yet—that they'd been detected. A regular merchantman wouldn't have picked up even the *slightest* hint of their presence until they were well within firing range. *Trojan's* sensors were the finest money could buy and even they hadn't noticed until it was too late to evade contact and pretend it was just a coincidence. "Let them think we haven't spotted them."

His mind raced. He knew better than to think there was *no* contact. It wasn't uncommon for random energy flickers to trigger alarms, but the contact was too solid—too artificial—to him to cling to the delusion. Anyone creeping into attack position was almost definitely hostile…hell, the rules of engagement laid down by the Alphans and enforced by the rest of the Galactics would be on his side if he opened fire first and asked questions later. There was no obligation to let a hostile ship get into point-blank range, not when the first salvo might be the last. Better to protect his own ship by opening fire on the enemy and swearing blind he'd never seen their ship.

Which might not be possible, he reminded himself. *The rules are for little powers.*

He scowled. He'd been forced to take a course in galactic law before he'd been granted his shipping licence and his instructor had made it clear the rules only applied to those without the power to stand up for themselves. The Galactics—the Alphans, the Pashtali, the other races that commanded immense military power—could do whatever they liked, while the smaller powers had to follow the rules to the letter. Even now, the Pashtali were mounting a savage public relations campaign against humanity, insisting the human race was cheating…never mind the immense disparity between the two powers. Leo clenched his teeth in frustration. The Galactics weren't stupid. He doubted any of them *really* believed the Pashtali. But the lies provided an excuse to sit back and do nothing while the galactic superpower ground Earth into the dust.

And now someone is coming up behind us, he thought, coldly. *It* has *to be an enemy.*

They'd timed it well, he noted. *Trojan* couldn't reach the crossroads and escape before the vectors converged and the enemy ship opened fire, nor could she dart back to the previous crossroads or break contact. If *Trojan* had been a proper freighter, if her IFF signal hadn't been more than a set of artfully crafted lies, she might be in some trouble. The freighter was huge, easily twice the size of the average cruiser, but she was as ungainly as a wallowing pig. There was no hope of breaking contact, not unless the enemy ship chose to let them go. Leo was fairly sure it wasn't going to happen.

"Tactical," he said. "Run preliminary activation programs."

"Aye, Captain," Lieutenant Walker said. He was an older man recalled to the colours, half his body replaced by cyborg implants that made him look like a patchwork man. The Solar Navy normally disapproved of such heavy augmentation, but the Solar Navy was too desperate for manpower to care. Besides, Walker was on a modified freighter, not an actual warship. "Activation program coming online...now."

The lights flickered. Leo gritted his teeth. The freighter's design called for two fusion cores—she could operate with one, in a pinch—but the engineers who'd converted her into a Q-Ship had installed four more. Powering up their main weapon *still* drained their power reserves, something he'd believed impossible until they'd put their ship through her paces a few, short months ago. It was disconcerting...hell, the risk of suffering a sudden power failure wasn't the worst of it. The groundhogs might write books where incoming ships had sensors so capable they could tell when their target was powering up its weapons, but it was impossible...normally. This time, there would be flickers of radiation when they brought their weapon online. The radiation shielding should provide some cover—he'd tested the armour thoroughly, during the trials—but it was hard to be sure. The Pashtali sensors were reputed to be good. Better than Alphan sensors? No one knew.

"Beginning charging procedure," Walker said. His voice was flat, betraying nothing of his inner turmoil. They'd get one shot, just one. If it worked, they'd be heroes; if it failed, they'd be dead. "Countdown begins...now."

"Hold fire until they are well within range," Leo reminded him, as if they hadn't drilled endlessly for this moment. "Wait for my command, unless they fire first."

"Aye, Captain."

Leo nodded stiffly, keeping his eye on the display. The enemy ship was closer now, entering missile range. Too close for his peace of mind, yet too far away for a guaranteed kill. They had the edge, if they opened fire...what did they want? Who were they? Pashtali? Vulteks? Pirates? Or perhaps even scavengers, the last remnants of races who'd been driven from their homeworlds and forced to live on the edge of galactic society? It was a chilling thought. If the war was lost, the human race might be reduced to nothing more than a handful of survivors, roaming the galaxy in search of a new home. And if they found one, their tormentors would be quick to snatch it...

No, he told himself. *That isn't going to happen.*

His eyes never left the enemy ship. She was still cloaked, her identity hidden behind a masking field, but the tactical computers were slowly putting together a picture of her true nature. Carola was *very* good at her job. The power curves suggested a light cruiser, perhaps an oversized destroyer...Leo wondered, if their opponent *was* a cruiser, why they were sneaking around rather than simply charging up and opening fire? It struck him as a little pointless. Did they suspect *Trojan's* true nature? They might...no, if they did, they'd have held the range open and blown his ship away well before he could retaliate. His lips twitched with grim amusement. In hindsight, calling his ship *Trojan* might have been a mistake.

But then, our naming conventions make no sense to the Galactics, he reminded himself, dryly. *Any more than their naming conventions make sense to us.*

"Captain," Carola said. "The enemy ship will be in position in two minutes."

"Three minutes to full charge, sir," Walker added. "She might see something..."

Leo nodded, curtly. His ship's exterior was no different from the thousands of other human-designed freighters working the spacelanes. The interior...if they were boarded, they'd have a *lot* of questions to answer.

Not, he suspected, that they'd ever have the chance. If a major power realised what they were carrying, they'd probably be disappeared; the ship going to the nearest military shipyard for analysis, while the crew vanished into a black interrogation chamber. His heart twisted. He was a brave man, but the thought of having his mind slowly dismantled by alien mind probes was terrifying. It was never easy to calibrate the probe for different races and a single mistake, committed by aliens with little experience with human minds, would be enough to reduce him to a drooling wreck. And...he shook his head. It wouldn't happen. He had strict orders to destroy his ship if there was even the slightest chance she'd fall into enemy hands.

And our mysterious friend does want us intact, he thought, grimly. It wasn't all bad—it gave him an edge, if the enemy was reluctant to destroy his ship—but it was worrying. *They'd have opened fire by now if they wanted us dead.*

His heart thudded as the range continued to close. The enemy ship was dangerously close. They were too close for anyone, even the insanely snooty Galactics, to believe they hadn't been spotted. The Galactics might *think* the younger races didn't know how to get the best out of their borrowed technology, and in some cases they were even right, yet...they were so close that even a simple automated program, with no more adaptive intelligence than a pre-invasion computer, would be sounding the alarm. And if they picked up a hint of the weapon being aimed at them...

"Captain!" Carola's voice rose with alarm. "They're decloaking!"

"Calm," Leo murmured. "There's no need for panic."

He leaned forward, bracing himself, as the enemy ship took shape and form on the display. A light cruiser...Pashtali in design, although old enough she might have been handed down to the Vulteks or simply sold to a younger race. The Pashtali could hardly be blamed if their outdated ships eventually wound up in pirate hands, after passing through so many owners they had no way to know where they would eventually land. He scowled, even though he knew he should be relieved. Earth was buying every ship it could, without asking too many questions, and toughening up the laws on starship transfers would actually make it harder to defend the homeworld. But, at the same time, too many ships wound up in pirate hands. They were a regular plague on the spacelanes…

The console bleeped. "Sir," Carola said. "They just ordered us to heave to and prepare to be boarded."

Leo raised his eyebrows. "Did they give us their IFF?"

"No, sir," Carola said. "The communication was in GalStandard Two."

"Interesting," Leo said.

He considered it for a moment. The Pashtali used GalStandard Two, and the fact the mystery ship used it suggested she was a Pashtali vessel, but it wasn't conclusive. There were quite a few other races who relied on the same artificial language to communicate…his lips twitched. The Alphans might have made a mistake, when they'd designed languages to allow cross-racial communication. There was no longer any ambiguity about insults that might, under normal circumstances, have been smoothed over. And that meant…

"Send them our IFF and manifest," he ordered. It was unlikely either would deter the mystery ship, but if they made themselves look a bigger prize the enemy would be reluctant to destroy them. "And request they allow us to proceed without further ado."

"Aye, sir," Carola said. There was a long pause. "They're repeating their earlier command and…missile! Incoming missile!"

"Aimed to miss," Walker grunted. "But close enough to prove they *can* put a warhead in our hull."

"Of course." Leo watched the missile lance past the hull and dart into the distance, before detonating. It was a clear warning there was no way the freighter could get out of range, even if she were given a head start. "Carola, request guarantees our cargo will be unharmed."

Carola grinned. "What cargo?"

Leo smiled back. The manifest was made up out of whole cloth, but he'd put it together with malice aforethought. If someone accepted it at face value, they'd believe *Trojan* was carrying valuable goods from Alphan Prime to Terminus, goods already sold to powers capable of making one hell of a fuss if they were stolen or destroyed in transit. The Pashtali—if the ship *was* Pashtali—might not dare blow his ship away. Sure, it would reduce faith in humanity's ability to ship supplies safely from one side of the galaxy to the other, but if someone worked out what they'd done it might widen the war. The safest choice, for them, was to capture the ship, then deliver the supplies themselves. And it would give them all the incentive they needed to keep closing the range.

"They've offered their guarantees," Carola said. "Sir?"

Leo keyed his console. "Bring us to all stop, then power down the drive and transfer all power to the main gun," he ordered. The range would close rapidly once his ship was seemingly dead in space. The enemy would reduce speed at once, just to keep from overshooting, but it would take several seconds for them to do it. "Tactical, are we ready to fire?"

"One minute, Captain," Walker said. "The gun is nearly charged."

"Prepare to open the gunport," Leo said. "And order all non-essential crew to the shuttle."

"Aye, sir," Carola said. He could *hear* the sudden trepidation in her voice. The shuttle *might* get away, if the gambit failed, but *she* would remain on the freighter to the bitter end. "They're on their way."

"Good." *Trojan's* crew was tiny, compared to a proper warship's crew, but that had its advantages. They'd have no difficulty evacuating the crew if the shit hit the fan. "They are to disconnect as soon as the hatches are closed."

"Aye, sir."

The tactical console bleeped. "Sir," Walker said. "The gun is ready to fire."

"Angle us into firing position," Leo ordered. "And open the gunport."

His heart raced. The armour had kept them safe, for the moment, but that was about to change. The radiation spike would be impossible to miss, once the gunport was open. How quickly would the enemy react? If they had their weapons dialled in on his hull, the best he could hope for would be a mutual kill. If…

"Energy spike," Carola snapped. "Captain, they're preparing to fire!"

"Fire," Leo snapped.

Walker tapped his console. The light dimmed, again, as the burner unleashed a hellish storm of energy into the enemy hull. The cruiser melted like snowflakes in hell, the ravaging fury stabbing through layers of armour and ripping through the vessel's interior as though it were made of paper. He sucked in his breath as the enemy drive field destabilised, an instant before the burner sliced through the fusion cores, depowering the ship. He was mildly surprised the ship hadn't exploded. The sheer power he'd unleashed was terrifying.

No wonder the Alphans ruled the galaxy for so long, he thought, morbidly. *They had the biggest sticks in the known universe.*

"Check for survivors," he ordered. There was no time to waste. They'd just lit up the entire system. If there was someone watching from a safe distance, they'd know what had happened. "And then prepare to resume our course."

"No survivors, as far as I can tell," Carola said. "What about their datacores?"

Leo shook his head. Datacores were hardened, but not *that* hardened. Besides, the enemy interior had been turned into a melted nightmare. The odds of finding a datacore in good condition were roughly akin to his odds of winning the intergalactic lottery and living long enough to claim the money. There might be something remaining, if they had time to go through the wreckage with a fine-toothed comb, but they didn't. The enemy ship was a dead hulk. Better to leave her death a mystery, rather than reveal what he'd done.

"No point," he said. He was tempted to search for genetic samples, in hopes of determining who'd flown the ship, but it was pointless too. The interior was too badly scorched. There'd be nothing of the crew left, not even atoms. "Helm, resume course. We'll report in when we reach the next relay station."

His lips twitched. It wasn't much, not in the grand scheme of things, but it would hopefully convince the Pashtali they needed to either stop harassing humanity's shipping or devote more ships and resources to prowling the spacelanes. Hopefully...he felt a sudden surge of hatred as his ship got underway, leaving the dead hulk behind. The Pashtali had jumped on a weakened human race and come very close to winning. Even now, the war remained in the balance...

... And he feared, despite everything, the end could not be long delayed.

CHAPTER TWO

POURNELLE SHIPYARDS, SOL ASTEROID BELT

THE PASHTALI SHIP was very...*alien*.

First Speaker Abraham Douglas felt a chill run down his spine as he surveyed the Pashtali ship, hanging in the midst of a network of struts and research modules. He was a well-travelled man and prided himself on keeping his composure even when confronted by very outré aliens, but the Pashtali ship just looked *wrong*. It was like a brooding spider...as if its designers had crafted a ship in their own image. The ship was hardly the first alien starship he'd seen—the Alphans regarded their ships as works of art—but its mere appearance was a grim reminder its designers had worked from very different ideas of how the universe worked. He sucked in his breath, taking a moment to gather himself. The Pashtali might be alien—very much so—but they were bound by the same laws of nature as their human enemies. Their tech wasn't *that* different.

He took another breath, studying the design thoughtfully. The Pashtali had clearly never intended to take *Crossroads* into battle. The vessel was heavily outfitted with armour and defensive systems, but hardly anything in the way of offensive weapons. Abraham wasn't surprised. The crossroads-generating ship had to be incredibly expensive, even by Galactic standards. They'd no more send her into the line of battle than he'd purchase an asteroid mansion for the express purpose of steering it into the sun. It had been sheer luck the human race had forced the Pashtali to surrender, when the Solar Navy had raised the siege of Earth, and hand over their ships. It might prove the key to winning the war or, at least, buying time for the human race to make allies and deter their enemies from continuing the fight. Who knew? Maybe the horse *would* learn to sing?

"First Speaker?"

Abraham turned, slowly. Commodore Roger Valentine stood by the hatch, hands clasped behind his back. He was a tall dark-skinned man with a bland, almost unremarkable face, wearing a naval uniform that had clearly seen better days. Abraham nodded, remembering the file he'd accessed during the flight to the shipyard. Commodore Valentine was the navy's leading expert in non-human technology, with a long career spent taking the best of Alphan—and other Galactic—tech and reverse-engineering it so humanity could put it into mass production. The Solar Navy's warships might be ugly—they'd never win any design awards—but they'd integrated ideas from right across the galaxy into a coherent whole. *And* they were a lot easier to repair than their alien counterparts.

"Commodore," Abraham said. "What progress have you made with the alien ships?"

Valentine smiled. "They were careful to destroy the datacores before they surrendered their ships," he said. "Under normal circumstances, it would be quite enough to keep us from putting the ships into service. However, we were able to jury-rig modified command networks which should, assuming everything works as planned, let us take the ships into combat anyway. They'll be difficult to control, but hardly inert hulks."

"Good." Abraham let out a breath. "We need more warships—and quickly."

"We were also able to recover a handful of IFF signals from the local buffers," Valentine added. "They may not be current—and they may well know which ships fell into our hands—but we might be able to use them to sneak up on enemy positions. Might."

"No guarantees," Abraham agreed. Earth had worked hard to obscure just *which* enemy ships had been captured, but he was uncomfortably aware too many alien powers had probably watched the battle from a safe distance. The Pashtali wouldn't have any problems purchasing the sensor records, if they thought to ask. "They will certainly suspect the worst."

"They may assume the ships are either destroyed or effectively useless," Valentine agreed. "But it would be unwise to count on it."

Abraham nodded. The Galactics rarely, if ever, used starships captured from enemy races. It was just too difficult to repair the ships, then operate them. The smaller races—including humanity—had no choice. Earth had learnt an awful lot about repairing and updating ships that had been in space longer than the entire human race, as well as controlling vessels designed for non-humanoid races. He felt a twinge of sympathy for the crews. The Alphans were humanoid, and they weren't *that* different from their former subjects, but their starships still felt *wrong.* It wasn't something he could put into words. And yet...

"We'll hope for the best, but prepare for the worst," he said, nodding to the porthole. "What about *Crossroads* herself?"

Valentine looked thoughtful. "The good news, sir, is that we understand how she does what she does," he said. "They use a brute-force approach to opening a makeshift crossroads into multispace, rather than the more elegant technology used by the Alphans, but it works. Given time and resources, we can duplicate it. We think they may have a degree more tactical mobility than the Alphans, but it's hard to be sure. The Alphans who spent the last month crawling over her refused to be drawn on the subject."

"They paid through the nose for access to the ship," Abraham said, curtly. "What's the bad news?"

"The design is very limited, sir," Valentine said. "The power requirements are off the scale. They can open a crossroads, after charging their power cells, then they have to wait for the cells to recharge before they can do it again. If our calculations are correct, they need at least an hour between crossroads. They also put a hell of a lot of wear and tear on their equipment too. *Crossroads* is easier to dismantle than their regular warships because they need to repair their systems, or even replace them, every few days. They even had a hull crammed with spare parts."

Abraham smiled, which boded ill for someone. "I assume there's no need to maintain the system when they're just travelling from crossroads to crossroads, without trying to generate their own?"

"We're not sure," Valentine admitted. "We think some of the systems need to be kept on standby at all times, even when the ship is deep within friendly space and doesn't have to jump out at a moment's notice. They were actually within a maintenance cycle during the Battle of Earth, which may have made it impossible for them to jump out and run."

"Lucky," Abraham said.

"Yes, sir." Valentine nodded to the alien ship. "We know how she does it, sir, and we think we can duplicate it. We also think we may be able to *counter* it."

Abraham leaned forward. "Counter it?"

"Like I said, it's a brute-force method," Valentine reminded him. "They basically generate a gravity field powerful enough to warp the fabric of space-time, eventually opening a crossroads into multispace. Given the nature of multispace, it's quite possible there are places they literally *cannot* open the crossroads, no matter how much power they redirect to their generators. They must have been surveying the multispace topography around Earth and the Occupied Zone for years, prior to starting the war."

"We know they were planning for quite some time," Abraham agreed. "We might not have time to match their work."

"It may not matter, sir," Valentine said. "If we use focused gravity beams, we might be able to disrupt their crossroads generator and prevent the crossroads from opening."

"Trapping their ships in realspace," Abraham finished. "Will it work?"

"Theoretically," Valentine said. "The concept was originally devised for use against the Alphans, sir, but their crossroads generators are so advanced they can literally integrate outside gravity pulses into their multispace portals and..."

Abraham held up a hand. "English, please."

"The Alphans can compensate for outside interference," Valentine said. He looked pensive. "If our research is correct, the Pashtali *cannot*."

"Which means we can lock them out of multispace," Abraham said. "Can we keep them from opening a crossroads and landing on top of us?"

"...Perhaps," Valentine commented, reluctantly. "It's hard to be sure. The math suggests it may be possible, but—again, given the nature of multispace—it might be nothing more than spitting into the wind. There'd be a hell of a lot of pressure on the counter-generator and no certainty it would actually work. Still, being able to lock them out of multispace will give us one hell of an advantage."

"If we have them pinned down," Abraham said. "They'll know it too, won't they?"

"Yes, sir," Valentine said. "They must have spent years working out the theory, then building the tech to turn theory into workable hardware. They'll have a far better idea of what the tech can, and cannot, do."

Abraham said nothing for a long moment. "And if they already have a countermeasure?"

"There's no way to be sure, sir, but we think that trying to open a crossroads under such circumstances will put a hell of a lot *more* wear and tear on their generators even if they succeed," Valentine said. "If nothing else, they'll have to stop for repairs in a hurry if they want to use the generators again."

"Which will certainly be expensive, for them," Abraham said. "Can you take the enemy warships into battle?"

"Yes, sir," Valentine said. "There will be shortages—again, they wiped the data cores before they surrendered—but we can overcome them.

However, we don't have anything like enough spare parts and once we start taking damage, it will be difficult to repair the ships."

"Noted," Abraham said. The Pashtali had never signed any interstellar treaties on interoperability. It was hard to escape the feeling that had worked in the Pashtali's favour. "Thank you for your time."

"You're welcome, sir," Valentine said. "Director Solomon is waiting for you."

Abraham nodded, shortly. He'd gone to some trouble to keep his visit to the shipyards as quiet as possible—the repair crews didn't have the *time* to down tools and put on a dog-and-pony show– but there was no way to keep his arrival completely quiet. He took one last look at the alien ships, then turned and stepped through the hatch. The modular corridors hummed with life, engineers and their support staff scurrying as if there was no tomorrow. Abraham gritted his teeth as he pressed himself against the bulkhead to let a pair of engineers push a trolley. There might not be *any* tomorrow soon enough, if the Pashtali refused to see sense and come to terms. They'd started the war, and gotten a bloody nose, and now couldn't back off without looking weak. It was frustrating as hell, not least because there was nothing Abraham could do to solve the problem. What sort of concessions could he offer that would make the Pashtali back off?

We could surrender tomorrow, unconditionally, and they'd still look weak in front of their peers, he reflected, sourly. *They'd still need to beat hell out of us…*

He shook his head as he stepped through the airlock and headed up towards the administrative modules. There was no way he could offer any terms, certainly nothing the Pashtali could reasonably accept. Public opinion would never stand for it. Hell, *he* didn't want to stand for it either. The human race had fought a far more powerful and aggressive alien force to a standstill…surely, a *rational* race would want to concede defeat as quickly as possible. It wasn't as if humanity could demand vast concessions. But the Pashtali had started the war and had made themselves look greedy and foolish as well as weak; now they needed a victory before someone jumped on them. It just wasn't fair.

The universe is not fair, he reminded himself. *And as long as there's no one willing to enforce the rules, the strong will always take advantage of the weak.*

Martin Solomon, Director and CEO of the Pournelle Shipyards Corporation as well as Minister for Industrial and Economic Development, rose to his feet as Abraham was shown into his office. He looked tired and drawn, after years of working to develop new ships and weapons, then months of hiding from the enemy fleet while desperately trying to repair the navy's remaining ships so they could resume the offensive. Even now, there'd been no relief, no chance to catch his breath. There was just too much to do before the hammer came down. Again.

"First Speaker," Solomon said. "I'm sorry I didn't have time to greet you earlier."

"It doesn't matter," Abraham assured him. "I enjoyed the chance to inspect the captured ships."

"We've learnt quite a bit from them." Solomon smiled as he poured two glasses of wine. "Mostly how *not* to do it, but quite a bit regardless."

Abraham raised his eyebrows. "How *not* to do it?"

"Their ships took more cues from the Alphans than they'd ever admit, I think," Solomon said, passing Abraham a glass. "They have their weaknesses, including a certain inability to carry out repairs while underway. They need a shipyard for repairs *we* could handle in deep space."

"Odd." Abraham sipped his wine. It might make sense for commercial ships, but warships couldn't always be withdrawn from the line of battle and sent home. "Why?"

"It does have its advantages," Solomon conceded. "Their ships are generally tougher than ours. Their hulls are solid shells, which can take more damage than our armour plating. The downside, though, is that when something *does* get through the hull it does a hell of a lot of damage. The hull traps the blast within the hull, leaving it bouncing around within the vessel rather than harmlessly burning away."

"Ouch," Abraham said. "I assume their interior armour isn't up to spec?"

"It's nowhere near as tough as the outer hull," Solomon agreed. His lips twisted into a cold smile. "The ships are tough, First Speaker, but nowhere near tough enough. We can take them down."

"And we have," Abraham said. He leaned forward. "How do we stand, production-wise?"

Solomon looked worried, just for a second. "Good news and bad. We've been able to resume production of warships and weapons, as well as converting freighters into makeshift warships to give us more missile platforms. The Alphans have also extended us a substantial line of credit, which has made it easier to purchase first-rate fabricators as well as warships from the other Galactics. However, we're reaching the limits of our capacities and I don't think we can expand them in a hurry..."

Abraham frowned. "I thought we were giving you all the resources we could muster," he said. "Is it not enough?"

"Sir, it takes one woman nine months to grow a baby," Solomon said. "That's a simple law of nature. Nine women cannot make a baby in *one* month. Right now, my personnel are overworked, which means mistakes creep into the production lines and, worse, we don't have the time or resources to train new personnel. We have too many undertrained personnel as it is, which is causing other problems. Ideally, I'd like to slow production a little and divert more experienced personnel to training duties, but that isn't going to happen."

"Shit," Abraham said. "I take it you can't use automated training programs?"

"They work for teaching the basics, sir, but a great deal of the things they need to know can only come from experience, and an experienced mentor," Solomon told him. "The training modules don't discuss how to take a component from one race and adapt it to work with another race's gear. Nor do they show where corners can be cut safely and where corners can *never* be cut. We're trying to rotate some of our newer personnel, the ones who passed the training course without ever putting their hands on actual hardware, through postings on freighters and industrial plants, but even *that's* a strain."

He shook his head. "The bottom line, sir, is that we need the war over as quickly as possible."

"So do we all," Abraham said, tiredly. "How long can you maintain your current tempo?"

"I'm not sure." Solomon leaned forward. "The longer this goes on, the greater the chance of a disastrous accident. We designed a system for replacing worn out components and personnel, prior to the war, but that's gone by the wayside now. We're effectively eating our seed corn, sir, just to push our limits as far as they will go. I don't think there's anything we can do about it, short of shutting down for a few weeks to rest and refit."

"Which is impossible," Abraham said.

"Until the end of the war, yes," Solomon agreed. "It's impossible to say for sure, sir, but my read on the situation is that we're going to have to slow down in six months, and that's if we're lucky. We may suffer an accident earlier that will make it impossible to maintain our tempo. I think"—his lips twisted—"we can pull some people off the production line to enhance our training program, but..."

He shook his head. "We're in trouble, sir. No two ways about it."

"I understand," Abraham said. "Is there no other way?"

"Not as far as we can tell," Solomon said. "There's nothing we can offer our people to make up for the simple fact they're tired and overworked. Wages? They don't have time to spend them. Perks? Ditto. Brothels? They're too tired..."

He shrugged. "We're still looking for alternatives, but realistically we're going to have to slow down soon. The equipment is running hot and so are the workers."

"I got the message," Abraham said, curtly. "What about recruiting non-human labour?"

"Much of it wouldn't be of any real use," Solomon said. "The minor races are reluctant to risk pissing off the Pashtali. The major races are less inclined to worry about their opinion, but their techs aren't trained to our standards. They have little or no experience of working with alien tech and it shows."

"Crap," Abraham said. "Do what you can."

"I will." Solomon sighed. "Just bear in mind that there will be an accident, sooner rather than later. And when it happens, production will slow to a crawl."

CHAPTER THREE

Earth Defence Force One, Earth Orbit

IT WAS NOT *HER* OFFICE.

First Admiral Naomi Yagami felt like a fraud as she sat behind Admiral Glass's desk and wore his uniform. She'd always thought she'd rise to flag rank eventually—the Solar Navy was painfully short of experienced officers—but she'd never expected to be promoted to fill a dead man's shoes. Admiral Glass had been the *de facto* founder of the Solar Navy, the man who'd guided the transition from the old Earth Defence Force to a proud spacefaring navy, the man who'd ensured that the navy remained intact, instead of being ripped apart by political infighting. And he'd died in battle...

She hated it. Admiral Glass should have gone into retirement, instead of dying. He'd done so much and yet...she wished, numbly, she'd been able to save him. No one suggested she'd let him die deliberately—everyone knew she'd done all she could—but she still felt guilty. She had no idea how to fill his shoes. She'd commanded starships, and fleets, but running an entire navy? It didn't help that so many officers had died in the fighting, ensuring that she had no choice but to promote the young and inexperienced. She suspected she wasn't the only one struggling with imposter syndrome.

Be honest, she told herself. *You'd be more worried about a junior officer who wasn't concerned about his ability to handle the job.*

She ran her hand through her hair, battling a surge of exhaustion. It was rare for an admiral to do her own clerical work, let alone wear more than two hats, but there was no choice. Admiral Glass's staff had largely been broken up and sent elsewhere. The Solar Navy had never had the time to develop a major bureaucracy and now it probably never would. She had too much to do, tasks that could normally be handled by her subordinates. It felt, sometimes, as though the Pashtali had torn the guts out of the navy, leaving only a skeleton behind. They'd be lucky if the navy was on an even keel by the time *she* had to retire.

The intercom bleeped. "Admiral," Ensign Joe Tasman said. "Admiral Morrígan and Captain Evensong are here for their appointment."

"Send them in," Naomi ordered, suppressing the urge to tell them to go away instead. "And have coffee sent in too."

"Aye, Admiral."

Naomi looked up as the hatch opened, pasting a calm expression on her face. Admiral Morrígan was a short dumpy woman who'd spent most of her career behind a desk, rather than commanding starships. Her file suggested she'd rotated into desk work five years ago and, somehow, had never been reassigned to starship or fleet command. Naomi wasn't sure what to make of it, although she was fairly certain the older woman wasn't incompetent. Admiral Glass wouldn't have stood for it. She was probably too good at her job to be allowed to return to space. Naomi hoped Admiral Morrígan didn't resent it.

"Admiral," Admiral Morrígan said. "I'm sorry we were delayed."

"It's ok, I worked on the paperwork," Naomi said. "As you can see, there's a great deal of it."

She sighed to herself. She had no idea how Admiral Glass had coped, when he'd been in charge. "Have you made any progress with fleet procurement?"

"We've obtained nearly a hundred starships of various classes from our sources, since last we spoke," Admiral Morrígan said. "However, the raw numbers tell a lie. Most of the ships are third- or fourth-hand at best, and in pretty poor condition. No one wants to sell top of the line warships these days, not to anyone. They'll make pretty good weapons platforms, with a little refitting, but not much else. The Pashtali will have no problems scything them down if they risk an open engagement."

"They may still have their uses," Naomi commented. Humans were *good* at refitting older ships and putting them back into service. "And the rest of the fleet?"

"There are shortages everywhere," Admiral Morrígan admitted. "We can fill some of the holes, Admiral, but the shortages will continue for months if not years. I'd prefer not to send the fleet into deep space, if it could be avoided..."

"If," Naomi said. "We may have to take the offensive."

She keyed her console, activating the holographic starchart. The former Occupied Zone glowed a warning orange, a grim reminder the Pashtali might have taken control of the zone, while—hundreds of light years away—Pashtali space glowed a baleful red. It was hard to comprehend the sheer magnitude of the alien empire, the sheer power they could bring to bear against the human race. She feared, sometimes, that all she and the Navy could do was kick and scratch on the way to the gallows. If the Pashtali decided to throw caution to the winds and throw everything they had at Earth, the Solar Navy couldn't hope to stop them.

But they'd be risking war with the Alphans, she reminded herself. *Would they really take the risk?*

"I would advise against it," Admiral Morrígan said, quietly. "We are in no state to mount any sort of offensive."

"And we're also in no state to sit on our butts and wait to be hit," Naomi growled. "How long will it be until they resume the offensive themselves?"

"We don't know, Admiral," Commander Evensong observed. "We know too little about them."

"How many ships do they have in service?" Naomi scowled at the chart. "How many ships can they redeploy to attack us? How many ships do they have in reserve and how long will it take for them to get the reserve ships into service? How long can they continue the war before the cost becomes too high?"

"Unknown," Evensong said. "We have some intelligence from the Alphans, and some more from our contacts across the known galaxy, but we know very little for sure. We can make educated guesses, yet..."

"We couldn't rely on them," Naomi finished. She studied the baleful red stars, her mind churning. The Pashtali had nearly two hundred stars under their control, which suggested they had one hell of a population and industrial base. The mere fact they'd produced *Crossroads*—and at least two other ships just like her—suggested they had the resources to expend on projects that could easily turn into boondoggles. "How long can they afford to wage war on us?"

"They do have other enemies," Evensong pointed out. "And they can't afford to weaken their border defences too much, or their enemies will jump on them."

Naomi nodded, sourly. The Pashtali were in a mess. They'd have gotten away with invading and annexing Earth and the rest of humanity's comparatively tiny handful of planets, if they'd carried out the operation quickly enough to ensure the other powers had no chance to intervene. Humanity just wasn't important enough to be worth saving. But instead, the Pashtali offensive had bogged down, making them look weak. They needed a victory—and fast, before someone else decided to take advantage. Naomi was mortally certain her counterparts were already planning how to win a decisive victory. It was what she'd do in their place.

"But they can still redirect enough ships towards us to cause real problems," she said. The Solar Navy had won the battle, but the cost had been terrifyingly high. "And perhaps even grind us down."

"Their best bet would be to launch a major offensive," Admiral Morrígan said. "They cannot afford to get bogged down."

"Admiral, they are already bogged down," Evensong said, quietly. "And if they launch a major offensive, they risk widening the war."

"They may be desperate," Admiral Morrígan countered. "Or they may even think the Alphans are bluffing."

Naomi nodded. The Alphans had dispatched nine warcruisers to protect Earth, but no one was sure what they'd do if push came to shove. Naomi wanted to think the Alphans would keep their word—they *had* sent ships, after all—yet it was hard to be sure. Humanity's former masters had been withdrawing into themselves for years, abandoning colonies and granting independence to a dozen client races. The only thing that had brought them out of their retirement was a chance to study *Crossroads* and even *that* wasn't enough to keep them involved. There was a very real chance the warcruisers had orders to withdraw if the Pashtali attacked in force. Earth had once been the key to the Alphan Empire. It wasn't any longer.

She keyed her console, bringing up the fleet lists. The raw numbers were impressive—she had nearly four thousand warships under her command—but the figures told a lie. Two-thirds of her fleet were primitive vessels, barely able to do more than launch missiles at their targets before they got blown away. A handful could do nothing more than draw enemy fire. She had hopes of ramming them into enemy targets, but it was unlikely the enemy would let them get close enough to ram. There weren't many *modern* warships in her fleet and those that were, she knew, would draw fire the moment they showed themselves. A smart enemy might discount the older ships completely, choosing to blow away the modern vessels. It was what *she* would have done.

Her heart clenched. They had enough combat power to *hurt* the Pashtali, if they came in fat and happy again, but not enough to *win*. They were bullies and she knew, from grim experience, that the only way to stop a bully was to convince him that he'd be hurt if he kept bullying. And yet, that wasn't easy. She doubted she could force the Pashtali to listen to reason.

They don't see any reason to listen to us, she thought. There *had* been peace talks, and they were still ongoing, but no one really expected them to get anywhere. The Pashtali had started by demanding humanity's complete surrender as a precondition, suggesting they weren't taking the talks seriously. *We need to force them to listen.*

She frowned, contemplating the problem. There was no hope of defeating and overrunning the enemy. Whatever victory they won would be limited in scope. And yet, that didn't mean victory was impossible. It just meant…her eyes narrowed as a thought crossed her mind. The enemy didn't have to be defeated, just weakened. At some point, the Pashtali would either sue for peace or get attacked by everyone else. They'd know it, wouldn't they?

They don't look remotely like us, she reminded herself. She was no xenophobe—the Solar Navy wouldn't have tolerated it—but the Pashtali were very alien. *They might not think like us.*

"If we decided to go on the offensive," she said slowly, "how long would it take to prepare?"

"At least three weeks, assuming we didn't take a fleet train with us," Admiral Morrígan said thoughtfully. "Realistically, six weeks would be a more accurate assessment. But if we stab into enemy territory, we'll be widening the war."

"Admiral, they stabbed at our homeworld," Evensong said. "They can hardly complain if we stab at theirs."

"The Galactics won't see it that way," Admiral Morrígan said. Her lips twisted in disgust. "One law for them, another for the rest of us."

Naomi nodded. The Galactics had organised the laws of war to suit themselves, without bothering to set up an impartial power capable of even-handed enforcement. The powers that could get away with breaking the laws were allowed to break them, the powers that couldn't got harassed by everyone else. She rubbed her forehead in exasperation. It was just like her old hometown. The people in charge could do whatever they liked, but if someone fought back it was *unfair.*

"I've had an idea," Naomi said. "If we can force them to react to us, for a change..."

She outlined her concept, piece by piece. The planning teams would have to take a look at it, to sort out the details and determine if it was feasible, then she'd have to take the updated plan to her political superiors and convince them to put it into action. If they refused...she rubbed her forehead. The choice was theirs. She might be the highest-ranking uniformed officer in the navy, but she was still under civilian command.

"Commander Evensong, work with the planning teams," she ordered. "Admiral Morrígan, have your staff prepare plans for a long-range fleet deployment."

Admiral Morrígan looked unsure, but nodded. Naomi nodded back in understanding. She didn't blame Admiral Morrígan for having doubts, not when the survival of humanity was in the balance. They had too many enemies, from great powers eying colonies and workforce to scavenger races watching for new targets. The Solar Navy was too weak to endure a long, drawn-out war. They had to convince the enemy to back off now or lose everything.

Unless the plan to set up a very distant colony goes ahead, Naomi thought, as she dismissed her two officers. *We might just survive long enough to rebuild and return to take the offensive...*

She shook her head. It wouldn't be *hard* to set up a colony—she'd heard whispers it had already been done, unofficially—but establishing one capable of rebuilding before galactic civilisation washed over it would be incredibly difficult. The colonists would have to build everything from scratch, unless they encountered a race willing and able to help. And that wasn't too likely. Anyone else they met would be more inclined to suck up to the Pashtali, rather than help a handful of runaway colonists.

The intercom bleeped, again. "Admiral, I have an updated intelligence report," Ensign Tasman said. "There was an encounter between one of our raiders and an enemy warship."

Naomi wished, not for the first time, that she was back on her command deck a very long way from Earth. It wasn't going to happen. She would never command another ship. The best she could do was fleet command, which wasn't quite the same. She wouldn't be in command of the ship...a good thing too, she reflected. She'd had to wear both hats during the Battle of Earth and it had been a nightmare. She had no intention of doing it again.

"Forward the report to me," she said. It was insane that they had no shortage of manpower and yet she couldn't build herself a proper staff. But then, they *were* very short on *trained* manpower. She made a mental note to look into possible substitutes, then shook her head. An experienced officer would know what was important and what could wait for later. A civilian would be much less capable of drawing the line. "And then send in more coffee."

"Aye, Admiral."

Naomi's console bleeped. She glanced at the report, skimming it quickly to hit the high points. *Trojan*, a modified freighter, had spotted and killed an enemy warship...Naomi's lips curved in dark amusement. The Pashtali had *seen* human burners in action, but they hadn't realised they could be mounted on freighters. Not yet...the report waffled a little, towards the end, as if the writer was unwilling to commit themselves. Naomi sighed inwardly. She'd been a starship captain. She *knew* how hard it was to be sure they were unobserved. For all *Trojan's* CO knew, there'd been an entire fleet of cloaked ships watching from a safe distance.

But at least she scored a kill, Naomi told herself, as her steward wheeled in a tray of coffee and sandwiches. It hadn't been easy to accept, at first, how the staff babied her; until she'd come to realise there weren't anything like enough hours in a day. She barely had time to jam a sandwich or two in her mouth, between meetings, briefings and more meetings. *We hurt the bastards.*

The thought mocked her as she read the report for a second time, then a third to make sure she hit the high points. The Pashtali had lost a light cruiser...big deal. They might not even notice the missing ship, not for a few weeks or months. When they did...she shook her head. It was unlikely anyone would care. One small cruiser wouldn't change the balance of power, although...

At least we know the overpowered burners can hurt their ships, she thought. The reverse-engineered weapons lacked the sheer power of the originals, which suggested the target might survive long enough to return fire even if fatally damaged. *And they'll have no way to know which freighters are Q-ships until it's too late.*

She switched the display back to the starchart and studied it thoughtfully. The encounter had taken place in the Occupied Zone, suggesting the enemy hadn't yet taken over every last inhabited star system. She supposed that wasn't really a surprise. Most of the systems were worthless, at least in the short term. The Pashtali wouldn't want to fritter away their strength by trying to hold them, not until they won the war. Besides, the Occupied Zone had been sliding into a full-scale civil war—several civil wars, between several different factions—when the *real* war had started. The Pashtali might be waiting, letting the wars burn themselves out, before they took control. Their enemies would be gravely weakened by the fighting.

Which is probably what they want, she reflected. The Alphans had done the same, when they'd invaded Earth. *The more rebels who kill themselves off now, the fewer who'll remain to fight when the real enemy arrives.*

"Admiral," Ensign Tasman said. "The First Speaker requests your presence at a meeting tomorrow morning. Should I clear your schedule?"

"Yes, please," Naomi said. She glared at the terminal—the paperwork was going to pile up while she was gone—then shrugged. It could be worse. Much worse. "Inform his office I will be pleased to attend."

"Aye, Admiral."

CHAPTER FOUR

SOLAR CITY, EARTH

"I HAVE THE LATEST SET OF POLLS, SIR," Rachel Grant said. She sounded as calm and professional as always. "Public opinion is still largely behind you, although there is a growing sense of concern about the ultimate outcome. The emergency measures are rubbing people the wrong way, sir, and they're probably alienating voters who will register their disgust at the election booths…"

She shook her head. "Fortunately, emergency housing measures and suchlike for refugees haven't provoked too many problems," she added. "Given time, that will change."

"Yeah," Abraham said. "I wanted this job, didn't I?"

He sighed. He'd never understood how many problems the government faced until he'd become the head of the government. He'd always wondered why the old government couldn't do anything…he groaned inwardly, reflecting *he* and his supporters now comprised much of the government and *they* were the ones who couldn't do anything. The war made it hard to lay anything more than very short-term plans, but still… he shook his head. He was starting to think his party would need a new leader, when the next election rolled around. The emergency measures had never been popular and even though the war wasn't over, too many people wanted them lifted.

"I couldn't say, sir," Rachel said, her expression artfully bland. "Did you have a chance to review the notes prior to the meeting?"

"No." Abraham cursed under his breath. It was petty and selfish—and he knew it—to think Nancy Middleton had had it easy, when she'd been the elected head of government, but he still thought it. "And it's time to begin, isn't it?"

"Yes, sir," Rachel said. "Ambassador Middleton is already in the meeting room."

"I'll review the notes later," Abraham said, although he doubted he'd have time. Seven years ago, he'd lambasted the government for hiring too many flunkies. Now, he wished he could go back in time and kick his past self in the rear. His staff was too small for the sheer scale of the tasks they faced. "Coming?"

He composed himself, as best as he could, as they made their way down to the underground complex. It had never been exposed and destroyed by the Pashtali, during their brief invasion and occupation, although no one was quite sure why. Abraham suspected they'd intended to base their puppet government there once they crushed resistance and took formal control of Earth. He doubted they'd never guessed it was there. Earth had taken too many cues from the Alphans and one of them was a collection of underground bunkers, to ensure the government survived if the planet came under heavy attack. The Pashtali *had* to have guessed the bunker was there.

But I wasn't, he reflected. *Perhaps they just wanted to play a waiting game.*

He stepped into the meeting room and nodded to Ambassador Middleton. The ambassador looked disgustingly fresh. Abraham told himself not to take it too personally. They were no longer rivals. He couldn't afford to feel resentment, let alone anything else. If she'd stayed in office instead of him...

We might be in the same mess, he reflected. *Or an entirely different mess.*

"Ambassador," he said, as Rachel poured them coffee. Abraham wanted something stronger, but he needed to keep his thoughts clear. "Did you finish speaking to the remaining ambassadors?"

"Yes, Mr Speaker," Nancy said. "My staff and I have spoken to them, trying to hammer out agreements. Not all of our possible allies are willing to talk too openly, even after we drove the Pashtali away from Earth, but..."

She shrugged. "The bottom line is that we have seven minor powers willing to sign on with us, if the war continues, and five more that will provide limited logistics support as long as it doesn't provoke the Pashtali. They're offering a considerable amount of firepower..."

"Yeah," Abraham said, quietly. Officially, he'd kept his distance from the negotiations. He couldn't afford to seem to be too interested if they blew up in humanity's collective face. Better to let the ambassador take the fall than risk the entire government. Unofficially, he'd kept abreast of them from the start. "And what do they want in exchange?"

"Long-term, they want us to win," Nancy said, curtly. "They want the Pashtali broken, Mr Speaker. They want to ensure the Pashtali don't pose a threat to them, or anyone, ever again."

"That may take some doing," Abraham commented.

"Short-term, they want us to do something about Terminus," Nancy said. She took a datachip out of her pocket and inserted it into an isolated projector. "As you can see..."

Abraham leaned forward as the starchart materialised above him. "Terminus is a major shipping hub," Nancy explained. "The system holds no less than seven crossroads, each one leading to a different set of shipping lanes. The planets have no intelligent life forms, so they've been settled by a multitude of different races and...well, they were allowed to remain reasonably independent as long as they didn't interfere with interstellar shipping. It's an entire system of free ports, sir, or at least it was. The Pashtali have placed the system under siege."

"I see," Abraham said. "And why do they want *us* to do something about it?"

"The shipping lanes link our prospective allies together," Nancy said. "As long as they have free access to Terminus, they can mass their forces and stand up to the Pashtali. Or so they say. If the Pashtali lay siege to the entire system, and block the crossroads, they can keep the other powers from massing. They need us to give the Pashtali the boot."

Abraham made a face. "And if we refuse, or fail, they pretend they don't even *know* us?"

"I think so." Nancy shook her head. "We proved the Pashtali can be beaten, but they still have most of their fleet. As long as they remain strong, and have unfettered access to Terminus, they can deter our prospective allies from doing anything to help us. They'll sell out for the best terms they can get, even if that means abandoning us. They'll have no choice."

"And if they're the ones holding Terminus, they can force the Pashtali to pay a high price for retaking the system," Abraham mused. He was no military man, but he knew the basics. "What's to stop them abandoning us the moment they get what they want?"

"The simple fact no one will ever trust them again," Nancy said. "None of our prospective allies are powerful enough to break their word on a whim, unlike the bigger powers. They can't afford to abandon us."

Abraham wasn't so sure. In his experience, there were times when people felt they had no choice but to break their word, even if it came at a price. What did honour and reputation matter, when the price of keeping the agreement was death and destruction? The Pashtali might be an overwhelming threat—they were—but they were also too strong to challenge openly, not unless there was no choice. He wondered, sourly, what he'd do if Earth had the option of staying out of the fighting. Would he abandon his allies to save his homeworld?

"I hope you're right," he said, finally. "Can they promise us anything now?"

"Not much," Nancy said. "They're too worried about Terminus."

"Don't they know the bastards don't *need* to use the crossroads any longer?" Abraham leaned forward. "They can generate their own now."

"I believe that concentrated a few minds," Nancy said. For a moment, she smiled in grim amusement. "I don't know for sure, because they were reluctant to discuss their contingency planning with me, but I had the impression they were considering securing Terminus before the Pashtali moved into the system and took over. It would have made a certain amount of sense. If they held the system, it would have kept the Pashtali from scattering them..."

"And if they'd moved quicker, they might not need us at all," Abraham said, slowly. "*Can* we liberate the system?"

"The admiral will have to answer that question," Nancy said. "We don't even know for sure what's happening there. All we know comes from their ambassadors here."

"Who are presumably in contact with their homeworlds," Abraham said. He made a mental note to look for independent confirmation. The Pashtali had more than enough firepower to convince an alien government to lie on their behalf. They'd lured a fleet into a killing ground before, back when the war started. Why wouldn't they do it again? "Can we trust them?"

"Can they trust us?" Nancy studied her hands thoughtfully. "We need allies. We need a way out of this war before our economy implodes or the Alphans abandon us or the Pashtali manage to win. This may be our one chance to put together an alliance that will threaten the Pashtali with actual defeat, not a draw. Can we afford to let it pass?"

"And if they're not trustworthy, we'll be sending a chunk of our fleet into the meatgrinder," Abraham pointed out. "How long will the Alphans protect us?"

Nancy made a face. "I don't know."

Abraham nodded, then raised his eyes to the chart. The Pashtali were expanding in all directions, taking control of strategic points that would allow them to lock up the shipping lanes and keep their enemies apart without expending much of their military power. It was galling to know that humanity was just one small target to them...his lips quirked as he realised they'd fucked up the timing. The Pashtali had started the next set of wars before crushing the human race, which meant they might be a little overextended…but by how much? No one knew.

"This is the one chance we have," Nancy said. "They're not talking to us, not seriously."

"No," Abraham agreed. The peace talks were a joke. The Pashtali had made that clear on the very first day. They presumably understood humanity as little as humans understood them, but it was impossible to believe that anyone who started the talks by demanding everything first and *then* haggling was taking them seriously. "We don't have the power to force them to take the talks seriously."

"Not alone, no," Nancy agreed. "But as part of a greater alliance…"

"If we can have the alliance," Abraham said. "We'll be taking a huge risk just proving we are committed."

"We're committed anyway," Nancy counted. "The Pashtali aren't going to go away, are they?"

Abraham laughed, humourlessly. "They attack us and somehow *we're* the ones who have to help them save face?"

"It's an old galactic custom," Nancy said. "And the only other option is fighting to the death."

"True." Abraham studied the chart. The human race *was* committed. There was nothing, up to and including outright surrender, that would convince the Pashtali to spare Earth. They'd been too badly battered by the fighting to accept surrender. They *needed* to make an example of the human race. "Damn it!"

"Quite," Nancy agreed. "If this works…"

"Start drawing up the paperwork, nail down the terms," Abraham said. "Speak to the ambassadors again, tell them what we want in exchange for doing their dirty work. And when we get independent confirmation of the situation, we'll decide if we want to take the offensive."

"We need allies," Nancy said. "We have to take the risk or…we'll be alone and then defeated."

"I know." Abraham scowled at the starchart. "But we need more than *just* allies. We need to knock the bastards out of the war before they knock us out."

He sipped his coffee. "And do you trust the Alphans to keep their word?"

"They have a long history of keeping their word," Nancy said, thoughtfully. "But none of us ever expected they'd just abandon much of their empire..."

Abraham nodded, curtly. He'd always imagined the road to independence would be slow and steady, long and perhaps bumpy. He'd thought he'd spend years developing independent facilities on Earth, claiming more and more autonomy within the empire...he'd even dared to wonder, at times, if humanity would have to fight for its freedom. Instead...the Alphans had just grown tired of their empire and let the human race go. It felt almost like a cheat, as if they'd been deprived of the chance to prove they could stand on their own two feet. He'd never really understood how much of the planet's economy depended on the Alphans, not until it was too late. And now...

"We never expected it," he said. "And how long will they keep their ships here?"

"I don't know," Nancy said. She looked oddly pensive. "I think they don't know either."

"No," Abraham said. He hated having to rely on something he couldn't control. It would have been better, in a way, if the Alphans had set a strict timetable. "What happens if we lose most of the fleet and *then* they decide to withdraw their ships?"

His mind churned. He'd never really thought of the Alphans as benevolent—they'd been imperialists first and foremost, who'd benefited hugely from all the benevolent things they'd done—but he knew there were worse masters out there. Humanity had been lucky. They could have been invaded and ruled by the Pashtali or...he frowned as a thought struck him. Was it a plan to weaken the human race all along, to force them to call their former masters back to rule? Or was he just being paranoid? The Alphans could have won a civil war, if they'd decided to keep Earth for themselves...

Although the system would have been incredibly banged up, he thought. *And it might not have been worth the effort.*

He studied Nancy for a long moment. She'd been a loyalist, back in the day. He had no reason to doubt her loyalties now, but…he shook his head. He was definitely being paranoid. He was tired and cranky and paranoid and…

"We're due to meet with the admiral shortly," he said. He checked his watch. The admiral should be on her way by now, unless a new crisis or three had exploded in the last few moments. "Hopefully, by then, we'll have the bare bones of a treaty or two."

"Nothing will be signed until Terminus is cleared of enemy ships," Nancy cautioned, warningly. "There's no way to change that, not in a hurry. They're not going to go out on a limb for us unless they're sure we're committed."

"And that there's a reasonable chance of victory," Abraham added. His lips twisted. They needed allies to win, but they could only get allies by winning…"We'll do our best, but…"

He shrugged, wordlessly.

• • •

Ambassador Yasuke kept his face under tight control as he finished reviewing the notes from the peace talks. He was no stranger to entitled arrogant ambassadors demanding everything they could get before talks got started—the humans joked about asses in ambassadors, which was often uncomfortably true—but the Pashtali were being absurd. They seemed to think the human race was going to give them everything, on a platter, and *then* hold peace talks? It made no sense. No one would agree to such terms and, if they did, there was no point in holding talks anyway. It was an insane mess.

He keyed his console, encrypting his private files. His superiors had hoped the talks would get somewhere, but it was clear they were going to be disappointed. The Pashtali just weren't taking them seriously. And yet, surely peace was their best choice? They'd attacked a dozen races, expanded their control too far too fast...why had they bitten off more than they could chew? Yasuke didn't like the implications. Did they think they could copy everything the Alphans had done, when they'd ruled the known galaxy? Or were they following a plan no one else could understand? Perhaps they thought they could smash everyone within reach, then take over before their targets could recover and fight back?

Which is as good a theory as any other, he thought, as he stood. *The Pashtali might think they can win by knocking everyone else down.*

He frowned as he made his way to the door. It was astonishing how his position had shifted in the last five years. He'd been a viceroy, then a powerless ambassador, then a powerful ambassador...it was confusing, something his people didn't handle very well. He'd wondered, at times, why he hadn't been replaced long ago. Perhaps he was considered the perfect representative, or...maybe his masters thought he'd gone native. Or they couldn't find a replacement. A person of *his* rank had a lot of say in his assignments. Earth hadn't been seen as an important posting until the Pashtali War had broken out.

No, he corrected himself. *It was one of the most important places in the empire, until we let it go. And then it became important again.*

"My Lord," his aide said, as he stepped into the antechamber. The human looked nervous. No one enjoyed being the bearer of bad news. "The Minister for Industrial Production sends his regrets, but he's running late. He should be here in twenty minutes."

Yasuke nodded and made his way to the window. The humans understood the value of being punctual. It was unlikely the minister intended to be insulting. He put the thought aside as he looked down on the city. The Pashtali had done a lot of damage, shooting up buildings and bombing troop concentrations, but the humans were already making repairs. They had an energy, he reflected ruefully, that his own people had lost long ago. He wondered, sometimes, if they'd replace his people as masters of the known universe. But it wouldn't be easy. There were too many threats lurking at the rim of civilised space.

If they survive the war, they'll go far, he told himself. *If.*

CHAPTER FIVE

SOLAR CITY, EARTH

"ADMIRAL," FIRST SPEAKER DOUGLAS SAID. "Welcome to Solar City."

Naomi nodded, shaking his hand. The flight over the city had been a grim reminder of the human costs of war; the lives ruined, the homes destroyed, the uncertainty overshadowing men and women who'd been forced to flee from the invaders. The Alphans had set up a food distribution network to end world hunger, when they'd taken control of the planet, and the provisional government had tried to keep it going, but it hadn't survived the invasion. Parts of the planet had too much food for their needs, while other parts were starving. Even now, too many people were desperately short of food and shelter. It was just another reason to end the war as quickly as possible, before the planet collapsed into chaos.

"You know Ambassador Middleton," Douglas said, indicating the other person in the chamber. "She's been handling negotiations with the lesser powers."

"A pleasure," Naomi said. She'd met Ambassador Nancy Middleton before, at Admiral Glass's funeral. She wasn't quite sure how the loyalist had ended up working for the independence activist, but she was pleased to see it nonetheless. It boded well for the future. If there *was* a future. The Pashtali were still out there. "Has there been any progress in negotiating with the Pashtali?"

"No," Nancy said, curtly. "We cannot determine if they are stalling for time, as some of our analysts think, or if they honestly believe we'll give them everything they want if they demand it loudly enough. Either way, we cannot reasonably give them what they want as a precondition and they're apparently reluctant to make any concessions to us."

Naomi sighed, inwardly. She wished she was surprised. The Pashtali were powerful enough to wait out the clock, secure in the knowledge Earth would collapse first. They might be stalling...or simply giving lip service to negotiations in a bid to appease galactic opinion. Or they might even think humanity would sell itself out for the best terms it could get...no, that made no sense. They'd be offering some kind of concessions if they honestly believed they could force humanity to accept an unbalanced peace.

"We have made more progress with the lesser powers," Nancy informed her, once they'd poured themselves coffee and sat down. "Some of them are willing to work with us, if we prove our willingness to continue the fight. They want us to liberate Terminus."

Naomi listened as Nancy ran through the whole story. She wasn't too surprised the lesser powers wanted a show of faith before siding with the human race, although it was awkward because the humans could hardly end the war unilaterally. It took one power to start a war and two powers to end it. And yet...she supposed it made a degree of sense. It would be easier to bend the knee to the Pashtali before joining the war, when the Pashtali might offer better terms in exchange for submission. As long as the Pashtali effectively ruled Terminus, they could keep their prospective enemies from joining forces...

She mentally collated Nancy's observations with her own plans. Her staff had drawn up a handful of options, each one existing—for the moment—solely on paper. A couple could be adapted to the new reality, if she went ahead with it...she took a breath. If she made a mistake...how, she asked herself, had Admiral Glass remained in command for so long? Each and every one of his decisions could have led to utter disaster...hell, the balance of power was so tilted against the human race that he could do everything right and still lose. And somehow he'd endured the pressure for nearly seven years before his death. She didn't know how he'd done it.

"My staff and I have been looking at options, purely on a contingency basis," she said, finally. She'd been cautioned political leaders didn't always like being told the military was planning operations, even if they never become anything more than ink on paper. It could be politically inconvenient if word reached the wrong pair of ears. "And they can be adapted to fit our needs."

Douglas leaned forward. "Can we win?"

Naomi hesitated. That was the rub, wasn't it? The war had to be won... at the very least, they had to go back to the *status quo ante bellum*. And yet, there was no way to force the Pashtali to negotiate on equal terms. They had to make the war too expensive to continue and yet...she scowled, inwardly. She had to make it clear to them, somehow, that any victory would be very limited in scope. There was little data on the enemy homeworld's defences, or on the defences surrounding their major worlds, but she had no doubt they'd be formidable. The massed power of the Solar Navy wouldn't be enough to crack them, even if the enemy warships were elsewhere. Her fleet would be bled white for nothing.

"There are some points I need to make, and make clearly," she said. She looked from one to the other, keeping her voice under tight control. They had to understand. "We will not win a total victory. There will be no victory parades on the alien homeworld. The best we can hope for, assuming everything goes our way, is a strictly limited victory. We must convince them that defeating us won't be worth the cost, a very difficult task. Ideally, we need to weaken them to the point other powers will jump on them—or they *think* they'll be attacked by other powers. Again, that will be a very difficult task."

"They do have enemies," Nancy said, slowly.

"Yes, but the enemy of my enemy is not always my friend," Naomi countered. "The Galactics might be quite happy to let us get beaten down, on the grounds we might pose a threat in the long run. Or they might be equally happy to let the war go on indefinitely, supplying us with ships and weapons to bleed the Pashtali instead of committing their own militaries to the war. They may dislike, even fear, the Pashtali, but as long as the Pashtali hold the whip hand the other powers will be reluctant to intervene too openly."

"Charming," Douglas commented. "You'd think they'd be able to stand up to the Pashtali."

"Interstellar power politics have always been about raw power, not principles," Naomi said, grimly. She'd spent enough time along the rim to be sure of it. "The Pashtali can get away with a hell of a lot, if the cost of bringing them to account is too high."

She took a breath. "We do have a window of opportunity, however," she said. "And we might be able to use it to win."

"But only a limited victory, as you said," Douglas commented. "What do you have in mind?"

Naomi took a datachip from her pouch and slotted it into the secure projector, then leaned back in her chair as the starchart materialised over the table. It was rare for admirals to give briefings personally—there were staffers for that—but she had no choice. The operational concepts were so highly classified that the officers who'd worked on them had been placed in lockdown, in a bid to ensure nothing—not even rumours—leaked. Naomi found it hard to believe anyone would willingly spy for the Pashtali, but she knew better than to assume it was impossible. The Pashtali could easily have recruited a handful of human turncoats and encouraged them to climb to the top. Hell, a mere five years ago, literally *everyone* in the navy had worked for an alien power.

And there are no shortage of isolated human settlements in disputed space, she reminded herself. *The Pashtali could probably hire mercenaries as well as spies.*

She put the thought aside and cleared her throat. "We have a brief window of opportunity, like I said," she started. "First, the Alphans are providing security for Earth. We have no idea how long the warcruisers will remain here, but while they do my staff believe the Pashtali won't risk a second invasion. The risk of starting a full-scale war with the Alphans would be too great."

"Unless they think the Alphans are bluffing," Nancy pointed out.

"It's a possibility," Naomi agreed. "Second, the Pashtali also have a string of border conflicts to handle before they turn their attention back to us. Most of those conflicts are minor, in the grand scheme of things, but my staff believe there's a non-zero chance of those conflicts either spinning out of control or the races and planets involved getting organised as a unit, given time. My staff didn't know, of course, that the races were already making approaches to us."

"It was highly classified," Nancy said.

Naomi nodded. "The basic operational concept was to take the fleet, all the warships we could muster, and raid along the edge of enemy territory, while *Crossroads* and the other captured ships slipped deeper into enemy space," she said. "Terminus wasn't on our original hit list, but there's no reason we can't strike the besiegers first. I'll have to direct a spy ship to investigate, just to determine what's really going on, before we commit ourselves. We can't risk heavy losses so quickly."

"You're gambling everything on one roll of the dice," Douglas commented. "Right?"

"In a manner of speaking, yes," Naomi said. "The truth is, Mr Speaker, that we are desperately short of everything from starships and missiles to trained and experienced personnel. We made a lot of progress, since independence, on filling the gaps in our order of battle—and replacing functions originally handled by the Alphans—but the war has left us eating our seed corn. Our position..."

She paused, considering her next words. Thankfully, Douglas was a student of pre-invasion human history. It was surprisingly rare, even now. The Alphans had never intended to suppress it, but Earth's history had seemed unimportant compared to the sheer immensity of galactic history. Naomi herself had been taught more about the Alphan Wars of Conquest in school than she had about battles fought by her ancestors, on both sides of the family. She'd made up for it since– she'd had plenty of time to read about human history—but she was painfully aware of the gaps in her knowledge. It was going to take years to bring human history front and centre.

"Our position is roughly akin to Finland, in 1940," she said. "We have trashed the attacking forces and sent them reeling back to think again, but we cannot hope to win a long, drawn-out conflict. They can just wear us down by raiding our lines, forcing us to burn up our resources and eventually lose the war. We have to gamble everything on striking deep into their territory, defeating them before they can defeat us. If we fail..."

"We lose," Douglas said. "Finland lost. Do you think we can win?"

"Finland did manage to maintain its independence," Naomi said. "I think that sitting still and waiting to be hit is a recipe for defeat. If we take the offensive, we might weaken them to the point they concede or get attacked by someone else."

She looked at the starchart. "And if you're right about the other powers joining us, if we liberate Terminus, we'll have a lot more options," she added. "But we need to know what's happening there before we commit ourselves."

"True," Douglas agreed. He sipped his coffee thoughtfully. "How long will it take to deploy the fleet?"

"At least a month, then another month to reach Terminus." Naomi grimaced. "Realistically, it might take longer. I'd prefer to keep the fleet away from the regular shipping lanes as much as possible. If someone notices us, they might sound the alert and then the Pashtali would know we were stabbing into their territory."

"Assuming they didn't write the whole thing off as a fleet of sensor ghosts," Douglas pointed out. "Or they chose to keep their mouths thoroughly shut."

"We couldn't rely on either," Naomi said. "Frankly, sir, I wouldn't rate our chances very highly. The Galactics may hope for our victory, on the grounds the Pashtali are worse, but that won't translate into active support. As long as they think the Pashtali will win, or remain a great power, the other races will be wary about taking our side. Why risk angering the Pashtali by *not* broadcasting a warning?"

"They'd risk angering us, if they did," Douglas said.

"We don't look anything like as dangerous," Naomi said, grimly. "The Pashtali outnumber and outgun us and that isn't going to change, not unless we come up with a silver bullet that renders their entire fleet obsolete. We simply don't have anything like as much leverage as they do and that isn't going to change either."

"Not in a hurry," Douglas agreed.

Naomi nodded in grim understanding. Earth—and the handful of majority-human colonies that made up human space—was *tiny* on a galactic scale, a star nation so unimportant that it was difficult to believe anyone could take it seriously. Douglas might be the head of state *and* head of government wrapped into one, but—as far as the Galactics were concerned—he was a comic opera character with delusions of grandeur. He would be lucky if any of them took him seriously, let alone treated him as an equal. It would take time—centuries, probably—for that to change. Earth was just too unimportant compared to the Pashtali and the other Galactics.

And some of them will be happier with the devil they know, she reflected. *They won't want to take a chance on us.*

Douglas let out a breath. Naomi didn't envy him. They'd said Admiral Glass was the one man who could lose the war—and *everything*—in an afternoon, but it was true of First Speaker Douglas too. If he did the wrong thing...Naomi knew, all too well, that their backs were pressed against the bulkhead. They could liberate Terminus, they could...but there was no guarantee the other races would keep their word. Naomi had no faith in treaties, particularly secret agreements never openly acknowledged.

The hell of it was that, if she was in their place, she'd probably consider breaking her word too.

"One final point, then," Douglas said. "Who'll be in command of the operation?"

"Me," Naomi said. "There aren't any other experienced candidates."

Douglas raised his eyebrows. "Really?"

"Yes, sir," Naomi said. "We didn't have many flag officers before independence. We rarely operated as part of a larger force and, when we did, we were normally under Alphan command. Afterwards, we had a few officers experienced in fleet command, but most of them died in the war. I am the most experienced fleet commander in service and I only took command of the fleet after my superior was killed."

"You'll be taking Ambassador Middleton with you," Douglas said. "She'll have wide authority to negotiate on Earth's behalf, should you lose contact with the government, and make temporary agreements with alien races. Or even the Pashtali, if they deign to talk to us."

"Yes, sir," Naomi said. She suspected it was a double-edged sword—the government wouldn't want the fleet doing anything that would make negotiations impossible—but there was no point in arguing about it. Nancy Middleton was an experienced diplomat. She'd know better than to try to push herself into the military command structure. "I hope we can lay the groundwork for successful negotiations."

"So do we," Douglas said. "Who'll be remaining here?"

"Admiral Morrígan," Naomi said. "However, sir, I must caution you that our ability to defend the planet, without the fleet, will be minimal. The planetary defences took one hell of a beating and we have been unable to do more than basic repairs, not when we had to devote everything to preparing the fleet. If the Pashtali attack, and the Alphans withdraw, we could lose everything."

"And we'll find ourselves fighting it out on the ground, again," Douglas said.

"Yes, sir," Naomi agreed. "However, if the enemy gains uncontested control over the high orbitals, we will lose."

"We might lose the homeworld," Douglas growled. "But we will not surrender."

Naomi kept her thoughts to herself. The PDC network had been badly degraded by the earlier invasion. The Pashtali would have no trouble landing a second army if they took control of the system, or even hammering away at the remaining PDCs until the planet was naked and helpless beneath them. Given time, and a constant bombardment, how long would it be until the planet surrendered? The Pashtali might hesitate to launch a genocidal bombardment—it would unite the rest of the known galaxy against them—but they could keep up the pressure more or less indefinitely. Douglas's government might not survive if the population became desperate for peace.

"As long as the Alphans remain here, we should be safe," Naomi said. "It is my duty, however, to discuss the worst-case scenarios as well as the best."

"True." Douglas looked tired but determined. "Return to your fleet, Admiral, and prepare for deployment."

"Yes, sir," Naomi said. "One other point; we cannot, we absolutely cannot, let the enemy have any idea of our plans. If they know we're heading to Terminus, they'll assemble a fleet to intercept and stop us. And that will be utterly disastrous."

"I see," Douglas said. "They'll know the fleet is preparing to deploy though, won't they?"

"Yes, sir." Naomi was sure *some* of the merchantmen passing through the system worked for the Pashtali. Even commercial-grade sensor recordings would be worth their weight in gold to enemy intelligence officers. "But as long as they don't know the target, we should be fine."

"We'll spread a few lies," Ambassador Middleton said. "Perhaps tell them we're heading back to Theta Sigma. They won't see it as a threat."

"No," Naomi agreed. "But they might not see it as very believable either."

CHAPTER SIX

JAMES BOND, TERMINUS

"IT'S QUIET," COMMANDER SARAH ANDERSON SAID, deadpan. "Too quiet."

Captain Thomas Anderson glanced at his wife and XO. "What do you mean?"

"We're approaching a bottleneck crossroads," Sarah pointed out. "So... where's all the traffic?"

Thomas nodded, curtly. The threadlines leading to Terminus were unusually thin and the crossroads unusually small, ensuring that traffic heading to and from the system was herded into a relatively tiny region of space. They should be seeing a *lot* more traffic in the threadline, from small independent traders to giant freighters and even warships. And yet, the threadline was disconcertingly empty. *James Bond's* sensors were only picking up three other ships, all keeping their distance. Sarah was right. It *was* too quiet.

"There really must be a blockade," he said. They hadn't heard anything about it, not until they'd picked up their orders from Earth, but there had to be a *reason* so few ships were passing through the threadline. "And that means...?"

He gritted his teeth as the countdown approached zero. The crossroads ahead of them was disconcertingly small, ensuring they'd return to realspace in an entirely predictable location .., and, if the enemy really *were* blockading the system, they'd be right under enemy guns. The system wasn't precisely a bottleneck—there were too many crossroads in the system—but whoever controlled it could put a sizable chunk of interstellar trade in a stranglehold. He wasn't keen on the idea of having his ship inspected, not by officers who knew what they were doing. *James Bond* might look like a harmless freighter, one of the countless independent traders making her way from system to system, but her sensor suite was the best money could buy. If the inspectors realised what it was, they'd ask some very pointed questions indeed.

Good thing we disembarked the kids, he thought, bracing himself for transition. It was tricky as hell to run a ship with only two crewmen, but it was better than the alternative. *They'll survive, even if we don't.*

The freighter shook violently as she passed through the crossroads, the display blanking and rebooting. Red icons flared to life...he cursed under his breath as they took on shape and form, customs and battle stations that really shouldn't have been there. They certainly hadn't been listed in the files. Beyond them, keeping their distance, he could spot a small fleet of enemy warships. Pashtali warships. They were far enough to keep them safe from a sneak attack, yet close enough to intervene if the shit hit the fan. He was mildly surprised the enemy hadn't mined the crossroads. But then, that might have been a step too far.

"We're being hailed," Sarah reported. "And they're not *quite* pointing their guns at us..."

Thomas scowled. If the enemy didn't have *James Bond* bang to rights, after she'd come through the crossroads, they were grossly overrated. The range was so short, relatively speaking, they'd have no trouble blowing the freighter away if they thought they saw something suspicious. And yet...he keyed his console, frowning as more and more data flowed into the passive sensors. It was a good sign, he supposed, that they weren't demanding transit fees. Yet.

"Send our IFF," he said. "And hope for the best."

Sarah nodded, her face grim. They'd gone to some trouble to prepare the fake IFF—it had been carefully crafted to make it look as though they'd been hired by someone who could and would kick up a fuss if the freighter was intercepted and searched—but there was no way to know how seriously the enemy would take it. The Pashtali might insist on searching the ship anyway, treaties be damned. Or they might check with the supposed employers, who would answer—honestly—that they'd never even *heard* of his ship and crew. And then all hell would break loose. They might have to destroy their own ship in order to keep their secrets from falling into enemy hands.

His heart sank as he surveyed the display. The Pashtali didn't *seem* to have the planets under control—they were surrounded by a multitude of defensive stations and platforms—but the crossroads were very definitely in their hands. No one could enter or leave the system without their permission, not even a first-rank interstellar power. He wondered, rather sourly, how they intended to get away with it...then, as he looked at the icons representing enemy warships, knew the truth. They'd get away with it because no other power could or would drive them out of the system. The smaller powers had been effectively isolated.

Sarah's console bleeped. "They're sending an inspection crew," she said. "And they want to check our holds before allowing us to proceed."

"Fuck." Thomas took a moment to calm himself. There was no way to escape, no way to get out of enemy range before they were blown away. "Implement stealth mode. Let them search the ship, as long as they don't look too closely at the sensors."

Sarah's face showed her doubts, but she didn't argue. Thomas knew what she was thinking. The vast majority of the ship was perfectly legitimate, from the cargo holds to the crew quarters...there was nothing, apart from the sensors, that should raise eyebrows. And yet, how could they be sure? The Pashtali might be harassing humans just for being human. He eyed the display as a shuttle detached itself from the hovering battlestation and flew towards his ship, the pilot showing off a little as he made his final approach. Thomas braced himself and keyed the airlock, preparing to receive boarders. As long as they didn't look too closely, he told himself as the shuttle docked, they should be fine.

A shame they're not human, he thought. *I know how to bribe humans.*

The thought made him smile—he hastily buried it—as the airlock hissed open, revealing a pair of Vulteks. Thomas blinked in surprise, then bent his head into the posture of respect. The bird-like aliens exchanged looks, then advanced—he couldn't help thinking of it as prancing—into the freighter, their beady eyes swivelling from side to side. Thomas kicked himself, mentally, for not expecting the Pashtali to send their clients to do their dirty work. The spider-like aliens didn't find human ships very comfortable. The Vulteks might have the same problem, but their masters didn't care what they thought.

"Papers," the leader stated. His face was weirdly immobile, as if he was wearing a rubber mask. "Now."

Thomas passed his ID datachip and waited. His superiors had gone to some trouble to give him a proper identity, one that didn't have any formal ties to Earth or the Alphan Empire. There was nothing to suggest he was anything other than an independent trader from an independent world somewhere in the midst of disputed space. And yet…the other Vultek kept glancing around, clawed hands twitching as if he wanted to rend and tear something into very little pieces. Thomas hoped the alien could restrain himself. The Vulteks had never liked humanity even before the Earth-Vultek War.

At least they're not interested in molesting us, he told himself. Interspecies sex wasn't precisely forbidden, but it was vanishingly rare even in the most liberal asteroid settlements on the edge of explored space. Spacers joked there was no *need* to ban it. *They might kill us, of course.*

The Vulteks carried out a desultory inspection of the ship, then left.

Thomas wondered, as *James Bond* received permission to head further into the system, just what their masters thought they were doing. The search had been so basic he thought he could have smuggled enough weapons to fight a small war past them. And yet...he scowled as it dawned on him the Pashtali were stamping their authority over the system. By taking control, by exercising authority and demanding everyone bowed the knee, they were establishing themselves as the boss. The hell of it was that it might just work. Terminus had always been an isolated system, carefully left politically independent to ensure no single power controlled it. And that meant whoever started to exercise control might win the system by default.

He keyed his console, steering a course towards the nearest planet, and kept an eye on the sensor reports. There were still no signs that the Pashtali were trying to control the planets themselves, but they hardly needed to bother. They could keep the system in a vise-like grip just by controlling the crossroads. The same factors that had made the system so interesting—and ensured it remained independent—were now being turned against it. Thomas frowned, inwardly, as the sensors kept updating. The planets looked ready and yet reluctant to fight.

"I've got us a berth," Sarah said. "I also put in a request to use their FTL communicator."

"We'll have to paraphrase everything first," Thomas said. "And make sure it doesn't draw attention."

He scowled. It was a risk—aliens rarely understood human idiom, but there was no reason they couldn't hire a human expert—yet it was one they'd have to take. An openly encrypted message would draw attention. Legally, the Pashtali weren't allowed to copy and decrypt the message, let alone insist on holding the freighter until the message was decrypted to their satisfaction, but no one expected them to honour their word. He'd just have to write a message that would be absolutely meaningless to anyone who didn't understand the code, then send it in the clear. Or in a code they knew their enemies had already broken.

Better not to use the code, he told himself. *We really don't want them looking too closely at us.*

The thought haunted him as they approached Terminus III. The planet had been a lifeless ball of rock when someone—the records weren't clear on who—had popped out of the nearest crossroads and surveyed the system. Terraforming attempts had been desultory at best, resulting in an atmosphere that was barely breathable and an ocean that—according to the files—was poisonous. It hadn't been enough to stop settlers from flooding the planet, establishing a cluster of sealed cities and orbital installations that tried to keep themselves as independent as possible. Thomas knew the type. Human or alien, he doubted there was anyone on or orbiting the planet who liked the Pashtali trying to take control. And yet, what could they do about it?

They'll be planning something, Thomas thought. *There'll be a resistance. But how do we get in touch with them?*

He dismissed the thought and looked at his wife. "I'll put the message together," he said. "You see if you can find someone willing to talk."

"Okay," Sarah said, doubtfully. "But we'll be lucky."

Thomas nodded, curtly. There'd be information brokers in orbit—there always were—but they'd be careful what information they sold these days. He keyed his console, trying to access the local network, yet there was nothing beyond a series of advertisements—mostly aimed at aliens—and a bunch of encrypted computer nodes. It wasn't really a surprise—there was no united government—but it was still irritating. They might not have time to locate anyone willing to talk.

If we stay here too long, the bastards might start wondering why we haven't gone on to our final destination, he thought. *And then they might want to take a closer look at us.*

He leaned back in his chair as they docked, taking a moment to check the atmosphere and everything else before he started writing the message. It wasn't an easy task. The message had to look innocuous, yet it had to contain all the code phrases his superiors knew to watch for. His lips twitched as he tapped out a particularly important section. Most spacers and traders—human and alien alike—had mates in every port. The message would look like a simple missive, addressed to his other wife. The fact he hadn't *got* a second wife was neither here nor there.

His eyes swept down the sensor records, checking and rechecking what he'd seen before adding it to the message. There was little hope of providing realtime updates on enemy positions—he had no idea what, if anything, Earth intended to do with the intelligence—but he could make sure his superiors knew the basics. The Pashtali had at least forty warships in the system, perhaps more, as well as battlestations and weapons platforms. It was hard to be sure, but he thought they were throwing together more battlestations all the time. They'd be needed to keep control of the system after the warships were dispatched elsewhere.

There is a war on, after all, he reminded himself, as he finished the message. *And they really have too many enemies for their own good.*

He sent the message, bracing himself for rejection. The Pashtali hadn't taken control of the local communicators, not openly, but he wouldn't be surprised to discover they were quietly interfering with the network. There was no way to be *sure* his message would reach even the first relay station. Would he even get a reply? His handler would put together a collection of vapid nonsense—he was sure of it—but would it reach him? He didn't know.

Sarah returned, looking grim. "The local brokers have gone underground," she said. "We don't have the contacts to find them."

Thomas stood. "Then we'd better go see if we can find a bar," he said. "We might get lucky."

He set the security system—he didn't want to come back to the ship and discover it had been looted—then followed his wife through the airlock and onto the station. It felt like a handful of older stations had been dismantled, then melded back together into a giant conglomerate of metal and atmosphere that was about as welcoming as a naval barracks. The air stank, although it was still breathable. He checked his emergency breather anyway—it was safely in his pocket, well within reach—and walked through the next set of airlocks. There were no further barriers, nothing to keep freighter crews from exploring the station. He gritted his teeth. He'd spent most of his adult life on the least savoury worlds along the fringe and even *they* had been more careful than this...

But there's no government here, he reminded himself. *They don't even have any laws.*

The thought mocked him as they made their way through the marketplace. The aisles heaved with visitors from a hundred different races, from galactic superpowers to scavengers. The stalls were crammed with everything from starship components to medical supplies, drugs, and illegal porn. His lips twitched at the latter before they moved on. One race's illicit erotica was a mystery to the others, with no shared agreement on what was completely beyond the pale.

Sarah nudged him. "You think that's genuine?"

Thomas followed her gaze. One storekeeper was advertising pieces of ancient super-advanced technology, displaying a handful of objects that *looked* alien...but might easily have been forged in a fabricator, rather than dug up on some long-dead world. It was possible they were real... but then, it was also possible he'd win the galactic lottery and become the richest man in the known universe. If they were real...no, they couldn't be real. The Galactics offered immense bounties for any pieces of ancient technology. Thomas had been told the bounties were paid too, after the technology was checked and verified. No one would bring the tech here, for a handful of credits, when they could get far more by taking it to the Alphans. Or the Pashtali. Or even to Earth.

"If it is, I'll eat my hat," he said. "It's probably forged."

He kept his eyes open as they made their way into a bar and bought drinks, then sat at a small table and studied the crowd. There were only a handful of humans, none of whom paid any attention to them. *That* was odd. Normally, humans were keen to meet other humans...Thomas frowned, inwardly, as his gaze moved around the room. There was an ugly tension in the air, a grim awareness the entire situation was hanging from a thread. He suspected it boded ill.

"We're being watched," Sarah said, so quietly he could barely hear her. "At least two people, both human."

"Stay alert," Thomas muttered. It was unlikely they were in any real danger, but it was impossible to be sure. "We'll go when we finish our drinks..."

He broke off as an immensely fat man separated himself from the crowd and sat down at their table, a twisted smile covering his lips. "You're new here, aren't you?"

"Yes," Thomas said. There was no point in denying it. "Just passing through, really."

The man leered at him. "And can I do anything to make your visit more comfortable? Booze? Girls? Boys? Girls and boys? Or even some hot little mamas with tentacles instead of hands..."

"We won't be staying long," Thomas said. The man was probably a fixer. There were hundreds like him in every free port. "We were wondering...what the fuck is going on with the warships out there?"

The man's smile didn't change, but his eyes went cold and hard for a long second. "Where have *you* been for the last few months?"

"Amanas," Thomas lied. The planet was on the other side of the known galaxy. No one would be able to disprove the story, not in a hurry. "We're only just heading back this way now."

"The Pashtali think they own this system," the man said. "And so far, no one has told them otherwise."

"Crap," Thomas said.

"I can give you an up-to-date briefing packet," the man said. "And I can give you the time of your life too. It'll be yours for a very reasonable price."

Thomas smiled, then started to haggle.

CHAPTER SEVEN

EARTH DEFENCE FORCE ONE, EARTH ORBIT

"ADMIRAL," ENSIGN TASMAN SAID, as Naomi passed through the antechamber. "I have the latest reports from the fleet for you."

"Forward them to my terminal," Naomi ordered. "And inform me when Commodore Valentine arrives."

She stepped into the office without waiting for his response, breathing a sigh of relief as the hatch closed behind her. The last two weeks had been nightmarish, with endless meetings and planning sessions broken only by brief pauses for meals and a few short hours of sleep before returning to the daily grind. The grim awareness she should be relieved, to say the least, that she wasn't being shot at didn't help. If her ship was under attack, she could at least fire back. Now, she had to tolerate people—and meetings—she would sooner throw out the airlock.

I don't know how Admiral Glass put up with it, Naomi thought, as she tried to focus. *There are too many things to do and too little time.*

She took a long breath, then another. The fleet's target remained a closely-guarded secret—only twelve people knew the truth and nine were in permanent lockdown—but she was all too aware rumours were spreading at the speed of light. Too many people were wondering, too loudly, why the entire fleet was heading to Theta Sigma. Too many others were asking why the fleet was even bothering, given that Theta Sigma and the rest of the Occupied Zone had been a poisoned chalice. Hell, no one was even sure what was going on in the former Occupied Zone. Theta Sigma hadn't been formally claimed by the Pashtali or anyone, really. For all they knew, the planet was still technically in human hands.

Not that it matters, really, she told herself. *We're not really going anywhere near the former Occupied Zone.*

She sighed as she made her way to her desk, trying not to groan at the mountain of paperwork awaiting her. There were too few staffers who could be trusted to handle the minor matters…she promised herself, when the war was over, she'd look for ways to lighten the load. The Solar Navy had never developed a major bureaucracy and, as absurd as it seemed, the lack had bitten them hard. She'd have to do something about it. And yet…she shook her head and sat down, flicking through the reports. The sooner the fleet was underway, the better. She might just have a chance to sleep for more than a handful of hours at a time.

And everyone else will get a chance to rest too, she thought. She hadn't realised how *easy* her life had been as a junior crewman, back before independence. Her past self had bitched and moaned and been a complete ignorant idiot, unaware of just how lucky she'd been. Now…she shook her head. Normally, she'd have been a captain or a commodore for several years before rising to flag rank. She hadn't expected to be kicked upstairs so rapidly. *If Admiral Glass was still alive…*

Her terminal bleeped. "Admiral," Tasman said. "Commodore Valentine has arrived."

"Send him in," Naomi ordered. "And send in coffee too."

She rubbed her forehead as the hatch opened. She'd drunk too much coffee over the last few weeks, but…what choice did she have? There were more advanced stimulants, all of which would give her a few hours of alertness followed by several more of complete lethargy. She could ask for them—very little was forbidden to admirals—but the price was too high. Besides, she would bring the hammer down—hard—on any junior officer who risked using them. She'd be leery about using them even as a last resort.

"Admiral," Commodore Roger Valentine said. "You wanted to see me?"

Naomi nodded, indicating a chair. She wished she knew the commodore better, but they'd never crossed paths until now. She'd been a line officer, while he'd been assigned to the advanced technological research division...the closest the old EDF had come to admitting it was trying to reverse-engineer Alphan technology before independence. Now...she'd read his reports with interest, but they'd never actually met. She wanted to get a feel for him before she put him in command of a fleet.

"Yes, Commodore," she said, as the steward wheeled a trolley into the chamber and withdrew as silently as he'd come. "Coffee? Sandwich?"

"Yes, please," Valentine said.

Naomi studied him thoughtfully as she poured them both coffee. "Your reports stated you believed the majority of the captured ships could be put into service very quickly, and I authorised you to proceed," she said. "How much progress have you made?"

Valentine sipped his coffee. "That's a difficult question to answer," he said, slowly. "From a technical point of view, the captured ships are ready for deployment. We have done what repairs we can, replaced some of the control systems and reprogrammed others, and rearmed the vessels with captured missiles and other supplies. However, we simply lack the trained repair crews to keep the warships running indefinitely. When they start taking damage, and they will, it will be impossible to fix on deployment."

He paused. "I've had volunteer crews working on the ships, and learning how to operate them, but there are limits," he added. "There's a good chance they'll take one look and *know* the ships are in unfriendly hands, even if we don't manage to...ah, *mess* up the IFF signals."

"They may well know which ships fell into our hands," Naomi said. If she'd been calling the shots on the other side, she'd have listed every starship that took part in the battle as *missing, presumed captured or destroyed*. It wasn't easy to change a warship's drive signature to make it unrecognisable and even *trying* would be far too revealing. "We'll have to assume as much."

"Yes, Admiral," Valentine said. "*Crossroads* is a different story. We assigned a larger crew and the ship was already crammed with supplies, although we're having to check them all for possible electronic sabotage. They may—may—have had time to upload subversive software into the components before they surrendered. Assuming that isn't the case, however, there are still limits. My best guess is that we will be able to use the crossroads generator four times at most before wear and tear renders the device useless, even with a full repair crew on hand."

"And that might be optimistic," Naomi said.

"Yes, Admiral," Valentine agreed. "We have no experience with this sort of technology. It's very much a brute force solution to the problem, unlike the far more elegant tech our former masters put together. It's possible the culminate decay will turn the generator into scrap metal before we make the fourth jump. We just don't know."

"I see." Naomi met his eyes. "For the moment, I intend to assign the alien ships to your command and use them to sneak up on enemy positions. Is that workable?"

"If the IFF codes we have are accurate, then yes," Valentine said. "But we cannot guarantee it. The codes we have were put together from scraps of recovered data and we won't know they're accurate—or not—until we actually try. We intend to stutter the signal, in hopes of disguising any inaccuracies, but I suspect they'll be reluctant to let us get too close until our *bona fides* are firmly established. Realistically, it won't work more than once."

"I wish I thought otherwise," Naomi said. Earth used a complicated—and rotating—set of IFF codes to prevent someone using a dummy code to get through the defences. She dared not assume the Pashtali were any less careful. "But we'll do everything we can to make it work."

"Yes, Admiral," Valentine said. "If nothing else, we'll make them a little more wary of their own ships."

Naomi had to smile, despite the tiredness pervading her soul. "They'll certainly have to recheck all their IFF codes," she agreed. "Speaking of which, did any of the secure communications nodes survive?"

"No, Admiral," Valentine said. "They were purged, then physically destroyed. There was literally nothing left but dust."

"Pity," Naomi said. It was difficult eavesdropping on enemy transmissions. A captured communications node would have made it a great deal easier, but the Pashtali had been quite within their rights to destroy them when they surrendered. "Will you be ready to depart on schedule?"

"I believe so," Valentine said. "We think there are no more unpleasant surprises waiting for us. If there are, our estimate may have to change, but overall we should have no trouble getting the ships underway. Once we take damage, though, our effectiveness will decline sharply."

"It would be a great deal easier if they made their ships as modular as ours," Naomi commented. "Why didn't they?"

"To be fair, their efficiency is considerably greater," Valentine said. "And they don't have to worry so much about splicing too many different components together with spit, baling wire and duct tape. But in the long run, their damaged ships have to go back to shipyards for anything more than basic repairs. *Crossroads* is the closest thing they have to one of our modular vessels and even *she* isn't easy to repair. I'm pretty sure they'd have stuck with their original concept if the generator didn't need to be repaired with every jump."

Naomi nodded, dismissing the thought. It was a curious design philosophy, and she didn't pretend to understand the mentality behind it, but it worked in her favour and that was all that mattered. She studied Commodore Valentine for a long moment, wishing she had someone else she could send in his place. He wasn't the only alien tech expert in her service, but he was easily the best. Under normal circumstances, he'd be too valuable to risk. And yet, what choice did she have? There weren't many humans who could operate alien ships easily.

"Report back to the shipyard and depart as planned," she ordered, reaching into her desk drawer to remove a datachip. "These are your secret orders, including a set of coordinates for the RV point. You are not to open them until you are in multispace and at least two days from Earth. Once you have the coordinates, you are to head straight for the RV point and wait there. The remainder of the fleet will join you shortly."

"Yes, Admiral," Valentine said. "We won't let you down."

Naomi nodded. It felt odd to be playing cloak and dagger games, and she doubted any watching eyes would *miss* the captured ships leaving the system, but it was well to be careful. They had to play a shell game, concealing which ships had left and which had remained…she hoped the stories about *Crossroads* being sold to the Alphans, carefully planted in the galactic media, had been convincing. She had her doubts about that too. The Pashtali might refuse to believe them.

"I'll see you at the RV point," she said, standing. "Good luck."

"Thank you, Admiral," Valentine said.

He stood, saluted, and left the compartment. Naomi watched him go, feeling a twinge of something she didn't care to look at too closely. His mission was a risky one, and the Pashtali would be unmerciful if they caught him, but…it was hard not to feel envious. He was in command of a small fleet—a flotilla, really—of captured ships, while *she* was responsible for the entire navy. The weight of the entire human race rested on her shoulders. She had no idea how Admiral Glass had coped with that, either.

Her terminal bleeped. "Admiral, Commander Evensong is requesting a meeting," Tasman said. "Can I send her in?"

"Yes, please," Naomi said. She eyed the coffee warily. "And then hold my calls."

"Aye, Admiral."

Commander Evensong looked disgustingly fresh as she stepped through the hatch. Naomi told herself, sharply, that such thoughts were unworthy of her. She was too tired…it would be wiser, perhaps, to leave the paperwork and get some sleep before she made a mistake that got someone killed. Or a lot of people killed. The higher the rank, she recalled her old instructor saying once, the higher the number of people you could kill through incompetence or malice. She hadn't thought of the old bastard in years…

"Commander," she said. She threw protocol to the winds and took a sandwich, motioning for Evensong to help herself. "What do you have for me?"

"We just received a message from one of our agents," Evensong said. "As per your request he made his way to Terminus and took a look around. The Pashtali are definitely laying siege to the system."

"I see," Naomi said. She hadn't distrusted the reports from the diplomatic staff, not exactly, but long experience had made her wary. Reports tended to grow in the telling if there was no independent verification. "Do we have any hard data?"

"He couldn't forward sensor records, no," Evensong said. "What he did tell us, however, is worrying. The Pashtali are setting up battlestations around the various crossroads, backed up by warships. Given time, he thinks they'll claim the system itself and dare the rest of the galaxy to do something about it."

"And no one short of the Alphans can," Naomi muttered. Terminus was an odd place, a strange combination of an open system and a bottleneck. As long as the Pashtali controlled the crossroads, they couldn't be dislodged…but if they lost that control, they were in trouble. It was curious. They were the second known race to develop crossroads technology, allowing them to jump into the target system behind enemy lines, and yet they seemed to be wasting resources on building pointless defences. "What do they know that we don't?"

Evensong raised her eyebrows. "I beg your pardon, Admiral?"

"They know they can bypass their own defences, and they'll assume others can too," Naomi said. "Why, then, are they building so many defences?"

"They may assume the lesser powers can't build their own crossroads generators," Evensong said. "Even if they did, the cost would be prohibitive for almost everyone. The defences may not be as solid as they once were, but they're not entirely useless either."

"No," Naomi agreed. She made a mental note to pose the question to the planning staff. "We'll need more hard data before we can plan an offensive."

"I believe the ship will be able to leave the system without impediment, although it is hard to be certain," Evensong said. "The Pashtali are not trying to keep ships from passing through the system, merely searching them as they pass. The searches aren't even very effective."

"But their real purpose is to make it clear the Pashtali are now in charge," Naomi said, tiredly. She'd seen it before, in the Occupied Zone. It was a fundamental tenet of interstellar law that whoever controlled the space owned it. The Pashtali had used it as an excuse to push the human race out. And Terminus didn't even have an official owner to contest the issue. "And it's working."

"Yes, Admiral," Evensong agreed. "The mood in the system is ugly, but as long as the Pashtali remain supreme it is unlikely anyone will challenge them."

Naomi nodded. "Then the sooner we proceed the better," she said. "If they get dug in, getting them out again will be impossible."

"Unless we're prepared to pay an immense price," Evensong said. "We could win the battle and lose the war."

Naomi barely heard her. There were too many other things she had to do, from reading and signing reports and requisitions to studying the reports from the simulated war games and authorising more training programs for the new recruits. She *knew* there was going to be a disaster, sooner or later, simply because of how many of her people were painfully inexperienced and unprepared. And yet, there was nothing she could do about it. There were no alternatives. There was no magical source of reserves she could call upon to fill the gaps in her roster. There was…

Evensong cleared her throat. "Admiral, permission to speak freely?"

Naomi scowled, drawn back to the immediate problem. "Granted."

"You are exhausted." Evensong met her eyes evenly. "You are trying to take too much on yourself and it is costing you. I know you don't have a proper staff, not yet, but you really need to take a break and get some rest."

"I wish that were possible," Naomi said. Evensong was in an odd position, as an intelligence rather than a line officer. She could speak freely and yet…"I don't have the time."

"Then find time," Evensong said. "Admiral, there are two weeks until the fleet departs. You need to be fresh, ready to take command, when the time comes. Get some rest now."

Naomi scowled. She didn't like being lectured by someone only a few years younger than herself. It didn't help that she knew Evensong was right. "Seeing we're talking freely, how did Admiral Glass handle it?"

"He had a staff," Evensong said. There was a hint of surprise in her voice. "He also had a better understanding of what he could, and couldn't, do as a flag officer. Much of his old staff has been dispersed, but you could pull together your own and put them to work."

"If I had time…" Naomi stood. "I take your point."

"I know, it isn't easy," Evensong said. She stood too, brushing down her uniform. "But Admiral Glass would not have approved of you working yourself to death. He'd have been the first to tell you to rest."

"I'll do what I can," Naomi said. She glanced at her schedule. Half of her meetings could be cancelled, or passed to Admiral Morrígan. The remainder could wait for the following day. "And thank you."

"You're welcome." Evensong shot her a jaunty salute. "And good luck."

CHAPTER EIGHT

ESS DAUNTLESS, SOL SYSTEM

"WELCOME BACK, ADMIRAL," Captain Janet Ruthven said. "It's good to see you again."

"Thank you, Janet," Naomi said. "It's good to see you again too."

She stepped through the airlock and took a long breath, a complicated mix of emotions welling up within her. *Dauntless* was her ship...no, she'd *been* her ship. She couldn't command the fleet as well as commanding her flagship...part of her wanted to argue she'd done just that, during the final stage of the battle over Earth, but she knew splitting her attention could easily have been disastrous. Janet deserved her promotion, Naomi told herself firmly, and would do a good job.

"Your staff are already on the flag deck," Janet told her. "They're looking forward to departure."

Naomi nodded. She'd been careful to ensure there was no formal greeting party, no suggestion *Dauntless* was going to fly *her* flag. She had no idea how closely the enemy—and supposedly neutral parties—were watching the system, but she dared not assume they weren't doing their level best to monitor fleet deployments. If they knew *she* was in command of the fleet...she shook her head. The Pashtali might not know her by name, or care if they did. They might even consider her a comic opera admiral, a fool who thought fancy uniforms and entitled attitude made up for a lack of ships and men. It was galling to think that was probably a good thing, although she doubted the Pashtali would be so inclined to underestimate her. They had every reason to take her seriously after she'd beaten their fleet and forced their survivors to surrender.

She smiled at her former XO. "How is the crew coping?"

"Well enough," Janet said. "I was lucky enough to keep a third of my officers and men, so we were able to establish and keep a gruelling training schedule. There were some minor incidents—new graduates thinking they know everything already, reservists having problems coming back to military discipline—but nothing we couldn't handle. *Dauntless* is in good condition, Admiral, and we are looking forward to taking the offensive."

Naomi scowled, inwardly. She'd gone to some trouble to make sure everyone was told—unofficially—that the fleet was going to Theta Sigma, but she didn't know anyone who actually believed it. She didn't even think the civilians believed it. The media had been relatively quiet, thank the gods, but fleet scuttlebutt insisted the navy was going somewhere else. Thankfully, none of the speculation had gotten close to the truth...she sighed inwardly, reminding herself her officers and men were trained to think for themselves. They were smart enough to realise the official story simply didn't make sense.

"We'll be underway soon enough," she said, vaguely. She'd distributed sealed orders to the flotilla commanders, ensuring they knew where to go once they were in multispace. The fleet would go into lockdown from that point too. If there were any spies on the ships, they wouldn't be able to alert their masters. "And then we'll see."

She sighed inwardly. The spooks had been watching for enemy spies, and putting out feelers in the hopes of feeding enemy agents false information, but so far the results had been minimal. Naomi wasn't sure what to make of it. The Pashtali *had* to understand the importance of human intelligence, didn't they? Perhaps they thought they couldn't make contact with human dissidents or turncoats, or perhaps they though such traitors simply didn't exist. It was quite possible there were no *Pashtali* traitors. God knew no one had succeeded in infiltrating *their* society.

We have to assume they have agents in ours, she thought. There'd been a *lot* of independence activists, five years ago, and some of them hadn't been shy about reaching out to alien powers. *And if they get a whiff of where we're going, the entire operation will be doomed before we even reach our target.*

The thought mocked her as she allowed Janet to give her a tour of the ship, pointing out all the improvements—and jury-rigged repairs—that had been made since Naomi had been promoted out of the command chair. It was a grim reminder the navy was desperately short of everything, even components that—prior to the war—had never been in short supply. Naomi knew it was probably worse for the Pashtali—their spare parts were custom-made—but it was no consolation. The Pashtali had the resources to buy everything they needed in bulk and stockpile them for years before they were needed. Earth didn't. And even with the credit and material quietly loaned to humanity, it still took time to build up the industrial base they needed to churn out more of everything. There was no way to get around the simple fact the navy was operating on a shoestring and would be for quite some time to come.

"You have a direct link to the bridge from the flag deck," Janet finished, as they stepped into the CIC. "You can even take command, if the bridge is taken out."

Naomi nodded, although she knew it was pointless. The bridge was the most heavily protected part of the ship. If it was taken out, the rest of the ship would probably be taken out too. The damage control teams were very well trained and practiced, but there were limits to what they could do. If the admiral assumed command in the middle of a battle, it would probably be to do nothing more than order the crew to abandon ship.

"Thank you," she said. "But hopefully that won't be necessary."

She looked around the CIC, feeling an odd twinge of amusement at the sheer lack of neatness. The compartment was crammed with consoles, projectors and chairs that looked as if they'd been stripped from a dozen different ships and stuffed into *Dauntless*. Wiring ran everywhere, linking the systems into the ship's command network so they could make contact with the rest of the fleet. It looked like a disaster waiting to happen, the sort of set-up that would have landed the crew in *real* trouble in the old days. The Alphans had always designed their ships for elegance, rather than efficiency. They'd poured scorn on humanity's attempts to refit old ships rather than producing newer vessels from scratch.

Her lips twitched. *We're going to have to drill the staffers to make sure they don't trip over the wires in the middle of a battle.*

"With your permission, I need to return to the bridge," Janet said. "I have too much work to do."

"And you can't fob it off on your XO," Naomi agreed. "I understand."

"He's currently supervising the training programs," Janet said. "Right now, we all need to be in two places at once."

Naomi nodded. "I'll speak to you later," she said. Protocol demanded Janet host a dinner for the admiral and his staff, once they were underway, but they didn't have the time. Naomi understood the value of protocol, and military formality, yet it couldn't be allowed to get in the way. They *had* to prepare the ships and crews for war. "And please let me know if you need anything."

"Shore leave," Janet said. "A beach, a book, and a hot date. I'm not picky. I'll even settle for a warm date."

"I wish," Naomi said. "There's little shore leave for anyone right now."

Her heart twisted. She'd done what she could, for her officers and men, but there hadn't been enough time to arrange more than a couple of days in the pleasure dens for everyone before the fleet departed. She had a feeling quite a few people had missed their slots, either because they wanted to remain at their posts or simply because their slots had been and gone before they realised they had them. The personnel department was falling apart at the seams, unable to cope with the sheer number of personnel passing in and out of the navy. She made a mental note to ensure the ships operated on a reduced schedule for the first week, giving the crew time to relax. It wouldn't be quite the same—a VR beach couldn't pass for a *real* one—but it was better than nothing.

It would have to suffice.

After Janet left, Naomi turned her attention to the main display. *Dauntless* was surrounded by hundreds of other starships, from purpose-built warships from a dozen races to converted freighters, passenger liners and manufactory ships. Her lips quirked. The liners had no place in the line of battle, but they hosted the repair and salvage crews she'd need to keep the fleet going. She'd had to argue long and hard to bring the manufactory ships with her—they'd been incredibly expensive, each costing five times as much as *Dauntless*—and yet, they might make the difference between victory or defeat. Earth had no bases, not even covert supply dumps, along the edge of enemy space. And if they had to go back home between missions, that lack would give the enemy a chance to recover and counterattack.

"Admiral," Commander Olson said. "We just picked up a message from fleet command. Observer Salix wishes to speak to you."

"I'll take it in my office," Naomi said. "Put him through."

She took a breath, composing herself as she stepped through the hatch. She'd tried to argue against allowing an observer to accompany the fleet, on the grounds she didn't need the distraction, but she'd been told it was a condition attached to the loans the Alphans had extended to Earth. She would have been happier if the observer had been based on one of the liners, where he could be accommodated in the manner his race took for granted...she shook her head in irritation. The observer had insisted on being on the flagship, something she *knew* was going to lead to problems. No one knew quite how to treat humanity's former masters these days. Should she bend the knee? Treat him as an equal? Or...or what? The protocol files were no help. They'd been written years ago, when human independence had been nothing more than a pipe dream.

She looked down at her uniform and sighed again. Her shipsuit was no different from the suits worn by officers and crew alike, save for the shoulder patch. She'd deliberately chosen not to wear a dress uniform when she'd boarded *Dauntless*, both to underline how serious matters had become *and* to deter her subordinates from wearing it themselves. She wasn't the only person who'd been jumped up several ranks, in the aftermath of the battle, and the last thing she needed was for one of them to start putting on airs. Someone would, she was sure. In the old days, she'd met quite a few officers who thought their rank made them superstars. Thankfully, Admiral Glass had cleaned most of them out of the EDF when it became the Solar Navy.

Her console bleeped. She sat down and braced herself, then pressed her finger against the scanner. A holographic image materialised in front of her. She bit her lip to keep from smiling. The Alphan's uniform was, by human standards, astonishingly fancy, with enough gold braid to pay her salary for a year. It was weird to reflect that, by *their* standards, it was a very simple uniform indeed. The alien might as well be slumming it.

"Admiral," Observer Salix said. He spoke in English, not GalStandard One. "I greet you."

"I greet you, Observer," Naomi said. She was astonished. She didn't know many Alphans who spoke English—her former CO had only spoken GalStandard One and flatly refused to learn even a handful of human words—and yet, this one did. She hoped it was a good sign. "I look forward to welcoming you in person."

"And I look forward to accompanying your ship," Observer Salix said. The phrase sounded slightly ridiculous in English. "I will be aboard shortly, alone."

Naomi hid her relief—and puzzlement. It was vanishingly rare for a high-ranking Alphan to travel without servants. Even their starship crews were treated like aristocrats. Naomi had been in fancy *hotels* that had had fewer luxuries than Alphan warcruisers. Was Observer Salix willing to slum it, just to observe the war, or was he expecting *her* crew to tend to his every need? She hoped not. She'd been careful to cut the number of support staff to the bare minimum. She didn't *need* a steward to make her coffee, when the man's berth could be given to a tactical officer or a repair technician or someone—anyone—who might be more useful in the long run. The Alphan was in for a nasty surprise if he thought he was going to be assigned servants. He was lucky he was getting his own cabin.

"You will be welcome," she assured him. "And I trust you will find the experience rewarding."

Observer Salix bowed his head as they exchanged a handful of additional pleasantries, their tongues stumbling lightly over the translated phrases. Naomi guessed the Alphan was an expert on human behaviour, probably one of the Alphans who'd been assigned to Earth for years and immersed himself in human culture. It was rare—the Alphans generally believed themselves to be the superior culture, with all others inferior by definition—but not unknown. The smarter Alphans had always realised that in order to lead humans, they had to know humans, and some of them had been very understanding indeed. She wished she had a copy of his file. He looked middle-aged, for an Alphan, but that was meaningless. The Alphans were known for their long lives. The alien in front of her might easily be old enough to be her great-grandfather.

"I will be joining you shortly," Observer Salix finished. "I bid you farewell."

"Farewell," Naomi said.

She raised a hand, then tapped her console, terminating the call. The holographic imagine vanished. She sat back in her chair, mentally replaying the conversation. It hadn't been anything like as informative as she'd hoped and yet...she had the nasty feeling she'd missed something. What? Observer Salix was clearly experienced with humans. He'd know better, wouldn't he, to dance around the subject if he truly wanted something? The Alphans might have an elegant flowery language, with unspoken social cues, but they had to know other races found it hard to read their true intentions. He'd have asked—or demanded—if he wanted something. Right?

The intercom bleeped. "Admiral, the warcruiser command just sent us an update," Olson said. "Observer Salix will be joining us this evening."

"Understood," Naomi said.

She sighed as she closed the connection. She'd have to prepare a suitable reception. Observer Salix seemed reasonable enough, but his superiors might take offense if she didn't lay out the red carpet for him. Or something. The First Speaker had made it clear they had to keep the Alphans on their side and if that meant applying tongue to buttocks...her lips twisted in amused disgust. The Alphans had never demanded *that* from their subjects—they weren't human—but their elaborate ceremonies sure as hell kept people in their place.

And they waste time, she thought. *No wonder they came so close to losing the war.*

She tapped her console, bringing up the buried personnel files. It had never been officially acknowledged, in the old days, but the EDF had quietly collected biographical data and crew reports on its alien masters. The humans had needed to know which of their superiors could be trusted not to freak out, if they were told something they didn't want to hear; they needed to know which aliens were incompetent, or abusive, or simply more inclined to spend time in their cabins than doing their jobs. The files were still there, hidden within the fleet's datacores. She searched them quickly, looking for signs Observer Salix had once served with the EDF. There were none. It was odd, given he was clearly experienced with humans. Had he changed his name? It was rare for an Alphan to do anything of the sort, but it wasn't impossible.

Her fingers danced over the keys, putting in a request for a copy of his file. The Alphans might refuse, with all the indignation of a woman who'd been asked to do something indecent, but it was possible they'd supply the file. And if they did...she frowned, wondering if she could rely on whatever was in the file. The Alphans rarely shared any such details with anyone—it was why the buried files existed in the first place—and even now, it was hard to believe they'd give the file without caveats. But if they really wanted an observer attached to the fleet…

She scowled as she brought up the starchart. The Alphans had an interest in monitoring the war, she conceded, but they didn't need to put an observer on her ships. They could have deployed recon ships to watch from a safe distance…were they monitoring her ships and crew, to see how they coped now the navy was cut off from its former masters, or were they wondering if humanity was now a threat? The Lupines had been primitive, compared to the Alphans, but they'd come very close to outright victory. She was *sure* the Alphans didn't want to go through that again, not with humanity. There were too many humans scattered across their empire for their peace of mind.

Worry about it later, she told herself. There was too much to do, before the fleet could finally depart. She'd taken Evensong's advice and cut down on the clerical work as much as possible—and recruited more staff to help her—but she still had far too many documents that needed her personal attention. *If we don't win the war, the humans in Alphan space might be all that remain of us.*

CHAPTER NINE

Solar City, Earth

"IT'S HARD TO SAY HOW MANY PEOPLE BELIEVE the cover story," Abraham said, as he took his seat. "The media is being surprisingly quiet, of course, but some of the independent analysts are questioning the official narrative."

"Of course," Nancy said. "It's what they do."

And you didn't quite *point out how I and my party made it easier for the analysts to undermine our security*, Abraham thought. *Not quite.*

He sighed inwardly. The Alphan Datanet had been a technological marvel and yet, it had been designed to restrict the free flow of information almost as much as it facilitated it. The human race hadn't needed long to figure out how the network censored dissident opinions, often banning—sometimes openly, sometimes covertly—anyone who questioned the official narrative. The Viceregal Government hadn't realised until it was too late that they were undermining their own credibility, ensuring that whatever they said was treated with utmost suspicion even if it happened to be the literal truth. Abraham and his party had committed themselves to liberating the datanet, to making it impossible for anyone—even them—to prevent people from talking. And now it had bitten them hard.

"They haven't worked out the truth," he added. "But they are convinced that something else is planned."

"It shouldn't be a major problem," Nancy assured him. "I doubt the Pashtali pay close attention to our media."

Abraham hoped she was right, although he dared not take it for granted. There were very few interstellar news networks and none of them were completely trusted. Hell, they hadn't even shown much interest in honest reporting, back when the Pashtali had been preparing the human race for the kill. They'd always been willing to repeat alien lies, rather than digging up the truth. That had changed, when the human race had won a battle it should have lost, but even now their reporting wasn't particularly accurate. Abraham suspected the Pashtali—if they bothered to pay attention—didn't believe a word. They *knew* they hadn't lost a million starships in the fighting.

"Still, the sooner the operation is launched, the better," Abraham said. "There's been no change, of course. They're still refusing to discuss reasonable peace terms."

"They've put too much of their credibility on the line to be satisfied with a handful of minor conquests," Nancy reminded him. "And their stalling makes things easier for us too."

Abraham nodded, curtly. The Pashtali could have offered to concede human independence, in exchange for control of the former Occupied Zone, and it would have been very difficult to convince his government to continue the war. The Galactics—including the Alphans—would have insisted it was a reasonable endgame, allowing the Pashtali to claim some spoils while leaving the human race independent. If the Pashtali had been honourable, Abraham might have been tempted to propose it himself. But he knew it would just guarantee a resumption of the war, a decade or two down the line, under far less favourable conditions.

Which is a joke, he reflected, sourly. *Right now, the conditions are pretty damn unfavourable.*

"We can hope," he said, finally. "The reports from Terminus suggest nothing has changed."

"And the fleet can strike," Nancy said. "If nothing else, we can force them to worry about their flanks."

Abraham scowled. They'd been over the whole plan, time and time and time again. They'd been so deeply immersed in the planning that he'd had nightmares about it, dreams of victory and defeat blurring together into a horrific mess that haunted his waking hours. They were gambling everything...he knew they had no choice, he knew they couldn't sit still and wait to be hit, yet it still felt like they were doomed. He could cancel the operation—the buck stopped with him—and yet he didn't dare. The operation *had* to go ahead.

"Yes," he said, quietly. "Are *you* ready to go?"

"Yes, Mr. Speaker." Nancy straightened. "My credentials are ready. The Galactics can verify them with Earth, if they wish. We've been over all the possibilities..."

"All the *anticipated* possibilities," Abraham reminded her. They'd never imagined the Pashtali might develop a crossroads generator, even though it was the holy grail of FTL research programs. The Alphans had proved it was possible, after all. "They may catch us by surprise."

"If they do, we'll handle it," Nancy assured him. "I have authority to handle most issues and refer the handful I can't to you."

Abraham smiled, humourlessly. "Just don't tell my party."

"Or mine," Nancy said. There was a hint of bitterness in her tone. "What's left of it, anyway."

There's hardly anything left of the Empire Loyalists now, Abraham thought, feeling a twinge of sympathy. The pro-Alphan party had come apart at the seams, when it became clear the Alphans weren't interested in maintaining control of Earth. It had its advantages—his party would hardly have allowed him to grant Nancy so much authority, if they'd thought she could leverage it for political advantage—but it also meant she was politically homeless. *And our own party might fracture soon too.*

He looked down at his hands. The Humanity League had had one purpose. Human independence. And they'd gotten it, which meant...they no longer *had* a purpose. Abraham had done what he could, steering the ship of state through the rocks and shoals of independence and war, but his party was still looking for a new purpose. It was just a matter of time, he thought, before the party split into two...

Better that than remaining the sole major party, he told himself, firmly. *The longer we remain in power, without having to contest elections we could easily lose, the more we'll lose touch with our voters.*

He put the thought aside. "Good luck," he said, standing. "And please keep me informed as best as possible."

Nancy stood and held out a hand. "Of course, Mr. Speaker."

Abraham shook her hand. "I'll see you when you return," he said. "Don't give away the homeworld."

"I wouldn't dream of it," Nancy said.

She headed for the door and stepped outside, closing it behind her. Abraham sank back into his chair, feeling old, tired and helpless. He was the First Speaker, the most powerful man on the planet, yet there was nothing he could do—now—to shape the course of events. The navy would do or die without him and...he'd done everything in his power to secure a victory, offered everything he could to galactic superpowers in a bid to get loans and warships and weapons transfers and yet it might not be enough. He didn't need to look at the starchart to know *just* how badly outmatched they were, to know that everything he'd done might be futile. If the Pashtali ignored their losses and brought the hammer down hard, the human race was doomed. It would be the end of everything.

But we might just weaken them enough to let someone else take them to bits, he reflected, as he forced himself to relax. There was no point in worrying about it now. *Who knows?*

The intercom bleeped. "Mr. Speaker," Rachel said. "Your two o'clock appointment is here."

"I'll be up in a moment," Abraham said. "Show him into my office when I arrive."

"Yes, sir."

• • •

"Well," the girl said. "It's been a while for you, hasn't it?"

Lieutenant Wesley Anderson tried not to flush as he sat up in bed. His company had been promised a week's shore leave before they rejoined the fleet, after assisting with disaster recovery on Earth, but through some curious alchemy it had turned out to be only two days before they had to report to the spaceport for the shuttle to the ship. He hadn't wasted time moaning and groaning about it—he'd been a spacer long enough to *know* shipping schedules changed all the time—when he'd heard the news. Instead, he'd made his way to the nearest brothel and secured a girl and an apartment. It wasn't quite what he'd wanted—he'd been having pleasant fantasies of mountain climbing—but it would do.

"Yeah." Wesley felt a twinge of guilt. A girl, even a whore, wasn't a bike or a car or something else he could buy and sell at will. She was...he wanted to believe she was a girlfriend, someone who would wait for him and be there when he came home, but he knew better. She sold a service and...he tried not to think about all the other men and women who'd used her too. "Months, really."

"I'm glad I was of service," the girl said. She cupped her breasts, holding them out to him. "Did you have a good time?"

"Yes." Wesley felt his manhood stiffen and glanced at the clock. He needed to be gone in twenty minutes and yet...there'd be no sex on the ship. Probably. There were privacy tubes, and prospective partners of both genders, but the marines would be kept very busy from the moment the fleet jumped into multispace. "Once more?"

The girl bent her lips to his manhood, her tongue playing with him long enough to bring him to the boil, then lay back on the bed. Wesley mounted her, feeling his manhood slipping deep inside her...she felt warm and welcoming and tight, her hips moving as soon as he was inside. The analytical part of his mind noted she was probably trying to get him off as quickly as possible—she didn't seem to care about her own pleasure—but the rest of him simply didn't care. He had no idea if the noises she was making were real or faked or some strange combination of the two. All that mattered was getting off one final time.

She lay back as Wesley came inside her, then pulled out. Wesley felt an odd little twinge of guilt as he rolled over and stood, heading straight for the washroom. The sergeant would be unamused if he was late to the spaceport and his CO would probably bust him all the way down to private if he delayed the entire squad. Or strangle him with red tape…he put the thought out of his head as he washed quickly, then dried himself and hurried out into the bedroom. The girl was still lying on the bed, arms and legs sprayed out in a manner he found a little disturbing. It bugged him, suddenly, that he didn't know her *name*.

"Don't let yourself give a shit about a prostitute," his old sergeant had said. "They act nice and talk nice and fuck nice, but the only thing they want is money and if you don't have money they'll toss you out harder than a jumpmaster."

Wesley dug into his pocket, found an unmarked cashcard and placed it on the table. "There's a tip for you here," he said. The girl didn't move. "And I hope I do see you again."

His stomach churned as his eyes wandered over the girl one final time—he wanted to ask her name, yet didn't dare—before he turned and walked through the door. The apartment was a lie, no more real than the average movie set. It sold a fantasy that would linger as long as the money held out, a fantasy of a pretty girlfriend or handsome boyfriend or both… it wasn't real. And yet, part of his soul cried out for him to forget the truth and go back to the girl and take her in his arms and…he shook his head, biting his lip. The fantasy wasn't real and the whore wasn't his girl and…

He reached the bottom of the stairs and walked outside. A long line of soldiers, marines and spacers were waiting outside, a number alternatively eying their watches and casting baleful glances at the doors. The line was moving remarkably fast—Wesley felt sorry for the girls—but it was still slow for bored and horny men who *knew* they had to get laid in a hurry before they were ordered back to the spaceport. He pretended not to notice a couple of very familiar faces, although he had no idea how *they* intended to have their fun and get to the spaceport in time. If they'd lost track of time, the sergeant would go ballistic.

His terminal bleeped, summoning an aircar. It swooped out of the skies and landed beside him, hatch already hissing open. Wesley clambered inside, feeling uneasy as the hatch closed again. He'd never been comfortable onboard self-flying cars and aircraft, even though he *knew* they were relatively safe. There was no human driver to take control in a hurry, if something happened the automatics couldn't handle or if they were simply overridden by subversive software. It was supposed to be impossible, but so was everything else until someone actually did it.

He took a long breath as the aircar flew towards the spaceport and grounded itself in front of the gates. Wesley stood and stepped out, allowing the guards to verify his ID before they allowed him into the complex. The spaceport had once been a purely civilian installation, but the military had taken over in the wake of the invasion. Giant aircraft—old-tech helicopters, modern antigravity shuttles and cargo haulers—clattered through the air, bringing in emergency supplies and carrying the wounded and dispossessed to safety elsewhere. Wesley had grown up on a starship and he couldn't help thinking the planetary surface was chaotic as well as unsafe, although he'd learnt to love the wilderness. There was no guarantee the refugees would find a safe home. He'd already heard rumours some of the poor bastards had been abused by their hosts.

Sergeant Keegan saluted as Wesley reached the hanger. "Sir," he said. "The shuttle flight has been put back to 1700."

"Ouch." Wesley remembered the marines at the brothel and guessed they'd heard the news first. They should have enough time to get laid and get to the spaceport, unless the schedule changed again. "Do we have any further updates?"

"No, sir," Keegan said. "We're still going back to *Dauntless*, but nothing beyond. It may not even be finalised until we actually reach the ship."

"Or even beyond," Wesley said. The Solar Marines were efficient, by groundpounder standards, but even *they* had problems maintaining a fixed schedule. It wasn't their fault. No one could be entirely sure a ship was going to arrive on time until it actually did and that was when there was only *one* ship involved. There were days when getting an entire fleet moving in the same general direction felt like a miracle. "We'll find out when we find out."

He stepped into the hangar and looked around. It was a mess, knapsacks lying everywhere as if they'd been thrown around the chamber at random. A couple of men were trying to get some rest, assuming there'd be no time to sleep once they were all on the ship; three more were playing cards, exchanging comical death threats as they threw matches onto the floor in place of actual money. Gambling wasn't forbidden—there was no way to keep spacers and soldiers from it—but gambling for money very definitely was. Wesley hoped the game wasn't getting out of hand. He'd made a few stupid bets himself when he'd been a lowly private—he cringed in embarrassment, every time he remembered them—and he feared the younger men would make the same mistakes.

And hopefully I will be as understanding as my LT was, he thought, as he sat down and opened his terminal. The older man had given him a stern, almost paternal lecture, on the dangers of agreeing to forfeits before finding out what they actually were. Being dumb enough to agree to flash the CO was one thing, being dumb enough to write someone a blank cheque was quite another. *He could have busted me down for being a dumb shit.*

The terminal filled slowly, the marines returning to duty after their brief leave. Wesley felt a strange mixture of envy and pity for the men who had homes and families on the planet. He hadn't seen *his* family since *James Bond* had departed months ago, heading back into deep space. Enemy space, probably. His father had hinted at all sorts of cloak and dagger missions, after Wesley had returned from capturing a Pashtali ship. Wesley still didn't know what the older man had had in mind.

He stood when the whistle blew, trying not to roll his eyes as they passed through *yet another* set of security checks. The spaceport crew seemed to think intruders could actually teleport into the complex...no, he knew better than that. They were worried about the marines getting loaded onto the wrong shuttles or being left behind...Wesley wondered, idly, what would happen if the shuttle loaded and departed while he was in the washroom. Who'd get in trouble for that?

Don't worry about it, he told himself. *There'll be enough trouble to go around if that happens.*

"Take your seat," Major Drache ordered. "We'll be departing shortly."

"Yes, sir," Wesley said.

He frowned. The older man looked as grim and unyielding as always. Wesley wondered, suddenly, if he'd taken any leave. Drache was the most controversial officer in the Solar Marines, a man who'd always be seen as having blood on his hands even though the inquest had proved otherwise. If he went out on the streets, he might be attacked—or worse.

And off to somewhere unknown, Wesley thought. Theta Sigma? He would bet his entire salary *that* story was a blatant lie. *Where are we going? Deep into enemy space? Or where?*

He smiled in anticipation. *And what are we going to do when we get there?*

CHAPTER TEN

ESS DAUNTLESS, SOL SYSTEM

"ADMIRAL," COMMANDER OLSON SAID. "The last of the formations has checked into the command datanet, and all secure communications links are now established."

Naomi sat back in her chair. It had taken nearly a week of frantic effort to pull together the remainder of the fleet, then drill her officers in what to do if—when—the command network fell apart. The Alphans had sworn blind that their datanets couldn't be shattered by enemy action, something only marginally believable before it had actually *happened* during the Lupine Wars. Naomi wondered, at times, what it said about humanity's former masters that they'd refused to accept reality, even when it was slapping them across the face. How many warcruisers had been lost, in the early days of the war, because their crews weren't trained to fight alone?

Her eyes wandered to Observer Salix. The Alphan had been surprisingly—astonishingly—polite and restrained, even though he really *had* to be slumming it. He hadn't demanded servants, or better food, or anything beyond a seat in the CIC. Naomi was sure he knew their target was somewhere other than advertised, but he hadn't demanded to know where they were going either. It was odd. Either Observer Salix had gone native in a way that would horrify his peers—which might explain why he'd been given the job—or he was up to something.

Or maybe I'm just being paranoid, she thought. *You should know better than to judge an entire species by a single member.*

She sighed inwardly. Her old CO had been lazy. He'd been too lazy to be abusive or unpleasant or interfere with her running the ship, but... it had been galling to know they'd been sitting on a powder keg and the lazy bastard hadn't even known it. They'd come far too close to an outright mutiny, with the underpaid and overworked junior crew seriously considering doing something stupid. And the asshole hadn't even bothered to say goodbye when he'd been ordered home...

"Good," she said, leaning forward. "Run through a *full* system check."

"Aye, Admiral," Olson said.

Naomi studied the display, trying not to wince. On paper, it was impossible to identify the command ships, let alone target them for destruction. In practice, it was all too possible. The network was designed to be confusing and yet any half-decent tactical officer would be able to pick out the relay ships, blowing them away to cut the remainder of the fleet into a handful of isolated formations. She just didn't have the network capacity to turn *every* ship into a relay node, which meant losing a single relay ship risked losing every ship in that formation. She'd drilled her crews in what to do and yet...she shook her head. There was no point in wishing for things she didn't have, not really.

If there was, I'd want an entire fleet of purpose-built warships, she mused. *And then I could scrap half the wrecks in my fleet.*

Her console bleeped. She glanced at the message—the final set of readiness reports had arrived—and then shrugged. Some of her captains had engaged in a little creative editing to make sure their ships weren't pulled from the line of battle, something for which—under better circumstances—she would have given them hell. Now, she needed every ship that could launch a missile or energise a beam...and to hell with the risks. If the older ships died, and they would, they'd at least buy time for the newer vessels. They'd have a chance to hurt the enemy before it was too late.

"Signal Earth," she ordered. "Inform Solar Base we are ready to depart."

"Aye, Admiral," Olson said.

Naomi felt a stab of guilt. She'd left Admiral Morrígan and most of her staff behind, with orders to do what they could to churn out more weapons and ships before the fleet returned home. It was unlikely they could do much of anything, if the Pashtali came calling. The Alphan warcruisers would be the only thing standing between Earth and utter destruction, once the fleet was gone, and if they were withdrawn the planet was doomed. Admiral Morrígan wouldn't even be able to die bravely. Naomi cursed herself for leaving with the fleet, even though—again—there was no choice. They *had* to knock the Pashtali off balance before it was too late…

Sure, her thoughts mocked. *And if they manage to stay balanced, they'll throw Earth into the fire and then hunt down the remains of the fleet.*

"Signal the fleet," she ordered. "We will depart as planned."

"Aye, Admiral," Olson said.

Naomi nodded, feeling the deck vibrate as *Dauntless* started to move. She felt a sudden twinge of loss as the icons on the display followed suit. She carefully didn't look at Observer Salix. The formation was only a formation by courtesy, the fleet looking more like a swarm of angry bees than a precise and elegant and perfectly balanced pattern. The warcruisers holding position near Earth were probably pointing and laughing, although they should know better. The Lupines had disdained precise formations and they'd still brought their enemies to the verge of total defeat.

We might have to copy their tactics, Naomi thought. *If only we had the ships to do it.*

She shuddered. Her ancestors had embraced suicidal tactics in desperation, crashing aircraft into wet-navy ships in hopes of buying their homeland a few more months of life, but the Lupines had taken it far—far—further. Their tiny ships hadn't seemed very dangerous, individually, yet they'd swarmed their targets and overwhelmed them through sheer weight of numbers. She hated to think about how many of the aliens had died in the opening battles of the war, but she had to admit it had been effective. They could replace their losses very quickly. The Alphans hadn't been able to replace a single warcruiser until well after the fighting was over. If they'd taken a few more losses, they'd have lost.

"Admiral," Olson said. "We will be entering multispace in five minutes. The far side is clear."

"Good." Naomi had fretted the Pashtali would try to mine the crossroads. It would be a waste of time under normal circumstances, as well as being flat-out illegal, but the fleet was so big it might be worth the effort. "Take us into the crossroads."

She felt her heart starting to race, again, as the crossroads started to loom on the display. It was hardly the first time she'd made transit—she'd been a spacer her entire adult life—and yet, she felt as if she was about to plunge into the unknown. Earth had deployed fleets before, but nothing so large...she tried not to think about the prospect of running into a smaller yet far more advanced enemy fleet. She might win through sheer numbers, if she took a page from the Lupine tactical manuals, yet the cost would still be staggering. It felt as though they were making a mistake...

Reality itself seemed to twist, a faintly queasy feeling passing through as they made transit. She knew it wasn't real, that it was a figment of her imagination, yet it felt as if she'd just stepped over a cliff. Multispace did that sometimes, a grim reminder it wasn't a safe place for matter-based intelligent life. The Alphans sneered at the idea that multispace might have intelligent life of its own, but there were stories...she wondered, at times, if there was any truth in the tales. It didn't seem likely and yet she wondered. All spacers did.

"Admiral," Olson said. "The fleet has completed transit."

Naomi felt her lips thin in disapproval. The transit should have gone quicker. It wasn't as if they were in a bottleneck system, with only a handful of ships able to make transit at any given time. The fleet's coordination would need to be worked on, clearly. They could have moved a great deal faster, without risking a collision or interpenetration. It was something she'd have to handle later, after the fleet was underway. They had to make a clean break before they altered course or they'd be shadowed all the way to their target.

"Order the fleet to proceed as planned," she said. The ships knew what they had to do, now they were in multispace. "And drop decoys as we go."

"Aye, Admiral."

"The enemy sensors are good," Observer Salix said. Naomi almost jumped. She'd practically forgotten the alien was there. "Do you think you can hide from them?"

"It will be difficult," Naomi said, concealing her irritation. "Multispace provides a great deal of sensor cover, but the fleet is too large to hide within the eddies for long. If they do have someone watching us from a distance, they may get a solid lock on our position. The decoys will make that harder, though, and we're hoping we can confuse them long enough to make a clean break."

She studied the display. Realspace was flat, at least in its natural state. Multispace was so incredibly folded and twisted that it was quite possible for two fleets to be practically on top of each other, with neither side being aware the other was there. The distortions along the threadlines were so intense that there was no way to be sure a starship's sensors were reporting accurately...and yet, with so many ships flying so close together, it was hard to believe they would remain concealed indefinitely. Observer Salix had a point. A lone scout, lying in the eddies, might just see them coming and signal ahead.

We'll see, she told herself. *And even if they do spot us now, we'll be moving in the direction they expect. We won't head to Terminus until after we pass the RV point.*

"Commander Olson, forward the updated reports to my office," she ordered, standing. "I'll review them this afternoon, then decide how best to proceed."

"Aye, Admiral."

Naomi had to remind herself to rest, as the days flew until they started to blur together. She no longer had to do clerical work– she was uneasily aware it was building up, awaiting her return—but there was no shortage of other things to do. The fleet held endless drills, the junior officers practicing their tactics while their seniors argued over how to proceed; the marines darted through the corridors, training on everything from boarding enemy ships to repelling enemy boarding parties. Naomi hoped and prayed, as the weeks wore on, that they were getting all their mistakes out of the way before they ran into a real enemy. Her simulations were as detailed as her programmers could make them, and she'd been careful to ensure that everything that could go wrong did, but a real enemy would be dangerously unpredictable. She felt her heart jump every time the display reported a possible enemy contact. If they knew she was on the way...

They do, she told herself, sharply. *There's no doubt about* that. *They just don't know where we're going.*

"The crew is holding up well," Janet assured her, one evening. They'd met for dinner, then a chat. "I was worried, at first, but being underway has sorted out most of our problems."

"That's good to hear," Naomi said. She rather envied the junior officers and crew. They didn't have her rank, but they didn't have her responsibilities either. "Were there any real issues?"

"Nothing too great," Janet assured her. "A couple of stills...one case of drunkenness, fortunately not when the idiot was on duty. They got a stern lecture and punishment duties, rather than the rope. I'll have to keep my eye on the engineer who put the still together, I think. He should have known better than to let the drinking get out of hand."

Naomi grimaced. No one had been able to *keep* naval crew from setting up stills and no one would try, as long as the operators were careful. If they got someone drunk...whoever had set up this still had been very lucky the drunkard hadn't been on duty or they'd have been in real trouble. They'd be lucky if they were *merely* dishonourably discharged without hope of reference.

"Also, one fight for no apparent reason," Janet said. Her lips twisted in dismay. "Both parties are on punishment duties too."

"Good." Naomi frowned, inwardly. If everyone was keeping their mouths firmly closed…something sexual? Or gambling? Or just one of those stupid fights started by someone saying the wrong thing? The crew were crammed into tiny compartments, with barely enough room to swing a cat. No matter how hard the officers and chiefs tried to distract them, there would be tension and sometimes that tension would lead to fights. "I…"

She stopped herself. *Dauntless* was no longer *her* ship. Hell, technically, *Janet* should leave such matters to her XO unless they really got out of control. "I think we're working out the kinks now."

"I think so too," Janet said. She took a sip of her tea. "Where are we really going?"

"We'll get to the RV point first," Naomi said. She wasn't surprised by the question. If there was anyone who really believed the official story, they were keeping very quiet about it. "And then we'll alter course."

Janet smiled. "You still can't tell me?"

Naomi grimaced. She trusted Janet and yet…she knew better than to break security regulations, even though the fleet was safely underway. It wasn't a matter of trust. Janet couldn't tell anyone, not now. And yet… she understood the reasoning behind the rules. The more people who knew the truth, the greater the chance something would leak and reach the wrong side of ears.

And we don't want to risk even the slightest chance of being detected before we reach our target, she thought. *If they know we're coming…*

She put the matter aside as the voyage continued. The universe seemed to shrink until it was no larger than her cabin, the CIC and a handful of other compartments. She forced herself to walk the decks, making a point to speak to the officers and crew even though it was technically against regulations. Some of them had been under her command, when the cruiser had been *her* ship; some were newcomers, learning the ropes from older and wiser hands. It felt wrong not to know their names. She'd known everyone on *Washington*, her first command…

But that was when the universe was a far simpler place and I was the XO, she thought. It was standard procedure for XOs to switch ships when they were promoted to command, although *her* career suggested otherwise. Janet's too, come to think of it. *It isn't so easy now.*

The thought haunted her as the fleet neared the RV point. If something had gone wrong…she'd had plans drawn up to cover every imaginable contingency, yet she was afraid of the *unimaginable*. Commodore Valentine and his flotilla might have lost control of their ships, or run into an enemy fleet that had blown them to dust, or…she breathed a sigh of relief as they emerged from the threadline and saw the captured warships, waiting for them. They'd made it! She waited until the IFF codes were checked and rechecked—she'd been all too aware the Pashtali would have no trouble operating their own ships, if they recaptured them—and then allowed herself to relax. The first stage of the plan had gone off without a hitch.

"Signal to all ships," she ordered. "The first set of sealed orders are now to be opened, then implemented."

"Aye, Admiral," Olson said.

Observer Salix caught her eye. "Did you give all the ships the same orders?"

"Not quite," Naomi said. The majority of the fleet would proceed to the *second* RV point, taking a course that should keep them well off the beaten track. It wouldn't be easy to avoid detection, but as long as the formation was carefully spaced out it was unlikely anyone would see *all* the ships. "A couple of ships have specific missions."

Observer Salix cocked his head. "And they are?"

"They're going to transmit a message for me," Naomi said, vaguely. She didn't want to discuss the rest of the plan. She had a rough idea of what she wanted to do, when she reached Terminus, but she needed up to date information. They'd been out of touch for nearly a month. Anything could have happened, anything at all. "And then they'll link up with us again."

She leaned back in her chair. The first set of sealed orders weren't too clear—beyond the coordinates of the second RV point—but her commanders were an intelligent bunch. They'd note the coordinates, take a look at a starchart and guess the final destination. She would be surprised if they didn't. They'd certainly have plenty of time to familiarise themselves with the intelligence reports, then work out what she had in mind. There was no point in keeping the secret any longer.

"The fleet is acknowledging, Admiral," Olson reported. There was a wealth of curiosity in his tone, carefully hidden. "They're ready to depart."

"Good," Naomi said. She came to a decision. "Once we're underway, I'll hold a holoconference. All captains and commodores are invited, no excuses. We'll discuss the plans, then move on from there."

"Aye, Admiral."

And hope they really don't see us coming, Naomi thought. Who knew what had happened on Earth? Someone could have talked or, more likely, someone could have shadowed the fleet despite her best efforts. *If they know we're on the way, we could be flying straight into a trap.*

CHAPTER ELEVEN

Terminus/Near Terminus

"THIS COULD GO VERY BADLY WRONG," Captain Thomas Anderson said, as *James Bond* undocked from the giant orbital station. "If they take a good look at us on the way out..."

"If," Sarah said. "They haven't looked too closely at us before."

Thomas nodded, curtly. *James Bond* had been in and out of the system four times over the last few months, using a different IFF every time. The Pashtali hadn't paid close attention, certainly not enough to notice the same ship was coming and going, but it bothered him more than he cared to admit. They might just be watching and waiting, although they might also be trying to imply their possession of the system wouldn't inconvenience the other Great Powers. They'd be more likely to get away with keeping the crossroads in their keeping if no one—at least, no one with the power to do something about it—thought the Pashtali wouldn't interfere with their trade.

His eyes narrowed as he studied the display. They'd spent a *lot* of time passively monitoring the Pashtali fortifications, as well as collecting data from the other ships passing through the system. The Pashtali had been building up their positions, slowly making their position effectively invulnerable. He had to admire their nerve, although the risk wasn't as great as it seemed. The only real danger was an alliance between the various lesser powers and, as long as they held the bottleneck system, there was no way to put an alliance together and coordinate an attack on Terminus, not without giving the Pashtali plenty of warning. He was surprised the lesser powers hadn't tried anyway. They were doomed to permanent subjugation if they didn't break out before it was too late.

The old boiling a frog problem, he reflected. *If you toss the frog into a pot of boiling water, the frog jumps out, but if you raise the temperature slowly the frog is half-cooked before he realises something's wrong.*

He scowled. The lesser powers *had* to know what was happening, didn't they? It wasn't *that* subtle. The Pashtali weren't even *trying* to pretend they hadn't taken the system for themselves. And that meant...he felt his scowl deepen as he recalled his orders. Perhaps something *was* up. The last set of orders from their superiors had had an unusual note of urgency, no matter that it was couched in romantic nonsense right out of a porno movie written by someone who'd never had sex, let alone a romantic relationship. His lips twitched. The Galactics who'd read the message—he was sure it had passed through a handful of communications taps—were probably rolling their eyes at human sexuality. He hoped they wouldn't realize there was a deeper message concealed within the nonsense.

"Course laid in," Sarah said. "Captain?"

"Take us out," Thomas ordered. "And keep all sensors stepped down to civilian levels."

"Teach your grandmother to suck eggs," Sarah teased. "I know what I'm doing."

Thomas accepted the rebuke in good grace. His wife had every right to be annoyed at his reminder, although they couldn't afford to do anything that might draw attention. There was no rhyme or reason to enemy patrols, no way to determine which ships were more likely to be stopped than others; he'd seen them harass harmless bulk freighters while allowing obvious smugglers to slip by without making any attempt to harm them. He'd thought they were playing favourites, allowing their allies to proceed while intercepting neutral or hostile shipping, but there was no pattern. For all he knew, they were flipping coins to determine which ships to scan or search. He didn't like it. He would be happier if he knew what was drawing enemy eyes to certain ships.

He calmed himself as the freighter picked up speed, thrusting towards the crossroads. It felt as if they were crawling across the system, even though he *knew* they were moving at unimaginable speed. The star system was just too *big*. He leaned back in his chair and watched as more and more data flowed into the secure datacores, from enemy battlestations to warships patrolling the system. His superiors wanted realtime data or as close to it as possible...he hoped, when he linked up with his contact, that whoever he'd been ordered to meet was understanding. As time moved on, the data would become steadily more and more outdated until it was worse than useless. He made a mental note to run projections, as soon as they were safely in real space. He dared not let his superiors think the data was perfect.

"They pinged our IFF," Sarah said, breaking into his thoughts. "We'll see..."

Thomas nodded, eying the battlestation and the handful of light patrol vessels orbiting the crossroads. There was no way they could outrun the tiny ships, if they demanded the freighter prepare to be boarded. He told himself there was nothing to alarm a search party, not unless the searchers inspected the sensors or the handful of other advanced components within the hull, but it was impossible to be sure. The IFF code was as bland and boring as possible and yet, if it drew attention...he reminded himself, again, that they'd been in worse scrapes. There was no reason to think the ship would be searched from top to bottom...

Sarah's console bleeped. "They cleared us to proceed," she said. "We did it."

"Take us into the crossroads," Thomas ordered. "And then set course to the RV point."

He kept a wary eye on the display as the crossroads loomed up in front of them. The Pashtali were making their control of the system very clear, simply by asserting the right to grant passage through the crossroads. It was hard to say how long they needed to assert control before they were recognised as the system's *de jure* owners—Galactic Law was a little vague-but he feared it wouldn't be long at all. Very few races had the power to push them out and the ones that did might find it easier to go along with the Pashtali's control, as long as they didn't push it too far. He hoped their recent defeat—over Earth—had convinced a few of the Pashtali's enemies it was time to push back.

And all the reports were so hugely exaggerated it was impossible to take them seriously, he thought. He'd downloaded a handful of reports from the battle, when they'd been looking for information brokers, and they'd insisted *millions* of starships had been destroyed in the fighting, along with more soldiers and spacers than existed in the known galaxy. *The Pashtali probably wrote the reports themselves, just to make sure no one believed the truth.*

His lips tightened. The Galactics weren't normally *subtle*. They didn't have to be. And yet, he had to admit it was a crafty trick. Instead of denying the battle had been lost, or insisting it had never taken place, they'd told the universe they *had* lost the battle...and exaggerated their losses so highly no one could possibly take the reports seriously. He wondered, idly, who'd come up with that idea. The Pashtali had quite a few client races under their banner. Perhaps it had been one of them.

And perhaps they should be on our side instead, he thought. *We're not the ones holding them in bondage.*

The freighter shuddered, slightly, as she passed through the crossroads. The display blanked, then rebooted. Thomas frowned, noting how few ships were passing along the threadline. It had been busier when they'd first entered the system and...he shook his head. Terminus was steadily being isolated from the rest of the galaxy. The only ships passing through the system were ones going to the lesser powers. He wondered, idly, if the Pashtali cared about the economic damage they were doing, just by taking control of the crossroads. It was quite possible they didn't give a damn.

"We'll be at the RV point in twenty minutes," Sarah told him. "What do you think we'll see?"

Thomas shrugged. Their superiors wouldn't have wanted near-realtime data unless they were planning *something* involving Terminus, but what? An attack? A covert mission? Or...or what? He considered the possibilities for a long moment, then shrugged and dismissed the question. They'd find out soon enough. He mentally reviewed his report, evaluating their final sensor records and tagging them with his own commentary. His superiors *had* to understand there was no apparent logic behind the enemy patrols, no sense of which ships would be searched and which left alone. It had to be deliberate policy. It was the only explanation that made sense.

The display bleeped as they approached the RV coordinates. Thomas sucked in his breath, feeling a flash of alarm. There were ships there... hundreds, perhaps thousands, of vessels holding position. He was painfully aware many would be nothing more than sensor ghosts or multispace reflections, images of starships hundreds of light years from their position, but there was still an entire fleet waiting for them. It was hard to resist the urge to reverse course and flee, even though he *knew* this fleet had to be friendly. The Pashtali could not have cracked the codes and, if they had, they wouldn't have sent such a big fleet to catch *James Bond*. Why bother? The freighter had been well within their grasp until she'd crossed the crossroads and vanished into multispace.

"My God," Sarah breathed. "That's a lot of ships."

"Yeah," Thomas agreed. "Even if only half of them are real, there's still hundreds of them."

And they're human, he thought, as he opened communications channels. *The Galactics would sooner die than fly such a ragtag fleet into battle.*

His heart twisted. The majority of the human fleet looked to be second-hand warships or converted freighters, with a solid core of human-built ships backing them up. Their raw numbers were formidable—he couldn't deny it—but cramming weapons and armour into freighter hulls wouldn't make them proper warships. They'd be slow and sluggish, and any *proper* warship would tear them apart within moments. And yet, what choice did the navy have? They didn't have *time* to build up the fleets they needed to take on the Pashtali, not on anything like even terms.

"Captain, they're ordering us to hold position," Sarah said. "And wait."

"They're going to attack Terminus," Thomas said. It was impossible and yet...why *else* would they travel so far from Earth? The Solar Navy was taking one hell of a risk. The Pashtali wouldn't expect the Solar Navy to attack them there—of course not—but taking so many ships so far from home meant Earth was uncovered. The Pashtali might win the war by dispatching a fleet to Earth, smashing the homeworld into rubble and declaring victory. "They're mad."

"Maybe," Sarah agreed. "Or maybe they have something up their sleeve."

"I hope you're right," Thomas said. He couldn't imagine *what*. "I really do."

• • •

"The enemy has emplaced battlestations near the crossroads," Commander Olson said. "But they don't seem willing to back them up with heavy mobile units."

Naomi nodded. It made military and political sense. The Pashtali didn't *need* an entire fleet to support the battlestations, not when there was no real threat, and keeping their heavy units away from the system made their presence look less threatening. She doubted anyone was fooled—the lesser powers wouldn't have risked approaching humanity if they hadn't thought they were in deep shit—but it didn't matter. It worked in her favour. The odds of breaking into the system before the Pashtali got organised and counterattacked were quite high.

"Copy the tactical data to Commodore Valentine," she ordered. "And inform him we'll go with Terminus-Three."

"Aye, Admiral," Olson said. There was a hint of doubt in his voice. "Signal sent."

"Good," Naomi said.

She understood his concerns. They'd wargamed the coming battle extensively, shifting the parameters time and time again until they thought they knew every last move the enemy could make and how to counter them. It was impossible to be sure, of course—there was no way to be sure *James Bond* had seen *every* enemy ship and fortification within the system—but they were fairly sure of breaking through the first crossroads. It would weaken the enemy drastically—they'd have no other way to escape, unless they ran the gauntlet—and yet there was no way to prevent them from signalling their homeworld. The Pashtali High Command would know their captured ships were being pressed into human service.

Which will hopefully make them a hell of a lot more paranoid, she thought. The alien ships were largely unique. The Pashtali didn't sell their purpose-built warships to anyone, even their own clients. It normally worked in their favour—they didn't have to worry about adapting them for other life forms—but not now. *They'll be much more careful about accepting their own ships at face value, once they know we can fly them.*

Her lips twitched in cold amusement—it wasn't uncommon for IFF codes to become outdated during wartime, which would be unfortunate for a perfectly genuine enemy ship approaching a paranoid outpost—before she dismissed the thought and returned her attention to the display. She'd expected the Pashtali to secure the various planets, but instead they'd more or less left them alone. The report from *James Bond* suggested the Pashtali didn't want to solidify their control *too* quickly—they wanted to get everyone accustomed to the idea of them ruling the crossroads before they moved on to the planets—but it hardly mattered. The planets were defended—there was a surprising amount of firepower protecting them—yet the lack of a central command and control network would cost them. She rather suspected it wouldn't take too long for the Pashtali to batter the defences into rubble, if they even bothered. A handful of lawless planets might be quite useful in the long run.

"Signal from *Trojan One*, Admiral," Olson said. "She's ready to proceed."

"Order her to depart as planned," Naomi said. "The remainder of the fleet, apart from the units on special duties, will follow in ten minutes."

She sighed inwardly. The closer they got to the crossroads, the higher the chance of being detected. No one would think anything of another Pashtali warship passing through the threadline—even the *Pashtali* wouldn't think much of it, unless their schedules were insanely tight—but the human fleet was quite another story. If someone saw it coming and reversed course, they'd have a very good chance of outrunning the fleet and racing through the crossroads to sound the alarm. There was no way to avoid the risk either. The threadline was too narrow for her to spread the fleet out, in hopes any passing freighter would only spot one or two vessels. She would just have to hope they could get to the crossroads before it was too late.

Assuming they see us from the moment we leave, they'll still need time to get ready to meet us, she thought. The fact the local defences *hadn't* gone on alert was clear proof the fleet's presence had gone unnoticed. *How long will it take for them to assemble their fleet and mine the crossroads?*

She ran the simulations as the timer started ticking down to zero. The Pashtali could slow her fleet down, even weaken them badly, if the Pashtali had time to start placing mines on top of the crossroads. It was a bottleneck—the entire *system* was- and there would be no way to crack the system without taking heavy losses. The techs had cautioned her they might not be able to use *Crossroads* to get into the system through the back door, explaining the local topography would work against them. If that happened…

There's nothing to be gained by worrying about it now, she told herself. She didn't want to use *Crossroads* if it could be avoided, not here. She had other plans for the captured ship that involved keeping its former owners in the dark as long as possible. *Focus on what you can fix instead.*

"Admiral," Olson said. "The fleet is ready to move out."

"Take us out," Naomi ordered. There was no need to give the order—the plan had been uploaded to the fleet the moment she'd viewed the realtime sensor data—but it had to be done. "And be alert for passing freighters."

"Aye, Admiral."

Naomi nodded, watching as her fleet slowly glided away from the RV point. The formation still looked ragged—the Alphans would die laughing, if they laid eyes on her fleet—but her ships and crews were as ready as they'd ever be. They'd spent the last month drilling endlessly, running everything from computer simulations to live-fire exercises. They'd gone through every plausible scenario and a few that were anything but. And they'd done well. The fleet might be a ragtag joke, by Galactic standards, but it was formidable. Win or lose, they'd go down fighting.

"Open a channel to the fleet," she ordered. Admiral Glass would have come up with something clever and inspiring, she was sure. He'd always known just what to say to get the best out of his people. She didn't have that talent. She'd just have to speak from the heart. "They thought we were weak. They thought we could be isolated and bullied into submission, that they could take everything we had without fear of consequence. Today, we show them they are wrong. Today, we show them what we can do. Today, we show them that we can *fight*."

She took a breath, feeling history peering over her shoulder. "This is the decisive campaign, one way or the other," she told them. "As a wise man said centuries ago, Earth expects everyone will do their duty."

Under the circumstances, she rather thought Lord Nelson would have approved.

CHAPTER TWELVE

TERMINUS

"CAPTAIN," LIEUTENANT MARQUEZ SAID. "We'll be passing through the crossroads in five minutes."

"Good," Commodore Roger Valentine said. It felt odd to be addressed as *Captain*—he'd been promoted years ago—but naval protocol insisted on it. "Prepare to transmit the IFF signal."

"Aye, Captain," Marquez said.

Roger nodded, feeling uneasy as he squatted on the desk. He'd seen hundreds of alien ships in his career, from starships very akin to human designs to weird structures and hodgepodges put together by scavenger races, but the Pashtali ship was incredibly alien, unsettling even to him. The interior felt like a strange cross between a beehive, an anthill and a spider's nest, the air hot and humid and crammed with bugs. It was hard to understand how the ship even *flew* with so much crap in the atmosphere, even if it was a cheap way to feed the crew. The bulkheads pressed down on him, somehow constantly suggesting they were on the verge of closing in and crushing the human crew. Roger rather suspected some of his officers and men would need to seek treatment after they returned home, despite having spent most of their careers working with alien tech. Pashtali ships were just too alien.

He scowled as he studied the display. They'd replaced the original datacores with human-designed computers, then searched the ship for hidden surprises, but it was impossible to be sure they'd found everything. There were just too many ways for the ship to signal its former owners, from distress beacons responding to outside probes to calculated fluctuations in the drive field, and if *he'd* been designing the ships he'd have made sure to include something that would raise the alarm. The Pashtali didn't sell their warships, which meant they'd assume one of their ships was friendly until proven otherwise, but they'd be wise to be careful if a ship arrived unannounced. It would cost nothing and save much.

"Take us through as planned," he ordered. Sweat prickled on his back. The IFF code was real, they thought, but it might be outdated. Or worse. It might belong to the wrong class of ship, or even the right ship in the wrong place. The Pashtali *knew* humans had a knack for refurbishing old warships and putting them back into service. Would they assume their ships couldn't be repaired? Or would they change their protocols anyway, just to be sure? "And then transmit as planned."

His stomach lurched as they passed through the crossroads. The Pashtali didn't seem to bother fine-tuning their drives, suggesting they were immune to transit shock or they simply didn't care. Roger suspected the former. The Pashtali were cold and cruel, but they were also calculating enough to know there was nothing to be gained by leaving their crew vulnerable. It might slow their reactions at the worst possible time. The display blanked, then rebooted. His eyes narrowed as a cluster of red icons, weirdly skewed, flickered into life. They'd fiddled with the translation software time and time again, but—no matter what they did—it had problems converting the sensor input into something humans could watch without a banging headache. The Pashtali saw the world very differently from their human enemies. It made him wonder if they got headaches from trying to access human databases.

They have clients who can do the dirty work, if they can't do it themselves, he reflected, grimly. *There's no reason to assume our databases are safe just because they might cause problems for whoever captured them.*

He scowled. It was impossible to be sure how much the Pashtali knew about their human enemies. Hell, the Pashtali had never seemed particularly interested in learning about any other intelligent race, save perhaps their handful of clients. And yet, they'd played to galactic opinion pretty damn well. Perhaps they'd gotten advice from a galactic PR firm. His lips twisted at the thought of a bunch of so-called influencers lecturing the spider-like aliens on how best to appeal to the rest of the known universe, then flattened as it dawned on him the thought wasn't funny. There were people out there who would cheerfully sell their enemies the rope the bastards needed to hang them.

"The IFF signal appears to have been accepted," Marquez said, slowly. "They're not making any threatening moves."

"Take us closer," Roger ordered. "And keep feeding them comforting lies."

A shiver ran down his spine as the range started to close. How close could they get before the battlestation ordered them to back off or simply opened fire? Galactic Law allowed someone to open fire without warning, if it looked like the unknown starship was closing to ram. In theory, the shooter had to be very sure the intruder could have nothing else in mind; in practice, the Pashtali could probably get away with almost anything, as long as they didn't bombard an entire planet into a lifeless chunk of rock. But he was flying one of *their* ships...he knew *he'd* hesitate if a human ship came at him like a bat out of hell and he assumed they'd do the same. Perhaps. The Pashtali weren't human. Their reactions were nowhere near as easy to predict.

And we need to be a lot closer for best effect, he thought. The battlestation was a pretty tough customer. She was larger than a battleship, with most of her extra mass devoted to armour and weapons. *If they order us to break off, we may have to open fire and hope for the best.*

He glanced at the timer. They'd been in-system for four minutes. If the plan went off without a hitch, the remainder of the fleet was six minutes behind. The enemy couldn't miss the first formations making transit, at which point they'd start wondering why *Trojan One* hadn't raised the alarm. And then...perhaps it was gross incompetence, rather than malice, but Roger didn't know any commanding officer who'd let it pass. The battlestation CO would probably order the cruiser to halt, then open fire if she refused to stop. It was what he'd do.

"Captain," Marquez said. "They're signalling us, demanding a code."

Roger sucked in his breath. They didn't *have* a second code. There might have been others in the datacores, but they'd been destroyed long ago. And that meant...the display flared red as the battlestation's targeting sensors locked onto the cruiser, a clear warning to stop or be fired upon. There were some races that might have ignored such a blatant threat, trusting in their reputations to protect them, but humanity wasn't one of them. Ironically, neither were the Pashtali.

He cursed under his breath. Three minutes to go...he wracked his brain for a way to stall, to slow the enemy long enough to get closer, but nothing came to mind. The patrol ships were already altering course, bringing their weapons to bear on the cruiser. It would be laughable, if the ship had been fully armed and manned, but *Trojan One* was neither. Her automated point defence would probably take out the patrol ships, and the battlestation's first salvo, yet she couldn't take a long engagement. The enemy might not be sure of what was going on, but they were playing it smart. They'd blow the cruiser away a long time before she could ram the battlestation.

"Open the hatches," he ordered. "Fire the missiles, then reverse course."

"Aye, sir," Marquez said.

Roger keyed his console, watching as the oversized missiles rocketed away from his ship and raced towards the battlestation. They looked almost laughable, compared to Galactic weapons, but the planners thought that would work in their favour. The enemy point defences would have no trouble targeting the missiles, then blowing them away well before they reached their target. If they were lucky…his lips curved into a cold smile as the patrol ships picked up speed, sweeping around the missiles and heading straight for the cruiser. It made sense, from their point of view, but it was still a terrible mistake.

If they'd fired on the missiles, he thought as he brought his own point defence online, *the mission might have failed completely.*

"Sir," Marquez said. "The missiles are lumbering into point defence range."

"Key them to detonate the moment the enemy opens fire," Roger said. The missiles were slow as well as oversized, but that would work in their favour too. The Pashtali would take their time, laying down every shot rather than trying to fill space with plasma bolts and railgun shells. "We don't want them to take the missiles out."

"No, sir," Marquez said.

Roger glanced at the timer—one minute—then triggered the point defence. Two patrol ships vanished from the display, the remainder spinning into a complicated evasive pattern that sent them corkscrewing towards their target. The battlestation opened fire a moment later, aiming missiles at *Trojan One* and point defence at the incoming missiles. Marquez whooped as the missiles seemed to triple in power, an instant before the burners sent ravenous steams of energy into the enemy amour. The battlestation seemed to shudder as the missiles twisted, the beams chopping through the outer hull and wreaking havoc on the interior. Roger almost felt sorry for the enemy crew. Anyone unlucky enough to be too close to the beams, as they sliced through the armour, would be fried before they knew what had hit them. The sheer power was staggering. The battlestation was designed to take heavy damage and keep fighting, but…he found it hard to believe anything could survive that. The normal precautions—hatches closed and sealed, crews in protective suits—would be practically useless.

If we did this to a ship, he thought as the first formations started to make transit, *she'd be atoms by now.*

The burners winked out. For a heartbeat, everything seemed to freeze. The battlestation was a twisted hulk, heat radiating into the cold of interstellar space. The remaining patrol vessels appeared unsure what to do, uncertain if they should try to close and ram *Trojan One* or reverse course and flee to one of the other battlestations. There was no trace of the enemy fleet—and the more distant battlestations—on the display, but Roger knew they were still there...and very aware of what had happened. It was the sort of trick that would only work once. The battlestation had been careless, allowing the decoy ship to get too close without checking its IFF and then declining to shoot down the missiles before it was too late. The remaining battlestations would be far tougher targets.

"Captain," Marquez said. "Admiral Yagami is requesting a status update."

Roger resisted the urge to point out they'd effectively killed the battlestation. It was possible—vaguely -there were survivors, but the battlestation itself was nothing more than a twisted hulk. There were no suggestions it could do anything to affect the battle, save perhaps soaking up a handful of missiles. He hoped the survivors had the sense to run up the white flag and surrender, before it was too late. If the human fleet didn't know the survivors were there, they wouldn't try to probe the wreck until after the battle.

If we bother at all, he thought. *The datacores will have self-destructed, if they weren't ruined by the burners, and the rest of the station is just a melted nightmare. We might just push it into the sun instead.*

"Inform her our first operation was a success, then request orders," he said. "And request resupply as quickly as possible."

"Aye, Captain," Marquez said. "We are ordered to remain in place, behind the crossroads, then return to the RV point once the remainder of the fleet has made transit."

Roger nodded. "Good," he said. "We've done our bit. Let's hope the admiral can do hers."

• • •

"They fell for it," Olson said. "The battlestation let the burner missiles get too close before it tried to shoot them down."

Naomi nodded. The human race had yet to duplicate the *real* burners, the energy weapons that made Alphan warcruisers the most feared warships in the galaxy. Human-designed burners had a tendency to either burn out or explode if they were pushed too hard, the latter threatening to set off a chain reaction that would blow the entire starship to atoms. It was costly to mount burners on missiles, and she'd doubted their value in open combat, but they'd proved their worth. The battlestation had been a formidable opponent, yet it had been taken out without firing more than a handful of shots.

"Transmit the signals, as planned," she ordered. "We will advance as soon as the remainder of the fleet has made transit."

She allowed herself a cold smile. Her counterpart on the other side had to be raging. If he'd had time to concentrate his ships, he could have advanced to the crossroads and sat on it, blowing away her ships as they made transit. The casualty rates would have been staggeringly high even if she'd carried the crossroads, bleeding her fleet white for very little reward. Instead, she had all the time she needed to mass her fleet and then advance further into the system. What would the enemy do? Try to slow her down? Or withdraw as quickly as possible?

Which would make life difficult for them, she thought. *They'd have to slip off the threadlines or risk being interned or destroyed. Either way, they won't be a problem for us any longer.*

Her console bleeped. "Admiral, this is Dennison in Comms," a voice said. "The FTL Transmitter is signalling urgently, using Pashtali encryption codes. We're currently trying to decrypt the signals, but we don't think we'll be able to read them for quite some time."

"If ever," Naomi said. She wasn't expecting anything beyond the awareness the enemy CO had managed to signal home. The Pashtali, if the spooks were to be believed, had repeatedly updated their encryption codes. It wouldn't be easy to break them and, given how alien the senders were, there was no guarantee the messages would be understandable even if they'd been sent in the clear. "Inform me when they stop signalling."

"Aye, Admiral."

"A curious decision," Observer Salix said. He'd kept his mouth shut during the first stage of the offensive, something that Naomi found a little surprising, but he was making up for it now. "Do you not want to silence the transmitter?"

"How?" Naomi grinned at her console. "There's nothing we can do, short of launching a kinetic strike, to shut the transmitter down. Not now. We'll deal with it later, if the locals don't switch sides."

Her grin grew wider. "And besides, we need the transmitter ourselves," she added. "Commander Olson, transmit the second set of messages and request they be relayed to their destination."

Observer Salix cocked his head. "You expect the transmitter to do as you ask?"

"They are *meant* to be neutral," Naomi pointed out. The Pashtali had made no attempt to seize or destroy the local FTL transmitter. It would have alienated nearly everyone in the known galaxy, maybe even turned them into the common foe. "And we are on the verge of taking the entire system. I don't think they'll refuse."

She sighed inwardly. The Pashtali were strong enough to get away with bullying the local staff. Humanity couldn't afford to do the same. If the Pashtali decided to *accidentally* launch a missile at the transmitter, risking mass slaughter and perhaps even genocide, the Galactics would do everything in their power to look away, while penalising humanity for the slightest misstep. There were times when she wondered why they should bother paying anything more than lip service to the rules, when everyone who could get away with ignoring them did. In the long run, Admiral Glass had always said, it would work out for the best. But in the short run...

No, she told herself. *We have to show we uphold the rules even when our enemies refuse to do the same.*

"Signals sent, Admiral," Olson said. "It'll be at least ten minutes before our messages reach the transmitter."

"Understood." Naomi had been a spacer long enough to know to account for the speed of light delay. Once the message reached the transmitter, it would be sent without further delay. "We'll see who's interested in helping now."

She glanced at the starchart, her thoughts racing. The lesser powers were on alert, she'd been told, readying themselves to take the offensive. Would they move, now she'd punched her way into the system? Or would they sit on their asses and let humanity do the dirty work? She didn't know. The planners had veered back and forth when the matter had been discussed, some arguing the lesser powers would act at once and others insisting they'd try to stay out of the fighting as long as possible. Naomi understood how they felt. She would have preferred to avoid a clash with a major power, if she'd been given the choice. The Pashtali were still overwhelmingly powerful. They'd been hurt, no doubt about it, but they might win the war.

But they're no longer overwhelmingly powerful here, she told herself. Her long-range sensors were tracking the enemy ships as their commander concentrated his forces. *And there'll never be a better time to drive them out of the system for good.*

"Admiral, there's been no response to our surrender demand," Olson reported. "They are still massing their forces."

"But not coming for us," Naomi said. She recalled some of the early simulations and frowned. The enemy CO might be wise to lure her away from the crossroads, then try to sneak around her to break through the crossroads and into multispace. "Plot an intercept course. We'll leave two squadrons on the crossroads, in case they try to sneak through, but take the remainder of the fleet to deal with their remaining ships."

"Aye, Admiral."

CHAPTER THIRTEEN

TERMINUS

OBSERVER SALIX HAD BEEN CAUTIONED, in no uncertain terms, to keep his background a secret from his human hosts. The fact he'd served in both the Lupine Wars, as well as having spent time as a commanding officer in the EDF, had been carefully unmentioned. There were no humans who recognised him from the old days—he'd had a little cosmetic surgery, just to be sure—and if anyone had put the pieces together they'd kept it to themselves. It was important the humans didn't realise just how much he understood, ensuring they'd always take the time to explain their thinking to him. And yet, it struck him as futile. They'd been a client race before being given their independence. The Alphans had never *had* to understand their human clients. The humans had no choice but to try to understand their masters.

And they did a better job of it too, he thought. *They know us much better than we know them.*

He kept his face under tight control. He'd read Captain Nobunaga's report on his former XO, now-Admiral Yagami. Captain Nobunaga had been a fool—that was clear, just by skimming his report—who'd failed to note much, if anything, about his subordinate. There was nothing positive or negative, nothing to suggest they'd spent years working together; nothing, even, to hint Captain Nobunaga had copied a handful of other reports or simply made his out of whole cloth. The report had been bland and completely useless. It was a shame the original EDF personnel had been withdrawn to fight in the wars before Admiral Yagami had been promoted to Commander. She might have gotten on much better with one of them.

"Contact in thirty minutes," Olson reported. "The enemy doesn't appear to have a plan."

"Which means they're up to something," Admiral Yagami said. "What?"

Salix had no answer. His orders had been vague on precisely *how* much help and advice he was to offer his hosts, but it didn't matter. The Pashtali had only a handful of options and yet they seemed to have decided to take the worst of them. They could be retreating into deep space to wait for relief, or jumping through one of the other crossroads, or even just trying to split up and evade the human ships long enough to break through the first crossroads. Instead, they were trying to make a stand...why? Did they think they could wear down the human fleet? It might be possible—it was the only explanation that made sense—but it struck him as a little pointless. But then, the Pashtali didn't have much regard for their own lives.

"Deploy additional probes," Admiral Yagami ordered. "And watch for cloaked ships."

"We loaned you a handful of our sensors," Salix said. "They shouldn't be able to conceal a cloaked ship from you."

He ignored her annoyed look. His superiors had made it clear he had two assignments. He was to watch the battles and study the Pashtali, in a bid to determine just how far they'd advanced over the last few years, but he was also to do the same for the humans themselves. It didn't sit well with him, given how closely his race and theirs had been linked together for centuries, yet he'd been given no choice. His superiors were worried. The humans might grow stronger, if they won the war, and eventually become a potential threat. And with so many other humans within the empire, and increasingly resentful of their lower-class status, who knew where that would end?

Poorly, he thought. *But what can we do about it?*

He put the thought out of his head as the range steadily closed. The enemy ships stood their ground, starfighters buzzing around their handful of capital ships like angry bees. Salix forced himself to consider what they might be doing. A squadron of warcruisers might hold position, relying on their burners to obliterate any foe stupid enough to close with them, but their commanding officer would be dishonourably discharged when he reported home...assuming he survived. The Lupine War had taught the Alphans a number of lessons, starting with the simple fact that a primitive enemy willing to soak up the losses and just keep coming was a terrifyingly dangerous opponent. Any *sane* commander would be trying to keep the range open, sniping his enemies from a safe distance. The Pashtali were steadily letting the chance to do that slip through their fingers.

The humans might have taken out their CO, but someone else will have assumed command by now, Salix thought. *They'll have sorted out who's senior by now, surely?*

"Admiral, we'll be in firing range in ten minutes," Olson said. "They're still holding position."

They're mad, Salix thought. He could understand the Pashtali willingly accepting the complete destruction of their fleet to weaken the human force—they had more ships to play with—but it was still odd. They'd gain more by pulling back and harassing the system, ensuring the lesser powers had to devote ships and resources to keep the Pashtali from raiding convoys and independent trade. *What are they doing?*

He put the thought into words. "Why would they hold position like that?"

"Good question," Admiral Yagami said. "I wonder..."

• • •

Naomi frowned, trying to keep her tension off her face as she studied the display. The enemy ships were showing up clearly on the display, all forty-seven of them. The largest ship was a midsized carrier, surrounded by starfighters, but the remainder were destroyers, frigates and a handful of light cruisers. It would make a powerful raiding force, if it chose to slink into the shadows and avoid contact with human warships, yet it was nowhere near strong enough to do more than give her a black eye. They hadn't even fallen back on one of the other battlestations. What on Earth were they doing?

Wrong question, she told herself. *If I did something like that, what might I have in mind?*

Her eyes lingered on the sensor display. Salix was right. The Pashtali shouldn't be able to get a cloaked fleet into firing position without being detected—the recon drones hadn't picked up the slightest hint there *was* a cloaked fleet—and yet the only explanation that made sense was bait in a trap. But if it was a trap, where were the jaws? If the Pashtali had a bigger fleet within the system, they wouldn't need to fuck around. And if they had a superweapon that could turn her ships into scrap metal, they would have used it by now. Hell, they'd have used it during the Battle of Earth. What were they doing?

Admiral Glass would know what they were doing, she thought. *He'd understand…*

Her mind seemed to go blank with shock, just for a second. She'd never thought the Pashtali would stoop to use a *human* tactic, but…they were the weaker side, for once, and that meant they needed to be cunning. And that meant…

"Deploy starfighters, antimissile formation," she snapped. They'd flown right into the enemy trap. There was no time to alter course, no time to even slow the ships to a relative stop. She had to admire the enemy nerve. If she was right, they'd stolen a human concept—one of Admiral Glass's concepts—and made it work. "Stand by point defence!"

Salix glanced at her. "Admiral?"

"They have spare missiles," Naomi growled. She was sure she was right. She'd wondered why the enemy ships were overclocking their drives...she knew now. "They've put the missiles in space, all drives and sensors deactivated to keep us from spotting them and are holding them at the ready so they can be thrown at us. They used their drive signatures to keep us from spotting the missiles and..."

The display sparkled with red icons. Naomi cursed. The enemy had noticed the sudden change in her formation, realised what it meant and reacted with commendable speed, trying to get their punch in before it was too late. They were punching well above their weight, she noted coldly; they'd deployed enough missiles to take a bite out of her fleet even if it cost them every ship they had. The pattern was a little odd, she reflected, as more and more data flowed into the display. They didn't seem able to choose a target or...her eyes narrowed as she realised the enemy were trying to cripple, rather than destroy, her ships. It made a certain kind of sense. Humans were good at repairing their ships while underway, but there were limits.

"All launchers, return fire," she ordered. The second enemy salvo would be a great deal weaker—she suspected they'd tried to strip their magazines bare to make the first punch as powerful as possible—but it would still be painful if it reached its target. "Hold back the antishipping strikes. We need to cover our ships."

She gritted her teeth as the wall of missiles converged on her ships. The Pashtali missiles were top of the range, fully equal to Alphan designs—they might even be a little better—and it showed. They were difficult to hit easily, between their relatively small size and the ECM field surrounding them. The starfighters did what they could, blasting vast numbers of missiles into dust, but the remainder kept coming. Naomi silently congratulated herself for insisting on running endless drills, back during the flight. Her point defence network wasn't as outmatched as she'd feared.

"Admiral, *Tulip* and *Monty* have taken heavy damage," Olson reported. "*Chesterfield* and *Grant* have both been destroyed..."

"Later," Naomi ordered. The remaining missiles were striking their targets now, their drives slipping into sprint mode as the range closed to zero. The damage mounted rapidly—starships crippled, starships destroyed—as the last of the missiles vanished from the display. She spoke a silent prayer for the dead, promising herself she'd review a full list when the battle was over. "The enemy fleet?"

"Taking heavy damage," Olson reported. "They're charging us."

Naomi nodded. It was the only thing the Pashtali could do, now. They'd planned an ambush, but the only way to make it work had been to hold their position until the range closed to the point the human ships could no longer escape. They couldn't reverse course now, let alone escape. Their only hope was to close the range as much as possible in a bid to inflict more damage before they were blown away. One by one, their ships died. She refused to relax, even mentally, until the last one was nothing but dust.

"Admiral," Olson reported. "Long-range sensors are picking up engagements near Crossroads Three, Five and Six."

"The other powers have arrived," Naomi said. She took a moment to study the display. The timing had been largely accidental—hopefully, the Pashtali would assume it had been deliberate. They'd certainly be a hell of a lot more paranoid about allowing FTL transmitters to remain active anywhere near their fleet. "Do they require assistance?"

"Unsure, Admiral," Olson said. "Crossroads Three appears to have been captured, but there's still fighting at Five and Six."

"Deploy squadrons to capture the remaining crossroads," Naomi ordered. "The remainder of the fleet is to return to Crossroads One."

"Aye, Admiral," Olson said.

Naomi frowned as she studied the display. There was no way to tell how quickly the Pashtali would react, but she was sure they would. Her fleet *had* to remain in control of Crossroads One, at least until the fleet got underway again, or they'd run the risk of being bottled up again. The Pashtali had tried the tactic once before, back when the war had started, and it had come very close to working. Here, she doubted there were any uncharted threadlines the fleet could use to escape. The smartest thing the Pashtali could do, under the circumstances, was hold her in place while grinding Earth into rubble.

"Order the communications staff to put together a signal for Earth," she said. "And then forward it through the local transmitter."

"Aye, Admiral," Olson said.

"Admiral," Salix said. "With your permission, I would like to write and send my report too."

"Of course," Naomi said, with the private thought no transmitter would *dare* refuse an Alphan. "Just be aware it might be intercepted."

She leaned back in her chair, studying the reports. Nineteen ships destroyed outright and a further twenty-five damaged, seven so badly they'd probably need to be scrapped. The report was very clear the ships couldn't be repaired without a shipyard—reading between the lines, Naomi suspected it was impossible even if they could get the ships home. She keyed her console, signing off on stripping the hulls of everything they could put to use elsewhere and then scrapping what remained. There was no point in trying to save them...she made a mental note to consider other uses, but drew a blank. They wouldn't even make decent decoys.

"You caught on to what they were doing," Salix said. The Alphan sounded bored, his haughty accent enough to get under her skin, but she thought she heard a note of interest under his tone. "What tipped you off?"

"We studied their battles," Naomi said. The Pashtali hadn't fought many battles with first-rank foes. Most of their engagements, the ones detailed in the records humanity had inherited from its former masters, had been against far inferior enemies. They hadn't needed to be tactically brilliant to rain kinetic projectiles on the Vulteks, when they'd started acting up, or blow up scavenger ships from well outside their own range. "They studied ours too. They took one of our tricks and made it work."

"Odd, for them," Salix observed. "And yet, it hurt you."

"Yes," Naomi agreed. On paper, the losses were minimal. They'd have been a great deal worse if the range had been considerably shorter. In practice, she wasn't going to get any reinforcements, perhaps not even missile replenishments. The Pashtali had lost the battle, but they hadn't lost the war. Not yet. "They're more ingenious than we thought."

And they always knew they weren't the top dog, her thoughts added. *The Pashtali always knew they'd have to pick a fight with the Alphans, sooner or later, if they wanted to take your place. They were planning how to do it for a long time. You were on top for so long you found it impossible to imagine being knocked down a peg or two. Even now, you find it hard to adapt to the new galactic order.*

"They are," Salix observed. "Unless they hired human mercenaries to help them fight."

"I'd like to believe that," Naomi told him. "But I very much doubt its true."

She glanced at Olson. "Inform Ambassador Middleton that we have secured the system and that she is free to contact the lesser powers, as planned," she ordered. If nothing else, at least three of the races had effectively declared war on the Pashtali. They would have to hang together or be hanged separately. "And caution her that, regardless of the outcome, we cannot remain here for long."

"Aye, Admiral."

Naomi nodded. The Pashtali hadn't expected her fleet to attack Terminus. She'd been fairly sure they hadn't been fooled by the story the fleet was going to Theta Sigma—if nothing else, they'd know by now the fleet hadn't arrived there—but they hadn't worked out where she was actually heading. And yet, they knew where she was now. How long would it take, she asked herself, for the Pashtali to put together a fleet to cut her off? Days? Weeks? How many ships did they have prepared for rapid deployment? How many ships could they pull back from their various wars without seeing their entire position crumble? The Spooks had done what they could, but most of their conclusions were little more than wild-ass guessing that couldn't be relied upon. She suspected she was about to find out.

We have to keep moving, she told herself. *If they pin us down, we're fucked.*

• • •

Salix had grown up in a universe where there was nothing, absolutely nothing, that could threaten his people. Very few races had the power to take down a starcruiser, let alone a warcruiser, and those that did knew better than to risk the retribution that would follow. The Alphans would crush them like bugs, then leave their remains as a warning for all who might consider following in their footsteps. They were the masters of the known universe and that would never change…

…Except it had. The Lupines had pushed the Alphans to the brink of defeat. Even now, even after watching the all-powerful warcruisers burning, it was still hard to wrap his head around what had happened. They were Alphans. They did not lose. And they hadn't…barely. They would have lost, he knew, if the humans hadn't fought for them. It would have been the end. It would have been the end of everything.

And now the Pashtali were making their own bid for power.

They should have known, Salix told himself, that *someone* would make their own crossroads generator. The warning had been passed through the years, from the very first day the Alphans had learnt to do it for themselves, only to be forgotten when it seemed no one else would ever match their feat. And yet, it was obvious that—sooner or later—someone would succeed. In hindsight…he looked at the humans, scurrying around their bridge, and felt an uncomfortable twinge of fear. The Pashtali had laid a trap, using an idea they'd stolen from the humans, yet it had failed. Sure, the balance of power had been on their side, but still…it felt as if something fundamental had shifted…

…And he wondered, despite himself, just where the future would go.

CHAPTER FOURTEEN

TERMINUS

"IT WILL BE OUR PLEASURE TO FIGHT ALONGSIDE YOU," Ambassador Graze said. "You have already proved you can fight and win."

Ambassador Nancy Middleton kept her thoughts to herself. Ambassador Graze's people—the Munoz—had done their best to stay out of interstellar affairs as long as possible, citing the rights of a self-spacefaring race to avoid being dragged into border skirmishes and outright war. They would be happier, she was sure, if they could stay out of interstellar affairs permanently, but that was no longer possible. She understood their feelings and yet she couldn't help feeling a certain degree of contempt. If the seven races that relied on Terminus for their access to the greater galaxy had allied before the Alphans started to wind down their empire, they might have been able to deter the Pashtali or—at the very least—make a stand under far better circumstances. A vigorous defence of the bottleneck system might have ground down even a full-fledged Great Power.

She studied the alien thoughtfully. The Munoz looked like mice, although mice with long sharp teeth and sharper claws. Their faces were immobile—it was hard to read any emotions—but their fur twitched constantly, as if it was being blown around by an invisible breeze. The files suggested *that* was how they showed their emotions...Nancy wondered, mischievously, why the files hadn't gone into great detail. The Alphans had never been particularly interested in other races, save for their clients, and yet she was sure *some* of them had studied the Munoz. Perhaps they hadn't bothered to record their findings or, more likely, the data hadn't been forwarded to humanity. The Alphans had never been inclined to keep humanity's databases up to date either.

"Let us be certain," she said. It was the kind of rudeness the Alphans would never tolerate, not from a client race, but the files insisted the Munoz preferred direct speech rather than endless diplomatic dancing around the topic. "You are willing to ally with us, to send your fleets to fight beside us and to remain with us, until we bring the common enemy to the table and convince them to end the war?"

The alien's fur rippled. "We and our allies are already committed to the war," he said, his voice atonal as always. "We will fight beside you until we win or lose."

Nancy nodded, thoughtfully. The Munoz—and the other races—had already dispatched their forces to Terminus. They'd had to hold some units back—the Pashtali no longer *needed* to hammer their way along the threadlines and punch though the crossroads—but they *had* made a sizable commitment. Crossroads One was surrounded by an ever-growing swarm of warships, weapons platforms and even a pair of makeshift battlestations, while minelayers waited for the order to start emplacing mines directly on top of the crossroads. Nancy suspected that at least *some* of humanity's new allies wanted to get on with emplacing mines, regardless of galactic opinion, but so far they'd refrained. She had no idea how long they'd hold back. In theory, the scoutships would spot an incoming enemy fleet before it reached the crossroads. In practice, no one knew for sure.

And the Pashtali are still immensely powerful, she reminded herself. *If they're willing to soak up the losses, they can retake Terminus, crush their new enemies and then turn their attention back to us.*

She leaned back in her chair. "Your military officers will accept our commands?"

"The units assigned to assist your fleets will serve under your command, within reason," Ambassador Graze said. A more diplomatic race might have left out the qualifier. "The units assigned to defend *this* system will serve under joint command."

"Of course." Nancy was starting to like the alien's bluntness. "We leave such matters in your hands."

"We have already agreed on a joint command structure," Ambassador Graze told her. "It will not be easy to maintain, but better that than"—he spoke a word in his own language; Nancy guessed it was an obscenity—"Pashtali domination."

"The prospect of being executed concentrates the mind," Nancy agreed. She hadn't expected the lesser powers to work together so well, but the groundwork had been laid well before the Battle of Terminus. They might well have been planning something—a desperate strike on enemy positions—well before the human race had shown the galaxy the situation wasn't hopeless. "I hope you will be able to defend the bottleneck indefinitely."

"As do we," Ambassador Graze said. "We also have a prospective first target for our joint operations. The Pashtali are currently laying siege to Tarsus and we think raising the siege would show, again, that they can be beaten."

"I imagine so," Nancy said, neutrally. "Military matters are outside my purview. The admiral would have to consider the matter."

"Of course," Ambassador Graze said, with no trace of the irritation a human might show under the same circumstances. He understood, perhaps better than she had a right to expect, that her authority was both vast and strictly limited. It went against the grain to be completely honest about what she could and couldn't do, as Ambassador-At-Large, but it worked in her favour. "We suggest, however, that the operation be mounted as soon as possible."

He stood, fur rippling as he bid her farewell. Nancy stood too and watched him go, then returned to her chair. The marines would escort the ambassador back to his shuttle and then wait at the airlock to meet the *next* ambassador. Nancy sighed and reached for a glass of water. It had been a long day, with so many breaches in diplomatic protocol she felt quite unmoored from reality. She was too used to the elegant dance of galactic diplomats, not the bluntness of races that saw no reason to pretend there wasn't an iron fist inside the silken glove. Her lips twitched in grim amusement. Her old mentor had once told her there was a right and proper way to say *give me what I want or I'll beat the hell out of you and take it anyway* and woe betide anyone who *didn't* follow it. Threats of violence were acceptable, apparently, as long as they were couched in the proper terms. What did it say about the Galactics, she asked herself, that they were more concerned with appearances than reality?

That they're no different from a housewife dabbing makeup on her cheeks to hide the bruises, she thought, sourly. *And pretending everything is fine while everyone else knows it damn well isn't.*

She reached for her datapad and hastily started to note her impressions of the meeting. It had been a busy week, first dickering with the alien ambassadors and then haggling with the corporations and tiny governments dotted across the system. Terminus's lack of a central authority, one with formal control over the system even if the reality was very different, was a major problem. Reading between the lines, she suspected some of the *governments* she'd encountered were semi-criminal organisations, existing on the borderline between grey and black affairs. She suspected the various lesser powers would eventually be forced to impose order, just to keep their claim to control the system itself. The Pashtali would certainly make a big song and dance about the alliance *not* controlling the planets, which would undermine their control over the crossroads…not, she supposed, that it would matter in the long run. No one cared about the formalities any longer. The matter would be decided by who had the biggest guns and the willingness to use them.

Which is depressing as hell, she reflected. *No one cares about right or wrong, just who is the stronger when push comes to shove.*

She sighed inwardly. Her mentor had pointed out, when she'd been young and naive, that naked force had settled more issues than anything else. If there was no strong power enforcing the rules, no one keeping aggressive powers from breaking them, the rules were meaningless. And if there *was* a strong power enforcing the rules, what was to stop that power becoming a tyrant in its own right? One could come up with all sorts of justifications to do whatever one wanted to do—the Alphans had insisted they'd invaded Earth for the planet's own good—but they were nothing more than a thin veneer of justification, the silken glove over the iron fist. Who cared what the Earthers of a few hundred years ago had wanted? All that mattered was that the Alphans had the strength and will to take the planet from its rightful owners. Hell, they'd made *themselves* the rightful owners.

The intercom beeped. "Ambassador, Admiral Yagami is asking for a moment of your time," her assistant said. "When do you want to speak with her?"

Nancy's lips twitched. There was no formal protocol governing the relationship between a fleet admiral and a roving ambassador, save for a handful of procedures humanity had inherited from their former masters. *None* of them were remotely appropriate for her current situation, although she rather wished they were. The human race would be far better off if the Solar Navy could hammer the Pashtali into rubble, leaving her to dictate terms to the survivors. But it wasn't going to happen.

"Inform the admiral I'll call upon her after I'm finished with the next ambassador," she said, tiredly. They might have done all the preparatory work over the FTL transmitters, but she still needed to meet the ambassadors in person. "And hopefully everything will be settled by then."

She smiled, again. Diplomacy was normally a slow process. It could take months to hammer out an agreement to proceed with talks, then sort out how the talks should be conducted before they got started. A major power intent on stalling could bog matters down by insisting on discussing the shape of the conference table and other trivialities, then raising objections to everything the other power proposed. But here...the lesser powers had no *time* to argue about such minor details. The bare bones of the alliance treaties had been hammered out very quickly, with only a handful of details remaining for her and her peers to work out over the last week. The Galactics probably wouldn't believe it, when the agreements were formally announced. It would be about as believable, to them, as the claim the Pashtali had lost *billions* of starships in the Battle of Earth.

And so they'll be surprised, she thought. *They really shouldn't be.*

• • •

"Admiral," Olson said. "The last of the supplies from local sources have arrived. The repair crews are inspecting them now."

Naomi nodded, rubbing her eyes. The system might not have a central government, or any shore leave facilities her crew could use, but it *did* have a surprisingly large number of independent spacers, engineers and quasi-legal repair yards. The sheer inventiveness of the local engineers was almost *human*. They had a habit of taking tech from a dozen different races and refurbishing it, even improving it, then selling it on to anyone with money and a reluctance to ask questions. Reading between the lines, Naomi was *sure* some of the repaired ships ended up in pirate hands, but right now she didn't have time to care. Terminus had been more than happy to sell her fleet everything it needed, at a price.

"Very good," she said. The fleet was ready to press on, more or less. She would have preferred more time—as well as a chance to give her crew some leave—but it wasn't going to happen. The spooks insisted the Pashtali would assemble their fleets as quickly as possible to retake the system. "How did the tactical simulations go?"

"The online simulations went well," Olson said. If he was surprised she hadn't been watching in realtime, he kept it to himself. "It may not work out so well in reality."

"No," Naomi agreed. The Solar Navy had no practice operating as part of a multispecies formation. It had never been required to serve alongside the Alphans, even when it had been the EDF. Now...everyone was being very cooperative, surprisingly so, but there were too many kinks that needed to be weeded out before she took the fleet into battle. A single misunderstanding in the middle of a fight could lead to disaster. "We'll have to find out soon."

The intercom pinged. "Admiral, Ambassador Middleton has arrived."

"Send her in," Naomi ordered. She glanced at Olson. "Go back to the flag deck and inform the tactical staff I want a full analysis by the end of the shift."

"Aye, Admiral."

Naomi stood as Ambassador Middleton was shown into the compartment. It hadn't been easy to know how to treat the older woman when she'd first arrived on *Dauntless*. Nancy Middleton's career had reached the very highest levels, then fallen, then started to rise again...Naomi didn't pretend to understand it. She supposed it spoke well of the First Speaker that he worked so closely with his former rival, rather than casting her into the political wasteland. But then, it had served a very practical purpose. The Solar Navy would have come apart at the seams if the new government had tried to purge loyalists from the ranks. It would have led to disaster, if not outright civil war.

"Ambassador," Naomi said. They'd been told to sort out a working relationship, rather than have their spheres clearly delineated by their superiors. "Thank you for coming."

"My pleasure." Nancy took the indicated chair. "I assume the Munoz sent you their proposal?"

Naomi keyed her terminal, bringing up the message, the starchart and the notes her staff had attached. She had gone through all the possible targets, when they'd been planning the operation, but she hadn't let herself get attached to any of them. Tarsus wasn't a bad choice, if the local intelligence reports were accurate. The system belonged to a spacefaring race that had told the Pashtali to pound sand, when the Pashtali had informed them they were part of the Pashtali Empire now and any attempt to resist would be severely punished. The fighting in space hadn't lasted long—the Pashtali had brought in overwhelming firepower—but the planet itself was heavily defended, forcing the Pashtali to land troops. So far, the honours were about even, yet it was only a matter of time before the Pashtali forced the defenders to surrender. The only thing keeping them from surrendering now, judging by the reports, was the grim awareness the Pashtali would punish the defenders harshly for daring to resist.

Bastards, she thought. *They can do what they like, to whoever they like, but if someone stands up to them it's unfair and illegal and they must be punished.*

"It seems like a workable concept," she said. "But"—her lips thinned as she eyed the chart—"the system isn't a bottleneck. We could beat the orbiting starships and hammer their forces on the ground, but the Pashtali would return in force and resume the invasion. There's no way to keep them off balance permanently."

"Unless they're too busy chasing us," Nancy said. "It would buy the defenders some time though, wouldn't it?"

"Yes, but not enough to save them," Naomi said. "Not in the long run..."

She frowned. She disliked the idea of risking her ships, and the newborn alliance, on a mission that could have no long-term effect, not unless the Pashtali completely changed their tune and abandoned the war. And yet, she had very little choice. She needed to both give the Pashtali a bloody nose—another one—and prove to the galaxy that humanity was serious about allying with other smaller powers to take down a big one. And...

"The system isn't a bottleneck," she repeated. "We could get very close to them without letting their scouts know we're there."

"And then put a knife in their backs," Nancy said. "That *would* make us look good."

Naomi wasn't so sure. "My ancestors won a great many battles, during the Second Global War," she said. "They still got heavily outproduced and crushed. We might be in the same position now."

"There are other powers that might side with us, if we show we can win victories and *keep* winning victories," Nancy countered. The determination in her voice was striking. "The Pashtali are not popular."

"Neither is the average school bully," Naomi said, tartly. "That doesn't mean everyone gangs up on him and beats him to a pulp."

She scowled. She'd known some terrible bullies in her time. Some had been expelled or imprisoned; some had shaped up and made something of themselves...she didn't know any who'd been forced to quit bullying by his peers. Or hers...she shook her head, dismissing the thought. The logic of galactic power was the same logic as the bully. If the bully looked strong, he got away with it; if the bully looked weak, everyone jumped on him. Her mood soured. It was true that most bullies were cowards, but the only way to trigger the cowardly reflex was to give him something to be scared of and that wasn't easy.

"I'll speak to my staff and draw up a rough plan," she said. "I'll also send scouts to Tarsus and, more importantly, dispatch the raiders into their space. We need to keep them off balance as long as possible, to ensure they don't win a victory."

"If possible," Nancy agreed.

Naomi leaned forward. "One other thing," she added. "Can we trust the lesser powers to stick with us?"

"I think so," Nancy said. "The Pashtali weren't offering them anything beyond the chance to bend the knee. Even if the Pashtali really intended not to demand more, at a later date, how could they be trusted? Us? We're meeting them as equals. We don't have the power to crush them, and they know it."

"A balance of power," Naomi said.

"More like enlightened self-interest," Nancy countered. "As long as we and they have common interests, we'll work together towards a common goal."

CHAPTER FIFTEEN

JAMES BOND, TARSUS SYSTEM

"THE NEW IFF CODES ARE LOADED into the transmitter," Sarah said, as the freighter approached the crossroads. "And they're as close to valid as possible."

Thomas nodded, curtly. He'd spent some time, before departing Terminus, trying to find out what the system's former masters had reported to their superiors, but he'd drawn a blank. The FTL transmitter was designed to wipe its records once it sent the messages—a common precaution, though irritating- and none of the other powers, corporations or criminal gangs invested in the system had recorded the outgoing messages. There was no reason to *think* the Pashtali would look at his ship too closely, but if they realised she'd passed through Terminus shortly before it fell they might start asking a few pointed questions. *James Bond* was hardly the only ship that fit that profile, yet...who knew? In their shoes, Thomas would be very paranoid indeed after losing an entire system.

If the Pashtali wear shoes, he thought. *Do they?*

He smiled at the thought, then keyed the helm console as the timer ticked down to zero. The Tarsus crossroads were immense, far too large to become bottlenecks, but that didn't mean the defenders couldn't monitor the crossroads and watch for signs of someone trying to sneak into the system. If they tried...he checked the IFF beacon, making sure it was pulsing out comforting lies. *James Bond* was just another tramp freighter, her crew moving from system to system, living life on a shoestring as they desperately tried to find contracts that would earn them enough money to keep their ship going for a few more months. The Pashtali might tell them to fuck off—or something along the same lines—but they probably wouldn't open fire without good cause. Probably. It wasn't easy to get the independent shipping community to agree on anything, but they'd unite in anger if anyone, even a great power, started to blow independent traders out of space. They had enough clout to make life very difficult for any government that refused to take a hard line with anyone who did.

The display blanked, then rebooted. Red icons flared up along the edge of the crossroads, then blinked to amber as it became clear the sensor contacts were nothing more than space junk. No, debris. The Pashtali had stormed the system, blown hell out of the handful of monitoring stations on the crossroads, then left the wreckage in place while laying siege to the planet itself. Thomas felt his stomach churn. There'd been no *need* to blow the stations away and slaughter their crews, nothing beyond pointless barbarity. They couldn't have kept the Pashtali from invading the system...Thomas wondered, suddenly, if they'd been wrong about the Pashtali being willing to keep the war relatively civilised. If they were feeling desperate...

"There are no active monitoring stations," Sarah said. "I'm not even picking up a standard beacon."

Thomas glanced at her, then back at his display. It was quite possible there was an entire fleet of cloaked ships holding position near the crossroads, or a handful of stealthed sensor platforms, but why bother? The Pashtali had every right to set up their own monitoring stations, secure in the knowledge Galactic Law would be on their side if someone blew them away. His eyes narrowed as the sensors collected more and more data, all insisting the ship was alone. Thomas knew better than to take that for granted. A lone ship, lying doggo near the crossroads, wouldn't be noticed by the passive sensors until she brought up her drives or active sensors. He reached for the console to do an active sensor sweep, then changed his mind. It would almost certainly draw attention they didn't want or need.

"Transmit a standard IFF pulse to Tarsus itself," he ordered, finally. "And inform them we'll enter orbit in five hours."

"Aye, sir," Sarah said. He could *hear* the smile in her voice. "I take it we're not in a hurry?"

"I see no reason to hurry," Thomas said. "We don't want them to think we're anything special, do we?"

He smiled, then sobered. The Pashtali were unlikely to look twice at his ship, unless they had some reason to be suspicious, but the locals might try to hire them. That would be ironic, if it got them caught. The locals would wonder why an independent freighter, a ship one bad day from complete failure, would decline a shipping contract, then complain to the Pashtali or the independent shippers. They might have to accept the contact, even if it meant going a long way out of their way. An independent—and desperate—captain who refused a contract was about as plausible a character as the gun-toting pacifist. Or the women whose first reaction to discovering a man spying on them was to fuck him, rather than screaming about perverts and demanding the man be beaten to within an inch of his life. The scriptwriters could create whatever characters they liked. The real world was rarely so obliging.

The display kept updating as more and more data flowed into the battle sensors. Tarsus was surrounded by dozens of energy signatures, suggesting the Pashtali were keeping the planet under a very tight siege. A handful of other ships were gliding through the asteroid belt, probably seeking out independent mining communities and forcing them to submit or die. The files insisted there had been at least five cloudscoops orbiting the gas giant, but there was no sign of them. Thomas cursed under his breath. It didn't matter who had destroyed the cloudscoops. Either way, the price of fuel within the sector was about to rise if it hadn't already.

And that meant independent shippers would find themselves trapped if they couldn't afford to pay.

It isn't as if it is hard to set up a cloudscoop, he thought. *We could skim the gas giant's atmosphere if necessary. But doing it while they're shooting at us will be impossible...*

Sarah's console bleeped. "I'm picking up a message," she said. "Text only."

Thomas frowned. That was odd, and normally reserved for formal warnings. "Put it though."

The screen lit up. BE ADVISED THIS SYSTEM IS IN REBELLION AGAINST ITS LAWFUL MASTERS. ALL INDEPENDENT SHIPPERS ARE ORDERED TO STAY CLEAR OF THE SYSTEM'S PLANETS AND ASTEROID SETTLEMENT AND REFRAIN FROM ALL NON-AUTHORISED CONTACT. ANY ATTEMPT TO DEFY THIS WARNING WILL RESULT IN THE HARSHEST CONSEQUENCES, UP TO AND INCLUDING ARREST, DETENTION, AND THE PHYSICAL DESTRUCTION OF YOUR SHIP. THERE WILL BE NO FURTHER WARNINGS.

"Charming," Thomas said. The message was worded oddly—he suspected it had been translated several times—but the meaning was clear. "How close do you think we can get before they come after us?"

"Not much closer," Sarah said. She nodded to the display. "The warning was transmitted the moment they picked up our message, or near enough to make no difference. There's no way we can get any closer under the guise of heading to the nearest crossroads, not now. The closer we go, the greater the risk of them hurling a missile at us."

"Yeah," Thomas said. "Or simply running us down."

His mind raced. There were plenty of tricks they could do to stall, if they needed to get closer, but he had a nasty feeling none of them would work. If they declared a major emergency, the Pashtali would probably insist on checking—and then searching—the ship before they were allowed to leave. Hell, Galactic Law insisted you had to help someone in distress, if you were in a position to do so without risk to yourself. The Pashtali might uncover the spy ship quite by accident, while upholding their responsibilities as a spacefaring power. It would be ironic, given how little attention they normally paid to interstellar treaties, but who knew? They had to be aware most of the galaxy was growing increasingly wary of them. They might think that helping a ship in distress was a good way to earn some brownie points.

"Inform them we are reversing course," he said, finally. There was no point in trying to get any closer. "You take the helm. I'm going to prep the makeshift drone."

Sarah frowned. "Be careful."

Thomas nodded, curtly, and headed for the hatch. Their superiors had worked out, in painstaking detail, how to take a handful of common or garden spare parts, the sort of components one could find almost anywhere, and put them together to make devices that were almost as capable as their military counterparts. A regular drone would be a red flag, if the ship were boarded and searched, but the components to make one wouldn't raise any eyebrows. Thomas made his way down to the machine shop, feeling a twinge of loneliness as he passed the cabins where his children had slept, then found the components and got to work. The drone took shape and form very quickly, a crude device that would nonetheless work long enough—he hoped—to get them some good visuals. He attached the laser communicator, did a complete systems check, then carried the device to the airlock. A flicker of the drive field would send it plummeting into the inner system, where it would fly past the planet and eventually plunge into the sun.

He keyed his wristcom. "Laser link established," he said. "Hold us steady."

"Of course," Sarah's voice said. "Cheeky bastard, aren't you?"

Thomas shrugged. A purpose-built drone would be larger—they were often twice the size of standard long-range missiles—and capable of operating without a realtime link to the mothership. *His* drone couldn't do anything more than take pictures and sensor records and would go dead, completely dead, if she lost the pinpoint laser link. And the tiniest shift in position, on an interplanetary scale, would be enough to put the drone well out of reach. She'd fly on into the sun and vanish, her passing completely unnoticeable...

Unless they've come up with something new, he thought, as he made his way back to the bridge. *There was all that talk about sensor gear capable of picking up a laser transmission from a distance.*

He frowned, recalling the vague reports, then shrugged. It might not be impossible, but it would require a technological breakthrough on an incredible scale. The Pashtali could not have done it...could they? If they had, surely the human race would have seen *some* sign of it before now. There wasn't a navy in the known galaxy that didn't use pinpoint lasers to steer recon drones into enemy systems, slipping them as close to enemy military bases as possible. If the technology to counter the lasers existed, the galactic balance of power would have been changed beyond all hope of repair.

"They're not making any attempt to come after us," Sarah reported. "They just ordered us away from the planet."

"They probably don't care if we use the crossroads," Thomas said. "They just don't want us anywhere near the planet itself."

He shuddered. He'd seen the reports from Earth, after the Pashtali invaders had been defeated. The spidery bastards had done a hell of a lot of damage, laying waste to a chunk of the planet and slaughtering hundreds of thousands of innocent people. God alone knew for sure *just* how many people had been killed. It had been nearly eight months since the invasion had been repelled and far too many people were still missing, their families clinging desperately to the hope they might have survived. Thomas doubted. Anyone who'd remained lost for months after the invasion was probably dead and gone, bodies dumped in a mass grave if they hadn't been vaporised by alien weapons.

Or they took advantage of the chaos to escape their old lives and reinvent themselves somewhere else, he thought. He understood the impulse. He'd have to do it himself, when the time came for him and his wife to retire. *But no one will ever know for sure.*

The console bleeped as the drone flew towards the planet. Thomas tensed, despite years of experience telling him the drone was practically impossible to detect. It had no drives, no active sensors, nothing to draw enemy attention beyond the pinpoint laser transmitter and *that* couldn't be detected unless a starship crossed the beam. And the odds of that happening were roughly on par with the Pashtali surrendering without further ado.

His lips twitched, then sobered. Tarsus was surrounded by at least a dozen Pashtali ships, including three planetary bombardment vessels. The planet's major cities were protected by PDC forcefields—the Pashtali couldn't batter them down without laying waste to the entire planet—but the enemy clearly had a strong position on the ground. It was hard to be sure, from such a distance, yet it *seemed* as if they were steadily grinding their way towards the nearest PDCs. How long would it be, he asked himself, before the defenders sued for peace?

Sarah peered over his shoulder. "How long has the fighting been going on?"

"Months, according to the reports," Thomas said. "They attacked Tarsus before the Battle of Earth."

"Whoops." Sarah smirked. "They should have concentrated on crushing us before picking fights with the rest of their neighbours."

Thomas nodded, although he wasn't sanguine about the prospect of the Pashtali biting off more than they could chew. Standard doctrine was clear. An invader who controlled the high orbitals could batter his enemies from well outside their own range, pummelling them until they surrendered, but one who *partly* controlled the high orbitals still had the edge. The Pashtali could secure their landing zones, using KEWs to keep the defenders from crushing the beachheads, while bringing in troops and vehicles to advance under the forcefields and eventually take out the PDCs. It was long and bloody, and most races preferred to avoid it as long as possible, but it could be done. The Pashtali seemed to enjoy it.

I suppose it does teach their targets that they really have been beaten, he thought, after a moment. *The groundhogs could insist that defeat in space doesn't mean defeat on the ground, if they wanted to delude themselves. It's a great deal harder to overlook a battle on the ground that leaves an entire planet in ruins.*

The drone kept transmitting, right up to the moment they lost the signal. Thomas swore under his breath. They would never know what had happened to the drone. It didn't *look* as though the drone had been spotted and destroyed—the enemy fleet wasn't blasting out of orbit, trying to run *James Bond* down before she could slip through the crossroads and vanish—but it was impossible to be sure. The Pashtali might have gotten lucky. Or the drone might have glitched and...he shook his head, hastily transferring the sensor records to the secure datacore. If the Pashtali came after them, they'd have to protest their innocence and hope for the best. Somehow, he doubted it would be enough.

"I'm getting too old for this," he said. "How about you?"

"When the war is over, we should go a *long* way from Earth," Sarah agreed. "Bid the kids farewell and head out into the unknown, trading as we go."

Thomas nodded. The prospect was very tempting. The kids were old enough to take care of themselves and there was nothing holding them back, save duty. And even *that* would end with the war. Perhaps. The agreement he'd made with the EIS, back in the old days, hadn't taken independence and post-independence wars into account. He'd done his duty—more than he was contracted to do—and besides, the ship was his. He could offer to send back reports, as he travelled into space that rarely—if ever—saw humans and hope it would be enough. It was a shame his old contact had retired, and Admiral Glass had died. They'd understood the realities of Thomas's work.

And they also would also understand the human race is fighting for its life, he reminded himself. *I should do the same.*

Sarah cleared her throat. "We're entering the crossroads now," she said. "For the record, I don't think they thought anything of us."

"Good," Thomas said. The Galactics looked down their noses at the younger races, including humanity, but better to be underestimated than to be taken as a threat. The Pashtali had thought humanity was an easy target, a year ago. He assumed they'd learnt better now. "Set course for the RV point. Admiral Yagami needs to know what we saw."

"Of course," Sarah said. She keyed her console, laying in the course, then leaned back in her seat. "Where do you think we'll be going next?"

Thomas shrugged. There was no answer. *James Bond* could fly around the rim of enemy space, and hardly anyone would notice or care, but the further she travelled into enemy territory the greater the chance she'd be detected. The Pashtali did everything in their power to keep independent shippers away from their worlds, making sure *their* freighters and crews were favoured so heavily no one else could compete. It was technically illegal, by Galactic Law, but it was impossible to do anything about it. He made a mental note to suggest that the matter be raised during the peace talks. It probably wouldn't get any traction, but it was worth a try.

"I have no idea," he said. The admiral might let them go home…no, that wasn't going to happen. *James Bond* was, as far as he knew, the only covert scout assigned to the fleet. If there were others, they'd make a point of not telling him. He didn't mind. What he didn't know he couldn't be forced to tell. "But I'm sure we'll find out soon enough."

"Yeah," Sarah agreed. "We really are getting too old for this, aren't we?"

CHAPTER SIXTEEN

ESS Dauntless, Tarsus System

"THEY'RE NOT TRYING TO MONITOR the crossroads?"

Naomi tried not to jump at Salix's sudden question. The CIC had fallen silent as the fleet inched its way through the crossroads and into the Tarsus System, even though it wouldn't make any difference whether the crew kept their mouth shut or organised a keg party with booze and hookers. It was an old cliché that sound didn't travel in space and there was no point in keeping quiet, but starship crews tended to be silent when they were travelling under stealth. It was just a human quirk, she thought, a pretence that they wouldn't be detected as long as they stayed very quiet. And it felt as though the observer had casually broken an all-powerful taboo.

"They may have a stealth ship watching from a safe distance," she said. It was what *she* would have done, if she'd had the ships and, more importantly, the time. The Pashtali might have withdrawn as many ships from Tarsus as possible, on the assumption they needed to concentrate their forces to retake Terminus before it was too late. "But it probably doesn't matter."

She glanced at Olson. "Deploy recon probes, then establish the command datanet."

"Aye, Admiral," Olson said. "Command datanet coming online…now."

Naomi nodded. The datanet had never been very solid, even before the fleet had been reinforced by ships from seven different races, but they'd done what they could to make it work. She silently blessed herself for ensuring the network was stress-tested before they encountered *real* stress. There were still problems in keeping the network together, and in establishing a shared language for operational commands, but it wouldn't collapse the moment they encountered the enemy. Her eyes tightened as the display filled with light codes, each one representing a ship or formation under her command. If the Pashtali could see her, they'd think she'd brought a hammer to smash an egg. It was overkill on a truly galactic scale…

It's important we win, she told herself. She wanted to think the Pashtali couldn't see her coming, but she dared not assume they couldn't. They probably had *something* watching the crossroads even if it was too big to block effectively. *We cannot let them have even a chance to win the coming battle.*

Her lips twitched. It was unlikely they could do more than irritate her, unless they had a much larger fleet lurking in stealth near the planet. *That* was unlikely too. If the Pashtali had had the ships to retake Terminus, they should have sent them at once without giving her and her allies all the time they needed to fortify the system. She suspected *that* meant the Pashtali were off balance, their fleets too spread out to be concentrated at a moment's notice. How long would it take, she asked herself, for them to put together a sizable fleet without uncovering their homeworlds? The spooks couldn't tell her. They just didn't have enough hard data to produce anything more than guesswork.

Observer Salix caught her eye. "Do they know we're here?"

"A very good question," Naomi said. The fleet was straightening itself out, falling into its ragtag formation as it glided away from the crossroads. "We are trying to be stealthy. We hope they won't see us coming. But we cannot rely on it. There are just too many cloaked ships trying to fly in formation."

She studied the display, her mouth suddenly dry. If the Pashtali didn't see her coming, she'd have no difficulty sneaking into range and opening fire. But if they did...how would they react? They didn't have anything like the firepower they'd need to stand up to her and, this time, they probably didn't have the time to set up a second missile swarm. Even if they did, they presumably knew it hadn't worked the first time. What would *she* do in their place?

I would know when to fold them and back off, she thought. There was no point in throwing away ships and men in a desperate and futile attempt to keep a system that was already lost. *But that would mean abandoning the troops on the ground.*

She cursed under her breath. She'd had to abandon troops during the Vultek War and that hadn't sat well with her, even though cold logic had told her there was no choice. The Pashtali would have to be insane to throw their ships away, trying to change what could not be changed, but...it had still bothered her. Would it bother them? The xenospecialists were still trying to put together a picture of enemy thinking, as if it suddenly dawned on them that a race that looked nothing like humanity might not *think* like humanity. The Pashtali weren't *really* spiders, no matter how much they looked like them. Would they bow to the god of military necessity, or would they refuse to abandon the troops on the ground?

And they will see us coming, she told herself. A handful of cloaked ships might escape detection as they made their way through the crossroads, but not an entire fleet. There were limits to even the best cloaking devices. *They'll have plenty of time to decide what to do.*

Her mind churned. Would they fight? Or run? Or bombard the planet? They *could* turn the entire world into a radioactive nightmare, if they were prepared to commit outright genocide. It would unite the galaxy against them, or would it? The Alphans were withdrawing from their empire and no one else had their power or prestige. Would the Pashtali gamble no one would try to stop them? Or...

She shuddered. If the galaxy didn't unite against them, others would retaliate. Tarsus—or what was left of a once-proud spacefaring race—certainly would. Humanity too, if Earth or one of her colonies was scorched clean of life. The Pashtali homeworlds could stand off an invasion force from anyone, save perhaps the Alphans, but it would be difficult to keep suicide squads from slipping through the defences and unleashing hell. Nukes, antimatter, chemical and biological weapons…no, it was unthinkable. The Pashtali wouldn't start a chain of events that would end with hundreds of worlds and billions upon billions of intelligent life forms dead. Would they?

Something else to worry about, she thought. *But not now.*

She stood in front of the display, trying to project an image of calm patience as Tarsus swelled in front of her. The recon probes were reporting back, signalling that almost nothing had changed since *James Bond* had been ordered to stay well away from the planet itself. The enemy fleet was altering its position, trying to concentrate its units…Naomi nodded, unsurprised. They'd seen the incoming fleet. They probably didn't have enough hard data to know just how big the fleet was, but they could probably guess. If the enemy CO at Terminus hadn't raised the alarm, when she'd crashed through the crossroads, he was probably lucky he was dead.

"Signal the fleet," she ordered, quietly. "Uncloak. I say again, uncloak and bring active sensors online."

Her lips twitched. The enemy fleet seemed to flinch. It was her imagination, probably, but it still made her smile. There were so many ships bearing down on the enemy position she could hardly blame them. The active sensors came online, revealing a handful of shuttles rising from the planet and heading to the fleet. Senior officers, being withdrawn before the hammer came down? Well-connected aristocrats, if the Pashtali *had* aristocrats? Or war criminals, denied protection under interstellar treaties? Or…she shrugged. It didn't matter. The enemy ships were already starting to thrust away from the planet.

"Alter course to intercept," she ordered. "We'll try to run them down."

She frowned as she saw the converging vectors on the display. The odds were against them, but if she was lucky the Pashtali would try to fire a shot or two for the honour of the flag. It depended on how daring the enemy CO was feeling. The smart thing to do would be to just keep building up speed, trying to keep the range as open as possible, even if they came into effective firing range for a few moments. The daring thing would be to close the range a little increasing the odds of a hit, but they'd have problems getting away afterwards. She could afford to fire enough missiles, even at that range, to swamp their defences.

"Admiral," Olson said. "They're piling on the speed."

Naomi nodded, concealing her annoyance. It was good to watch the enemy ships run before her—it would make good propaganda, if nothing else—but she wanted to smash the ships before they found friends and came back to reclaim the system. For all she knew, there were entire fleets of battleships rushing towards her. It was possible, too. The human race had spent six months assembling every warship they could build, beg, borrow or steal. The Pashtali had to be doing the same.

"Hold our current course for ten minutes, then detach two pursuit squadrons to shadow them all the way to the crossroads," she ordered. "If they keep running, one squadron is to take up position on the far side and watch for enemy reinforcements; the other is to hold position on the near side and wait."

"Aye, Admiral," Olson said.

Observer Salix caught her eye. "They're running for their lives," he said. "That's odd."

"It's the best thing they could do," Naomi said. "If they stood and fought, we'd blow them to hell. If they tried a long-range engagement, we'd throw enough missiles at them to smother their defences. Retreating is probably the best thing they can do. They know where the nearest reinforcements are, even if we don't. They'll link up with them and come back here with blood in their eye."

She glanced at Olson. "Detach a pair of scouts and order them to shadow the enemy ships as far as possible," she added. "If they find reinforcements, I want to know about it."

"Aye, Admiral," Olson said.

Observer Salix frowned. "The enemy will use the threadlines to evade the scouts."

"Perhaps." Naomi put firm controls on her temper. "It's worth a try. The scouts may find nothing, or they may lose the enemy, or they may locate the enemy fleet before it surprises us."

She kept her face blank, somehow. She didn't mind being questioned in private—Admiral Glass had always insisted people learnt through asking questions and listening to the answers—but being interrogated on her own command deck was irritating as hell. It probably wasn't good for discipline either. She knew it was important for her subordinates to understand the reasoning behind her orders—she'd had one superior who'd kept everyone in the dark as long as possible, only to cause a near-disaster when he'd been taken out in the middle of the engagement—but there were limits. She would have preferred the observer kept his mouth shut and waited until they were alone to ask questions.

But his role here is probably to observe us as well as the war, she thought. Observer Salix was so different from her old commander she was tempted to wonder if they were different races. It was impossible, but still. . .*I wonder what his report will say, when he sends it home?*

"Admiral," Olson said. "The enemy is still picking up speed."

"And overpowering their drives," Naomi said. She hoped their drive nodes would fail, although she doubted it. They'd have a far better idea of what their ships could take. "I think they won't stop running until they reach the crossroads."

She studied the display for a moment, then shrugged. There was no point in wasting any more time. They weren't going to intercept the enemy ships unless the enemy decided to commit suicide.

"Detach the pursuit ships now," she ordered. "And then order the remainder of the fleet to advance on Tarsus."

"Aye, Admiral," Olson said.

Naomi braced herself as the fleet altered course, swinging around to head straight at the planet. The enemy fleet was gone and was no longer in a position to do much of anything, but they'd left a *lot* of weapons platforms orbiting Tarsus. Her eyes narrowed as she spotted a handful of platforms opening fire, raining KEWs and plasma bolts on the surface. The bastards didn't seem to think the fighting was over, damn them. Were they aiming to do as much damage as possible before they were wiped out? Or were they up to something?

"Signal the enemy," she ordered, quietly. "Transmit the surrender demand."

"Aye, Admiral."

"They won't listen," Observer Salix predicted. "Why should they?"

Naomi gave him a sharp look. "Because they are doomed," she said, flatly. "They will be slaughtered if they try to continue the fight, either by us or by the locals. If they surrender to us, we'll treat them in line with interstellar treaties...if they surrender now. If they don't..."

"They'd still be surrendering to a very lowly race indeed," Observer Salix countered. "They might prefer to die."

"Really?" Naomi felt a flash of irritation. The Pashtali had surrendered—once—at Earth. They might be happier if it had been the Alphans or another Galactic race that had forced them into surrender, instead of uppity humanity, but the precedent had been set. It was unlikely the local Pashtali *didn't* know. The news had travelled all over the known galaxy. "If they want to die, they will."

• • •

Observer Salix kept his thoughts to himself as the human admiral turned away and busied herself issuing orders to her subordinates. It was hard to read human emotions, and harder still to understand them, but he was fairly sure she was annoyed. Humans were a prideful bunch, even after hundreds of years under alien rule. They didn't like the reminder that most senior races regarded them as children, rather than a mature race in their own right. And while they had a lot to be proud of, they also lacked the awareness of just how small their achievements were compared to their former masters.

To be fair, they did best the Pashtali more than once, he reminded himself. *But only through cheating.*

He hid his dismay at the treacherous thought. The Pashtali had been caught by surprise, first at Terminus and then at Tarsus. They had probably anticipated the humans trying to reclaim the Occupied Zone, perhaps crossing the border there and infringing Pashtali space. To attack a target so far from home...it sounded insane and perhaps it was, yet it really *had* knocked the Pashtali off-balance. And the humans had found allies.

Remarkable, he thought, with genuine pleasure. *Who would have considered it?*

His mood soured. The Alphans weren't used to treating other races as equals. The best they offered anyone, even their peers, was ill-hidden condescension. They weren't the only Galactics who refused to consider junior races their equals. The Pashtali didn't have allies, they had servants. And everyone else was just the same. The Alphans might have liberated Terminus, and made a big song and dance about doing it, but they wouldn't have just handed it back to the locals either. They would have come up with an excuse and kept it for themselves. But the humans had simply handed it over to the locals without a fight, or even an argument. It was insane, by the standards of good galactic behaviour, and yet...

It might have worked out in their favour. They could have held the bottleneck system and dared the locals to kick them out. Better human masters than Pashtali, right? They could have held the system against the Pashtali too, if they dug in...there was nothing to gain by abandoning the system and a great deal to lose. Except, it had won them allies and friends—true friends. The alien ships accompanying the human fleet was proof enough of that! And...they'd been cunning, too. By convincing the various lesser powers to work together to fortify the bottleneck, they'd not only won themselves a lot of influence, but also made it harder for their allies to switch sides. Observer Salix had no idea how much of it was intentional—and how much sheer luck—but it didn't matter. It was against galactic principles, against the cold law of the jungle the galaxy had observed since time out of mind, and it had worked. The humans had come out ahead.

And what does this mean, he asked himself, *for the rest of the galaxy?*

"Admiral," the little human operator said. "The Pashtali on the ground are refusing to surrender. The local government is requesting we clear them out."

"Drop KEWs on them," Observer Salix advised. It was unfortunate there would likely be innocent locals amidst the enemy targets, but it was a small price to pay for liberating the planet. "Crush them from orbit."

"They're too intermingled," Admiral Yagami said. "We need to land troops to flush them out."

Observer Salix leaned forward. "The locals don't have troops of their own?"

"Not in position to intervene quickly," the little human said. "They're too dug in to take the offensive."

"Quite," Admiral Yagami said. "Alert the Marines. They are to prepare for rapid deployment."

"Aye, Admiral."

Observer Salix frowned. It was insane. Crazy. And yet, the humans had a saying. Crazy like a fox, crazy enough to work…the death toll was going to be high and yet…

The locals are going to think the humans took risks they didn't have to take, just to keep their casualties down, he thought. No other race would put the lives of aliens ahead of their own, even if they were allies. *How will this work out for them?*

Bracing himself, he leaned in to watch.

CHAPTER SEVENTEEN

TARSUS, TARSUS SYSTEM

"YOUR TARGETS ARE THE BUG-LIKE THINGS," Captain Arcos snapped, as the shuttle ploughed into the planet's atmosphere. "If any of you shoot a frog, you'd damn well better be able to justify it!"

Lieutenant Wesley Anderson nodded, feeling sweat trickling down his back. The armoured combat suit was supposed to maintain his temperature at a reasonable level, but somehow he felt both hot and cold as the shuttle continued her descent. It wasn't the first drop he'd made—he'd jumped a dozen times during training and several more during his initial deployment—yet it was his first drop into a combat zone. The live feed from the shuttle's sensors showed enemy missiles and energy weapons, rising to target the shuttles as they dropped towards the ground. It seemed impossible they'd survive long enough to deploy, even though the decoys were absorbing much of the enemy fire. He wished they'd had time to secure a proper landing zone on the far side of the border, then march overland to their target. But there'd been no time.

The military life, he reflected. *Long hours of boredom, followed by moments of screaming terror.*

"Jump in five," the jumpmaster called. "Brace yourself."

Wesley gritted his teeth, reminding himself he'd been through worse. He hadn't backed out on his first drop and he wasn't going to back out now, not that he could. He'd have been in deep shit if he'd backed out when they'd been on the ship, but at least it would have been possible. Now, he was committed. The suits were already being shoved towards the hatch. He frowned as he watched the live feed—a missile flashed past, so close he was *sure* he could reach out and touch it—and then drew back, cursing himself. If there was a missile out there with the shuttle's name on it, he wouldn't see the incoming shot. They'd be dead before they knew what had hit them.

The shuttle lurched. Something had exploded, far too close for comfort. Someone was praying over the command net—Wesley started to mute them, then stopped. It would make it impossible to hear if they had something more important to say. The Marines around him were brave men—cowards didn't get through Boot Camp—but right now they were as helpless as the alien civilians on the planet below. They couldn't do anything, other than wait for the drop and rely on the pilot to save their lives. The sheer helplessness grated. Wesley had been trained to always take the offensive, but now all he could do was hang in his suit and wait.

"Fifty seconds," the jumpmaster said. A low rumble echoed through the suit as it glided forward. "Forty seconds..."

Wesley felt a sudden *shove* as the suit was thrown into the atmosphere. His automatic systems took over, sending him plummeting towards the ground. He barely noticed as the suit picked up speed, his HUD feeding him a steady stream of data from stealth probes and the orbiting starships. The enemy were on the move, but to where? He frowned as a kinetic projectile flashed past and hit the ground, raw energy marking the destruction. A smart enemy would be trying to surrender by now, he was sure. Their starships were gone, leaving them alone and encircled on a very hostile world. The frog-like natives were probably gearing up to push the invaders back into the sea.

Unless they think their tormentors will return, Wesley thought. It wasn't impossible. The briefing had made it clear that the fleet had to move fast and break things, rather than risk getting bogged down. *They might be afraid to lift a hand against the Pashtali for fear they'll retake the high orbitals and then retaliate.*

He braced himself. There were more flashes of light on the ground, faint impressions of alien cities that looked decidedly weird despite being combat zones. His suit reported that the air was breathable, but with some contaminants that might be harmless or might be chemical weapons unleashed by one side or the other. Species-specific toxins were banned by galactic conventions, from what he'd been taught at Boot Camp, but the Pashtali cared little for such niceties. He shuddered in disgust. They could have dusted the entire planet with a lethal virus, waited a year and then moved into the dead world and taken it for themselves. There was no one who could have tried to stop them.

The ground came up and hit him, the suit's antigravity units kicking in a bare second before he would have hit the surface and gone splat. There was no time for shock, no time to catch his breath as the rest of the squad landed around him. His HUD was already filling with tactical updates, precise notations of where his fellows waited intermingled by vaguer notes of prospective enemy positions. He looked around, noticing the strange combination of alien buildings behind him. The hive-like Pashtali structures contrasted oddly with buildings that seemed to be made from mud and wood, strikingly human-like even though they rested within pools of water. He looked down and realised they were standing in mud. The ground felt both stable and slippery.

"They're retreating from their forward posts," the drone operator warned. The tactical map updated rapidly, showing a stream of enemy soldiers heading towards the human positions. "I think they're trying to concentrate..."

The ground shook as more KEWs hammered down. Wesley hoped they'd wipe out most of the enemy troops before they encountered the humans, but he knew that was wishful thinking. The two groups of aliens were too closely intermingled for indiscriminate orbital strikes. Only a complete idiot would assume there was a way to separate the friendlies from the enemies and kill the latter without harming the former, but he'd been cautioned there were a lot of complete idiots in politics. The human race couldn't afford an incident enemy propaganda would turn into a full-scale atrocity, even though the enemy had committed an entire string of atrocities themselves. It wasn't fair—no one with half a brain would believe it was possible to be entirely sure of one's target in a war zone—but it was an inescapable reality. They'd just have to be as careful as possible and hope for the best.

He snapped orders as the squad advanced, taking up firing positions and waiting. The Pashtali weren't being as foolish as they looked, even though they were exposing themselves to orbital fire. If their forward units fell back to the occupied cities, they could use the civilians as human—alien—shields and hold out long enough for their fleet to return and drive the human ships away. Even if their fleet didn't return, winkling them out would be long, costly and devastating. He gritted his teeth, reminding himself that the local civilians didn't deserve to be slaughtered for being in the wrong place at the wrong time. They might be alien, but they still deserved to live.

The ground shook, again. The enemy were firing missiles in all directions, some aimed at the starships and shuttles overhead and others on the landing zones. Wesley cursed as a nuclear warhead broke through the hastily established point defence network and detonated right on top of a human position, wiping out a command post and a number of human troops and...he told himself the armoured suits were tough, that they were designed to thrive in very hostile environments, that if they weren't at ground zero there was a very good chance the wearer had survived. It didn't matter. The command post was clearly out of contact and would remain so for the foreseeable future. The command network had already adapted, ensuring the chain of command remained firmly in place. The enemy were drawing closer...

"Shit," someone muttered.

Wesley was inclined to agree as the Pashtali came out of nowhere and charged. It wasn't the first time he'd seen the spider-like aliens, but it was easily the worst. A writhing mass of spidery legs and tentacles rushed towards him, a creeping nightmare that reflected humanity's worst phobias. He'd grown up on a starship and spent most of his life meeting aliens and yet merely seeing them charge made his stomach churn and his legs turn to jelly. He wanted to freeze and he wanted to run and...

The Pashtali opened fire, snapping him back to himself. They might be horrific, but they were hardly supernatural monsters. They were a threat. Threats could be killed.

"Fire," he snapped.

The enemy line wavered as plasma bolts and railgun shells tore through flesh and armour as if it was nothing more than paper. The enemy didn't recoil, despite hundreds—perhaps thousands—being killed in the first seconds of fighting. They kept coming, heedlessly trampling over the dead and wounded. Wesley kept firing, feeling uncomfortably as though he was fighting an all-consuming fire with water. The flames could be kept at bay, but never quenched...and they'd reach for him the moment he lost control of the hose.

An alien exploded, body scattering blood and guts everywhere, the horror lost within an entire liturgy of horrors. The Pashtali just kept coming, charging to their deaths. He swore as he realised his plasma cannons were on the verge of overheating. They needed to stop firing and yet they couldn't, for fear of being overrun...

A red icon flashed up on his HUD. Corporal Slattery was dead, blown to hell by her own weapons. The line wavered...Wesley keyed his communicator, requesting fire support from the nearest available source. They were at danger close ranges, where there was a very good chance orbital fire or surface-based missile batteries would accidentally hit his position instead of the enemy, but there was no choice. The enemy were firing as they came...most of the bolts flashed over their heads, but if they tried to run they'd be shot in the back. He thought he saw a handful of spiders carrying packs and realised, too late, they were suicide runners. The leader exploded, taking out a fire team. Wesley's line wavered and broke.

"Get down," he snapped, as a trio of KEWs struck the enemy lines. The ground heaved so violently he found himself flat on his face, with no clear memory of how he'd gotten there. "Get back!"

He crawled back as the ground shook, time and time again. It seemed incredible that anything could survive such a bombardment—each shot had to be taking out hundreds of aliens—but the Pashtali just kept coming.

Why? Didn't they know they could surrender?

He knew so little about his enemies...were they insect drones, willing to sacrifice themselves for the good of the hive, or did they just think there was no point in trying to surrender? It was possible. The locals might be disinclined to show mercy, even if they were sure the Pashtali ships would return to take revenge. Wesley understood. Humans had never liked being under enemy control, even without the shame and humiliation of being helpless, and when that control snapped...

A pair of hovertanks glided into position, guns yammering as the retreating squad took cover behind them. Wesley took a moment to catch his breath, then peered west. The enemy were *still* coming, charging out of the smoke and firing. Some seemed more capable than others, advancing from cover to cover rather than simply running to the sound of the guns. Soldiers? Had they sent a tidal wave of civilians ahead of them, hoping they'd soak up human fire? It was sickening. He knew humans had done their fair share of sickening things over the years, and to each other rather than to alien life forms, but he couldn't recall any mention of anyone doing anything like *that*. The sheer inhumanity would give humanity's worst monsters pause.

He raised his heavy rifle and snapped off a shot at a pair of advancing aliens carrying a giant missile launcher between them. The first alien fell; the second pointed the launcher at the nearest tank and hit the trigger, firing before he was blasted down himself. The missile slammed into the tank, punching through armour and turning the interior into a fireball. Wesley winced. The tank armour was tough, and he'd seen tanks shrug off hits that would turn an armoured suit into paste, but anything that got through would kill the tankers before they had a chance to bail out. Their remaining armour trapped the blast inside the tank, making sure the crew were screwed. He muttered a silent prayer for the dead as the enemy pushed forward, flowing across the ground like a horde of angry ants. He wondered if that was precisely what they were. Some Pashtali appeared to be individuals, others little more than biological robots.

The horror raged on as more and more aliens slammed into his position, pushing the humans back by weight of numbers. The slaughter was sickening. Each plasma bolt or railgun shell went through dozens of aliens, but there were always more. He gritted his teeth as another suicide runner blew a hole in his lines, hastily plugged with orbital fire before the Pashtali could take advantage. They just kept coming...he was sure, now, that they were unwilling to surrender, and had determined to take a few humans with them before they died. And...he glanced at the overall tactical display, shaking his head in disbelief. How many aliens were there? It felt as if he'd personally killed their entire army and they were still coming...

"Incoming shells," someone snapped. "Duck!"

Wesley barely moved as shells rocketed overhead and crashed down on the enemy lines. The ground heaved, once again. He felt numb as the Pashtali advance seemed to stagger—for a moment, he thought they'd finally broken—before resuming the charge. It was incredible. It was impossible. It was...he saw an alien rear up and put a plasma bolt through his own brain, the superhot pulse burning through alien flesh and pushing onwards into the next few targets. They staggered, some falling and others somehow carrying on even though shock alone should have killed them. It was just...

He felt the ground shift under his fleet and looked down, realising—in a flash of horrified insight—what was about to happen. His legs started sinking—he screamed a warning to his men as he kicked down, relying on his servos to launch him into the air. It was dangerous as fuck—the moment he flew up, he was exposed to enemy fire—but there was no other choice. The ground below him boiled, more aliens swarming out of the tunnel and charging at the humans. Wesley cursed and snapped orders to fall back as the line came apart, more and more aliens boiling upwards or charging over the muddy ground. The second tank was blown to hell by a suicide runner, the crew barely having enough time to bail out before it was too late. It didn't save them. They were gunned down before they managed to run to the rear.

"Move," he snapped. The ground shuddered as KEWs slammed down, trying to collapse the tunnels. He was morbidly impressed they'd even been dug under the bombardment. The prospect of being trapped underground would have deterred even the bravest human from trying the same tactic, but...the aliens had made it work. He supposed the spider-like aliens were more used to burrowing than their human counterparts. The interior of their starships looked like giant anthills. "Hurry..."

The ground heaved, once again. Wesley turned and ran as more hover-tanks appeared to lay down covering fire. The aliens just kept coming... was there no end to the slaughter? How long had they been fighting? It felt as if they'd been fighting for hours or days or even...he checked his suit and blinked in surprise. An hour? A mere hour? He felt a shockwave, the impact nearly throwing him to his knees. He'd thought his guys could handle anything, but...

He breathed a sigh of relief as they linked up with their reinforcements, hastily digging trenches and converting abandoned alien buildings into makeshift strongpoints. The net kept reporting enemy troops popping up behind the lines...probably coming out of tunnels or lurking in muddy pools. He wondered, suddenly, if the Pashtali were amphibious. If they could draw oxygen directly from water, instead of using breathers, the sea behind the human position might not be the impassable barrier they'd thought. He keyed his communicator, relaying his concerns to his superiors. The Pashtali were desperate. They might try to use the sea to mount a counterattack anyway.

A sudden wave of exhaustion overcame him. He felt as if he'd been fighting for days, not hours. He felt...he took a long breath, silently grateful none of his men could see him clearly. The suit bleeped, offering a handful of stimulants. Wesley keyed in a *no*. They were too dangerous, unless the situation was beyond desperate, and even then he'd have second thoughts. The risk of a bad reaction was just too high.

"Here they come," someone shouted. "Brace yourself!"

Wesley staggered up and took his place. And the slaughter went on.

CHAPTER EIGHTEEN

Base Camp, Tarsus, Tarsus System

DEAR HOLY FUCKING SHIT, Naomi thought, as she surveyed the remnants of the alien bases and cities. *What the fuck are we fighting?*

She'd thought she was inured to horror. She'd seen the aftermath of battles in space—the dead, the wounded—and toured the wreckage after winning the Battle of Earth, but this was different. Dead bodies—mainly Pashtali—lay where they'd fallen, as far as the eye could see. The handful of human and other bodies mixed amongst them seemed grossly outnumbered, yet...her gorge rose as she saw a headless corpse, lying on the muddy ground. She took a breath and regretted it, instantly, as the stench of hundreds of thousands of rotting bodies assailed her. It had only been a day since the battle had ended, with the death of the last Pashtali, yet the atmosphere was tainted. Worst of all, the heat and moisture were encouraging the bodies to decay quicker.

Her stomach churned. The Pashtali were insane. They could have surrendered, they could have gone into POW camps and waited for liberation or a prisoner exchange, but instead they'd fought to the death. It made no sense! They really *were* mad. She had promised to accept surrender and she'd meant it, and...she swallowed hard, tasting bile. How many

Pashtali had been killed in a day? It was impossible to even guess how many bodies lay in front of her, decaying in the sun. Thousands? Hundreds of thousands? She doubted she'd ever know.

She heard someone throwing up behind her and carefully didn't turn to see who it was. Nancy Middleton? Olson? One of the shuttle crew? She'd thought it important to see the aftermath of the battle, to gaze upon the bloody scene of death and...she shook her head, cursing her own mistake. It was easy to forget that icons on the display weren't *just* lights on the display, that they represented starships crewed by intelligent beings and when they died their crews died too...here, there was no escaping the reality of what they'd done. She and her forces had had no choice—they'd offered to accept surrender, they'd promised safe conduct—but she still felt as though she'd done something awful. She wondered, morbidly, what galactic opinion would make of it. They had plenty of footage proving the Pashtali had had every chance to surrender—she would have accepted it, right up to the end—but they hadn't even deigned to reply. The nasty cynical part of her mind figured the Pashtali spin doctors were already spreading lies. Too many Galactics would believe them.

"God," Nancy Middleton said. The older woman looked decidedly green around the gills. "Why...? Why...?"

"I don't know," Naomi said, tightly. "But I don't like it."

She kept her face under tight control. There was no point in continuing to try to figure out why the Pashtali had refused to accept defeat until killed to the last being. Aliens were alien and the Pashtali more alien than most. Their army might have thought it would be slaughtered if it surrendered, or it might calculate that killing a handful of humans was worth the cost, or it might not have been able to think much of anything. There was very little data on the Pashtali in the files and much of what they *did* have was contradictory, to the point she wondered if the Alphans had been deceived. Perhaps the aliens they'd fought had been nothing more than worker bees or army ants, completely expendable to their superiors. Or... it was just insane. The word kept echoing through her mind and yet...

We know some of them are intelligent, she told herself. *Are the rest of them just organic robots, or what?*

"Right now, it doesn't matter," she said. She'd wanted to see the scene for herself and now she had. "We can't linger, not for more than a day or two. Do you have a meeting lined up with the local government?"

"Their ambassador," Nancy confirmed. "They insisted he'll be meeting us at Town Seven,"

Naomi grimaced. There'd once been several cities and hundreds of towns within the occupied zone, but the fighting had reduced most of them to rubble. They were lucky many of the locals had managed to get out, either before the enemy advance had swept over their homes or when the humans had come in to liberate them, yet an uncomfortably large number of locals had been caught in the storm and killed. The local government didn't seem inclined to blame the humans for the deaths, thankfully, but she still felt guilty. Perhaps she could have convinced the Pashtali to surrender, if she could have found the right words, or even to sit on the sidelines and wait for the larger war to be resolved one way or the other. She knew she'd done her best and yet, she'd wonder—for the rest of her life—if there'd been a way to avert it, to save innocent lives.

No, she told herself, as a pair of shuttles flew overhead. *They were determined to do as much damage as possible, to us and their unwilling hosts, in their last few hours of life.*

Nancy met her eyes. "My aircar is due shortly," she said. "I'll see you back on the ship?"

"Please," Naomi said. She took one final look at the nightmarish scene, promising herself she'd do everything in her power to make sure the Pashtali got the blame they so richly deserved, and then turned back to the shuttle. "Good luck."

Olson joined her as she stepped through the hatch. The younger man looked as green as the ambassador...Naomi felt another twinge of guilt. She wasn't sure why she'd insisted on her assistant accompanying her. It wasn't as if she *needed* his presence. If he'd needed to tell her something, he could have done it—just as easily—over the communicator. And besides, if something happened to Naomi, her successor would need Olson to ensure he caught up with everything he had to know before the shit hit the fan. Again. Naomi was careful to ensure her senior officers knew as much as possible, but any sudden change in command would bring confusion in its wake.

"Admiral," he said. "*Daffodil* has returned, and reported she lost track of the alien ships."

Naomi nodded, curtly. She hadn't expected the scouts to be able to track the alien ships all the way to their reinforcements, although she'd allowed herself to hope they might. If she had a chance to bite off and destroy a chunk of the alien fleet, before it could be reinforced...she shook her head, dismissing the thought. The engagement would have been chancy even if they'd had an opportunity to make it work.

"*Hazel* has yet to return," Olson added. "She might have better luck."

"We'll depart as planned, unless she brings us very good news," Naomi said. She took her seat and closed her eyes. The shuttle's atmosphere tasted of dead and rotting bodies. She felt as if she should pass through a biohazard screening when she returned to the ship. "We can't stay here."

She felt another twinge of guilt. Tarsus hadn't lifted a finger to assist her, not when she'd chased the enemy fleet away nor when she'd landed troops to take out the enemy positions on the ground. They'd done nothing to anger the Pashtali and yet, she had a nasty feeling the Pashtali would take their anger out on Tarsus anyway. It was sickening and yet very in character for a race of interstellar bullies. How *dare* someone fight back against their would-be enslavers? How dare someone come to liberate the slaves? She suspected the locals would be completely quiet, refusing to commit themselves, until the war ended with a clear winner.

They have a point, the cynical part of her mind noted. *Their orbital defences are gone and their planetside fortifications are badly battered. They cannot use the crossroads as bottlenecks, ensuring they cannot keep the Pashtali out of their system...*

"I also have an updated report from the FTL network," Olson said, holding out a datapad. "Task Force Skinsuit is proceeding towards its target."

"And let's hope the enemy aren't ready for them," Naomi said. The Pashtali might have assumed no one could fly their starships. They knew, now, that that wasn't true. "If nothing else, we'll keep them off balance."

She took the datapad and sat down, feeling uncomfortably grimy. She hadn't felt so filthy in years. The shuttle hatch closed and the craft took off, clawing its way into orbit. Naomi scowled as she glanced through the brief statement, then turned to the updated reports from the fleet. The ships were as ready to depart as they'd ever be. And...

Her heart clenched. She'd lost two hundred Marines on the surface, according to the final count. It was a tiny figure, compared to the hundreds of thousands of dead aliens, but it still hurt. Eighteen bodies had yet to be recovered, if indeed there was anything left of them...she wondered, numbly, what the locals would do if they found the bodies after the fleet departed. Legally, they were supposed to return the body to the nearest human consulate; practically, they might be better off destroying the body and pretending they'd never seen it. Who knew how the Pashtali would respond if they returned in force? They had never struck her as being petty and spiteful before, yet what they'd done to Tarsus had been *incredibly* so.

We might still find the missing bodies, she told herself, although she knew it was unlikely. The post-battle assessment teams would have located the fallen, even if they hadn't had time to recover them. *And then we can give them a proper burial.*

She looked at her aide. "Inform the fleet we will be departing as planned," she said, firmly. The longer they stayed, the greater the chance of the Pashtali pinning the fleet down and tearing it to shreds. "There's no longer any point in staying here."

"Aye, Admiral."

• • •

Under other circumstances, Nancy Middleton thought she would have found Town Seven—or whatever the locals called it—surprisingly charming. It looked very much like an old-style human village, the kind of habitation that had only been preserved through human determination to retain something of their past, resting within a pool of shallow water. A deeper lake sat right next to the village, ripples within the water suggesting the wildlife was slowly returning after the fighting had come to an end. She thought, as the aircar dropped to the muddy ground, that humans who lived in similar environments would have built their homes on stilts, to keep them safely above the waterline. The locals didn't need to bother.

She composed herself, despite suddenly feeling a mad urge to giggle at the collection of humanoid frogs waiting for her. They looked like cartoon characters that had stepped into the real world…she bit her lip, dismissing the thought before it could show on her face. Tarsus had been a self-spacefaring world before the invaders had arrived, which was more than could be said for Earth, and they might know enough about humans to read her expression. Besides, they probably found her appearance just as comical. She was tall, by their standards, and almost insanely thin. In their shoes, she might wonder how she could walk upright without tripping over her own feet.

"I greet you," she said, in careful GalStandard Four. It wasn't her favourite language—she understood it better than she spoke it, and she had to think to avoid mispronouncing the words—but the locals couldn't speak GalStandard One or Two. Their mouths just couldn't form the words. "I speak for my people."

The leader stepped forward. He barely came up to her chest. Nancy resisted the urge to kneel. It was hard to escape the sense she was dealing with a child, even though she knew better. She bit down hard on that reaction, too. The alien in front of her might not be the head of government—an ambassador could be thrown under the shuttlecraft, his diplomacy declared the work of a rogue who'd exceeded his authority if it blew up in the government's face—but that didn't mean she shouldn't take him seriously. His government would be offended, even if it was hoping the human ships would leave before the Pashtali returned. They didn't want their system to become a battleground. Again.

"I speak for my people," the alien said. His voice was low and raspy. Nancy was surprised he didn't use a voder. The tone bothered her, even though she knew it was just her perception. He wasn't trying to be offensive. "We are grateful for your help."

Nancy nodded, keeping her face bland. "We are grateful for the chance to offer it," she said, picking her words carefully. GalStandard Four had always been a little more flowery than GalStandard Two. "And we will soon be departing your system. Your worlds will be yours again."

She thought she saw surprise on the alien face. Galactic history *teemed* with liberators who'd kicked out the old masters, then established themselves as the new. The Pashtali had certainly told the galaxy they were liberating their conquests from their former masters...not, she was sure, that anyone actually believed them. It just provided a fig leaf to do nothing about it. Here...she was certain the locals had braced themselves to discover that the human fleet intended to keep the system, even if they didn't take the planet itself. They might be better masters than the Pashtali, but they'd still be masters.

And the Pashtali would return and kick us out, she thought. *And then they'd become the masters once again.*

She sighed, inwardly. She'd read a story once, written in the days before the galaxy had forced itself upon the human race, in which Earth was conquered by an alien race that was fighting a war with another race, pressing the humans into service as sepoys. They'd told their human servants the second race was utterly monstrous, a plague that had to be eradicated. And then the second race had invaded, kicked the first race off humanity's homeworld, and told the humans they'd been duped. It was the first race that was monstrous....

And the planet kept changing hands, until there was nothing left of the human race, she thought, cold despite the heat. *They were both monsters who cared nothing for the innocent lives crushed beneath their feet.*

"You will not impose unequal treaties on us?" The leader lifted his eyes to meet hers. "Or insist on trading agreements?"

"No," Nancy said. The human fleet could impose whatever it wanted, now, but that wouldn't last. Besides, they'd made a good start by dealing with other races as equals. She wasn't about to throw it away now. "The planet is yours. We hope you will trade with us, under galactic protocols, but we do not insist on it."

She couldn't read the alien races, but she was sure they were staring at her in stunned disbelief. She'd felt the same, when the Alphans had told her they were abandoning Earth and leaving the human race to its own devices. It had been hard to believe, back then, and it was hard to believe now. She sighed inwardly. Leaving the system to its own devices was the best thing they could do. The Pashtali would need to think long and hard to come up with an excuse to invade for a second time...

Not that that will slow them down for long, she thought. *But they'll look like the aggressor in front of the entire galaxy.*

She kept that thought to herself—she doubted the Pashtali would lose sleep over the matter, not when it was unlikely the galaxy would unite against them—as she briefly discussed trade deals. The system didn't have much to offer, beyond the right to make transit through the crossroads. The once-proud industrial base was nothing more than ruins, save for a handful of asteroid settlements that had gone doggo before the enemy started to look for them. They would rebuild, if they were given the chance. And if they did, they might be grateful to humanity for saving them.

"We thank you for your kind offers," the alien said, when they'd finished. "My government will debate the matter and reply directly to yours."

"Of course." Nancy bowed her head. "My government will be very eager to hear from yours."

She sighed to herself as she took a step back. She knew they intended to stall as long as possible, first to make sure the fleet actually departed on schedule and second to wait and see if the Pashtali intended to respect their newfound independence. The locals might have preferred to have the human fleet point its guns at their homeworld, making it very clear they'd been forced to concede whatever the humans wanted. But then, like the aliens in the story, the Pashtali might not accept such an argument. It was a great deal easier to dispute such claims when *you* weren't the one being held at gunpoint.

But the galaxy would know we'd bullied them, she reflected, as she boarded the aircar for the flight back to the camp. It might be necessary, to await the wrath of the system's former masters, but it would look bad in the long run. The Pashtali would certainly make a big show of how they were liberating the world from its human invaders, and the human race would wind up with egg on its face. *And the only thing worse than a bully is an unsuccessful bully.*

She shook her head. They'd done all they could, as little as it was. And now it was time to go.

CHAPTER NINETEEN

SYSTEM P-25, PASHTALI SPACE

THE PASHTALI DID NOT, as far as anyone had been able to determine, name either their ships or their worlds. Commodore Roger Valentine found it difficult to imagine a species with such a lack of imagination—and he *knew* the Pashtali had to have some, or they would never have climbed into space without help—and yet there were no suggestions the xenospecialists were wrong. It was possible, he supposed as the tiny squadron glided into System P-25, that the planets and ships had names in the alien language, but if so they'd never been translated into any galactic tongue. Perhaps it was an insane security precaution. Or perhaps they honestly didn't feel the need to share anything of themselves with aliens.

I suppose they do have a reason to be annoyed, he thought. Earth had barely been poking its way into space when human history had run into a brick wall and stopped dead. The Pashtali had been a major spacefaring race when they'd encountered the Alphans and discovered, to their horror, that they had no say in galactic protocols. It would have been galling to have laws imposed on you even if you agreed the laws were generally *good* laws. *Galactic history would be very different if they'd been the ones to make it into space first.*

He put the thought out of his mind as he studied the sensor display. System P-25 was a major shipping hub, located perfectly to support either a renewed drive against Earth or an offensive against Terminus. Hundreds of ships were gliding around the system, either going to and from the crossroads or plying the lanes between the various planets. The three major worlds were heavily defended, if the files were accurate, and for once he had no reason to doubt them. The Pashtali had invested heavily in the system's infrastructure. He was sure they'd be certain to invest in defences too.

Which means that getting too close to the planet is likely to be impossible, he told himself firmly. Task Force Skinsuit might be flying Pashtali ships, but if they hadn't changed their IFF codes after the Battle of Terminus he'd go spacewalking without a spacesuit. They *knew* humans could fly their ships now. *But we don't have to get too close to make a splash.*

"Captain," Marquez said. "Long-range passive sensors have picked out a handful of industrial nodes orbiting the planets."

"Add them to the target list, when we start firing kinetic projectiles," Roger ordered. He doubted more than a handful of the ballistic projectiles would strike their targets—it was hard to target something from light minutes away, even if the defenders weren't on alert—but it would keep the enemy off balance. "Any convoys?"

Marquez peered down at her console. "I think one is forming up now," she said. "But it's hard to be sure."

Roger nodded. The Pashtali system was surprisingly ordered—the majority of industrialised systems had hundreds of starships and spacecraft swarming around—but it was still hard to work out what was going on, not from a safe distance. The Pashtali were randomly sweeping space with active sensors, as if they hoped to catch intruders sneaking into their system. Normally, he'd consider it a waste of effort. Here, it might work in their favour. The Pashtali *did* have intruders in their system.

They'll be putting a hell of a lot of wear and tear on their systems, he reflected. It was a grim reminder that, despite everything, the Pashtali had money and resources to burn. *But they can afford it for a while longer.*

"Keep an eye on the convoy," he ordered. "And alert me when it starts to move."

He scowled as he sat back in his cramped chair, keeping an eye on the display. They'd intercepted a handful of transmissions, as they'd made their way to System P-25, but none of them had been particularly helpful. The Galactics were broadcasting wildly exaggerated claims, from human fleets bombarding the Pashtali homeworld into submission to the entire human fleet wiped out with a single shot. The only Pashtali message they'd intercepted had been indecipherable, to the point he wondered if it was a decoy intended to make them waste their time. It might have that effect, even if it was unintentional. If it drew on cultural aspects the human race didn't share…

"Captain," Marquez said. "The convoy is departing the planet and setting course for Crossroads Three."

Roger smiled, coldly. "Plot an intercept course, then move us into position," he ordered. He'd picked their current location with malice aforethought. Crossroads Three linked to threadlines that headed further into enemy space, rather than leading outside their empire. It was just possible they'd be less wary about escorting convoys in safe territory. They'd learn better in a hurry, if his plan worked. "And prepare to start launching kinetic projectiles."

His heart raced as the ships glided into position. The convoy was being surprisingly careful—he wondered, grimly, if he was about to make a fatal mistake—and sweeping local space constantly with active sensors. There was a better than even chance they'd spot his ships—or, at the very least, detect hints there were cloaked vessels nearby. He hoped they'd hesitate to open fire, if they realised he was flying one of their ships, but that wouldn't last. After Terminus, they wouldn't let *any* ship nearby unless it had the right codes.

"They'll enter optimal firing range in thirty minutes," Marquez reported. "But they may see us earlier."

"We'll play it by ear," Roger said. "Patience."

He smiled again as he studied the enemy ships on the display. Their active sensors were a serious problem -they might easily detect his ships before they were in the right position—but they did give their targets a slight advantage. He could pick out their locations nearly as easily, using their own sensors to track them. Nine destroyers—or vessels of a similar mass—escorting thirty-seven heavy freighters. It was impressive, by his standards, and yet it was nothing to a great power. Thirty-seven freighters? The Pashtali had *thousands.*

"They can afford to lose a few," he muttered.

Marquez looked up. "Sir?"

"Never mind," Roger said. "Just thinking out loud."

His mind raced. The Pashtali rarely—if ever—hired freighters from outside their empire. It wasn't clear if they let their *clients* fly freighters within their space. They didn't need to bother, normally, but now...his lips quirked. On paper, losing a handful of freighters would be little more than a minor nuisance. They might not even notice. In practice, it would be a different story. They'd have to redeploy freighters to cover the gap and then redeploy smaller ships to serve as escorts...hell, they'd need to deploy bigger ships to make sure they could ward off raiders. And that would weaken the forces they could throw at Earth or Terminus. It was unlikely his raids would convince the Pashtali to come to the table, but it was possible. They'd certainly have trouble rebalancing themselves...

Unless they decide to just grit their teeth and take it, he thought. *Or use our attacks to galvanise public opinion.*

He scowled as the enemy ships came closer. The Pashtali had attacked *Earth.* They'd pushed the human race to the brink of defeat. The galaxy could hardly complain if the human race took the war into enemy space, could they? And yet they would. They'd insist it was dangerous, that it would escalate the war...as if a direct attack on humanity's homeworld was anything but! He wasn't blind to the risks, but...he gritted his teeth. The Galactics might talk about the rule of law, yet it was nothing more than a thin veneer of legality spread over a galaxy where the strong did as they pleased and the weak suffered what they must. Why...

The display flashed red. "Captain," Marquez said. "They've spotted us!"

"Fire," Roger snapped.

He'd considered trying to bluff, in the certain knowledge the Pashtali would hesitate to open fire, but it had seemed pointless. They didn't have the right codes and they'd just been caught sneaking around the system. He watched as the first salvo of missiles rocketed away from the squadron, aimed right at the enemy ships. The destroyers were already shifting position—whoever was in command was sharp, he noted ruefully—but it was too late to save themselves. Their point defence hadn't been prepped to back up the active sensors.

"The enemy fleet is breaking orbit," Marquez reported. "At least four squadrons, perhaps more. They're coming right at us."

Roger nodded. "Fire a second salvo, then transmit the prepared packets and reverse course," he ordered. "I think we've overstayed our welcome."

He ignored Marquez's snort as the enemy ships started to die. It was a shame they had no time to try to capture the freighters—their cargo might have been useful—but the enemy fleet was already heading for their position. He didn't dare risk a battle. His ships were undermanned, without a proper point defence network. The cruiser shuddered as she emptied her missile launchers, then started to come about. The electronic warfare packets might do some damage—Roger wasn't hopeful, but it was worth a try—as they assailed the local communications network. If they got through the firewalls, the enemy would have to waste quite a bit of time taking the system offline and repairing the damage.

"The kinetic projectiles are inbound," Marquez said. "They should do some damage."

"We'll see," Roger said. There was no shortage of space junk to compress into kinetic projectiles. They could afford to launch hundreds of shots for one or two hits. "Right now, trigger the drones and then take us straight to the crossroads."

"Aye, sir," Marquez said. Her fingers danced across the console. "The drones will go live in five minutes."

Roger nodded, silently accessing the situation. The enemy convoy had been shattered. A handful of ships had survived, but it didn't matter. The enemy fleet was piling on the speed, pushing its drives to the limit, yet it probably wouldn't manage to close the range enough to be sure of a hit in time to keep his ships from escaping. He wondered, idly, if they'd try to fire on him from extreme range. It was the sort of tactic the tactical manuals insisted was worse than useless, costing the attacker hundreds of missiles with no assurance of a hit, but it might just work. His ships didn't have the point defence they needed to survive a running battle.

They know what these ships can do, in the right hands, he thought, coldly. *Do they know we didn't manage to capture or repair* all *their systems?*

He glanced at the timer. The enemy fleet was *really* picking up speed. Warcruisers were supposed to be the fastest capital ships in space—they could even give gunboats and patrollers a run for their money—and yet the Pashtali ships were pushing their drives right to the limit. They were so intent on running his ships down that they didn't seem to care they were risking drive failures...did they think they could recapture the ships before it was too late? Or...or what? Did they think they had to be destroyed before their secrets fell into enemy hands? His lips twitched. It was a little late for *that*.

They might think we took the datacores intact, Roger thought. *If they don't think we can fly the ships without them...*

His mind raced. Was that possible? There were no major differences between Pashtali technology and the rest of the Galactic races and the minor differences could be overcome by someone who knew what they were doing. The ships felt very alien, and everything from their control systems to units of measurement were a little weird by human standards, but they could cope. Could the Pashtali? They were so different, they might not be able to cope with human ships, so different they might assume humans might not be able to cope with their ships either. Did they think Task Force Skinsuit was crewed by *turncoats*?

"The drones are going live," Marquez said. "The enemy will see them shortly."

Roger nodded and waited. The drones were primitive, even by the standards of scavenger races. There'd been no way to convince the Solar Navy to let him take some of the latest Alphan drones, not when they might fall into enemy hands. His crews had patched together the drones, deliberately overpowering them to suggest some ships were using their drive fields to conceal others. The Pashtali might think they were being conned—they'd certainly notice the drive fields weren't very localised—but would they take the chance?

It might not be as much of a chance as it looks, he told himself. *The planet is heavily defended. They might take the risk of splitting their forces—and it is no risk at all.*

His mind raced. The Pashtali had to see the drones. They had to. What would they do?

"They're maintaining pursuit," Marquez reported. She sounded personally insulted. "They're ignoring the drones."

"Smart of them," Roger said. It would be interesting to know if the Pashtali had seen through the deception, or if they'd merely decided the planetary defences could handle the illusionary fleet, but it hardly mattered. "Maintain course and speed."

"Aye, sir," Marquez said.

Roger keyed his console, checking the flight vectors. If nothing changed, the squadron should be able to slip into the crossroads and vanish before the enemy fleet made transit. Going off the threadline was dangerous, but it was probably their best bet...particularly if they did it before the enemy ships jumped. He briefly considered making a stand; if he'd been in command of a proper squadron he would have done so, but under the circumstances, it was too risky. His ships were in no state for an engagement, even if they would be lying in wait on the far side of the crossroads. The crossroads was too big to force the enemy to come at them one by one.

They may be lucky there are so many crossroads within this system, he thought wryly, *but none of them are actual bottlenecks.*

"They're opening fire," Marquez said. "A light salvo..."

"Testing our defences?" Roger didn't like the look of it. If his ships defended themselves, they'd reveal that their point defence was not up to scratch. If they didn't even try to defend themselves...he scowled, weighing the odds. Whoever was on the other side was a smart cookie. If his defences had been at full capacity, the bastard would know better than to hurl good money after bad. "Hold our course and plot targeting, but only bring our weapons online at the last moment."

"Aye, sir," Marquez said.

Roger gritted his teeth. The enemy commander had put him in an interesting spot. He dared not fight back and yet he had no choice. If any of his ships took damage, they'd have to be abandoned. He didn't have the spare parts or the crews to do repair work even if he wasn't under fire. And yet, holding his fire until the last moment would be dangerously revealing. If the enemy commander was as smart as Roger feared, he'd draw the right conclusion and fire a full salvo. If...

"Push our drives into the red," he ordered. That was a risk too, but—again—there was no choice. "I want to be through the crossroads as quickly as possible."

"Aye, sir," Marquez said. "Our point defence will go live in ten minutes."

"Good," Roger said. Nothing, not even a warcruiser, could outrun a missile. It was possible they could *outlast* the incoming salvo, forcing them to burn out and go ballistic before they slipped into attack range, but he dared not count on it. His counterpart would have run the calculations and concluded his fleet could land a blow even at extreme range. "They really don't seem to have fallen for the drones, do they?"

"No, sir," Marquez said. "But even from this distance, there's something pretty screwy about their signatures."

Roger said nothing as the clock ran down to zero, the point defence opening fire. It had had plenty of time to work out how best to take out the missiles, picking them all off before the range could close to nothing. He leaned forward, wondering why the enemy commander hadn't fired a second—and much bigger—salvo. The range was long, but not that long...

They may think it would be just a waste of time and resources, he thought. *Or they might think they can catch us in multispace.*

His lips twisted into a brief smile as they crashed through the crossroads and into multispace without bothering to slow down. The raid hadn't been a complete success, but...they'd sneaked into the system, effectively destroyed a convoy and gotten out again. They'd also learnt things he would have preferred not to know about enemy sensors...he made a mental note to try to find a way to get word to Admiral Yagami. If she didn't already know, she needed to.

"Captain," Marquez said. "We're out of the threadline. They shouldn't be able to see us."

"Not unless they come after us," Roger agreed. It wouldn't be easy. There were too many possible vectors and the odds of guessing the right one were low. The Pashtali would need hard data to get it right and they didn't have any. "Signal the squadron. We'll keep moving to the RV point, then consider our next move."

"And there I was hoping for some shore leave," Marquez said, deadpan. "No sunny beaches for us, sir?"

"Not unless you want to take leave on a Pashtali world," Roger said. There'd be no shore leave until they returned to human space, which would be quite some time in the future. "But we'll see what we find as we trail our coats though their space."

"Yes, sir," Marquez said. "Perhaps they're hiding an entire planet of beaches within their empire."

"Perhaps," Roger agreed. "I wouldn't bet on it, though."

CHAPTER TWENTY

SOLAR CITY, EARTH

"WE RECEIVED A FORMAL COMPLAINT from the Pashtali," Rachel Grant said. "Apparently, the fleet attacking Tarsus was a direct breach of galactic protocol and they want the Admiral's head on a platter."

First Speaker Abraham Douglas snorted, then sobered. "Is anyone moving to back them up?"

"Not according to the Foreign Office," Rachel told him. "Not *yet*, anyway."

"They're waiting to see who comes out on top," Abraham said. "You'd think they'd notice the locals didn't *want* to be invaded."

He frowned as he recalled the messages from the fleet. The Pashtali had fought to the death, literally. There were no prisoners, not even a handful of enemy wounded captured because they couldn't continue the fight. The Pashtali had died in droves, throwing away their lives in a desperate bid to kill as many humans as possible before they were wiped out. It was a grim reminder they *were* alien—and that the cost of victory, even a semi-favourable truce, might be terrifyingly high.

But then, the cost of defeat is murder, he thought, sourly. *There's no way to discuss surrender on terms if the enemy refuses to treat with us seriously.*

"Yes, sir," Rachel said. "There's been no noticeable reaction, as far as we can tell. The Pashtali still look too strong to challenge openly."

"Charming," Abraham muttered. The human race had won a pair of victories in quick succession, embarrassing their enemies, but he knew all too well they could be reversed at any moment. Admiral Yagami's report pulled no punches. The Pashtali might already be heading back to Tarsus. Terminus would be harder to retake, unless they were willing to risk one of their few crossroad-generating ships, but they could do it. "Is there any response to the Terminus Accords?"

"Again, nothing noticeable," Rachel said. "It's hard to say for sure, sir, but—reading between the lines—they may feel the mice have decided to bell the cat."

Abraham made a face. It was, he felt, a disturbingly accurate analogy. The mice might well vote to bell the cat, but if the cat refused to cooperate who was going to force it? There was no way for the tiny mice to force the cat to wear a bell, just as there was no way for the lesser powers to force the Galactics into doing something they didn't want to do. The Terminus Accords might lead to a fundamental shift in the balance of power, but the Galactics had every reason to be sceptical. They might wind up being nothing more than ink on paper. Hell, that might be wildly optimistic.

"We'll just have to wait and see, too," he said. "If they do come to see the alliance as a threat, they'll try to stop us."

He studied the starchart, his mind peering into a possible future. No lesser power could stand up to a greater power, not if it stood alone. But an alliance of lesser powers? Collectively, they'd control enough ships, crossroads and resources to give even a great power pause. If they hung together...they might be hanged together, his mind noted in a flicker of dark humour, but they'd certainly make the bastards work to hang them. The Accords might not survive their first conflict—the Pashtali could still turn the war around—yet if they did...

It helps no one likes or trusts the Pashtali, he told himself. They could offer honourable agreements, and mean to keep them, only to discover no one trusts them enough to accept.

Rachel cleared her throat. "We have been able to secure more loans from other powers, with surprisingly generous terms," she said. "A full briefing is in your terminal and..."

Abraham held up a hand. "We can worry about that later," he said. "How is the public taking recent developments?"

"It's hard to say," Rachel said. "Generally, news of the two victories went down very well. I don't think there'll be any immediate push for peace on any terms, not even from the handful of MPs who think the war will end badly or are morally opposed to fighting a war even if the enemy gives us no choice. There are some concerns about escalating the war, as we have struck into enemy space and given them a black eye—a *second* black eye. They fear the Pashtali will find it harder to swallow their pride and offer terms we can accept."

She paused. "There is also some feeling we should have kept Terminus—and perhaps even Tarsus—for ourselves," she added. "It isn't a very strong sentiment, not yet, but it's something to keep an eye on. If either system becomes economically powerful and important, I think there will be voices arguing we threw away something we desperately needed."

Abraham rolled his eyes. "Are there really so many empire-builders out there?"

"Polling is an imprecise science," Rachel said, her tone adding *as you know perfectly well*. "It is never easy to gauge how many people truly hold such feelings. The people arguing the case for a human empire insist we're the best ones for the job, or that we have a right to keep whatever we grab, but we don't know how numerous they truly are. The man in the street doesn't really grasp the reality of interstellar politics, or the distance between Earth and Terminus. He just sees that the Solar Navy captured a system of priceless strategic value and simply handed it over to a bunch of aliens who couldn't bring themselves to lift a finger in their own defence."

"It isn't as if they *could* stand up to the Pashtali," Abraham pointed out. "By the time they realised they needed to work together, it was already too late."

"Yes, sir," Rachel said. "But the average man in the street doesn't understand the cold realities."

"And would he prefer to expend undue effort on keeping a system that will get us nothing, but more enemies?" Abraham fought to keep the irritation out of his voice. "We can't hold the system, so we may as well give it up in exchange for an alliance and trade agreements."

"Right now, very few people understand the reality," Rachel said. "All they see is that we won the system, fair and square, and then simply gave it up."

"The irony is killing me," Abraham said. "Were we so bad when we were the opposition?"

His face twisted in remembrance. How long had it been since he'd been an up-and-coming politician, free to snipe at the government from the opposition benches without having to take any responsibility? He'd called himself the government's harshest critic and he'd had no qualms about blaming the government for not doing the impossible. Now...he knew precisely how Nancy Middleton had felt. She'd been wrapped in chains, bound by the cold realities of interstellar politics, unable to move freely...he wondered, suddenly, why she didn't hate him. He was starting to dislike the new men on the benches, the ones as carefree of consequences as himself. How would they cope when they came face to face with all the messy little realities, from funding shortfalls to greater powers bullying lesser powers? They'd be caught in a trap of their own making.

We promised a land of milk and honey and freedom if we were elected, he reminded himself. *We were lucky there was no real opposition, back then, to capitalise on our failure to deliver the impossible. Now...*

Rachel shrugged. "It is possible to learn how to fly a shuttlecraft by reading technical manuals," she said. "It isn't so easy to actually *do* it. One can say the same for politics."

Abraham nodded, conceding the point. "We may have to bring some opposition MPs into the cabinet," he said. There'd be disagreement from his own supporters—he could name three MPs who'd be furious if he made any overtures to the opposition—but he had enough clout to push it through over their objections. "If the opposition wins the next election, they'll need a realistic idea of what they can and can't do."

"Yes, sir," Rachel said.

"I'll give it some thought," Abraham said. "Are there any other issues?"

"A handful," Rachel said. "On one hand, from an economic point of view, the costs of the war are continuing to bite. There's no easy way to defray them. We have enough food and suchlike to keep the population alive, and the refugee situation is finally under control, but the economic projections are gloomy. Even if the war ended tomorrow, sir, we'd probably still go into a recession. Inflation is on the rise and there's nothing much we can do about it."

She grimaced. "Capital flight is also on the rise," she added. "And there's not much we can do about it either."

"No," Abraham agreed. There was no way to keep the rich from moving their savings into alien banks or investing in alien industries. He wasn't sure quite how that would work out, if the Pashtali won the war, but... right now, it was something that couldn't be helped. The economy was already fragile and trying to clamp down on currency transfers would only make it worse. "Put together a team to look at the options, then produce recommendations. We should be able to find some incentives to keep capital from fleeing our worlds."

"Yes, sir," Rachel said. "On the other hand, there is a minor but growing problem. There's a certain undercurrent of irritation we lied to them about the fleet's destination, even amongst people who understand we had no choice. They feel *they* could be trusted, and should be, although they don't extend that consideration to anyone else. It may lead to problems in the future."

Abraham made a face. "The more people who knew the truth, the greater the chance of a leak," he said. *Someone* would have blabbed.

Someone—accidentally or no—would have gotten word to the alien ambassadors. There was no way to be sure, either, the Pashtali didn't have spies on Earth. Human history was *full* of traitors who'd betrayed their countries and gotten away with it. "If one of the news broadcasts told the universe, the Pashtali might have believed them."

"Believed the news?" Rachel allowed herself a smile. "They'd have to be *very* alien."

"Hah." Abraham had gone to some trouble, when he'd been in opposition, to fight for a free press. It was irritating, now that he was the one in charge, to admit there were some things that really should be kept *out* of the press. Reporters simply couldn't be trusted to apply common sense during their endless search for scoops...sure, some could be reasoned with, but others were so desperate to make names for themselves that they'd compromise national security without a second thought. "We couldn't take the chance."

He stared at his hands for a long moment. The government needed to be trusted if it were to survive. The Alphan Viceroyalty had been trusted, despite everything, until the Solar City Massacre. His government was nowhere near as stable. The days when he and his allies had been able to rule freely were gone, now the opposition had rebalanced itself and was regaining power. He could justify his decision to lie, if anyone asked, but lying was habit forming. Too many people already thought the ability and willingness to lie was an essential requirement for being a politician. And he'd technically proved them right.

"We'll continue to monitor the situation," he said, finally. He wasn't planning on staying in his post, after the war. Someone—he forgot who—had cracked governments needed to be changed as often as diapers, for pretty much the same problem. He could go into semi-retirement and sit on the backbenches, offering his advice to his successor. "If it turns into more than quiet grumbling, we'll decide what to do then."

"Yes, sir." Rachel glanced at her datapad. "You have two meetings with alien ambassadors, at 1300 and 1500, then dinner with Richard Hawthorne to discuss them. I suggest"—her tone hinted it was more than a mere *suggestion*—"that you get something to eat before the meetings. The Telic will be very offended if you eat in front of them."

Abraham nodded. The Telic were an odd race, by human standards. On one hand, they had sex as naturally as breathing and saw nothing wrong with doing it in public. On the other hand, they regarded eating in front of strangers as taboo and considered sharing a dinner table to be roughly akin to shitting on the pavement. He'd glanced at the files and noted even children rarely ate with their parents and, once they were taught how to eat, were expected to eat alone. But then, they were hardly the weirdest alien race humanity had encountered ever since the invasion. There were races so alien it was hard to have a conversation and be sure you were talking about the same thing.

"I'll grab a sandwich," he said. He'd once thought government ministers had endless banquets. He now knew they never had the *time*. "And then make sure to wash before I meet them."

"Eat and drink plenty," Rachel advised. "You literally *cannot* do either in front of them."

"I read the file." Abraham reminded her, although he understood. The Telic were pretty close to being a great power. If they sided with humanity, they'd be powerful and capable allies and their mere presence might convince others to join the alliance too. If they chose to stay aloof, other powers might do the same. The fact they'd insisted on talking to *him*, rather than an ambassador, was a good sign, but it also meant the risks of fucking it up were alarmingly high. "I'll behave."

Rachel flushed.

• • •

It would not have surprised the Earth Intelligence Service, Ambassador Yasuke considered, to discover the Alphans had several different intelligence-gathering networks on Earth. They had ruled the planet for hundreds of years, easily long enough to forge links to talented humans and offer patronage in exchange for service. Some had been openly recruited, others had been warned to keep their true allegiances quiet or—in a few cases—didn't know who read their reports. A number had gone silent, after independence, but others remained on the payroll. Yasuke had no qualms about keeping the lines of communication as open as possible.

We need to know what they're thinking, he thought, as he read the report. *And how their politics are shifting during the war.*

The report was surprisingly wordy, for something put together by a human. His own race would never use one word when fifty would suffice, but his human contact seemed to think he was being paid by the word. Yasuke allowed himself a cold smile at the thought. The payment wouldn't change, even if the contact had just written a handful of lines. It wouldn't do to imply the agents wouldn't be paid for their work. It would just make it harder to recruit spies.

All the more so because we no longer control the planetary intelligence and counter-espionage networks, he reflected. *The days when we could offer patronage and titles are long gone.*

He put the thought aside as he mentally compared the report to the official statements from the human government and the reports forwarded to him from the fleet observers. The humans had won two victories, both of which looked spectacular even though the fleet observer had been quick to point out they were little more than pinpricks at best. The spy went into more detail about how many ships had been lost and how many weapons had been fired off, but...overall, there were no major differences. The humans had won and, in doing so, they'd won allies.

Which is interesting, he mused. *Isn't it?*

It was something that had honestly never occurred to him—or to any of the other major powers. The universe was divided into great and lesser powers, the former doing as they pleased and the latter doing as they were told. The Alphans had clients, races they patronised; they didn't have allies, even amongst self-spacefaring races. The cold laws of the universe, the laws of the jungle, were immovable. One got what one could grab, one kept what one could keep…one ruled when one was strong and knuckled under when one was weak. And yet, the humans were making actual *allies*? It was hard to believe they took the Terminus Accords seriously—the Galactics had agreed the Accords were nothing more than a PR stunt—but they'd handed Terminus over to the other powers without hesitation. It was madness. By every sane galactic standard, they should have kept the bottleneck system until they were forced out. Instead…

"Insane," he muttered. "But it might work."

His mind churned. The Pashtali were still overwhelmingly powerful. Given time to concentrate their forces, they could reverse humanity's victories…*couldn't they*? Tarsus was probably helpless before them, if they returned in force, but Terminus? They did have a crossroads generator now—*that* was a reality everyone would learn to accept—yet it wasn't anything like as flexible as they presumably hoped. It certainly didn't match *Alphan* capabilities. And that meant…Terminus was effectively impregnable unless the Pashtali were prepared to take horrific losses while punching through the bottleneck.

And that means the humans have a secure rear area, without needing to expend their ships and men defending it, he thought. *They have allies.*

It was a curious situation and yet, he could see the advantages. The collective firepower of eight lesser powers might be enough to deter even the Pashtali, if they thought the alliance would hold together for more than a few months. And then…what did it mean for the galaxy? How many lesser powers would join up, seeking protection from their betters? And what did it mean for *his* people?

He stared at the report, without reading it. In truth, he had absolutely no idea.

CHAPTER TWENTY-ONE

ESS DAUNTLESS, SYSTEM P-34

"THE MUNOZ ARE DOING WELL, ADMIRAL," Olson reported, as the fleet glided through a crossroads and into System P-34. "The Pashtali are taking a beating."

Naomi nodded. She'd been nervous about relying on her allies to clear the crossroads, despite weeks of simulations and joint exercises, but the aliens had done well. They'd thrust through the crossroads, projecting an image of being strong without being *too* formidable, then brought in the rest of their squadrons when the Pashtali chose to stand and fight. Her lips twisted into a grim smile as the last of the enemy ships vanished from the display. They should have fled the moment they'd seen the ships emerging from the crossroads. It might have saved their lives.

And they would've added their ships to the enemy fleet being gathered to confront us, she thought, coldly. The scouts hadn't located any trace of an enemy fleet, beyond a handful of pickets and guardships monitoring various crossroads and star systems, but she was morbidly sure it was being assembled and prepared. She'd trailed her coat through a handful of enemy systems, none particularly important, in hopes of keeping the enemy guessing about her movements, yet she knew it was just a matter of time before the Pashtali tried to do something. *They have to stop us before they start losing control of their own systems.*

She allowed herself another smile. The Pashtali had tried to lay claim to the Occupied Zone by weakening humanity's grip on it, then insisting the absence of any effective control over the sector gave them the right to send ships to patrol, protect their convoys and effectively take over. There was a certain sense of pleasure in turning the logic on them. The more systems she raided—punching out defences, hammering ground bases, destroying passing convoys—the weaker the enemy would look, eventually convincing other races to send ships to 'secure' the star systems... and, effectively, take control for themselves. It would be a while before anyone worked up the nerve to try—the Pashtali were still terrifyingly powerful—but she was sure someone would. Eventually. If the Galactics thought the Pashtali Empire was on the verge of collapse, they'd want to grab what they could before someone else got there first.

"Detach two raiding squadrons to the planet, with instructions to clear the enemy presence," she ordered. "And remind them that, if they run into something they can't handle, they are to back off."

"Aye, Admiral," Olson said.

Naomi nodded. The system wasn't particularly important in the grand scheme of things. The files had been vague, but—reading between the lines—it was clear the natives had barely mastered the wheel when the Pashtali arrived and took over. They were so lowly on the galactic scale, thanks to their masters, that they didn't even reach the level of clients or even scavengers. They had no hope of independence, let alone power in their own right...she shuddered, all too aware humanity could have gone the same way, penned up in enclaves and left to die. She wished she could do something for them, beyond blowing away the Pashtali bases on the surface, but there was nothing. There was no way she could defend them when the enemy returned to retake the system.

We should be able to do something, she thought, but nothing came to mind. She didn't even have time to pick up a handful of aliens and take them away, settling them somewhere far from enemy space. Or did she? She had a pair of empty troop transports that could be repurposed, if there was time. *If we try...*

She tapped her console, issuing orders. There was no way to know what would happen if they tried, but she owed it to herself to make the attempt. She couldn't hope to evacuate the entire planet, yet if she could lift off a breeding population and move them to Terminus or all the way back to Earth...

Her lips twitched in amusement. Earth might not be welcoming, but colony worlds tended to be more progressive. And who knew where it would go?

"Admiral," Olson said. "*James Bond* signalled. She made transit through Crossroads Two and...I'm afraid it isn't good news."

"Spit it out," Naomi ordered. "What happened?"

"System P-33 is a bottleneck," Olson said, as the sensor reports appeared on the display. "And they're ready for us."

We nearly fucked up the timing, Naomi thought. She'd sent *James Bond* ahead of the fleet, with orders to pass through a handful of systems, but if the enemy had realised the fleet had arrived in P-34 they might have refused to allow *James Bond* to transit into the threadline from P-33. A few minutes more and the aliens would have had a chance to stop her dead. *We got lucky.*

She frowned as she surveyed the defences. The defenders hadn't let the grass grow under their feet. They'd towed battlestations from the other crossroads to provide additional firepower, then—if she was any judge—started to lay minefields too. If they hadn't been doing that when *James Bond* passed through, they'd sure as hell be doing it now. She hadn't been able to keep P-34's defenders from alerting P-33.

"The scout only picked up fourteen warships, holding position near the crossroads," Olson said. "However, there might be more ships lurking under cloak."

Naomi nodded. She doubted it—the Pashtali couldn't afford to keep throwing away ships, not when they needed to meet her fleet with one equal or greater—but it was possible. They'd never have a better chance to bleed her white...she tapped her console, exploring the possibilities, then frowned. A direct assault through the crossroads would end badly. If she won, she'd pay such an immense price that the enemy would have no trouble mopping her up; if she lost, she lost.

Fortunately, there was another option.

"Signal the fleet," she ordered. "We will proceed to Crossroads Two and make transit into multispace, then link up with *Crossroads* before advancing to P-33."

"Aye, Admiral," Olson said.

"Detach two scouts and send them ahead," Naomi added. "I want a clear topographic analysis of the multispace region surrounding the crossroads, with their best guess of which parts of multispace correspond to P-33."

"Aye, Admiral."

Naomi forced herself to relax as the fleet picked up speed. There was no point in worrying about the coming battle, not yet. If they found a place they could open a crossroads, they'd do it; if they didn't...she keyed her console, bringing up the starchart. There were fewer threadlines in the region than she'd expected, but they could make their way around P-33 without crashing into the system and being whittled down on the defences. Given time, they could even make their way to a different crossroads and enter the system without challenging the defences at all.

But we need to create an impression of unstoppable momentum, she reminded herself. *A long delay between attacks will give them time to rebalance and counterattack*

She studied the starchart for a long moment, recalling the latest—and already outdated—messages from Earth. The human race had new allies; some were willing to take the field, some only willing to supply money and support without putting themselves in danger. The latter would be fairweather friends, she was sure, but there was no point in complaining about it as long as they didn't switch sides *too* quickly. The realities of galactic power weren't easy to ignore. The longer she kept the enemy off-balance, the more races that would either side with humanity or start picking at the still-breathing corpse of a once-great empire.

"Admiral," Olson said. "Signal from Major Lollard. His force has made contact with the locals and they've accepted his offer of transportation. He requests permission to assign the POW ships to the mission too."

Naomi hesitated, then nodded. She should have thought of that. The POW ships were uncomfortable, even by military standards, but they were designed to hold thousands of intelligent life forms and keep them alive long enough to reach their destination. If the Pashtali were seemingly reluctant to surrender, the ships could be put to other use. The aliens wouldn't be POWs, but...

"Do it," she said. "And assign a destroyer squadron to escort them back to Terminus."

She told herself, as more and more reports came in from the planet's surface, that she'd made the right call. The natives had been crushed so badly they'd forgotten almost everything of their pre-contact culture, yet they'd been denied any role in the alien empire...they weren't used even as soldiers or brute labour. She was surprised the Pashtali hadn't simply exterminated them. Genocide would—in theory—bring the entire galaxy crashing down on the perpetrators, but the system was so isolated it was quite possible no one would notice. Her lips thinned . The Pashtali might not have deliberately set out to exterminate the locals, but they were pushing them down the path to extinction. The aliens she'd rescued might wind up the last of their kind.

The thought haunted her as the fleet reached the crossroads and slipped into multispace, her scouts buzzing ahead to watch for minefields and other nasty surprises. How many races had died out, crushed so completely they simply couldn't recover? How many races had become scavengers, dependent on their betters for the technology they needed to survive? How many had been penned up, unable to rise? She had no answer. She doubted she ever would.

There has to be a better way, she thought. *Somehow...*

She stood and made her way through *Dauntless*, touring the decks as she'd done when *Dauntless* had been *her* ship. It was a strange experience, as if disparate parts of her life were blurring together. The crew were respectful, of course, but...she wasn't the old lady any longer. She spoke to a handful, trying to gauge their mood and morale, even though she knew the answers might well be worthless. It would be a brave crewman who told his admiral he was down in the dumps...

Her lips quirked. Morale was high, for the moment. It wouldn't last forever—the ongoing mission and the lack of shore leave would start to grate soon, no matter how many entertainment nights the captains tried to offer, or how many illicit stills were quietly ignored as long as crewmen didn't report for their shifts drunk—but it would last long enough. She hoped. It was impossible to say how long it would be before they could stand down and go home, or even orbit a cosmopolitan world long enough to get some leave. No one knew when—if—the Pashtali would see sense and come to the table before the war was fought to the bitter end.

It doesn't matter how many perks we offer the crew, she reminded herself. *They need to be off the ship for a few days, away from the uniform, away from their duties and the discipline and...*

She smiled at herself. She'd often thought her commanding officers—and the admirals above them—hadn't grasped that point. And yet, she understood their concerns—and their thinking—a little better now. There was no time to slow down, no way to pull ships out of the line of battle and give them and their crews a little rest. Operational tempo had to be maintained, regardless of the wear and tear on the ships and crew. They could *not* afford to let the enemy go on the offensive.

It isn't as if we can stop them, she thought, as she entered her cabin to rest. It was a short flight from P-34 to P-33, but she could get a few hours of sleep before returning to the CIC. *We can only keep piling on the pressure and hope they break.*

Sure, her thoughts mocked. *And what happened to your ancestors when they tried the same tactic and lost?*

She told that part of her to shut up. If there had been any other options, she would have taken them. Now, she was committed.

• • •

"It seems rather pointless to save the local primitives," Observer Salix said, as Admiral Yagami joined him on the CIC. "Why waste berths on your ships?"

"Leaving them to die would be inhumane," Admiral Yagami said. She sounded tired, as though she hadn't slept very well. "And who knows what they might become, if they were given a chance?"

Salix said nothing for a long moment. The Alphans had written and imposed Galactic Law on the vast majority of the known galaxy, but they hadn't done it out of the goodness of their hearts. The law was designed to legalise everything they'd done, from taking control of a number of vital systems to rubber-stamping the *de facto* enslavement of primitive races. He had no illusions about the law, or the simple fact it was hard to convince anyone—these days—to enforce it against the Great Powers. And his people had no real concerns about primitive races. They would hardly go to war on their behalf.

And yet, the humans had deployed ships to rescue a bunch of primitives from alien domination.

It puzzled him. The Munoz and the others had something to offer—ships, personnel, a reason to fight—but the primitives had nothing. They had nothing except sticks and stones…they didn't even have insights into Pashtali thinking or technology from being subjugated that might justify the expense. The human race was going to have to pay for their care and feeding, as well as everything else. The more he thought about it, the less sense it made. And yet…

"They can give you nothing," he said, finally. "Why help them?"

"It costs us very little," Admiral Yagami said. "And it may wind up being very useful."

She turned away and continued to snap orders as her fleet split in two, one force launching missile pods through the crossroads while the other headed to the RV point. Salix leaned forward, watching with interest. The missile pods wouldn't do much, if any, damage to the enemy defences, but they'd keep enemy eyes focused on the crossroads. Would they realise the humans had brought their captured crossroads generator all the way from Earth? Salix was mildly surprised they'd gone to all that trouble. His people would have paid through the nose to get their hands on the alien ship and take it apart, just to see how it worked. The Pashtali hadn't come up with something new, although it was hard to be certain. They'd certainly surprised everyone when they'd opened crossroads in the middle of the first major engagement.

And there's no way to know how many other ships they have that can open crossroads, he reminded himself. The official estimates had been vague to the point of uselessness. Half the analyst team had been in deep denial, despite the sensor records the Solar Navy had forwarded; the other half had veered between insisting there was only one crossroads generator and suggesting there might be an entire *fleet* of them. *They have to have more than one, but how many?*

"Admiral," Olson said. "The fleet has reached the deployment zone."

Admiral Yagami glanced at Salix. "How do your ships handle the gravity flux?"

"They adapt," Salix said. He didn't know the technical details—the few who did were rarely permitted to leave the homeworld and never allowed to leave the empire—but he'd been on warcruisers that had jumped into combat zones before. "The Pashtali generators are nowhere near as advanced as ours."

"So it would seem," Admiral Yagami said. He thought he saw hesitation, even concern, on her face. Relying on alien technology had to gnaw at her, although there was little in her fleet that was purely human. He couldn't fault her. The crossroads generator had been put together by a very inhuman race and the slightest mistake could be disastrous. The only way to be sure the control system worked was to try it. "Signal *Crossroads*. They are to open the gateway in five minutes."

"Aye, Admiral," Olson said.

Salix braced himself. The Alphans would never admit it, at least not to anyone outside their own race, but their grasp of multispace theory was nowhere near as advanced as they claimed. They could still be blindsided—the storm that had raged between Earth and Alphan Prime had caught them by surprise- and there were places, despite their best efforts, where efforts to open a crossroads were doomed to fail. He'd been told that the first research into generators had been hit or miss, and it had taken years to come up with something that produced anything more than a brief ripple in the gravity field. The Pashtali had had to start at the beginning. There was no way, he was sure, that they'd caught up so quickly. It was impossible.

A low shudder ran through the ship as a gravity wave slammed into their hull. Space—multispace—was twisting, shockwaves running through the twisted fabric as it tied itself into a knot, then tore open into a gateway. Alarms howled—Salix felt a flicker of panic as the gravity field seemed to grow stronger—as the ship shook again and again. It was as if the drive field was pushing the ship in all directions, simultaneously, before lurching forward. He heard someone retch behind him and started to turn, then stopped. The sense they were about to step out of an orbital tower's airlock and plummet to their deaths was overwhelming…

Well, he thought. *The Pashtali generator is still no match for ours.*

It wasn't much, he reflected sourly, but it was all he had.

CHAPTER TWENTY-TWO

ESS DAUNTLESS, P-33 SYSTEM

NAOMI FELT AS IF SHE'D BEEN PUNCHED in the belly. Twice. She hadn't felt so bad since she'd gotten into a fight as a teenage girl and her assailants had held her down and pounded her chest until the teacher had pulled them off and sent them to be punished. She'd needed weeks to recover…she swallowed hard, trying to convince her body the feeling was nothing more than her imagination. The transit had been rough, as if the crossroads hadn't been tuned properly, but it hadn't done any real damage. They'd made it through the crossroads before it started to collapse back into nothingness.

They must be less vulnerable to transit shock than us, she thought. Her staff looked as if they'd been through the wringer and even Observer Salix looked uncomfortable. *Or they haven't been able to work the bugs out of the system yet.*

"Tactical report," she snapped. "Where are we?"

Olson coughed as he bent over his console. "Roughly ten thousand kilometres from our planned arrival coordinates," he said. "I'm feeding the data to *Crossroads* so they can refine their calculations."

"Later," Naomi said. Ten thousand kilometres was nothing, on an interplanetary scale. She would be more concerned if they'd appeared right next to the crossroad defences, or within the planet's atmosphere. "Fleet status?"

"No major damage, some minor," Olson said. "A handful of officers and crew were rendered comatose by transit shock. They've been relieved and dispatched to sickbay."

Naomi allowed herself a moment of relief. It could have been worse. A lot worse. They'd work on their calculations later, now that they had some hard data to slot in beside the simulations, but right now it wasn't a problem. She leaned forward as more and more data flowed into the sensors. The Pashtali had to be reeling. They'd towed nearly every battlestation in the system to the crossroads, only to have her fleet drop out of multispace between them and the planet. Her lips twitched. They'd done it to a human fleet—twice. They should have considered the possibility of someone doing the same to them.

"Transmit a formal demand for surrender," she ordered. The Pashtali ships were already bringing their drives online, readying themselves to plunge into the crossroads. They would have to flash past her squadrons, before her ships recovered from the shock and opened fire, but they could probably do it. She wasn't too concerned. There was no way to keep the Pashtali from signalling for help. "And then prepare to advance on the crossroads."

She scowled. Ideally, she would have preferred to leave the defenders alone. The battlestations weren't dangerous unless her fleet ventured into range. Leaving them to die on the vine would have suited her. But she only had one *Crossroads* and the techs had reminded her, time and time again, that there was no way to know how many times she could use the alien tech before it burnt itself out. The sooner she cleared the crossroads, the sooner she could bring in reinforcements from Terminus or lure other great powers into the collapsing empire. If the Pashtali remained in place, they could insist they owned the system...

"No response, Admiral," Olson reported. "They're merely bringing their weapons online."

"And they'll have no trouble targeting us either," Naomi said. "Signal the fleet. Prep for a long-range engagement, then key the courier drones for launch.

"Aye, Admiral."

Naomi braced herself, assessing the situation. The battlestations couldn't move under their own power—their station-keeping thrusters weren't designed to do more than nudge—but they were already bigger than battleships and their designers had crammed their hulls with weapons and sensors. Their commanders might even be deploying free-floating missiles too. The trick had worked once before and it might work again. She just didn't have *time* to let them wither and die on their own. And yet, the battlestations were formidable opponents. A missile duel would be costly, even if she won; a close-range duel might easily turn into a complete disaster.

We do have a plan, she thought. *But we may not be able to pull it off.*

The display sharpened as the range steadily closed. The enemy battlestations were overloading their active sensors, running so much power through the sensor nodes that they'd start to burn out within hours. The haze was so intense she was morbidly *sure* they were deploying free-floating missiles and weapons pods, relying on the sensor glare to hide them. Not bad thinking, she reflected, although the wear and tear on their systems would make repairs a nightmare. But then, there probably weren't going to *be* any. They had to know there was no point in trying to hide the battlestations. Her fleet knew precisely where they were.

"A missile duel will be immensely costly," Observer Salix commented. "Do you intend to risk a close-range engagement?"

"No," Naomi said, biting down hard on her annoyance. He was only verbalising her earlier thoughts. "I have a trick up my sleeve."

"A warcruiser squadron would slice the battlestations apart from middle range," Observer Salix continued. "Are your burners up to the task?"

"Not at the moment," Naomi said. "Like I said, I have a trick up my sleeve."

She looked at Olson. "Fire the first salvo, then the drones and decoys, then the second salvo as soon as we enter the powered missile envelope."

"Aye, Admiral," Olson said. "Two minutes to engagement."

Naomi nodded and took a step back, silently asking herself if the enemy stations would open fire first. She might just impale herself on their fire, if the range kept closing, and even if she didn't it would force her to keep her distance a little longer. There was nothing to be gained by opening fire outside her powered missile envelope. The missiles would go ballistic well before they reached their targets, making themselves easy pickings for enemy point defence.

And if they can be induced to shoot themselves dry, so much the better, she thought. *But it probably won't matter in the long run.*

"Admiral," Olson said. "We will enter engagement range in thirty seconds."

"Proceed as ordered," Naomi said, quietly. Questions ran through her head. Did the enemy know what she had in mind? How quickly could they react, if they knew? How long had they spent thinking about defending the system...long enough to work out what she had in mind and come up with a counter? "Fire as soon as we cross the line."

"Aye, Admiral," Olson said. "Firing...now."

Dauntless lurched as she unleashed her first salvo, the rest of the fleet following suit. A tidal wave of missiles, a wall of seemingly unstoppable destructive power, blasted from the tubes and raced towards the enemy battlestations. They returned fire a second later, belching a wall of death at the human and allied ships. Naomi gritted her teeth as the drones and decoys followed the missiles, the latter projecting enough sensor ghosts to confuse even Galactic sensors. She'd been hesitant to use any of the borrowed tech for the mission—the Alphans would not have thanked her for giving their potential enemies a sneak peek at their latest technology—but she needed every edge she could muster. There would be no second chance.

"Admiral," Olson said. "The second salvo has been launched."

"Signal all ships," Naomi ordered. "Reverse course. I say again, reverse course."

She leaned forward, watching the tidal wave of missiles slam into the enemy point defence. It was an unstoppable force, but it was meeting an immovable object. The battlestations were putting out enough point defence to tear great holes in the tidal wave, vaporising hundreds of missiles before they could reach their target. Others were decoyed away, their warheads fooled by ECM beacons, or wasted themselves on starfighters. It looked as if only a hundred or so were going to reach their targets...

But they're not paying any attention to the courier drones, she thought, as the drones raced *past* the battlestations and into the crossroads, flickering and vanishing into multispace. *They needed to take them all down and only took out a handful or so.*

"Admiral, the drones are through the crossroads," Olson reported. "The timer starts now."

"Fire the third salvo," Naomi ordered. They were right on the edge of effective range, and many of her warheads would go ballistic before they reached their targets, but hopefully it wouldn't matter. "And then stand by point defence."

She braced herself as the enemy missiles crashed into her formation. There were a lot of them, more advanced than she'd realised; she cursed under her breath as a number steadfastly refused to be decoyed and threw themselves on her defences. If the Alphans hadn't quietly upgraded the fleet's tech, this would have been a costly engagement. As it was, her losses started to mount sharply. The hell of it was that she was better off with the enemy trying to take out her ships, rather than damage as many as possible. In the long run, that would have served them better. It was no comfort.

The display updated as the missile pods and converted freighters made transit, the latter shooting off additional missiles instead of hesitating long enough to reorientate themselves and giving the enemy a chance to blow them away. A handful struck the remaining mines and died, but the remainder got their missiles off at point-blank range. Naomi felt her lips curve into a savage smile as the enemy battlestations started to die. They could normally have warded off the assault—the system was a bottleneck—but they couldn't handle an attack from both sides at once. It was odd that they hadn't considered the possibility. Surely, they should be aware of the potential of their own technology.

The British invented tanks and aircraft carriers, she reminded herself. *But it was the Germans and Japanese who figured out how to use them to best advantage.*

Dauntless shuddered as a missile detonated against her hull, the enemy fire trailing off as—one by one—the remaining battlestations died. Naomi allowed herself a moment of relief, even as she repeated her offer of surrender. There was no answer. Again. She shook her head in disbelief as the last battlestation hurled a final salvo at her ships, before a direct hit punched through its armour and detonated inside the shell. Naomi doubted the entire crew was dead—the battlestation was too solid—but they couldn't fight any longer.

Why the hell weren't they surrendering?

"Admiral," Olson said, formally. "We have cleared the crossroads."

"Signal the planet," Naomi ordered. "Inform them we are now in control of the system, in line with Galactic Law, and that they have"—she glanced at the display—"four hours to evacuate the orbital infrastructure so we can destroy it. Any resistance will result in further devastation. There will be no further warnings."

"Aye, Admiral," Olson said.

Naomi drew in a breath as the display updated. Hundreds of ships were fleeing the planet, heading towards the other crossroads or out into interplanetary space. Most were harmless; interstellar freighters passing through the system, unaware they were heading straight into a war. There was nothing to be gained by trying to run them down and blowing them away, not when they'd spread the story far and wide. The Pashtali could write off Terminus and Tarsus as poorly defended systems, but not P-33. The human fleet had stormed the system, then taken out an entire cluster of battlestations while only suffering minimal losses. There was no way in hell the Pashtali would be able to keep *that* from spreading.

"They'll pull back behind their forcefields," Observer Salix said. "Do you intend to land troops?"

"We don't have the numbers for a long, drawn-out campaign," Naomi said. The planet was mostly Pashtali. The handful of alien enclaves were too small to offer any real assistance, even if they wanted to. The files hadn't said much about the enclaves, beyond the mere fact of their existence, but there couldn't be much more than a few hundred thousand aliens on the surface. Hell, that might be optimistic. "We'll settle for clearing the orbitals and leaving the planet alone."

The Alphan seemed surprised. "You're not going to attempt to seize the industrial base?"

"They wouldn't let us take it intact," Naomi said. She'd considered it, but the Pashtali were disinclined to be reasonable. She had a feeling they'd sooner blow up their industrial nodes—which they could replace quickly, if they'd planned ahead—than risk allowing her to cart them off. They'd certainly wipe the datacores before she could stop them. "Better to destroy it than risk trying to snatch it."

She frowned inwardly as she keyed her console, bringing up the starchart. Where next? The Pashtali might have assumed she wouldn't be able to break into the system—they would have been right, if she hadn't had *Crossroads*—and, if that was the case, they might be setting ambushes around P-27 and P-28. Might. The scouts hadn't been able to track alien movements and report back...two scouts had vanished, which suggested they'd run into something they couldn't handle. The alien fleet? Scouts weren't that well-armed or defended...that they'd vanished, perhaps been killed, didn't mean they'd run into anything bigger than a light cruiser. There was no *proof* there was a major enemy fleet lurking around the two systems...

A thought struck her and she looked at the Alphan. "What would *your* people do if they knew there was an alien fleet smashing through your rear?"

Observe Salix seemed surprised by the question. "It would depend on how powerful the fleet was," he said, finally. "If we thought it was too large to challenge without a major deployment, we would concentrate on protecting vital targets and forcing the fleet to engage fixed as well as mobile defences. Why do you ask?"

"The enemy knows we're here," she said. "What are they going to do about it?"

Her mind raced. The Pashtali had committed a classic error, dispersing their forces before crushing the human race into the dirt. They now had too many conflicts along their borders, conflicts they couldn't shut down in a hurry. They'd take heavy losses if they pushed for a hasty decision, weakening their military, and they'd be seen as weak if they abandoned the conflicts and pulled out. *And* their former enemies might sign the Terminus Accords. It might be the beginning of the end.

Except we could do real damage if we kept poking into their space, she thought, as she studied the threadlines. *The border conflicts are minor. If we thrust into their core systems and lay waste to their industrial base, they could lose everything. Would they concede the border wars—for now—or risk keeping them going?*

She had no answer. Human history had plenty of examples of governments feeding blood and treasure into unwinnable conflicts, including some that had cost the governments the wars and their very existence. The Pashtali might be just as foolish, or they might cut their losses…except that doing so might not be an option. Human governments had often had the chance to back out. The Pashtali might be chased back to their core worlds by their enemies…who had every reason to want revenge and no reason to assume any treaties they made with the spider-like aliens would be honoured any longer than strictly necessary.

Her eyes narrowed. *If I was in charge of the enemy fleet and I knew P-33 had been attacked, I'd mass my fleet at P-30, perhaps P-21, and plot an intercept as soon as I thought I could face the human fleet on even terms. It would give me the best chance to force an engagement, if I thought I could win, or back off and fall back on heavy fixed defences if I thought I was outmatched. And that means...*

She took a breath. *We can't afford an engagement on equal terms, which means we need to avoid those stars. But we also need to carry the fleet deeper into their territory, which means we'll have to go the long way around...which will slow us down. Do we have a choice?*

Olson cleared his throat. "Admiral, we are nearing the planet," he said. "There's no indication they've evacuated the platforms."

Naomi scowled. There was no way to *know*, short of boarding the platforms and searching them and she didn't have time. And they knew it too. She studied the display for a moment, even though she knew there were no other options. The Pashtali had been warned. The cold-blooded part of her mind pointed out that, if they hadn't evacuated the platforms, slaughtering the trained industrial workers would work in humanity's favour. The rest of her recoiled at such logic. The Pashtali might be willing to commit mass slaughter, but she wasn't.

"Target the platforms as planned, then open fire," she ordered, tiredly. They just didn't have the time! Legally, they were in the clear—they'd secured the system and issued a warning—but the Pashtali wouldn't see it that way. "And then prepare to set course for P-39."

"Aye, Admiral," Olson said.

"An interesting choice," Observer Salix said. If he had any concerns about the kinetic bombardment, he didn't show them. "There are few targets in the system worthy of your attention."

"Yes, but it will give us access to more threadlines and make it harder for them to determine where we're going," Naomi said. "There are also fewer bottlenecks, which will also make it harder for them to pin us down. In fact, it might be worth trying to trick them into thinking we're going to veer through P-31. They'd want to believe it."

The Alphan cocked his head. "Would they not realise the unlikelihood?"

"Perhaps, but they'd want to believe it," Naomi said. She knew it was a lie—she knew only a complete idiot would walk into such a perfect site for an ambush—and she still found it hard to convince herself the enemy wouldn't try it, if their positions were reversed. "The most convincing lies are always the lies the mark wants to believe."

CHAPTER TWENTY-THREE

SYSTEM P-20, PASHTALI SPACE

"WE JUST INTERCEPTED A MESSAGE from the Telic to the Pashtali," Marquez reported. "Apparently, the Telic are very concerned with the lack of security along the border and are sending their own warships to protect their shipping."

"A bluff?" Commodore Roger Valentine looked up from his console. "Or a genuine threat?"

"It's hard to say," Marquez said. "Obviously, I don't know what the Pashtali said in response. They may say nothing and dare the Telic to cross the line. Or they may inform the Telic that crossing the border in force will be seen as an act of war and treated accordingly."

Roger allowed himself a smirk. The Pashtali had weakened humanity's control over the Occupied Zone and used it as an excuse to take the sector for themselves, all perfectly legal under Galactic Law. He hoped they were enjoying the taste of their own medicine. Admiral Yagami was clearly giving them a very hard time if the Telic thought they could get away with even threatening to send ships into enemy territory. Perhaps the Pashtali thought there was a good chance the Telic would wind up shooting at Admiral Yagami...no, that was unlikely. The Telic would have an excellent claim to the disputed sectors if they defended them against the human hordes. He doubted the Pashtali would take the risk.

The enemy of my enemy is my enemy's enemy, he reminded himself. He couldn't remember who'd said it, but it was a fundamental truth of galactic politics. *No more, no less.*

"See if you can pick up any response," he said, wryly. "It'll be interesting to see what they say."

"Yes, sir," Marquez said. "But they may say nothing."

Roger nodded, then turned back to his console. The squadron had been sneaking into P-20 for the last four days, gliding towards a planet surprisingly close to the local crossroads. The Pashtali had turned it into a bottleneck system, even though the crossroads was a little larger than the typical bottleneck. He had no idea what they'd been thinking—the resources they'd funnelled into the defences would have been better spent on mobile units—but it hardly mattered. Roger suspected they were doing everything in their power to reinforce the defences as quickly as possible, now the human fleet had made its way into their rear. Perversely, it might even work in their favour. Admiral Yagami would bleed her fleet white if she tried to punch through the defences and take the system.

And there's no proof she actually wants to come here, Roger thought. He studied the starchart for a long moment. Perhaps the Pashtali had wanted to deter their prospective enemies, without deploying a major fleet. Or perhaps they just wanted to tax everything that went through the crossroads. *The system isn't that important—and smashing the defences and local industries won't be worth the cost.*

He grimaced—it was yet another reminder they were badly outmatched—and concentrated on the mission. The Pashtali defences were firmly focused on the crossroads, to the point he wondered if they thought Admiral Yagami *was* planning to punch through the defences and take the system. It was unlikely and yet...he frowned as he studied the mobile units orbiting the planet, far enough from the crossroads to be safe from surprise attack and yet close enough to race to back up the fixed defences if possible. Perhaps there was something to be said for the enemy defences after all. A prospective enemy might take a handful of worthless systems, but they couldn't get any closer to the *important* systems without punching through the defences first. They certainly couldn't make their gains permanent as long as the Pashtali could hide behind their fixed defences, build up their fleets and retake the offensive.

Not that it matters, he told himself. *We don't have time for a long, drawn-out conflict.*

His console bleeped. They were in range. "Signal the squadron," he ordered. "Start deploying ballistic missiles, as planned."

"Aye, sir," Marquez said.

Roger's heart started to race. They were moving at unimaginable speed and yet, on an interplanetary scale, they were practically crawling towards their targets. The missiles would be moving slowly, too, as they were launched into space. They were so tiny it was unlikely they'd be noticed until they went live, but if they *were* spotted before they reached attack range they'd be wiped out within seconds. Roger doubted that the Pashtali would ask questions before opening fire. Anything that crept so close to a crossroads was almost certainly hostile.

Or a starship crewed by complete idiots, Roger thought. The universe had no shortage of fools, including some who somehow managed to get their hands on starships. *They'd probably think they were doing the universe a favour as they blew them away.*

He braced himself. The missile guns—imparting velocity to the missiles without bringing their own drives online—were primitive, so primitive the techs were *sure* the Pashtali wouldn't suspect their existence. Roger hoped they were right. The Galactics might bask in the glow of their technology, but most of them understood a rock could beat a laser under the right circumstances. He'd studied the fighting on Earth, during the Alphan invasion, and it was clear the planet's defenders had given the invaders a very hard time. If the Alphans hadn't controlled the high orbitals, and blasted the defenders from high overhead, the fighting might have gone the other way. His lips twitched in cold amusement. It must have galled the invaders to watch their armoured vehicles get turned to scrap by tanks so primitive they belonged in a museum.

"Twenty minutes to attack range," Marquez said, as the last of the missiles were propelled into interplanetary space. "No sign we've been detected."

"Not yet." Roger said. The enemy fortifications were surrounded by a sensor haze. It was just possible they'd pick up *something*, despite everything. And then...what? The missiles were designed to be hard to spot, but there were no guarantees. "They'll see us soon enough."

Sweat prickled down his back as he waited, the seconds ticking by one by one. It was a shame the Pashtali had changed their IFF codes, making it impossible to get the squadron into firing range without raising the alarm. They'd tried to figure out the underlying logic, in hopes of working out a viable IFF code, but they'd found nothing. Roger suspected the codes were randomly generated and assigned. It was what he'd have done, in their place. They didn't have time for anything else.

And it's how we do it, he reminded himself. *They might start taking pages from our book.*

He leaned forward as the last seconds ticked down. The passive sensors couldn't track the missiles—they were effectively invisible—but as long as they remained on course their locations were easy to predict. The enemy didn't seem to have noticed them...

"ECM pulses online, ready to activate," Marquez said. "At your command..."

"Let the missiles go live first," Roger said. The missiles were slipping into the sensor haze now. A decent analysis algorithm would spot them, or *something*, and raise the alarm. He wouldn't be comfortable giving a computer the authority to open fire, not without a human in the command loop, but the Pashtali might feel differently. It would be interesting to see if they did. The Galactics had never produced true AIs and it might be possible to trick an unintelligent system into firing on the wrong side. "I wonder..."

The sensor console bleeped an alarm. "Sir, we're picking up enemy ships transiting Crossroads Three," Marquez said. "They're heading directly towards Crossroads Two."

Roger cursed his luck. The enemy fleet was already in the system, already closer than he wished...the display updated, projecting the enemy trajectory. The speed of light delay meant the display was already outdated, with the enemy fleet dangerously close. Not close enough to catch the squadron, if they brought up theirs and fled, but close enough to be a major threat if he stuck around. There were too many ships...his eyes narrowed as he realised his squadron wasn't the target. The enemy ships were heading to intercept Admiral Yagami.

"Fuck," he muttered. He brought up the starchart, then shook his head. He had no idea where Admiral Yagami was, or where she was going. Did the Pashtali? Probably. The human fleet had to make its presence very noticeable, which had the obvious disadvantage of telling the enemy where to go. "That isn't good news."

"No, sir," Marquez agreed. "The planetary defenders are also breaking orbit."

Roger nodded, studying the in-system display. The Pashtali were probably drawing mobile units from each and every star system they passed, rather than allow Admiral Yagami to meet each squadron individually and defeat them in detail with overwhelming firepower. It was what *he* would have done. The Pashtali could not afford to be defeated, or even *look* defeated. The vultures were already scenting weakness, gathering at the border in hopes of snatching a share of the spoils. How long would it be, he asked himself, before one vulture made a move and drew the others after it? Not long, if he was any judge. The Pashtali had too many enemies for their peace of mind.

And the admiral might not even have the slightest idea the enemy fleet is on the way, Roger thought, worriedly. His most optimistic estimate suggested the Pashtali would intercept the human fleet in two weeks. His most pessimistic estimate...he doubted Admiral Yagami would risk getting too close to the potential bottlenecks, but she *did* have to make the enemy look weak. *They might run her to ground inside a week.*

He glanced at Marquez. "Prepare a laser communications packet and attach our stolen codes to the message header," he said. "I want the message relayed through their network as quickly as possible."

"Aye, sir." Marquez sounded doubtful. "If they know we copied their IFF codes, they might guess we copied their communications codes too."

Roger nodded, curtly. In theory, the Pashtali communications relays were supposed to forward all messages without question. In practice, they might keep the messages in the buffer until they were sure the signals were harmless. Roger was fairly sure that was exactly what they'd do, if the message appeared to come out of nowhere. The duplicated message headers should authorise the relay stations to forward the message, by making them look like perfectly legitimate *Pashtali* signals, but there was no way to be sure. And if they realised what the human techs had done…

They might just have deduced it already, he reminded himself. The entire stunt might be worse than useless. *But we have to try.*

Marquez's console bleeped. "Sir, the missiles will go live in two minutes…"

"Signal the squadron," Roger ordered. His planning had been very loose, thankfully. They weren't bound to an impractically tight schedule. "We will give them one minute of ECM, as planned, then break contact."

He frowned. "And send the laser signal to the FTL relay now."

"Aye, sir," Marquez said. "Signal away…now."

Roger forced himself to relax. The laser signal, with the message headers, should reach the relay station well before the operators realised the crossroads was under attack. There was no reason, he told himself firmly, for them to think there was anything odd about the message. It hadn't even looked as though it had come out of empty space. They were close enough to the defences for the operators to think it had come from the crossroads…

The display washed red. "Sir," Marquez said. "They've seen the missiles!"

"Bring the ECM online now," Roger snapped. The missiles were keyed to go live, if the warheads realised they'd been detected, but it had become a race against time. How long would it take for the enemy to react? Their point defence wouldn't be completely powered down, would it? They were on a *crossroads* in the middle of a war. The enemy could pop through at any moment and they knew it. "And start pulsing!"

"Aye, sir," Marquez said. "The enemy fleet is accelerating!"

Roger nodded, cursing under his breath. The Pashtali had gotten lucky. The arrival of their fleet had thrown off his planning. Their point defence was already pulsing, spitting death at the missiles and the sensor ghosts surrounding them. He doubted, somehow, that many of the missiles would reach their targets. The Pashtali had been surprised—they'd probably thought the system was relatively safe—but they'd reacted well. A number of missiles were already gone. The remainder were being targeted now.

And we can't get any closer, he thought. *We're already too close for comfort.*

"Signal the fleet," he ordered. "Deploy ECM drones and aim them at both the defences and the enemy fleet, then come about and retreat as planned."

"Aye, sir."

Roger felt the captured ship's gravity twitch as she started to move, gliding away from the defences. The enemy had a solid lock on them now… he wondered, in hindsight, if it wouldn't have been better to avoid bringing up their ECM, but there was no point in worrying about it now. One battlestation had been hit, the burner carving through the armour as if it wasn't there at all. He'd hoped for better, but it hardly mattered. The real goal—remind the enemy they were no longer safe behind the lines—had been accomplished.

"Deploy a second set of drones," he said, as the display bleeped an alert. The enemy sensors had a solid lock on their hulls. Their ships were turning to give chase. Thankfully, it was unlikely they'd be able to run his ships down before they slipped through the crossroads and vanished. "Try to steer them away from us."

"Aye, sir," Marquez said. The display sparkled with red icons. "Sir, they've launched starfighters."

They can't be flying those craft themselves, Roger thought, clinically. The Pashtali weren't good flyers, generally preferring to leave starfighters to their clients. *And they're just throwing those craft away?*

He kicked himself, mentally, as the starfighters raced from their motherships. They would be operating well beyond their effective range, to the point they were unlikely to return to their carriers before their life support ran out, but the Pashtali didn't care. They thought little of their own lives. They'd have no qualms about sending their clients to die. Even if they'd had time to outfit the starfighters with extension packs, in hopes of giving the pilots a chance to survive, the odds would still be against them. He made a mental note to try and turn the incident into propaganda. The Galactics wouldn't give a shit—client races owed their patrons everything—but the clients themselves would be concerned. Who knew? It might even be enough to convince the clients to rise and try to kill their masters.

"Stand by point defence," he ordered. Normally, the starfighters wouldn't be a serious threat unless they were armed with missiles or torpedoes. Now, with his ships manned by skeleton crews, he couldn't afford to take any damage. "Link the ships into the datanet, then fire as soon as they come into range."

"Aye, sir," Marquez said. The range was closing rapidly. "The drones don't seem to have had any effect."

"Send the destruct command." Roger wasn't surprised. He hadn't expected the deception to work—and, if it had, it wouldn't have lasted past the moment the squadron opened fire on its tormentors. "Don't leave anything behind for their techs."

"Aye, sir," Marquez said. "Enemy starfighters entering range…now."

Roger leaned forward, watching as the starfighters charged into the teeth of his fire. Their pilots were good, he noted sourly, although their flying showed they knew they were on the verge of running out of life support. The Pashtali didn't seem to have come up with any new weapons either, although their torpedoes were quite bad enough. His ships had to fight hard to keep them from striking their hulls and inflicting real damage. He cursed as he saw a torpedo hit one of his ships, narrowly missing a drive node. The damage wasn't significant, but without a shipyard it was dangerously close to lethal. He briefly considered ordering the crew to jump onto their shuttle and abandon ship, then dismissed the idea. The starship was still useful. As long as they got through the crossroads…

"The enemy are pressing their assault," Marquez said. "I think they don't have any hope of returning home."

"No," Roger agreed. He felt a twinge of sympathy for the pilots. They deserved better patrons. The Alphans had never sent humans to *die*, throwing away their lives as callously as one might discard a burnt-out component. "Watch for suicide tactics. They might try to ram us."

His eyes narrowed as a pair of enemy starfighters did just that, ducking and weaving as they closed on his ships. They were blown to dust bare kilometres from their targets. Roger allowed himself a moment of relief, then another as the squadron passed through the crossroads and vanished down the threadline. He snapped orders, commanding the fleet to lay mines. It was unlikely the enemy would give chase, not when they had to catch Admiral Yagami, but it was just possible they'd try. The mines would make life interesting for anyone who did.

And they'll make a fuss about it in front of the galaxy, he mused. *Will it cost them badly? Or will it rebound on us?*

"Get me a damage report from the wounded ship," he ordered. They'd have to do something with her, unless they could carry out repairs. He doubted it. "And then set course to our next target."

"Aye, sir," Marquez said. "Do you think Admiral Yagami got our message?"

"I don't know," Roger said. The message *should* have been relayed, but if the Pashtali blocked it…"I think we'll just have to wait and see."

CHAPTER TWENTY-FOUR

ESS DAUNTLESS, P-39

"ADMIRAL," OLSON SAID. "I think we have company."

Naomi frowned as she glanced at him. "Company?"

"Our recon shell picked up hints of cloaked ships, holding station too close to the fleet for comfort," Olson said. "I think we're being shadowed."

Naomi felt her frown deepen as she studied the display. The fleet had made its way through the threadlines, avoiding a pair of star systems that might have been able to decimate her fleet if she tried to punch through, and they'd done everything they could to avoid being tracked, but she'd been sure the Pashtali had a rough idea where she was going. They wouldn't expect her to go *off* the threadlines...she shook her head. She'd done that once before, in the opening days of the war, and it had nearly cost her everything. They'd been lucky to survive long enough to get home.

She considered her options carefully. The enemy might think they hadn't been detected. Not yet. If she did nothing to alert them, they might remain in a state of happy innocence until...she worked out how to turn their presence to her advantage. Or...should she detach a pair of ships to chase the enemy spies away? They were close enough to get some solid data and relay it to the planet, which would forward it to the enemy fleet...where *was* the enemy fleet? She was rather surprised they'd made no attempt to mine the threadlines to keep her from flying around the sector…

But then, that would alienate the rest of the galaxy, she thought. The latest updates from Earth had been clear. Galactic opinion didn't favour Earth—and that was unlikely to change—but it no longer favoured the Pashtali. The vultures were gathering, preparing to feast on the carrion. *They really don't need more enemies.*

"Hold our current course," she said, finally. "And prepare to implement Shell Game."

"Aye, Admiral,"

Naomi nodded to herself. The Pashtali sensors were supposed to be good, but even *they* would have trouble picking out individual ships amongst her fleet. And that meant…she could keep them guessing. There was no *need* to take her entire fleet to hit P-39—the system had only a handful of fixed defences and no mobile units—and she knew it. If she sent a handful of units elsewhere…

We already left Crossroads *and her escorts in multispace*, she reminded herself. *We can't afford to detach too many other ships.*

Olson started. "Admiral, we just picked up a message relayed through the FTL network," he reported. "Preliminary message headers indicate it's from Commodore Valentine!"

"I see," Naomi said. She'd been cautioned there was no way to be sure they *could* get a message into the enemy relay network. She'd ordered Commodore Valentine to refrain from trying unless the situation was urgent. "Can you decrypt the message?"

"Yes, Admiral," Olson said. His voice rose in alarm. "Admiral, they spotted an enemy fleet making its way through P-20!"

Naomi brought up the starchart and studied it. "When's the message time-stamped?"

"Two days ago," Olson said. "It was relayed through at least two stations before reaching us."

"Two days," Naomi repeated. "Their fleet was at P-20 two days ago."

She considered it carefully. The code was a very simple one that should have been nothing more than nonsense to any alien eyes, but she knew better than to take that for granted. The aliens might not be able to read the message, yet they'd be able to guess its contents from context and context alone. Her old instructors had made that clear, using the example of an indecipherable message from a house to a fire station. The message was unreadable, but anyone who looked at the context could tell it was reporting a fire…

Her eyes lingered on the starchart. The enemy fleet had had two days. Assuming it had pushed its drives to the limit, which was unlikely, they might be approaching P-39 now. Or they were already in the system… she frowned as she studied the display, trying to assess if their shadows were merely the trailing edge of the enemy fleet. The message hadn't been anything like detailed enough, not for her peace of mind. The Pashtali wouldn't risk an engagement unless they were confident of victory. And that meant they were trying to bring overwhelming fire to bear on her.

"Signal the fleet," she ordered. "The battlecruiser squadrons are to proceed to the planet and turn its orbital defences into scrap metal. The remainder of the fleet is to advance to Crossroads Two."

"Aye, Admiral," Olson said.

Naomi nodded, cursing multispace's weird trajectories under her breath. She could bring the entire fleet around and retrace her steps, but that would narrow the gap between her ships and the enemy fleet. Perhaps. There was no way to know where it was hiding. If it wasn't in the system already, would it try to pop through Crossroads One or Two? Or did it have a crossroads generator with it? The message was woefully short on actual detail. She understood the problem—a detailed message would almost certainly run afoul of enemy censors—but she needed more. If there was a crossroads generator with the enemy fleet, her tactics would be worse than useless…

"Admiral," Olson said. "Long-range sensors are picking up enemy ships transiting Crossroads One."

"Interesting," Naomi observed. It would have been more efficient if the Pashtali had popped out of Crossroads Two. They must have suspected she wasn't planning to fly through P-39 on her way to P-40. It wasn't an unreasonable guess, but it was wrong. "Signal the carriers. On my command, I want those cloaked ships chased away."

"Aye, Admiral," Olson said.

Naomi tapped her console, detailing the battle plan. The enemy had played it safe, giving her a chance to lure them into a threadline...a *mined* threadline. It was hard to be sure how many ships were breathing down her neck—they were flying in close formation and using overlapping drive signatures to conceal their precise location, just like her—but they'd made a mistake. They'd soon have to choose between running a minefield gauntlet and letting her go, unless they managed to run her down before she made transit. *That* wasn't going to happen.

Not unless they've managed to improve their drives beyond all recognition, she thought. The analysts hadn't noted any major improvements in alien drive tech, although the Pashtali could easily have decided to keep the drive improvements a secret until they managed to spring the trap. She doubted it. Right now, the Pashtali needed to look as intimidating as possible to deter their many enemies. They might have waited to refit their ships before kicking off the war. *No, they can't have made too many improvements...*

"Launch recon probes," she ordered, calmly. "I want a good look at that fleet before it gets any closer."

"Aye, Admiral," Olson said.

Naomi leaned back in her chair and waited. The Pashtali would have to decide, soon enough, if they wanted to overload their drives trying to run her down or simply let her go. She hoped they'd go for the latter, although she knew it would be the former. They'd be insane to let her go...and yet, if the recon probes weren't being spoofed in some way, the enemy fleet was just plodding along. Were they intent on keeping up the pressure, without actually trying to close the range? Or were they up to something?

The puzzle nagged at her mind as the minutes ticked by, one by one. She knew she should leave the CIC and take a nap, as the minutes became hours, but she didn't dare. The Pashtali fleet was strong enough to deter her from bringing her fleet around and forcing the issue, yet it seemed content to keep its distance and shadow her. What was it doing? She supposed they could be trying to intimidate her, to keep her from taking out planetary defences and orbital industries, but...it was odd. The Pashtali could afford to soak up heavy losses. She could not. In their place, *she* would be trying to close the range as quickly as possible.

"Admiral," Olson said. "The enemy fleet is launching starfighters."

"Interesting," Naomi said. The enemy starfighters would be operating right on the edge of their range, even with extension packs. They were going to have to get in, launch their missiles and get out again before they ran out of life support and died. "I wonder..."

She put the thought aside as the swarm of red icons closed on her ships. "Signal the carriers," she said. "I want a full Combat Space Patrol surrounding the fleet, and point defence targeting enemy starfighters and missiles as they close to attack."

"Aye, Admiral."

• • •

Observer Salix was unsurprised, as the range between the human fleet and the enemy starfighters closed, to note that the capital ships were keeping their distance. Starfighters were pretty much expendable, as far as most races were concerned, particularly the ones flown by client races. The Pashtali weren't known for treating their clients very well, not even the handful of races that had started to develop technology themselves before they discovered the galaxy was full of predators. The Pashtali risked little by engaging the fleet at a distance and gained much if the starfighters inflicted any real damage. If nothing else, they could wear down the human crews before the real fighting began.

He leaned forward, studying the battle with cold clinical interest. The human pilots were *good*. Their starfighters weren't the most advanced in the galaxy—they certainly didn't match Alphan designs—but their pilots knew how to get the best out of them. The enemy pilots—Vulteks, he guessed—were just as good, as well as determined to hurt their targets even at the cost of their own lives. They struck hard, with damage mounting rapidly. He heard the humans curse as a pair of outdated warships exploded, followed by a third staggering out of the line of battle; he told himself, firmly, not to point out that it could have been worse. The outdated ships had soaked up missiles and starfighters that could have killed a far more advanced vessel.

The battle raged on, more enemy starfighters spewing from their carriers to attack the human vessels. They seemed to be staggering their attacks, keeping up the pressure; they seemed determined to ensure the humans were worn out, by the time the enemy fleet finally caught up with them. And yet...he frowned, puzzled. The Pashtali would have done a lot *more* damage if they'd launched all their starfighters at the human fleet, all the more so as the humans weren't trying to launch counterattacks. The more he looked at it, the more it didn't make sense. The fighting was going on and on and yet the enemy didn't seem inclined to close the range.

They're either trying to grind the humans down, he thought, *or they're waiting for something.*

He felt the ship shudder as a missile struck her hull. Alarms howled, red icons flashing on the display before flipping to yellow or green. No major damage...Salix tried not to show his relief. He was no coward, but he didn't want to die as a mere observer. He'd been promised a promotion when he returned home...*if* he returned home. He didn't want to think about the possibility of dying here...

"The battlecruisers have reported in, Admiral," the human communications operator said. "The planetary defences have been taken out, along with a handful of orbital stations."

A shame they can't bombard the surface too, Salix thought. *But the Pashtali would probably try to claim the humans wantonly slaughtered innocent civilians.*

The ship shuddered, again. Salix forced himself to relax. There was no shortage of stories about Alphan observers who'd been in command right from the start, their hosts recognising their natural superiority and granting them complete authority without even being asked, but most of those stories were nothing more than flattering nonsense. He had no authority on the human ship. There was nothing he could do, except watch and silently plan his report to his superiors. And hope the humans didn't accidentally get him killed.

• • •

Naomi tried not to rub her eyes.

The fighting had raged for hours, enemy starfighters sweeping towards her ships to skirmish with the CSP and launch missiles at her hulls, then withdrawing to rearm before returning to the fight. The damage was mounting steadily, despite the best efforts of her repair crews, and she had a nasty feeling the enemy fleet was just waiting for her to be weakened before closing for the kill. And yet, the fleet continued to keep its distance. What was it doing?

They have to have scraped up every ship they could and combined them into a single fleet, she thought. She wasn't facing the *entire* enemy fleet, but there was a very good chance they'd massed every ship in the sector and pointed them at her. If she took the fleet out, the Pashtali would be so gravely weakened they'd be unable to keep the vultures from taking big bites out of their territory. *No wonder they're playing it safe.*

She scowled as she watched the battle continue to unfold. Earth couldn't afford to lose her fleet, either. She was tempted to reverse course, close the range and fight it out, but—win or lose—it would be disastrous. The Pashtali might lose the sector, and a few others, yet humanity would lose its freedom. There were too many powers who saw Earth standing up to the Pashtali and saw a potential threat. And that meant…

"Admiral," Olson said. "We'll cross into multispace in thirty minutes."

"Unless they try to close the range now," Naomi said. She doubted the enemy could catch up with her in time. Perhaps they wanted an inconclusive battle, secure in the knowledge they had shipyards within easy reach. Her ships would need weeks to reach the nearest friendly shipyard, if they were lucky. "What are they doing?"

"Holding the range open," Olson said. "They're not even trying to close to missile range."

Naomi cursed under her breath. Something was wrong. Something didn't quite make sense. And yet, what? She forced herself to think, evaluating the various possibilities. The enemy were holding the range open—the thought went through her head, time and time again—instead of trying to close with her. Was she right? Was she facing the only major enemy force in the sector? Or did they have a trick up their sleeve?

Perhaps I should have kept Crossroads *with us*, she thought. She knew the crossroads generator would be a priority target—the enemy would throw everything they had at the captured ship, if they spotted her—but it would be so much easier if they could just drop into multispace and vanish. The Alphans had made ruthless use of the technology over the centuries. *If we could just run for our lives...*

"Admiral," Olson said. Alarm rang through his voice. "The enemy fleet is picking up speed."

"Curious," Naomi commented. "It's too late to keep us from escaping..."

Her mind churned. What were they doing? They'd left it too late to do much of anything, save chasing her out of the system. Was *that* the point? Or...she wondered, just for a moment, if they intended to drive her towards one of the bottlenecks. It was possible, she supposed. If they forced her to crash into a heavily defended system, they might weaken or destroy her fleet without taking any real damage themselves. And yet...she wouldn't let them do *that* to her. She'd sooner take the fleet off the threadlines and make her way through uncharted space than flirt with destruction. The enemy had to know that, didn't they?

Unless they are really wary of losing too many mobile units of their own, she thought. *If they look weak, everyone else will jump on them. They might destroy us at the cost of being permanently reduced to a minor power. No one will ever let them rise again.*

"Signal the fleet," she ordered, calmly. If the Pashtali were willing to let her escape into multispace, she'd do it before they found a way to stop her. "We will make transit as planned and set course for P-40, mining the crossroads behind us."

"Aye, Admiral," Olson said.

"And deploy a flight of recon probes," Naomi added. "I want to make sure the crossroads isn't already mined."

"Aye, Admiral," Olson said.

Naomi forced herself to wait. The Pashtali might have been trying to drive them into a minefield...if they'd had time to lay one. She doubted it, but...they had to check, just to be sure. The Pashtali were alien, with thought processes that made the Alphans look practically human, yet they weren't *that* different...

They might have something clever in mind, she thought. *But what?*

Her unease grew as the fleet neared the crossroads. There was nothing. No mines, no weapons platforms, nothing. It was...puzzling. The enemy fleet behind her was accelerating slowly, telegraphing its every move like a novice. Either the enemy CO was an idiot or he was up to something, but what? She refused to believe he was an idiot. The Pashtali had been in space well before the human race had discovered fire. And they couldn't afford to lose. They wouldn't have put a known idiot in command of their fleet...

The display sparkled with red icons. "Admiral," Olson snapped, as alarms started to howl. "Enemy ships, coming through the crossroads!"

Shit, Naomi thought. She saw her own mistake now, too late. Her inexperience had cost her dearly. *We flew right into a trap!*

CHAPTER TWENTY-FIVE

ESS DAUNTLESS, P-39

"ADMIRAL." OLSON SOUNDED as if he were reading a list of the dead. "I'm picking up at least forty capital warships, emerging from the crossroads."

Naomi felt a flicker of panic, which she squashed ruthlessly. She'd made a deadly mistake—she'd assumed the fleet behind her was *everything* the Pashtali could scrape up—and now it was going to cost her. The enemy had played their cards well. They'd forced her into a position where she would have to either force her way through the newcomers, bleeding her fleet white in the process, or break off and let them drive her into interstellar space. If she'd had *Crossroads* with her...

They'd have blown her away first, she thought, numbly. *Instead, she might just escape while the rest of us get blown away instead.*

She cursed under her breath. Her fleet's inexperience—*her* inexperience—had gotten them killed. She was going to lose hundreds of ships and thousands of spacers—and so were her allies. The alliance was going to die with her ships and humanity was going to lose the war and...a thought crossed her mind. It was going to be tight. Very tight. But it might just work. Might.

"Signal the fleet," she ordered. "All missile-armed ships are to fire on Enemy Two. Launch every missile we can. Then we alter course"—she drew out a vector on her console—"as quickly as possible."

"Aye, Admiral," Olson said. "But they'll run us down."

"If they have time," Naomi said. "If they have time."

"They will have time," Observer Salix said. He sounded as calm as a man ordering dinner, not someone facing certain death. "Do you not want to consider surrender?"

Naomi swallowed the sharp response that came to mind. "There's no point," she said. The Pashtali had never been very kind to prisoners. Observer Salix might be safe—the Alphans wouldn't be pleased if he was killed—but everyone else would be lucky if they were just dumped on a barely-habitable world and told to turn it into a paradise or else. It was more likely they'd simply be murdered. The Galactics probably wouldn't bother to do more than file a token protest. "They won't accept surrender."

She glanced at her communications operator. "Signal *James Bond*," she ordered. "She is to contact *Crossroads* as quickly as possible, with the following orders..."

Observer Salix listened quietly, then leaned forward. "Do you think you can survive long enough to make it work?"

"It's all or nothing," Naomi agreed. "But the other options are worse."

Dauntless shuddered as she unleashed a full broadside, the remainder of the fleet following suit. The Pashtali returned fire a moment later, their missiles lancing towards her fleet. Naomi gritted her teeth as their point defence datanet came to life, binding their ships together into a single entity. The datanet was good, better than hers. She cursed as hundreds of missiles vanished, while a handful of surviving missiles punched through the Pashtali defences and slammed into their hulls. A number of ships exploded. A handful more simply vanished.

Decoy drones, she thought, dispassionately. *They're better than we thought.*

She braced herself as the enemy missiles targeted her ships. They'd been rumoured to be second only to the Alphans, she recalled, and it looked as though the rumours were true. The enemy missiles refused to be drawn onto the decoys...worse, they evaded her point defence as they closed the range. She swore out loud as more damage started to mount up...she realised, numbly, what the enemy starfighters had been doing. They'd weakened her defences before the enemy sprang their trap.

Good thinking on their part, she admitted, sourly. *They had us completely fooled.*

The thought taunted her as the fleet slowly turned away and picked up speed. She'd made a huge mistake and a great many of her subordinates were about to die for it, even if her plan worked. It was quite possible *she* would die for it...she pushed that thought out of her mind and concentrated on the display. The Pashtali seemed surprised she hadn't rushed to the crossroads, blasting through the blockade despite the certainty of losing much of her fleet. Did they think she was planning to double back once their fleets united and gave chase? It was unlikely. As long as they were between her and the crossroads, they'd tear her to shreds if she tried.

"Admiral," Olson said. "Commodore Macarthur suggests we retreat to Crossroads One."

"Enemy One will keep themselves between us and the crossroads," Naomi said. The Pashtali weren't likely to let her escape through the *other* crossroads, not now their trap had been sprung. "But angle us as if we're planning to race to the crossroads. Let them think we have nothing better in mind."

"Aye, Admiral," Olson said.

"They won't underestimate you again," Observer Salix said. "This isn't an attempt to drive you out of their space. This is an attempt to destroy you."

"Yes," Naomi agreed, biting down the urge to point out that was blindingly obvious. She raised her voice. "Signal the carriers. I want a third of our starfighters configured for antishipping strikes, then directed to slow the enemy fleet as much as possible. Make it clear I want cripples, not kills."

"Aye, Admiral," Olson said.

Naomi's thoughts hardened as she concentrated. Observer Salix was right. The Pashtali were unlikely to underestimate the human race a second time. The Galactics tended to look down their noses at races that hadn't developed spacefaring technology for themselves, assuming their clients considered GalTech nothing more than magic spells that defied rational explanations. They weren't entirely wrong—there were scavenger races that used tech they literally didn't understand—but humans had been studying alien tech since the original Alphan invasion. It might be advanced—there was no doubt about it—yet it wasn't magic. It could be beaten.

And just because we don't know how to produce it doesn't mean we don't know how to use it, she thought. The flicker of hope was growing into a fire. *If they give us just enough time...*

The enemy fleet picked up speed, moving with a ponderous inevitability. It didn't seem worried by the human starfighters buzzing through its formation, although its point defence killed a bunch of them before the remainder could close on their targets and salvo their missiles into the enemy drives. It went against the grain to cripple, rather than kill, the starships, but there was no choice. If they didn't escape today, it didn't matter what happened tomorrow.

"Deploy mines," she added, as the two fleets continued to converge. "Slow them down as much as possible."

"They'll have no trouble avoiding the mines," Observer Salix pointed out. "This isn't a crossroads."

"Yes, but they'll still have to evade them," Naomi countered. "And every time they do it they'll give us a few more seconds."

She scowled as she studied the starchart, silently assessing the enemy plan. It was incredibly difficult, even for the Alphans, to coordinate a battle across interstellar distances. The Pashtali had been lucky to make their ambush work...in hindsight, she thought they might have been smarter to mine the crossroads and then close in to finish off the remains of her fleet. But that wouldn't have been so public...

And they did one hell of a lot of damage, even if they just let us go now, she told herself, grimly. *They caught us with our pants down and forced us to run.*

"Signal from *James Bond*," Olson said. "They're making transit now."

"Good," Naomi said. She allowed herself a moment of relief. *James Bond* wasn't a proper stealth ship. She'd feared the Pashtali wouldn't allow her to make transit—or simply realise they'd seen the same ship several times before and blow her away. "And now we wait."

• • •

Observer Salix was not pleased.

The fact the Pashtali had carried out an ambush was disconcerting. It was hardly the first ambush they'd carried out during the war—they'd started the war with an ambush—but they'd managed to predict the fleet's course and get into position without the humans realising they'd flown into a trap. He had to admit, at least to himself, that the ambush might have snared a warcruiser formation just as effectively, if not more so. It was a grim reminder that the Pashtali had advanced more than the Alphans had realised, in the years since the Lupine Wars. They might be more of a threat than his people wanted to admit.

And I might die on this ship, unable to report home, he thought. The human plan was a sound one—on paper—but there were too many holes for his peace of mind. Too much could go wrong...the human admiral had missed a trap and she might be flying straight into another one. *That would be bad.*

He kept his face impassive with an effort. There was no way to be *sure* the Pashtali would return him to his own people, if they took him prisoner. They might simply take him to a hidden lab and dissect him, taking his body to pieces bit by bit to unlock secrets his race had kept carefully hidden. Who knew what they could do, if they gained access to his genetic code and the details of gene-engineered improvements spliced into his DNA over the years?

The development of targeted viruses is forbidden, he reflected. *But they've already shown a frightening lack of concern for galactic law.*

His eyes sought out the light codes on the display. The alien ships were keeping pace with the human starships, unwilling to break free and abandon their allies. *That* was impressive. Observer Salix had to admit the humans had done well, when they'd forged their alliance...normally, in galactic history, alliances lasted as long as they were convenient and not a moment longer. But then, the Pashtali had made it clear they weren't interested in anything other than total domination. They would have been wiser, he reflected, to try to split the alliance.

It would have made them look weaker in the short term, he reflected. *But in the long term it would have served them well.*

"Admiral, the enemy fleet is evading the mines," the little human said. "I don't think any of their ships were hit."

A desperate tactic, Observer Salix noted. There'd been no time to lay a proper minefield and then lure the enemy onto it and even if there had been, the odds of catching the enemy fleet were very low. Minefields were only really effective at crossroads and threadlines, which was partly why they were banned. *But if it slowed the enemy down a little...*

He braced himself. The Pashtali were still picking up speed. There was something slow and steady about their acceleration curves, suggesting they weren't in any hurry to run the humans to ground. It wasn't unexpected. There was no *need* to risk burning out their drives. The humans had nowhere to run...unless, he supposed, there was an uncharted crossroads on the edge of the system. It was possible, but unlikely. The Pashtali had certainly had ample time to survey the system for additional crossroads.

And they wouldn't have been shy about telling everyone, if they'd found one, he reflected, wryly. There was nothing to be gained from keeping a crossroads secret, certainly not one so far from their homeworlds. *They could have collected a fee from every ship that wanted to use it.*

He sat down and waited. There was nothing else he could do.

• • •

"Admiral, we're coming up on Point Sisko now," Olson said. "So far, no change."

Naomi nodded. She felt as if she'd passed through tiredness and entered a whole new realm of exhaustion. Her body was fizzing, drunk on fatigue poisons and stimulants she would normally have banned...she hoped the plan worked before her body ran out of endurance and collapsed. The Pashtali were picking away at the human fleet, sniping at their defences and trying to get starfighters into position to take out sensors, weapons and drives. She'd lost track of how many ships had fallen out of formation, only to be blown away by enemy missiles. She thought a handful of cloaked ships had made their escape—she'd cut them loose, using decoys to hide their absence- but it was impossible to be sure. They might end up being the only survivors of her fleet.

The timing is too tight, she thought. The Pashtali had taken a risk—and she was taking a greater one. She'd had to make up the plan on the fly. *This could go badly wrong...*

Alerts flashed up on her display. The Pashtali were shooting her ships to pieces. She could repair some of the damage, perhaps all of it, if she had time...she didn't. The enemy were forcing her to wear out her drives, putting enough wear and tear on her systems—and her crews—that her entire fleet was likely to come apart sooner rather than later. It was the downside of how they'd taken ships from a dozen race, she supposed; the refits were alarmingly fragile, when the enemy started pouring on the pressure. The purpose-built ships were doing better, but they were still suffering. She silently blessed the techs who'd worked so many backups into the system. The fleet would have shattered by now if they hadn't built so much redundancy into the network.

"Admiral," Olson said. "The crossroads is opening!"

Naomi allowed herself a flash of relief. "Contact the fleet," she ordered. They'd made it! Barely. "All starships are to fire one final broadside at the alien fleet, then proceed through the crossroads as fast as possible."

"Aye, Admiral."

Dauntless shuddered as she unleashed her missiles one final time, then lunged into the crossroads. Naomi hoped—prayed—*Crossroads* could keep it open long enough to get the entire fleet into multispace, then slam the door shut before the enemy ships could give chase. The sudden appearance of the crossroads *had* to have shocked them. The Alphans hadn't tried to open a crossroads from multispace to allow a fleet to escape... they'd never even considered, as far as she knew, a tactic that involved having the generator on the wrong side of the crossroads. It might not be even possible, for them. The brute-force technique was inelegant, to say the least, but it did have its advantages.

We could rig up fixed crossroads generators to allow access to multispace, she mused, as the enemy fleet—too late—started to pick up speed. They'd clearly never considered the prospect of someone opening a door from the wrong side. *Why did they never think of it?*

"Admiral, *Crossroads* reports she is under immense strain," Olson said. "She can't keep the crossroads open for much longer."

"She is to keep the crossroads open as long as possible," Naomi ordered. The remainder of the fleet was powering through the vortex, gliding into multispace. "And then close..."

Dauntless shuddered. Naomi winced as, on the display, the crossroads started to twist in impossible directions before snapping out of existence. A starship was bisected by the closing crossroads, sliced in half so effortlessly...she felt sick, sick and tired. She didn't know how many ships remained on the wrong side of the crossroads, completely at the mercy of an enemy that had never showed any. Cold logic insisted she'd done the right thing—she'd preserved most of her fleet, including the allied vessels—but she still felt guilty. She should have been on the last ship out.

Admiral Glass would have scented the trap, she thought, morbidly. The nasty part of her mind wondered if her superiors would bother with a court-martial. She'd been so blind...they might just march her to the nearest airlock and toss her into vacuum. No, they'd want to make an example of her. She'd been promoted well outside her competence zone and it showed. *Admiral Glass would have known precisely what to do.*

She caught herself with an effort. The stimulants were wearing off. Her thoughts were wandering, as if she was drunk on duty...her lips quirked, wondering just how many charges could be crammed onto a court-martial assessment. Losing a battle *and* being drunk on duty? She had to fight to keep from giggling. It was just insane.

"Admiral." Olson looked as bad as she felt, if not worse. "The...ah, the fleet has completed its transit. Losses are..."

"Signal the fleet," Naomi ordered. She'd think about the losses later, about the men and women who'd died under her command, when her brain didn't feel as though it was full of mush. "The beta crews are to take the helms and proceed to a safe location, somewhere off the threadlines. The alpha crews are to report to their racks for a long rest."

Olson blinked. "Admiral?"

"Do it," Naomi said, curtly. If she was exhausted past the point of sanity, the rest of the crew wouldn't be any better. They'd be seeing things soon enough, if they weren't already. The beta crews could get the fleet somewhere safe, before the Pashtali worked out where they'd gone and gave chase. It wouldn't be easy to calculate the precise location in multispace that corresponded to their exit point in real space, but the Pashtali could do it. "Order them to lay mines as the fleet leaves. We might get lucky."

"Aye, Captain," Olson said. "I..."

"Pass command to Commodore Foxe, then go get some rest yourself," Naomi ordered. She stood on wobbly legs. It felt as if it would be a minor miracle if she got to her sofa before she collapsed. She wanted to sleep and never wake up. "And that's an order."

"Aye, Admiral."

CHAPTER TWENTY-SIX

ESS DAUNTLESS, MULTISPACE

"HOW BAD IS IT?"

Naomi rubbed her forehead. She'd slept for hours, then awoken briefly to eat and drink something before going back to sleep and she still felt tired. The stimulants were taking longer than they should to leave her body—she'd simply taken too many– and it was all she could do to keep herself from going to sickbay and demanding more. The doctors should say no, if she asked, but would they? She cursed the drugs under her breath. There were medical treatments to counter the physical effects, as someone came off the drugs, but the mental effects were much harder to handle. She'd be yearning for the drugs for days and weeks before she finally returned to normal.

And there's no time to go on leave, she reflected, sipping her coffee. It tasted foul. She wasn't sure if that was a side effect of the drugs or a simple reflection of how much she'd drunk in the last few hours. Her stomach churned unpleasantly. *I'm just going to have to hope I can handle the withdrawal.*

She took a breath. "It isn't good," she said, with masterful understatement. "We lost a bunch of ships, along with their crews, and several more are damaged beyond immediate repair. We can't fix them without a shipyard, so we'll have to turn them into suicide runners if we can get them to our next target."

Her head spun. Who'd have thought the *Pashtali* would take such a risk? They could have played it safe...instead, they'd split their fleet—a big no-no, according to all the tactical manuals—and tried to mousetrap her. They'd timed it perfectly...she wondered how they'd done it, then scowled as she realised the answer. Humans weren't the only ones who could send seemingly innocuous messages over the FTL network. The Pashtali had probably done the same, using alien codes in hopes the messages would pass unnoticed. She made a mental note to get the analysts to go through the records, in hopes of picking out the messages, before deciding it would probably be futile. There were a *lot* of messages and, with a little care, the senders could make sure it looked about as harmless as the rest.

And we can't start blowing up transmitters either, she reminded herself. *That would get everyone mad at us.*

"We lost the battle," she conceded. "But we didn't lose the war."

"That's good to hear," Nancy Middleton said. The ambassador sipped her coffee. If she thought it was unpleasant, it didn't show on her face. "What are we going to do now?"

"I suppose the real question is this," Naomi said. "Are our allies going to stick with us?"

"Good question," Nancy agreed. "I believe so, but it is hard to be sure."

Naomi nodded, curtly. The Pashtali would demand Terminus, as the price for allowing the allies to withdraw from the war, but the allies would be reluctant to give up the bottleneck system. The Pashtali would have no trouble breaking up the alliance, if they controlled Terminus, and then teaching the lesser races a lesson one by one. It was unlikely the Pashtali would settle for anything less...she keyed the display, bringing up the starchart. They might try to secure the systems on the near side of the bottleneck, but it wouldn't give them the edge they sought. No, the allies would remain allies...

Unless they think our doom is certain, she thought, coldly. *If they think they'll be beaten, they'll sell out for the best terms they can get.*

She wondered, morbidly, what *she* would do, if she was in their place. Would she accept defeat and sell out her allies, or would she fight to the last? She wanted to fight—she hated the idea of simply giving in and rolling over—but would it be worth the cost? If there was no hope of victory...she scowled as she studied the display. What would she do, if the choice was between surrender or total annihilation? Would she surrender or would she fight to the last?

If it was just me at stake, I would fight, she told herself. *But if it was the entire human race...*

The thought haunted her. She couldn't comprehend, not really, how many humans there were. Hell, no one knew for sure. There were humans who'd settled in the Alphan Empire and humans who'd migrated to isolated colonies or headed far beyond the rim of explored space, but...there were over fifteen *billion* humans in human space. She couldn't grasp the numbers...they were her parents and siblings, her friends and families, her fellow naval personnel and everyone else and if they were all going to die...She'd wondered, years ago, why the human governments had surrendered so quickly, when Earth had been invaded by the Alphans. She knew now. The situation had been hopeless, with the entire planet and its population at stake.

Nancy cleared her throat, drawing Naomi's attention back to her. "I will speak to them, as they repair their own ships," she said. "Do you have anything you wish me to tell them?"

"We lost the battle, but we didn't lose the war," Naomi said. "We'll make repairs, then we'll resume the offensive."

If they don't find us first, her thoughts added. It should be impossible. The fleet had moved away from the crossroads and threadline. Her worst-case estimate suggested it would take at least a day—more likely three—for the Pashtali to reach the point they'd entered multispace and the fleet simply wasn't there. *But if they bring up a crossroads generator of their own...*

She put the thought out of her head and leaned forward. "We have to retake the offensive as quickly as possible, both for our own morale and for the good of our allies," she said. "And we also need to send messages to Earth."

"I dare say our allies want to do the same," Nancy said, dryly. "Can they?"

"Once we complete our repairs, yes," Naomi said. "Frankly, even sending a courier to the nearest system would risk detection. We don't want to give them another shot at us."

"Of course not," Nancy agreed. "Can you guarantee a victory?"

"No," Naomi said. She stared at her fingers. "But I do intend to pick a target that cannot hope to stop us."

How sporting, her thoughts mocked. She shook her head sourly. *It wasn't as if they ever gave us a sporting chance.*

"If you can find such a target," Nancy said. "Is there one?"

"Yes," Naomi said. "The majority of the star systems on the edge of their territory are poorly defended. They probably denuded them of starships and starfighters to reinforce the fleet they aimed at us. The real problem is finding one that is significant enough to hurt them, without risking a major clash with their fleet. I'll give the matter some thought."

"And get some more rest too," Nancy told her. She smiled, rather wanly. "If I'm allowed to give you orders, that's an order."

Naomi's lips twitched. "Naval regulations are rather vague on the matter," she said. On one hand, Nancy Middleton was a guest onboard *Dauntless*; on the other, as a roving ambassador, she had some authority as well as connections at home. She didn't have command—there was no way she could—but it would be a foolish officer who didn't at least pretend to take her concerns into account. "I will try to get some rest when I have a chance."

"Go now," Nancy advised. "You don't have anything to do for a while, do you?"

Naomi scowled. The ambassador was right and yet, she felt she should be doing *something*. She hadn't been an admiral long enough to forget that flag officers touring damaged ships tended to get in the way more than anything else, but she *wanted* to walk the decks and try to convince the crews the fight was far from over. The Solar Navy had been in tight spots before when the war had started. A flash of *déjà vu* ran through her. They'd been forced to hide in multispace when the Pashtali had jumped the fleet, starting the war...

And we had a survey ship with us, one capable of locating an unexplored threadline, she thought, grimly. *We don't this time.*

"There's plenty of things I need to do," she said. "But..."

"They can wait," Nancy told her. "Go rest. You won't be any good to us if you start seeing things while you're on duty."

The intercom bleeped. "Admiral," Olson said. "I have the latest reports for you."

"Bring them in," Naomi ordered. She looked at Nancy. "You go reassure our allies. I'll rest as soon as I can."

"Good." Nancy stood. "And if you need a sympathetic ear, I'm here."

Naomi nodded, although she knew she wouldn't take the ambassador up on the offer. She didn't have *anyone* she could talk to, no one who wasn't under her command. She thought she understood, now, why there'd been commanding officers who'd brought their civilian partners on deployment with them. They could go back to their cabins and confide in their partners, discussing their fears and weaknesses in a way they never could with their subordinates. Naomi had never liked the practice—she'd had quite enough of civilians who thought they shared their partner's rank—but she was starting to understand it now. In hindsight, perhaps she should have found someone...

It was too late, the day the war broke out, she thought. *And now it would be pretty much impossible even if we were back at Sol.*

The hatch hissed open. Nancy stepped aside to allow Olson to enter, then left. The hatch closed behind her. Naomi allowed herself a moment of relief—Nancy had more common sense than most civilians, human or alien—and then pointed her aide to the seat Nancy had vacated. Olson looked ghastly; his face pale, dark bags under his eyes, a faint sheen of sweat on his forehead...Naomi hoped, grimly, that he'd had the sense to ensure his backup checked his work. It wasn't easy for anyone to admit their work might be flawed, but it had to be done. The alpha crews were so tired they were already making mistakes.

"Admiral," Olson said. "I received the latest set of updates. Repair efforts are well underway. We think some ships on the scrapped list can be repaired, if we cannibalise parts and weapons from the remaining ships; there shouldn't be any problem in crewing them, as we'll be taking crewmen from the scrapped vessels and distributing them around the fleet."

He paused. "The SAR sweep has also been completed," he added, passing her a datapad. "We have a final total of four thousand, three hundred and seventy crewmen dead, injured, or simply missing and presumed dead."

"Over four thousand," Naomi muttered. "Shit."

She scowled at the datapad without seeing it. The Solar Navy wasn't *that* big. They couldn't afford to lose so many trained men, not in a single battle. She tried to tell herself that the missing spacers had been captured by the enemy, that they'd be recovered through prisoner exchanges after the war, but she knew better. The Pashtali hadn't had much of a chance to take prisoners, even if they wanted to. The missing crewmen were almost certainly dead. She wondered, grimly, how many of the injured would follow them into the grave. The fleet's medical facilities had been pushed to breaking point. Even a comparatively minor injury, something that could be easily handled in a planetside medical centre, would be fatal if it wasn't treated in time.

"Yes, Admiral," Olson said. "There's...ah...there's also a report from *Crossroads*. She's lost two of her four gravity generators. Her CO reports she can no longer produce a reliable crossroads on demand."

"They told us she wouldn't last forever," Naomi mused. She looked up at him. "What *can* they do?"

"Produce gravity pulses, apparently," Olson said. "Her CO requests permission to leave the fleet and return home."

"Denied," Naomi said. "We can't repair her, even if she goes home."

"I don't think so," Olson agreed. "The gravity generators are incredibly fragile. Once they started to fail, they triggered a chain reaction that tore the entire structure apart. Realistically, we should have been servicing the generators every time we used them. The CO seemed a little surprised we managed to get them as far as we did."

"We'll keep her with us, for the moment," Naomi said. An idea crossed her sleep-deprived mind but refused to come into focus. "If nothing else, the Pashtali will want to retake her intact. We can use her as bait in a trap."

"Yes, Admiral," Olson said. He took a breath. "The repair crews think the majority of the work can be completed in a week. They did caution they may run into problems they cannot easily solve or run short of spare parts as well as manpower and expertise, but most of the damage can be repaired fairly quickly. The ships we believe to beyond repair, of course, are a different story."

"We need to focus on the smaller repairs first," Naomi said. She liked the idea of salvaging the badly damaged vessels, but she doubted it was possible. "The ships that are beyond easy repair will have to be put aside, at least for the moment."

"Aye, Admiral," Olson said. His face took on the indefinable air of a man who knew he was about to deliver bad news, the kind of news that wouldn't be well-received. "The downside, however, is that we are currently cut off from the fleet train and the stockpiles we set up at Terminus, which means we will almost certainly run out of supplies. The repair officers want to call the fleet train here, so we can make use of their supplies..."

"Which runs the risk of the enemy shadowing the fleet train to our current location," Naomi mused. She'd worked hard to keep the exact location of the fleet train a secret, ordering the freighters to remain cloaked and to give any possible enemy contacts a wide berth, but she had a new respect for the Pashtali. If they spotted the fleet train, they'd do everything in their power to destroy it. "I think we'd be better off linking up with the fleet train as we take the offensive again."

"Yes, Admiral," Olson said. He was too tired to conceal his concern. "When do you intend to take the offensive?"

"As soon as the fleet is ready to go," Naomi told him. "We don't have time to waste."

She sighed to herself. They hadn't been able to pick up any messages, but she'd bet good money that the Pashtali were telling the universe they'd beaten the human fleet. The longer the fleet remained in hiding, the harder it would be to regain momentum when they retook the offensive. Their allies might stick with them—Naomi certainly hoped so—but neutral powers might stay clear or start tipping towards supporting the Pashtali. And the Galactics might change their minds about sending escort vessels into their territory.

"Ask the tactical deck to start looking for possible targets," Naomi said. "We want to make an impact, without too much risk."

Olson looked decidedly unimpressed. Naomi hid her amusement. She'd have felt the same way, when she'd been a junior officer. There was no way to avoid risk. Even *trying* smacked of cowardice. And yet, what choice did they have? They had to avoid a major confrontation until they were ready. She could easily win a battle and lose the war if the victory was costly as hell…

"Aye, Admiral," he said, finally. "I'll see to it at once."

Naomi nodded. "And go get some sleep," she added. "That's an order."

"Aye, Admiral," Olson said, again. "I…"

He bit his lip. Naomi wondered, idly, if he was about to protest he was needed on the CIC or suggest that she too got some sleep. It didn't matter. She'd already had the lecture from Nancy Middleton and she would get some rest, as soon as she read the report from *Crossroads*. She trusted Olson to summarise the gist of the report, and not miss out any important details, but there might be something in the report she needed to read for herself. Who knew what else the captured ship could do?

"Dismissed," Naomi said. "Go rest."

Or find a partner and go to the privacy tubes, her thoughts added. *Or do something—anything—as long as it helps you rest.*

"Aye, Admiral," Olson said. "One final matter—when do you want to hold the funeral service?"

"Once we've completed the repairs," Naomi said. It went against the grain not to hold the funeral service as quickly as possible, but the fleet was in dire straits. The living came first. Always. They'd pay their respects to the dead later. "Right now, we have to focus on preparing to retake the offensive."

Olson stood. "Aye, Admiral."

I probably made that point a little too well, Naomi reflected, as Olson stepped through the hatch. *But it needs to be said.*

She sighed as she stood and made her way to the sofa. She'd rest for a few hours, to let her body recover, then go back to work. By then, hopefully, the tactical staff would have a few possible targets for her. If they found somewhere important...ideally, somewhere a little off the beaten track, somewhere the enemy wouldn't expect her. Travelling off the threadlines was a risk, but what wasn't? They needed to evade the enemy fleet until they were ready to face it.

The war is not over, she told herself firmly, as she lay down and closed her eyes. *We lost a battle. But we didn't lose the war.*

CHAPTER TWENTY-SEVEN

SOLAR CITY, EARTH

"THE INTERSTELLAR MEDIA IS DEMANDING answers, sir," Foreign Minister Richard Hawthorne said. "They want to hear our side of the story."

"And we have none to give." First Speaker Abraham Douglas looked at Admiral Danielle Morrígan. "We don't, do we?"

"No, sir," Admiral Morrígan said. "The Pashtali claim they met our fleet in battle and defeated it. We have no independent verification, naturally, and they have declined to provide any hard sensor data to either us or neutral powers. That's fairly common, unfortunately, but in this case it makes it impossible to verify what they're telling us."

"Of course," Abraham agreed, dryly. It was possible to fake anything, he'd been assured, from love letters to diplomatic notes designed to trigger off a war, but it was far from easy to fake a full-scale battle. It was difficult to fake hard sensor data—there would always be something a little *too* neat about faked data—yet very few powers would simply hand over raw data for analysis. It would tell their rivals too many things about their capabilities. "So we *know* nothing?"

"Yes, sir," Admiral Morrígan said. She paused, worrying her lower lip. "That said, the Pashtali are unlikely to lie outright. If they got caught in it, their credibility would be shot to hell. It would be an absolute gift to their enemies, including us. We assume, in the lack of any real data, that there was an engagement and we *didn't* come out on top."

Abraham felt ice gripping his heart. "And how *badly* did we lose?"

"The analysts think we lost the engagement, but it wasn't a total defeat," Admiral Morrígan said. "Assuming the Pashtali are telling the truth about the timing of the engagement, it's been a week. If they destroyed the entire fleet, or forced it to surrender, they would be parading the remains on all the news channels, or making Admiral Yagami recite prewritten speeches about human aggression and suchlike in front of the entire universe. They would have scored one hell of a propaganda victory, but they didn't. The analysts think the majority of their fleet escaped the trap."

"But they don't *know*," Abraham repeated. "Right?"

"No, sir," Admiral Morrígan said. "Like I said, we have no independent verification. We have been unable to determine if there were any neutral observers with hard sensor data on the scene, nor have we been able to make contact with the fleet. Our allies have also been unable to make contact with their squadrons. They know as little as us."

"Unless we believe everything the Pashtali are telling us," Abraham said. "What do the analysts make of their statements?"

"The Pashtali aren't offering any real specifics," Admiral Morrígan said. "That makes us think the battle took place, but that it wasn't a total defeat. They might be more willing to share hard sensor data if they thought there was no chance of anyone being able to make use of it, at least in the next few months. We may not know for sure until we get in touch with the fleet, or what remains of it."

She leaned forward. "Sir, the battle took place hundreds of light years away. It might be several weeks before we have *any* solid data."

"I see." Abraham was familiar with the realities of interstellar travel and communications—and how long it could take, at times, for reliable data to travel from one side of the explored galaxy to the other. "Richard, how do we stand with our allies?"

Hawthorne frowned. "The Terminus powers are still with us, from what they've said. They are in a poor position, strategically speaking, and the Pashtali don't seem willing to offer more than vague promises in exchange for them leaving the war or turning on us. From what we've heard, they want Terminus and they're prepared"—his voice turned scornful—"to pinkie-swear they won't take the rest of the star systems if they're allowed to keep the bottleneck. I don't buy it and nor do our allies. They're still massing their fleets to hold the bottleneck at all costs."

"Which may come back to bite them, if the Pashtali have a second *Crossroads*," Abraham observed. "Do they?"

"Unknown, sir," Admiral Morrígan said. "We assume they have more than one, but—as far as we can tell—they only sent one against us. We simply don't know."

"The first starship of a new class is always massively expensive," Martin Solomon commented. "The designs prove impractical, or need to be adjusted at short notice, or the early trials prove the ship needs extensive modifications before entering active service. Hell, we've had ships spring leaks in the hull because the designer had no practical experience and made a simple but potentially fatal mistake. The later ships are always cheaper because the bugs have been worked out of the design, and the construction crews know what they're doing. Our calculations about how much *Crossroads* cost the Pashtali might be accurate, for a given value of accurate, but they might be able to produce more later, for a cheaper price."

Abraham frowned. "Can you calculate how many more they might have?"

"No," Solomon said. "We just don't have the insight into their industrial base for anything more than wild-ass guessing. If we assume they intend to build *Crossroads*-class ships and nothing else, they'll be able to churn out somewhere around a hundred or so within the next five years.

However, that seems unlikely. My office thinks a more reasonable figure is five to ten ships of her class."

"Practically speaking, we didn't have a clue she existed until they jumped our fleet," Admiral Morrígan cautioned. "No one else knew, from what we have been able to determine. It's quite possible they have an isolated shipyard, either in one of their core systems or even somewhere in interstellar space and finding it will be difficult."

"Agreed," Solomon said. "There are just too many variables."

"I understand." Abraham looked at Hawthorne. "And the rest of our allies? And the neutral powers?"

"The Alphans have said nothing," Hawthorne said. "My office has asked their ambassador for any intelligence they might have, from the sector, but so far we haven't had any reply. The Galactics as a whole seem to be waiting to see what happens—they haven't backed down on their threats to escort ships through the edge of enemy territory, yet they haven't gone through with it either."

"The battle was only a week ago," Admiral Morrígan said. "They may have dispatched ships and we simply don't know about it, not yet."

"True," Hawthorne agreed. "But they would be keen to try to avoid a clash with the Pashtali. Or us."

He met Abraham's eyes. "The situation is still very much in flux, sir," he said. "The Pashtali are wobbling. Their grip on their empire and a number of crossroads and bottlenecks is looking shaky, and their problems are accelerating. The vultures are gathering, looking for ways to bite off chunks of their territory or even impose the right of free passage. The Pashtali have always been reluctant to allow free passage and free trade and, in doing so, they have made a lot of enemies. At the same time, they are still a major power. Their enemies may fall back if the Pashtali seem likely to win the war."

"Of course," Abraham agreed, sourly. "The strong do whatever they like and the weak suffer what they must."

"Yes, sir," Hawthorne said. "We are making progress. It is just very *slow* progress."

He shook his head. "There's been no change in their talks with us," he added, after a moment. "The script hasn't changed since the fleet departed. I don't think their representatives are aware of how things have gone. Frankly, I stand by my original conclusion. They're stalling to the point of absurdity. My guess is that they're not even *trying* to keep us talking, not any longer."

"It wouldn't be the first time one arm of the government lost track of what the other arms were doing," Abraham said. "Have they not tried to use the victory to pressure you and your representatives?"

"No, sir." Hawthorne grinned. "If I went by what was discussed in the sessions alone, I'd say there were neither victories nor defeats. Their reps don't seem aware of them. They just seem to be blindly following orders."

"Which could mean their government hasn't decided what to do," Abraham said. "Or that they're trying to determine how badly the defeat will weaken our position."

"The public is already aware that *something* has gone wrong," Jenny Geddes said. The Interior Minister scowled. "There's no way to block civilians from accessing interstellar news networks. Most of them aren't particularly trusted, not here, but enough are that word is starting to spread. We're getting hundreds of questions from families of military personnel and there's nothing we can do about that either. My office has been pushing the line of no independent verification, and I have staffers reminding people that the Pashtali have a long history of dishonesty, but I can't promise it will have any effect. We don't know enough to tell the world."

"We don't even know enough to lie," Henry Travis said. The Vice Speaker scowled at the display. "Assuming the fleet really was destroyed, or at least crippled, where do we stand?"

"We lose," Admiral Morrígan said, simply. "The best we could hope for, under the circumstances, would be becoming an Alphan Protectorate. Again. The worst...total occupation, perhaps even total extermination. The Pashtali have shown a frightening lack of regard for interstellar law and civilised norms, sir, and they might assume they can get away with attempted genocide. Some humans would survive, we think, but as nothing more than a scavenger race. We wouldn't be able to rebuild in a hurry."

Travis swallowed. "I see."

"There's no way to sugar-coat it," Admiral Morrígan said. "We staked everything on one roll of the dice. We are committed."

"And there's no way to back out, not without surrendering," Travis said. "Right?"

"Effectively so," Hawthorne agreed. "If we want a protector, we'll have to offer them more than goodwill."

"We also need to shore up our financial situation," Zoe Walker said. The Finance Minister looked around the table, her eyes grim. "We are dependent, right now, on loans from various interstellar powers. If it looks like we'll be unable to repay those loans, they'll start calling them in. And then the economy will be fucked."

"So we don't pay," Travis said. "We are in the middle of a war. We can refuse to hand over anything we need for our defence."

"Which will make it harder to get loans in the future," Zoe snapped. "The interstellar bankers rely on trust, sir, and confidence their debtors will repay them. If we refuse to pay our debts, or hand over the collateral, they will see us as a bad risk and then they'll simply decline to loan us anything more."

"We may not live another year," Travis said.

Abraham barely heard the argument. The stakes had already been high, but now they were stratospheric. There was no way to know what had *really* happened...he wished, suddenly, for verifiable data even if it proved that Admiral Yagami and her fleet had been blown to dust. At least he'd *know* what happened...right now, he and his team were faced with making policy blind, without any solid awareness of what had really happened to the fleet. The only good sign was that the Pashtali hadn't demanded their immediate surrender or else. It was a hint, at least, that Admiral Morrígan and her analysts were correct and the fleet had survived the engagement. But he dared not rely on it.

If they know how many ships we had, prior to the engagement, they'll know how big a chunk they tore out of our navy, he thought, numbly. *They might decide they can wage war on the rest of their neighbours first, then turn their attention back to us. We couldn't rebuild in time to meet them.*

"Mr. Speaker," Zoe said. "We have to pay our debts."

"And we will, if we can," Abraham said. "Remind the bankers that we may be all that is standing between their homeworlds and the Pashtali."

He knew, even as he spoke, it was unlikely to impress the bankers. Earth was a very minor power. The Terminus Powers were all lesser powers. They might be formidable, as a group, but the Galactics wouldn't be impressed. Not yet. They might not see Earth as a bulwark between them and a deadly enemy, but just another minor power that had defaulted on its loans and needed a spanking. To him, Earth was the centre of the universe. To them, Earth didn't even rate a mention.

We beat the Pashtali once, he reminded himself. *Too bad the rest of the galaxy only takes notice when it suits them.*

His bleeper chimed. "Sir," Rachel said. "Ambassador Yasuke requests an immediate interview with you. He's already on his way."

Abraham grimaced. The Alphans were normally sticklers for protocol. They weren't supposed to depart for diplomatic meetings until they *knew* there would be someone waiting for them...he couldn't recall, *ever*, a meeting that had been held with practically no notice at all. And yet...there was no point in trying to delay matters. If the Alphans thought the meeting was vital enough to dispense with protocol, they were probably right.

"We'll discuss the issues later," he said, standing. "For the moment, we'll maintain a strict *no comment* policy and, if pressed, note we're waiting for hard data."

He left the chamber, formally dismissing the meeting. There were no objections. His cabinet had grown up in a universe controlled by the Alphans. They *knew* how unusual it was for one to demand an urgent meeting. Abraham's mind churned as he made his way to the elevator and headed up to his office. It boded ill, he felt. If the Alphans withdrew their support, and the warcruisers protecting the system, Earth would be hopelessly vulnerable. All hopes of victory would go with them.

"He's landing at the pad now," Rachel said, as he left the elevator. "I'm having him escorted to the diplomatic chamber."

"Let's hope he's in an understanding mood," Abraham muttered. Ambassador Yasuke was more insightful and relaxed than most Alphans, but by human standards he was still incredibly prideful and quick to stand on his dignity. "Can you arrange for tea and biscuits?"

"Of course, sir," Rachel said. "Good luck."

Abraham tried not to show his concern too openly as he stepped into the room. Ambassador Yasuke was already being shown in through the opposite door, his escorts standing back to allow the door to close. Abraham groaned inwardly. Protocol demanded he stand to greet the alien ambassador, but it was too late for that. The meeting had been thrown together far too quickly for anyone's peace of mind.

"Ambassador," he said. His mind raced. Should he apologise? Or should he assume the alien would understand why protocols hadn't been followed? "Thank you for coming."

"Thank you," Yasuke said, as if he *hadn't* been the one to request the interview. "My government insisted I meet with you at once."

Abraham felt cold. "They did?"

"Yes." Yasuke held out a datachip. "Our...*sources*...within the Pashtali Empire were able to get some live footage of the recent engagement between your fleet and theirs. It was a defeat, I am sorry to say, but not a total one. Your admiral was able to break contact and escape into multispace."

"I..." Abraham found himself at a loss for words as he took the chip. "I...on behalf of my government, I thank you."

"You are welcome," Yasuke said. "I'm afraid that certain details were removed from the footage, but enough remains—we hope—for you to verify it."

"We understand," Abraham said. The Alphans had spies within

Pashtali space? It wasn't really a surprise—every government worthy of the name had sources everywhere they could—but...he had the odd feeling he was missing something. "My analysts will study the footage as soon as possible."

Yasuke bowed his head, a polite acknowledgement. "My government has also asked me to inform you that they intend to continue supporting your war effort, through both a minor military deployment and open lines of credit. We have attempted to discuss a possible peace with the Pashtali, but they have refused to make any concessions at all, either to you or your allies. We believe they think the war is far from lost."

"They may be right," Abraham said. "Is your government willing to provide military support?"

"Not as yet," Yasuke said. "Perhaps not ever."

Abraham nodded, concealing his annoyance. The Pashtali would back down, wouldn't they, if the Alphans threatened to cross the border and join the war? They'd have to be insane to pick a fight with the Alphans, as well as the other Great Powers. Earth couldn't convince the major powers to join the war, but the Alphans could...right? But he knew better than to expect it. The Alphans had taken heavy losses in the last war. They didn't want to get into another one, not if it could be avoided.

Nor do we, he thought.

"We understand," he said. The Alphans wanted a buffer state between their empire and the Pashtali, not a war fought out to the finish. "And again, we thank you."

"We will discuss other matters later," Yasuke said. He stood and bowed, then retreated to the door. "For the moment, we wish you well."

"And you," Abraham said. "Your escorts will take you back to your aircar."

Abraham stared at the datachip as the alien ambassador stepped out. Hard data...it was what they needed. He doubted the Alphans would provide faked data and it would be easily disproven when the analysts went to work. And yet...he was sure they were missing something. But what?

CHAPTER TWENTY-EIGHT

ESS DAUNTLESS, P-23

OBSERVER SALIX WOULD NEVER have admitted it, certainly not to his hosts, but he found human adaptability more than a little disconcerting. The humans had taken one hell of a beating and yet, after a week of hard work, were ready to return to the fight. There was no way his own people could have matched it, he conceded ruefully. It wasn't just that their ships were harder to repair without a shipyard—that could be changed, now they *knew* their ships could be damaged—but...it was a zest for life, a willingness to innovate that his people had lost long ago. Half the repairs were patchwork messes that should not work, yet did. The ships were ready and raring to go. And their crews seemed to feel the same way.

It was perplexing. The humans had been beaten. They'd lost dozens of ships and thousands of crewmen. Their morale had started to plummet, then steadied and slowly started to climb again. They'd buried their dead, launching the bodies into multispace with due honours, before returning to their duties with a grim determination to continue the war. There was no way to be sure, of course, but Salix was entirely confident that the Pashtali had yet to repair their damaged ships. They might not even have started. If that was the case...

He stood on the human CIC, watching as the fleet emerged from the crossroads under cloak and headed into the transit system. P-23 was little more than a lone star and a handful of asteroids—hardly worthy of any real attention, although two had been turned into free-floating habitats—but there were five crossroads that allowed the system to be used as a transit point. He was mildly surprised the Pashtali had bothered to settle the asteroids, although he suspected they were just trying to make sure no one disputed their claim to the system. It might have been a waste of time, a few centuries ago, but now...he shook his head. The system was too deeply within their empire for anyone else to take and hold it for long. He honestly wasn't sure if Admiral Yagami was doing the right thing.

But it will poke them in the eye, he thought, coldly. The human analysts insisted the mere presence of their fleet, sitting in P-23, would force the Pashtali to respond. Salix couldn't disagree with their logic, even though he doubted the system could be held. If there'd been a set of bottlenecks, the humans could have bled the Pashtali, but the crossroads were all too large to be effectively mined. *They'll scramble and throw the humans back into multispace and then...what?*

His lips twitched. The fleet had picked up a handful of signals as it popped in and out of realspace, confirming that the galaxy was doing the equivalent of holding its breath, waiting to see what happened. The Pashtali had been telling everyone they'd won a great victory, but no one seemed to believe them. They had a poor reputation for telling the truth, although—in this case—their claims were generally accurate. Earth had confirmed there'd been a battle, but not said anything beyond that. Salix suspected it was the smartest thing they could do.

"Admiral," the little human said. "We are reaching Point Gudrun."

"Good," Admiral Yagami said. "Deploy the stealthed probes, then hold us here."

"Aye, Admiral," the human said.

Salix glanced at the human admiral. "Do you not fear detection?"

"The only active sensors in the system are orbiting the habitats,"

Admiral Yagami said, calmly. "We'll stay well clear of them as long as possible. They have no mobile units patrolling the system, so we should be safe enough."

They could have the entire system riddled with passive sensor platforms, Salix thought. He didn't bother to say it out loud. The human knew it as well as he did. There was no way to spot a passive platform, save by bringing up active sensors and that would advertise their presence to the entire system. *They'll just have to hope they remain undetected until they reveal themselves.*

He sat down and forced himself to wait. P-23 wasn't particularly important or well-defended—the humans could destroy the habitats pretty much effortlessly, if they were willing to commit butchery—but it was just a matter of time until a major convoy passed through the system. The Pashtali were straining every sinew to reinforce their outer systems, tightening their defences at bottleneck systems and preparing logistics for a renewed push against Earth or Terminus. Admiral Yagami had calculated the fleet would have a good shot at capturing, or blowing away, the next convoy. They couldn't hold the system, but they could force the Pashtali to respond to their provocation. And who knew what would happen then?

"A shame we don't have any updated convoy details," Admiral Yagami observed. "Do you have any intelligence reports you haven't shared with us?"

It took Salix a moment to realise he was being teased. "No," he said, concealing his annoyance. Humans were flippant when his people took refuge in stiff formality. "If I knew such details, I would not have been assigned to your ship."

The human took no visible offense. "It would be useful to have an agreement on interstellar free trade," she said. "You know, one that was actually enforced."

"It was not easy to come up with the agreements we have," Salix said. "And no government is willing to commit itself completely to..."

The console chimed. "Admiral, we have multiple ships transiting

Crossroads Two," the little human interrupted. "Half of them appear to be Pashtali freighters."

And more coming all the time, Salix noted. The Pashtali convoy was huge. *They really are desperate, aren't they?*

"Plot an intercept course," Admiral Yagami ordered. "Where are they heading?"

"Looks like Crossroads Five," the human said. "I'd say they're heading to Terminus."

"Or their nearest base to the bottleneck," Salix said. "Can you take the escorts?"

Admiral Yagami smiled, coldly. "Oh, yes."

• • •

Naomi had feared the worst, even though the fleet had stayed well away from surveyed threadlines as it made its way to P-23. The system was impossible to defend and yet its central location suggested the Pashtali would be wise to station a major fleet in the system, where it could respond to threats in any of the adjoining systems. She had very little hard data on what was actually stationed in the system and much of it was so outdated she suspected she'd be better off without it. But they'd entered the system to discover it was emptier than she'd expected. The Pashtali had probably withdrawn the defending ships so they could join the fleet that had jumped her earlier.

And they probably want to tempt us into attacking the habitats, she thought. *If we did, we'd lose galactic sympathy in a heartbeat.*

She smiled, coldly, as the enemy convoy took on shape and form. Seventy freighters—more freighters than Earth had ever risked in a single convoy—escorted by over thirty warships of varying size. It was unlikely pirates would pose any real threat to the escorts—pirates tended to be wary of tangling with warships—but there were quite a few races eying Pashtali space and wondering what they could snatch while the former owners were concentrating on the human threat. The Pashtali needed to make it clear they were in control, before it was too late. She was about to show the galaxy they were not.

"We'll be in optimal firing range in thirty minutes," Olson reported. "The fleet is ready to engage."

"Target the escorts," Naomi ordered, coolly. "We'll give the freighters a chance to surrender."

She glanced at the starchart, her mind churning. The settlements would signal the enemy fleet, the moment the convoy came under attack. How long would she have to loot the freighters before enemy reinforcements arrived? It was impossible to know. The closest enemy systems were only a few hours away, but would they have anything to send? How many ships had the enemy pulled from their regular duties and combined into their fleet? Hell, where *was* the fleet? She hadn't seen it since the last engagement. And she *knew* she hadn't done anything like enough damage to render the fleet unfit for battle.

Her heart pounded as the seconds ticked away. P-23 was the ideal system for an ambush—there were five possible escape routes, none of which could be barred to her—but the Pashtali knew it. They must have thought about it. And that meant...did they think she might take the risk of going further into their space? She had no idea, but they'd already surprised her once. And that meant...

They are not gods, she told herself, severely. *And they cannot adjust the realities of interstellar warfare on command.*

"Admiral," Olson said. "The escorts are closing on us. They'll be within detection range in ten minutes at most."

"And they might spot us earlier," Naomi agreed. There were some races that regarded escort duties as dishonourable, and only assigned such missions to the dregs of their militaries, but the Pashtali didn't seem to share that attitude. The odds were good they'd spot something and growing higher with every passing second. "Fire the moment they spot us."

"Aye, Admiral."

Naomi kept her eyes on the display, silently betting with herself when detection would become inevitable. The enemy sensors were supposed to be good...good enough to spot a fleet of cloaked ships? The range was ticking down rapidly. The fleet was barely moving, doing nothing more than station-keeping, but...

The display flashed red. "They saw us," Olson reported. "Firing...*now*!"

Dauntless shuddered as she unleashed a full broadside. The enemy escorts didn't hesitate. Their point defence came online with alarming speed, even as they struggled to form a defensive wall between the raiders and their charges. Naomi was morbidly impressed as more and more of her ships wobbled out of cloak and opened fire, launching a tidal wave of missiles at the enemy ships. Some might escape, if they turned and fled before the range closed. But they'd have to abandon the freighters to their fate.

"Their point defence network is alarmingly good," Observer Salix commented. "They are taking down too many missiles."

Naomi nodded, curtly. It didn't matter. She'd fired so many missiles that *some* were bound to get through the defences, each hit weakening the enemy position and making it more likely the next missile would get through too. The enemy barely managed to fire back a handful of missiles—none of which made it through her point defence—before she wiped out the escorting warships. None tried to flee. Naomi wondered, idly, if they were brave or foolish. She'd brought so much firepower to the engagement the outcome had been practically predetermined.

"Admiral," Olson said. "The last of the warships has been destroyed."

"Signal the freighters," Naomi said. They looked a little confused, some trying to stand their ground while others were backing off...not, she was sure, that they had much chance of getting out of range before it was too late. Freighters handled like wallowing pigs at the best of times. There was no way they could escape her ships, even if they scattered. They'd left it too late. "Inform them that this is their one chance to surrender or be destroyed."

She braced herself, unsure what to expect. If the freighters surrendered, she could capture and loot them; if they refused, she could legally blow them away. And yet, she wasn't sure if she had *time* to take possession of the freighters. How close were the enemy reinforcements? How long did she have?

"No answer, Admiral," Olson said.

Naomi gritted her teeth. The hell of it was that she understood the enemy position. Seventy freighters and their supplies were pocket change to the Pashtali—all the more so if the ships were crewed by their clients—while to her they were manna from heaven. She needed the supplies, or at least they thought they did. Blowing up their own ships to keep them from falling into her hands made one hell of a lot of sense...

"Signal the freighters," she said, tiredly. The Pashtali wouldn't care, but the rest of the galaxy might take note she'd tried to save the crews. "Inform the crews that they have five minutes to abandon ship, then their vessels will be destroyed."

"Aye, Admiral," Olson said. "I am..."

He broke off as the display flared with light. "They're charging us," he snapped. "Closing to ram!"

"Belay my last orders, fire at will," Naomi snapped. The enemy freighters were sluggish and normally they wouldn't have a hope of catching her ships, but her ships were practically unmoving. They didn't have time to reverse course and run. "Take the freighters down, now!"

She gritted her teeth as the fleet opened fire. The enemy freighters kept coming, shedding lifepods as they charged. She should have anticipated suicide tactics. They couldn't save the freighters and they wanted to prevent her from capturing the supplies, so why *not* turn them into suicide runners? She braced herself, watching as a trio of freighters vanished from the display. The remainder kept coming, suddenly more threatening than freighters had any right to be. She kept herself steady, watching the enemy lifepods fleeing in all directions. The nasty part of her mind wanted to fire on them, even though it was both uncivilised and against galactic law. She told that part of her mind to shut up. They had to avoid being branded as barbarians or they could forget about any support from the interstellar powers...

Interstellar powers that are willing to turn a blind eye to blatant rule-breaking, as long as the power breaking the rules is too strong to challenge, she thought bitterly. *What is the point of being a good little girl and following the rules if everyone else breaks them at will?*

The display cleared. Naomi felt a moment of relief, followed by irritation. The freighters had soaked up missiles she couldn't afford to lose, even though she intended to link up with the fleet train shortly and resupply. Who knew what she'd encounter, between P-23 and the RV point? She intended to travel off the threadlines as much as possible, but the enemy had surveyed the sector long ago. They might guess at her route and arrange a second ambush.

"Admiral," Olson said. "The last of the freighters has been destroyed."

"Signal the settlements," Naomi said. "Inform them we are departing the system and they can pick up the lifeboats at leisure. And then set course for Crossroads Four."

"Aye, Admiral," Olson said.

Observer Salix cleared his throat. "Would it not be wiser to head for Crossroads Five?"

"No," Naomi said. She was pleased with the brief engagement, enough not to be annoyed at his questioning. "We don't know where the enemy fleet went, after the last engagement, but if they want to intercept us here, they'd have to come through Crossroads Five. Four adds an extra four days to our journey, yet it will make it harder for them to intercept us and easier for us to evade them if they outguess us. It can be done."

She leaned back in her chair. "And besides, it will give us a chance to send a messenger ship to an independent FTL transmitter," she added. "We need to check in with Earth and determine our best course of action, once we resupply."

"The Pashtali should let you use their transmitters," Observer Salix said. It was hard to be sure, but Naomi thought he was being sarcastic. The observer was hardly a fool. He might be irritating, but he wasn't stupid or ignorant. "They signed various treaties..."

Naomi shrugged. They were too deep within enemy space to rely on access to enemy-controlled transmitters. The systems on the edge of the empire had to be kept open, unless the Pashtali really wanted to provoke an incident, but here? She shook her head. She was unwilling to risk even trying, for fear of telling the Pashtali something they desperately needed to know. If they figured out how to sift the human messages from the torrent of alien signals, they'd start blocking them before they could reach their destination.

She put the thought out of her mind as the fleet crossed the system, making sure to evade the settlements as much as possible. She'd gambled on an easy victory to restore her crew's morale and it had worked, although the suicide runners had been a nasty shock. Next time, she'd make a point of blowing away the freighters after a single warning. And after she resupplied…

We need to find a way to lure them into a fight on our terms, she thought. She had ideas, but none of them were gelling. Not yet. Once they were in multispace, she'd discuss the matter with the tactical analysts. They might come up with an idea she could put into practice before the Pashtali managed to capitalise on their victory. *The longer we trail our coat around their space, the greater the chance they'll run us down again. And the next time we won't be able to open a crossroads and run.*

She frowned. What if…?

The idea was vague. It might not work. The enemy would have to dance to her tune and any military officer worthy of the name knew a plan that depended on the enemy doing what you wanted was doomed to fail. There was a very real chance the enemy would simply refuse to take the bait. But if they did, it might end the war on human terms.

And if it doesn't, she told herself, *we'll still give them one hell of a fright.*

CHAPTER TWENTY-NINE

JAMES BOND, ANTIGEN SYSTEM

"THE PASHTALI MUST BE FUMING," Sarah observed. "Will you take a look at that!"

Thomas smirked. Antigen was a transit system on the edge of enemy space—only a handful of threadlines and crossroads from Terminus—and, right now, it was playing host to battle squadrons from a dozen different powers. His smile grew wider as his sensors spotted a convoy, heavily escorted by warships, gliding from a distant crossroads and heading straight for the planet. Sarah was right. The Pashtali, who technically ruled the system, had to be hopping mad. There was no way they could convince the other powers to remove their warships without threatening war and there were too many other powers involved to risk their threats turning into reality. The whole situation had become an uneasy stalemate. He wondered, idly, what the Pashtali intended to do about it.

They may just wait and hope it all blows over, he thought, as *James Bond* signalled her arrival to the local traffic control. *But the longer they allow those warships to remain there, the greater the chance they'll get to stay there permanently.*

He watched as more and more data flowed into his sensors. Antigen had always been surprisingly disorganised—the system had been settled by several different races, like Terminus, before the Pashtali had taken control—but right now it was borderline chaotic. Hundreds of starships—freighters as well as warships—cluttered up the system, taking advantage of the confusion to smuggle goods and weapons through the crossroads or directly to the planet or asteroid settlements. Earth had very limited intelligence on the planet's political makeup, but with so many subject races under enemy control it was clear *some* of them were looking for ways to escape or minimise Pashtali control. He didn't blame them for trying, even though they risked heavy repression. They'd never have a better chance to win their independence, or at least a better deal. The Pashtali couldn't bring reinforcements to the system without drawing in more warships from hostile powers.

"Picking up an acknowledgement from three different warships, as well as the high orbitals," Sarah said, wryly. "They all seem to have bought our transponder."

"Good." Thomas let out a sigh of relief. They'd jiggered the drive nodes as much as possible, as well as adjusting the IFF beacon to tell the locals a series of comforting lies, but he was starting to fear they'd pushed their luck too far. The Pashtali would eventually notice the same ship under a handful of different IDs and ask a few pointed questions, if they didn't simply pop a missile into her hull. Here, at least, that wasn't going to happen. It could start a war. "How many docking orders have we been sent?"

"Just one," Sarah said. "They want us to dock at Orbital Five."

"And they'll search us before they let us go onto the station," Thomas said. "I hope you're ready for it."

"I'll get undressed now," Sarah said. "They can provide their own lube."

Thomas snorted at the weak joke, then settled back to watch the display as *James Bond* glided towards her destination. Antigen had been settled for years and it showed. The orbitals were a halo of space stations, asteroid habitats, industrial nodes and orbital anchors, the latter connected to space elevators running down to the planet below. It was impossible to get an accurate count of how many spacecraft were orbiting the planet, from giant freighters and warships to tiny shuttles and worker bees. His lips twitched in amusement. There was no way in hell the Pashtali had had any real control over the system, even before the other warships had arrived. If there hadn't already been smuggling rings and rebel cells in the high orbitals, he'd quit his post and go live on a planet.

"I'm getting too old for this," he said, as they were overshadowed by the giant orbital station ahead of them. "I really am."

"Yes, dear," Sarah said, with suspicious affability. "Would you like me to make you a nice cup of hot milk, before you go to sleep in the sun?"

Thomas made a rude gesture, then concentrated on exchanging electronic handshakes with traffic control before they were allowed to dock. The Pashtali—or their clients—were checking and rechecking everything, either trying to catch the newcomers in a lie or merely to be assholes. He wouldn't bet against the latter, not when the Pashtali *had* to be furious at losing effective control over the system. It was a tried and tested way to register their disapproval without starting a shooting match, then a war. None of the warships overhead would go to bat for a lone freighter, not when the Pashtali were well within their legal rights...

A dull thump echoed through the ship as they docked. The outer airlock hissed open a second later, triggered by the station. Thomas schooled his expression into calm immobility as the inner hatch opened, a chill running down his spine as the first alien *flowed* into the freighter. The Pashtali looked too much like spiders for his peace of mind, even though he *knew* their evolutionary history had to be very different. *Real* spiders couldn't grow beyond a certain size without collapsing under their own weight, although that didn't stop the dangerous ones from being *very* dangerous indeed. He bit his lip, cutting off *that* line of thought as three more Pashtali advanced into the chamber. Even their *movements* were uncanny.

"Sit on the deck, remain here," the leader ordered. He spoke through a voder, stripping all trace of emotion from his voice. "Do not move until we give permission."

Thomas shrugged, exchanged glances with Sarah and sat. He'd have been happier if the search had been conducted before they'd docked at the station, allowing him to trigger the self-destruct if the Pashtali discovered anything dangerous or incriminating. Now, triggering the destruct charge would damage the station, something enemy propaganda would blame on the human race. Sure, *James Bond* was—at least on paper—an independent freighter and centuries of galactic precedent insisted an entire race could not be held accountable for the crimes of a few, but he doubted the Pashtali would let such a golden opportunity slip by. They'd insist the whole incident was a terrorist strike aimed at killing as many people—of all races—as possible. Or something. And too many bystanders would pretend to believe it.

He kept his face as calm as possible—the Pashtali *might* be able to read human expressions, or have access to someone who could—as the aliens explored his ship. There was nothing particularly incriminating in the cargo hold, nothing to suggest they'd accepted goods from pirates or travelled anywhere near Earth or Terminus, but it was hard to be sure. The Pashtali were, in theory, obliged to tolerate anything that wasn't specifically illegal, yet...he swallowed hard, wishing he could hold his wife's hand. For all he knew, they were planting evidence they could then claim to have discovered...he told himself, firmly, they wouldn't bother. He still wished he had a working internal monitoring system. It would be neat to have some record of their visit.

The Pashtali returned, chattering in a language he didn't recognise. Their own? The Pashtali *had* been a self-spacefaring race long before they'd encountered the Alphans, long enough to maintain much of their own culture and society. He'd been told that a surprising amount of *Earth's* society had come from the Alphans, even with the attempts to revive some aspects of the native human culture. The aliens stepped back and glided out the hatch, the last one telling the humans they were cleared to proceed before departing. Thomas allowed himself a sigh of relief as he stood and closed the hatch, careful not to say anything out loud. It was quite possible the Pashtali had dropped bugs throughout the ship, just to see if their guests said anything incriminating. It was what *he* would have done.

Sarah held up her hands, signalling a message. *Search the ship?*

Do it, Thomas signalled back. It was a shame the kids were no longer with them—they'd have to search the ship individually, just to make sure every last inch of space was covered twice—but better that than taking them into danger. *And then we can get started.*

He keyed the terminal to log into the local datanet and download an updated *précis* for the system, then removed the detection tools from the cabinet and started to search the ship. The Pashtali had been everywhere, including some of the smaller cargo compartments; he scowled as he noted how they'd torn open a couple of shipping crates, then left the debris on the deck for him and his wife to tidy up. He waved the scanner over the cargo, breathing a sigh of relief once he was sure the searchers hadn't hidden any bugs within the crate, then continued the search. Sarah would check his work, just to be sure. He hoped the Pashtali hadn't come up with anything new. His instructors had told him that surveillance technology advanced all the time, racing against counter-surveillance technology. If there was a bug in the ship his sensors couldn't detect, they were in deep shit.

They wouldn't waste something like that on us, he thought, coldly. *If they suspected us, they could have taken us off the ship at once and dissected her at leisure.*

"Clean," Sarah said, when they'd finished. "You want to go for dinner, or to sell our crap?"

"Better sell first," Thomas said. Independent freighter crews needed to sell their wares as quickly as possible, if only to build up a surplus of local currency. The Pashtali might notice if they didn't and start asking why. "You get us a place. I'll arrange shipment."

"Aye, Captain," Sarah said.

Thomas checked the *précis*, noted all the careful evasions written into the official download, then changed into a basic shipsuit before leaving the ship and stepping onto the orbital station. The air stank of hundreds of different races, all jammed together; he took deep breaths, forcing his body to grow used to it. It wouldn't do to show his discomfort in front of potential clients. There were no customs facilities on the far side of the airlock, nothing to keep him from taking whatever he liked off the ship. That wasn't uncommon. He suspected the Pashtali monitored the online sales network, to ensure nothing illicit was being traded, as well as inspecting anything that went down to the surface. Reading between the lines, the enclaves below were restive. It felt like Theta Sigma before the war.

Serve the bastards right, he thought, although he knew an uprising would be futile unless the rebels seized control of the high orbitals. The foreign warships were unlikely to intervene in what was so clearly an internal matter. They might care a great deal about the orbital installations, and the crossroads, but the planet's surface wasn't any of their concern. The Pashtali had clear title. *But what will happen if all hell does break loose?*

The sense he was sitting on a powder keg just waiting to explode grew stronger as he made his way into the market hall. It was a truly immense compartment, large enough for hundreds of intelligent beings from dozens of different races to meet and mingle, but instead of a melting pot the crowds were gathered in clumps. Violence hung in the air, as if gangs were just waiting for the signal before they drew their weapons and started slaughtering each other. There were no police in evidence, not even the customs officers who'd searched his ship. Thomas was silently relieved that Sarah had remained on the ship, even though she'd be pissed when he returned. If something happened to him, she could get *James Bond* back to friendly territory and report home.

He kept one hand near his pistol as he made his way to the merchant office. The guards on the hatch—Vulteks, carrying enough weaponry to fight a small war—eyed him suspiciously, then checked his ID before stepping aside and allowing him to proceed. Thomas walked through the hatch and blinked in surprise, almost coming to a halt as he spied the alien behind the deck. An Alphan? It was vanishingly rare, these days, to see an Alphan outside their own territory. Thomas had the disconcerting sense the ground was shifting under his feet. What was an *Alphan* doing here?

They're not all snobbish bastards who'd prefer to sit in squalor than make an effort to clear up the mess, he reminded himself. *Some of them are actually quite reasonable, in moderation.*

"I greet you," the Alphan said. "I am Driscoll of Tarn."

"I greet you." Thomas bent himself into the Posture of Respect. It had been years since he'd had to do it, back when Earth had been an Alphan possession, but his body still remembered. "I wish to conduct business."

"Of course," Driscoll said. The Alphan managed an expression that might just have been an attempt at a human smile, if the watcher used his imagination. "I have already downloaded and accessed your manifest. I believe I can sell most of your goods within two days."

And does that mean you have buyers who can be lined up in short order, Thomas asked himself, *or do you intend to sell the goods to yourself and then sell them onwards at a considerable mark-up?*

He leaned forward. "We would be honoured by your assistance," he said. Alphans *liked* having their rears kissed, metaphorically if not literally. "It has been a long flight and we are desperate for a rest."

"I can advance you a suitable sum, if you wish," Driscoll said. He made a show of inspecting his datapad, although Thomas was entirely sure he already had the contents memorised. "The exchange rate of local currency to GalCreds is not good and growing worse, I am afraid, but if I pay you the advance in local currency you can use it straight away."

Thomas leaned forward. "The exchange rate is normally very stable," he said, taking advantage of the opening. "Why is it growing worse?"

Driscoll showed little expression, but Thomas knew his people well enough to read the worry. "The situation is currently in flux," he said. "There are too many warships in the system for comfort, with a serious possibility of the system becoming neutral ground or a war zone. If the former, the local currency will have to be disconnected from the Pashtali currency; if the latter, money may mean very little unless it is converted into GalCreds."

"At a truly ruinous rate of exchange," Thomas commented. "I heard the war was getting worse."

"The interstellar shipping lanes are growing dangerous," Driscoll agreed. "The Pashtali are no longer capable of protecting commercial ships through their territory. They appear to have lost at least a dozen convoys, perhaps more. The other powers are making a bid to provide the protection themselves, which will undermine Pashtali control..."

Thomas nodded, concealing his impatience. He already knew all that, at least in general terms, but Driscoll might know something he didn't. It was quite possible he was an information broker, on the sly, or even an intelligence agent keeping his people appraised of what was going on outside their territory. Or both. Information brokers often had close ties to intelligence services, even if they didn't work for them directly. Thomas had done the job himself as a younger man.

"I heard the humans intend to strike at the core of the enemy empire," he said, when Driscoll paused. "Is that true?"

"It's a possibility," Driscoll agreed. "You are human yourself. Does the war not concern you?"

"Only as a trader," Thomas lied. It wasn't uncommon for independent traders to have no loyalties at all, beyond their ship and crew. The Vulteks outside probably had no more loyalty to the Pashtali than Thomas himself. "I would like to see a human victory, but I wouldn't risk my ship for it."

"No doubt," Driscoll agreed. "It is difficult to sort truth from fiction. The Pashtali have beaten the human fleet—they say—but the humans insist their fleet survived and the fact they carried out a very public attack on a transit system is proof they are telling the truth. Or so galactic opinion believes. There are rumours the human race is coming here, or going there, or just trying to pour on the pressure in hopes of getting the Pashtali to crack."

"But you don't know," Thomas said. "Which systems are safe, for us?"

"Life isn't safe," Driscoll told him.

Thomas tried to hide his surprise. The Alphans were incredibly cautious, by human standards. Their forefathers might have built a vast empire, with blood and treasure and a certain amount of good luck, but the current crop was incredibly cautious, unwilling to take the risks their forefathers had considered perfectly acceptable. They minimised risk as much as possible, over-engineering their ships and technology to make it as hard as possible for something to go wrong. Their homes, even the poorest, were so comfortable and safe they put even the richest mansions on Earth in the shade. And yet, *this* Alphan accepted the risks that came with living? It was odd.

"I can sell you an updated starchart," Driscoll added. "But the information will be outdated very quickly."

"If it isn't already," Thomas said. He leaned forward. "How much of an advance will you offer us?"

"Ten thousand local credits," Driscoll said. "To be taken out of the sale of your goods."

Thomas blinked. That was a small fortune. Or was it? If the local currency was sinking so rapidly, the sum might soon be worthless. It might not even be enough to buy a mug of coffee!

"Shit," he said. "Too much currency leaving?"

"As fast as it can go," Driscoll agreed. "Shall we start haggling?"

"Yeah," Thomas agreed, slowly. They'd have to signal Earth—and the fleet—as quickly as possible. "Let's haggle."

CHAPTER THIRTY

P-16, Pashtali Space

"SHIT," MARQUEZ SAID. "MINES!"

Roger glanced at her. "They mined the crossroads?"

"The space around the crossroads," Marquez said. "Clumps of self-powered mines, ready to make their way onto the crossroads on command."

Roger cursed under his breath. There was little point, normally, in mining a crossroads unless it was a bottleneck. It was incredibly wasteful to scatter mines over such a vast area of space when it was statistically unlikely the incoming ships would interpenetrate with the mines or simply materialise close enough to the minefield for the mines to kill them before their point defence blew the mines into dust. The Pashtali hadn't quite taken the risk—the mines were no threat to anyone right now—but they could be guided onto the crossroads at any moment. He frowned, stroking his chin as a thought occurred to him. The space beyond the minefield appeared to be empty, but there could be a small fleet of cloaked ships—or even a handful of powered-down missile pods—lurking in the vastness of interplanetary space.

"Keep us as stealthed as possible," he ordered. If he was any judge, the Pashtali would have strewn sensor platforms around the crossroads as well. "We don't want to draw attention."

"Yes, sir," Marquez said. "They don't seem to have noticed us."

"No," Roger agreed. "But that could change."

He keyed his terminal and brought up the starchart. P-16 sat on a direct line from P-23 to P-1, the enemy homeworld. Anyone who wanted to batter their way into the very heart of enemy space practically *had* to go through P-16, unless they wanted to go a *long* way out of their way or risk travelling through unstable regions of multispace. They'd intercepted messages carrying rumours, suggestions the human fleet intended to capitalise on its victory at P-23 by attacking P-1 itself. The Pashtali probably wouldn't believe the tales—the human fleet wasn't strong enough to tangle with the homeworld's defences—but they couldn't afford to entirely discount them either. He supposed that explained the minefield. A few hours of warning would give the defenders more than enough time to move the mines onto the crossroads and bring up mobile units in support.

And given how rough multispace is around this system, he mused, *they can be fairly sure we won't be dropping in behind them.*

Sweat beaded on his back as they inched off the crossroads and into interplanetary space. The passive sensors picked up nothing, beyond warning beacons surrounding the minefields. He wondered, suddenly, if the minefield was nothing more than smoke and mirrors. The mines were too small to spot with optical sensors and bringing up active sensors would paint a giant target on their hulls, forcing the tiny squadron to turn and run instead of completing the mission. He toyed with his terminal, trying to determine possible angles of approach to the primary planet, but drew a blank. They simply didn't know enough for their conclusions to be anything more than guesswork.

There have to be limits to how many minefields they can scatter around, he mused, as they kept going. *The odds of us hitting a mine are vanishingly low.*

He kept his face under tight control. He'd been a spacer long enough to understand, at a very primal level, just how tiny his entire squadron was on an interplanetary scale. The odds of them passing within a few hundred kilometres of a mine were still very low. No one, not even the Pashtali, could emplace enough mines to guarantee a hit. And yet, he felt as if he was taking one hell of a risk. They were blind. The first warning they'd get of a mine was hitting it. He would almost have been happier if the enemy were shooting at them.

"No contacts, beyond the beacons," Marquez said. "I think we're safe."

"Keep your eyes open," Roger ordered. "We'll pause once we're past the outer shell."

Or where we think the outer shell is, his thoughts added. *There's no way to be sure we're clear of the minefields unless we bring up the active sensors and that will get us killed.*

He sighed inwardly and concentrated on the live feed from the passive sensors. P-16 was surprisingly active, with hundreds of drive signatures boiling around the planets and asteroids, but almost all of the signatures appeared to be Pashtali. There were only a handful that seemed to belong to other alien races, all so far from the planet that he suspected they'd been ordered to keep their distance. The planet itself was surrounded by dozens of drive signatures, flying in such a tight formation he was sure they were yet another convoy. His lips twisted. They'd had to give the last two convoys they'd encountered a wide berth after noting their escorts were alert and ready for trouble. It would be satisfying as hell to strike a convoy so deep in enemy space. If the stories about other powers were actually true...

Marquez looked up. "I think we're clear of the minefields now," she said. "We're certainly clear of the beacons."

Roger nodded. Legally, the Pashtali were supposed to inform passing ships about the minefield so they could keep their distance. It made a certain amount of sense if the minefield was emplaced on a bottleneck, although—like a number of other interstellar protocols—it was often honoured in the breach rather than the observance. Practically speaking, he suspected it didn't matter. The beacons didn't provide any *precise* data that could be used for minesweeping. They just warned ships to stay clear or else.

"Shape our course towards the planet," he ordered. "And keep us well clear of the shipping lanes."

"Such as they are," Marquez said. "The system is a little more organised than most, isn't it?"

"Yeah," Roger said. "And it gives us a *lot* of targeting opportunities."

His lips twisted. Earth's asteroid belt was a teeming mass of mining ships, legal habitats, semi-legal habitats and a decentralised government that resisted instruction from both Earth and Alphan Prime with as much determination as it could muster. There were only a handful of core mining stations and losing them, while painful, wouldn't be enough to bring Earth's industries to a grinding halt. The cloudscoops were bigger targets, and very noticeable against the gas giants, but Earth's spacers and miners had long-since perfected the art of skimming the gas giants atmospheres for fuel. Here...he rolled his eyes at just how *centralised* the system truly was. There were four asteroid smelting complexes and at least thirty cloudscoop, all easy to spot even with passive sensors. Taking even *one* of them out would do untold harm to the system's industrial base.

And we can slip a nuclear-tipped ballistic missile into range very easily, he thought. It would never have worked on Earth, but here...*We might be able to do them a hell of a lot of damage for very little risk.*

"Signal the squadron," he ordered. "We'll proceed to the planet. The rest of the squadron is to split up and approach the mining platforms, then attempt to destroy them at"—he glanced at his display—"1700."

"Aye, sir," Marquez said. "That should be more than enough time to get everyone into position."

Unless we get detected ahead of time, Roger thought. The planet and the mining platforms were both surrounded by active sensors, sweeping space constantly for threats. The cloaked ships would be fine, in theory, as long as they kept their distance, but...one minor mishap would reveal their presence. *Splitting up the squadron raises the risks of detection...*

"Get some rest," he ordered. They had fifteen hours to wait. More than enough time, he hoped, for the alpha crews to catch some sleep and a shower, then return to their stations before the shit hit the fan. "I'll see you at 1500."

"Aye, sir." Marquez didn't sound happy, but she understood. "You get some rest too, sir."

Roger nodded and made his way into his makeshift cabin. It still felt weird, as though he was camping in a very alien environment, but he was too tired to notice or care. There was no point in trying to remodel the ship, beyond the very basics. The analysts had already gone through the captured vessels with a fine-toothed comb, learnt everything that could be leant and cleared them for service. Roger knew the entire squadron was rated as expendable. There was no point in wasting resources making the ships comfortable when they were all going to be destroyed, sooner rather than later.

He shook his head, crawled into his sleeping bag and closed his eyes. Sleep didn't come easy. He knew the odds of detection were very low, and would remain low until they reached their target, but it didn't feel that way. He felt like a fly crawling across a stained-glass window, all too visible to eyes below. And yet...he took a breath and forced himself to sleep. The alarm rang seconds later. He had to check his terminal to be sure he'd actually slept for nine hours.

Fuck, he thought numbly, as he took a quick shower. The Pashtali seemed to enjoy showers as much as their human enemies, although their showers produced warm mist instead of streams of water. *If we ever do this again, we need to arrange for better facilities for the ship.*

He finished showering, changed into fresh clothes and nibbled on a ration bar as he made his way back to the bridge. The sheer alienness of the ship surrounded him as the corridor tilted upwards, reminding him of an anthill rather than a starship...he wondered, idly, if it was whimsy or an attempt to make the crew feel at home. The latter seemed rather more likely, although it was impossible to be sure. There were quite a few

Galactic races who wove their notion of whimsy into their starship designs.

"Captain," Marquez said. She was back early—Roger hoped, grimly, she'd managed to get enough sleep. She looked fresh, at least. "I think you should see this."

Roger peered at her console. The enemy convoy was still forming up. It was...

"Shit," he muttered. "That's not a convoy, that's an entire fleet!"

"Yes, sir." Marquez glanced at him. "We just got a clear look at it. "Fifty-seven warships, ninety-two freighters of varying designs and... and sir, they've got a *Crossroads*."

"Are you sure?" Roger bit down on the comment a second later. Of *course* she was sure. The crossroads-generating starships were very noticeable. They were so big and powerful they were impossible to miss. "Just one?"

"Yes, sir," Marquez said. "Nothing else in the fleet comes remotely close to a *Crossroads* in size or power. I don't think even their battleships could power a crossroads generator for more than a few seconds."

"Unless they've managed to miniaturise the generators and trim down the power requirements," Roger observed. He'd never seen an Alphan generator, but they *had* to be a great deal smaller than their Pashtali counterparts or they couldn't have fitted into warcruiser or starcruiser hulls. "Is there any hint of gravity fluctuations around any of the other ships?"

"No, sir," Marquez said. Her hands danced over her console, checking and rechecking just to be sure. "But the fact they've brought a *Crossroads* suggests they don't think they have a choice."

Roger nodded slowly. A *Crossroads* was a big and very obvious target. Her function was no longer a mystery, ensuring she'd be the primary target for any enemy force that crossed her path. The Pashtali couldn't hope to replace her in a hurry, unless they really *had* committed most of their industrial base to churning out more of her class. It would be amusing if they did, Roger reflected. It would be pretty much suicide to focus on a single-use ship at the expense of everything else.

His thoughts churned. The fleet was clearly getting ready to depart for the edge of enemy space. How long did they have before it set out? He studied the sensor display, silently trying to work out the answer, then dismissed it as beyond calculation. The fleet might be on the verge of departure, or it might be waiting for additional reinforcements from the inner worlds. Either way...fifty-seven front-line warships were a major threat, even if they were clearly concerned about their supply lines. The mere fact they'd brought a fleet train with them was clear proof, as far as they were concerned, that they didn't intend to remain at P-16 indefinitely. No, they had to be heading to the border.

They shouldn't be able to pin Admiral Yagami down, not again, he thought. *But if they take up position and send out scouts, they might just be able to locate her and close in for the kill.*

"We can't guarantee getting a message into the interstellar communications network, can we?" He didn't need to hear her answer to know the truth. The Pashtali controlled the planet completely. The files were vague, but it seemed fairly certain there were no offworld enclaves on the surface. They didn't *need* to let anyone else use their communications network and, even if the message had the right access codes, they might hesitate before forwarding it onwards. "There's no way to warn the fleet?"

"Not from here, no," Marquez said. "We could risk sending a message, when the balloon goes up, but they'd have ample time to lock down the FTL transmitter and store messages in the buffer until they've been inspected."

Roger cursed under his breath, cold equations pressing down. They had two hours before the first ballistic missiles were launched, two hours before the entire system went on high alert. And yet, trying to send the message ahead of time might be disastrous. If the Pashtali realised what it was, they'd draw the right conclusion and put their entire system on alert and *that* would be just as bad. The rest of the squadron would fly right into the teeth of enemy fire.

He found himself writhing in indecision. Admiral Yagami *had* to be warned. Yet the mere act of *trying* to warn her could bring destruction down on his squadron...a price he would pay, he conceded ruefully, if he knew it would ensure the warning reached its destination. But there was no way to be sure...cold logic demanded he withdraw now and fly to the nearest open transmitter, yet even that ran the risk of abandoning the rest of the squadron. He asked himself, numbly, what Admiral Yagami would do? Could she write off the squadron to save her fleet?

Probably, he thought. A handful of captured enemy ships, against ninety percent of humanity's remaining ships and trained crews? It was no contest. *And I might have to do the same.*

He took a breath. "We have a recon probe left, don't we?"

"Yes, sir."

"Program it to send the message to the FTL transmitter at 1700, followed by a wide-beam propaganda broadcast," he ordered. The broadcast would irritate the Pashtali, and hopefully they'd assume it wasn't meant to do anything else, but it would also order the rest of the squadron to abandon the plan to link up at the first RV point and go straight to the second. "And then reverse course. I want to be halfway to the crossroads by 1700."

Marquez blinked. "Sir?"

"We need to warn the fleet and we cannot guarantee the transmitter will forward the message," Roger said. There was a very good chance he'd be put in front of a court-martial board, perhaps for deserting his comrades in the face of the enemy, but he couldn't think of a better plan. He didn't have time to recall the other ships, even if he could do it without alerting the enemy. "We have to get to another transmitter before it is too late."

"Yes, sir," Marquez conceded, reluctantly.

"Program the drone," Roger ordered. "And then deploy it in stealth mode."

He sighed inwardly as he keyed his console, updating his log. It was unlikely Marquez and the rest of his crew would get in trouble for following his orders, even ones that risked leaving the rest of the squadron dangerously exposed, but it was well to make it clear the orders were his and his alone. He didn't want to give anyone even the slightest hint he'd called a council of war in hopes of seeking consensus, not when the outcome was unlikely to be good for anyone involved. The admiral would understand, but would the paper-pushers back home?

"Drone launched," Marquez said. "Bringing us around...now."

Roger nodded, studying the enemy fleet on the display. Small craft were buzzing around the warships, probably restocking their arsenals before the fleet departed. He wondered if the enemy CO had drawn starfighters from the planet's defences, perhaps even insisted on taking half the mobile force too. It wasn't impossible. P-16 had enough fixed defences to give the fleet a very hard time, even without mobile units to back up the defences. Admiral Yagami might be able to take control of the system itself, but the planet would remain outside her grasp.

Not that she'd take the risk, Roger thought. *This close to the enemy home systems, even a victory would lead rapidly to a defeat.*

"We'll be passing through the crossroads in four hours," Marquez reported. "We could drop the cloak..."

"No," Roger said. He had no idea if there were any mobile units lurking near the crossroads, but there was no point in taking chances. "They could try to steer the mines into our path if we did."

He sighed, feeling haunted. They had to run, they had to take word to the fleet, and yet it felt as though he was running away. But what choice did they have?

None, he told himself firmly. *Admiral Yagami* must *be warned.*

CHAPTER THIRTY-ONE

ESS DAUNTLESS, P-42

NAOMI HAD HALF-EXPECTED, as the fleet made its way from P-23, that they'd be ambushed by the enemy force that had nearly beaten them earlier. She'd probed every system carefully, and deployed scouts to monitor their threadlines even when they were staying away from the shipping lanes, but there had been no sign of the enemy fleet. It was perplexing. The Pashtali didn't believe their own propaganda, did they? Or did they really believe the rumours about her fleet heading towards their core worlds?

They have to be more than a little paranoid about us now, she thought. *We shouldn't have been able to bounce back so quickly.*

She stood in her ready room, studying the nearspace display. They'd linked up with the fleet train—her crew were conveying supplies as quickly as possible—as well as more ships from the Terminus powers, including some makeshift warships. She wasn't sure how useful they'd be, in a real battle, but it gave her more mobile units as well as deepening the allied commitment to the war. The cynical side of her mind wondered how much firepower had been held in reserve to protect Terminus itself, or to hint the alliance would be amiable to switching sides if the Pashtali make the right offer, but she could hardly blame the allies for considering their exit strategy. If *Earth* could leave the war with her independence, and her pre-war territory, would she do it? Naomi wanted to think otherwise, but she suspected the answer was *yes*. There were limits to how long they could continue the war before they simply ran out of resources.

"Impressive," she said. "What do you make of it?"

Observer Salix showed no visible reaction. He'd been surprisingly quiet during the last few days, to the point Naomi had started to wonder what he was thinking. The Alphan had kept to himself...it was rare, of course, for his race to socialise with races they regarded as lesser—which was pretty much everyone—but still...

"You have developed a fine system for transhipping supplies and personnel," Observer Salix said, finally. "It is no match for a network of fleet bases, of course, but workable."

"We don't have any fleet bases so far from human space," Naomi reminded him, sardonically. The closest human base—Theta Sigma—was hundreds of light years away, assuming it was still intact. She was surprised the Pashtali hadn't trashed the system out of spite. Given the chaos on the surface, it was quite possible they'd assumed the rebels would do the work for them. "We have to rely on freighters."

"Indeed," Observer Salix agreed. "And very good they are too."

Naomi tried not to shoot him a hard look. *Something* was clearly bothering the alien. He hid it well, but she'd spent two-thirds of her career under an Alphan CO who couldn't care less about the humans under his command. She knew how to read them and...he was clearly perturbed by *something*. What? The convoy slaughter? It had been perfectly legitimate under the laws of war. Or...

Her lips twisted? Romance troubles? A 'Dear John' letter? It was unlikely. Alphan reproduction was a closed book to their clients, let alone everyone else. Besides, from what little she did know, they didn't take romantic attachments as seriously as their former clients. They didn't seem to have them...she wondered, idly, how much of the whispered rumours were anywhere close to the truth. It would be ironic if the suggestion their prudishness concealed a wildness was actually true.

She cocked her head. "Do you want to talk about it?"

The alien showed a hint of surprise. "About what?"

"You're distracted by something," Naomi said. It was risky to suggest she could read the Alphan—he wouldn't want sympathy from her, any more than she'd want sympathy from the lowest crewman on the ship—but she wanted to know. "Do you want to talk about it?"

"I'm just considering the future," the alien said. "There are too many Galactics involved now."

Naomi nodded, though she had the odd feeling she was being misled. There were at least *nine* major powers sending their warships to enemy space, either to secure the crossroads or to escort convoys through the threadlines. The Pashtali hadn't made any official comment, as far as her intelligence staff had been able to determine, but everyone agreed they had to be furious. There was no way they could kick out the other powers without destroying her fleet, allowing them to claim they'd secured the shipping lanes, and she had no intention of letting herself be destroyed. The attack on P-23 had succeeded beyond her wildest dreams. It had proved, beyond all doubt, that the Pashtali couldn't protect ships passing through their territory.

Serve the bastards right, she thought, with a flicker of dark amusement. *They did it to us first.*

She met the observer's eyes. "Do you think they'll impose some kind of truce on us?"

"I do not know," Observer Salix said. "It is possible they'll press for some kind of agreement that allows both sides to back off, without being able to declare victory, but the Pashtali are unlikely to honour the truce for long."

Naomi nodded, curtly. The Pashtali could play nice for a while, while building up their fleet, and then resume the war at a time and place of their choosing. This time, they wouldn't try to be clever, or to come up with a nice little excuse to take a perfectly legal bite out of Earth's territories. They'd strike at Earth directly and then swing round to finish off the colonies, smashing humanity's resistance in the first moments of war. Or something along those lines. They wouldn't give humanity time to rebuild, not again. They might even devastate the orbital industries rather than try to take them intact.

"You can put together some kind of treaty monitoring system, can't you?" She knew, even as she spoke, that it was unlikely. "Or something to keep them from blatantly breaking the agreement as soon as possible?"

"Perhaps." Observer Salix seemed unconcerned. What was *really* bothering him? "We'll see..."

The intercom bleeped. "Admiral," Olson said. "We picked up a message from Commodore Valentine. I believe you should see it at once."

"Bring it in," Naomi ordered. She looked at Observer Salix. "Duty calls, I'm afraid."

Observer Salix took the hint—surprising, in a race that normally paid little attention to subtle prompts from their lesser—and left the compartment. Olson arrived a moment afterwards, carrying a secure datapad in one hand. Naomi's eyes narrowed. A secure datapad meant trouble. If Commodore Valentine had sent a secured message to the fleet...

"Admiral," Olson said, holding out the datapad. "It's not good news."

"It rarely is," Naomi said. She feared it was just a matter of time before the raiders pushed their luck too far and vanished. "Let me take a look."

She scanned the report quickly, her eyes narrowing. The raiders had probed P-16 and discovered, to their horror, that the enemy were massing a fleet there, one clearly ready to depart. She looked at the date and time stamps and frowned. The message had been sent three days ago and the fleet had been sighted six days ago...it could be on its way by now. She keyed her terminal, bringing up a starchart. If the Pashtali knew where to find them, they could be on their position in three days.

By which time we'll have completed the resupply and headed elsewhere, Naomi thought, coldly. *Do they know it?*

"They may not realise how quickly we can resupply the fleet," she mused. The Solar Navy had perfected the art of resupplying ships without a proper fleet base. The Galactics preferred to rely on their bases, when they had them. "If they think we'll still be here..."

She raised her head and met Olson's eyes. "Send a copy of the data to tactical," she ordered. "I want their assessment as quickly as possible."

"Aye, Admiral."

Naomi studied the chart thoughtfully. The enemy fleet was powerful. She could take it, perhaps, but the cost would be high. Too high, unless she prepared the battleground ahead of time. That wouldn't be easy. The enemy had a second *Crossroads*. They could drop out of multispace anywhere they liked, time and conditions permitting. She felt a twinge of unease. They could come out right behind her, if they got the timing right. And even if she won the battle, the *first* enemy fleet could beat her.

Or they combine the two fleets into one and chase us back out of their territory, she thought, tiredly. *What are they planning?*

Her eyes narrowed. The enemy would have problems running her down. They'd have to find her first, then prepare a second ambush... no, that trick wouldn't work twice. This time, she could make sure they didn't have a chance to herd her into a trap. Hell, she could stay off the threadlines and dance around them, careful to avoid a major clash. If the other Galactics stayed out of the fighting...

She sucked in her breath. "They're not coming for us," she said. "They're going to Terminus."

Olson frowned. "How can you be sure?"

"They can't guarantee finding us, let alone beating us," Naomi said. "Ideally, we'd keep our distance from their fleet and force them to chase us, again, as we drive through their systems and hammer their defences from outside their own range. They know it too. They can't block us from doing it unless they divide their forces, which will give us the chance to pick off their formations one by one."

"Or invite interstellar intervention," Olson agreed. "The

vultures are already gathering. If they look weak, they look vulnerable."

"Yes." Naomi mentally drew a line on the chart. "But if they go to Terminus, if they break into the bottleneck system, they can drive our allies out of the war and prevent us from drawing on their resources. At best, they can open an artificial crossroads, pin the defenders against the primary crossroads and defeat them; at worst, they can turn the bottleneck into a liability and prevent anyone from entering or leaving the system."

Olson frowned. "But wouldn't that risk angering the other powers, thus providing an excuse for intervention?"

"Perhaps," Naomi said. "But the Terminus powers are at war with them. They can sell it as a perfectly legitimate military operation, particularly if they launch an invasion through the bottleneck—or around it."

"They can't go through the bottleneck, not unless they're willing to soak up immense losses," Olson said. "Unless they have some other trick up their sleeve..."

"They could use captured ships themselves, or missile pods," Naomi said. "But you're right. It would be easier if they could get into the system another way."

She stroked her chin as she studied the display. Terminus was, if the techs were correct, a difficult system to open an artificial crossroads. The local region of multispace was so tangled, by the gravity surges and extra-dimensional forces that had produced the bottleneck, that trying to get into position to open a crossroads would be dangerous. Or so she'd been assured. The Terminus powers had surveyed the systems carefully, before the Pashtali had tried to take it for themselves, and they'd concluded it was very hard to navigate safely. Even the Alphans would have trouble...

Or so we think, she thought. Was she wrong? Did the Pashtali think they could get away with risking a direct attack? Or that they could put a cork in the bottle and keep humanity's allies locked away for the next few years? *What are* they *thinking?*

"They have to win quickly," she mused aloud. "What are their options? How can they win the war?"

Olson ticked off points on his fingers. "Destroy our fleet. Occupy Terminus. Invade Earth. Again. Destroying our fleet might be the easiest to accomplish."

"Yes." Naomi frowned. Invading Earth would mean a direct clash with the Alphans and probably every other Great Power jumping on them. Occupying Terminus would be incredibly costly, unless they had something up their sleeve. A traitor? Not impossible, but unlikely. Perhaps they did intend to hunt down the fleet, except they'd never be sure where the fleet *was*. Unless..."Oh."

It struck her in a moment of insight. "Terminus is a bottleneck," she said. "That's why they wanted it in the first place. But it links to other systems, which they might be able to access with a *Crossroads* and then invade Terminus from an unexpected direction. Do it properly and they might be able to get their fleet into Terminus before any warning reaches the defenders...hell, they might even time it so the warning ensures they get their fleet moving and yet caught in transit. If they get it right..."

"It's a little elaborate," Olson pointed out. "Too many things could go wrong."

"They can back off, if they lose," Naomi countered. "They can open a second crossroads and escape."

She thought she understood the enemy's way of thinking. Deploy a fleet to pin down the defenders and seal off the bottleneck. Keep them looking in one direction, while moving forces into position to strike from another. If the timing didn't work out, they could either keep possession of the target system—and force the defenders to absorb heavy losses while liberating it—or back off completely. It would be chancy, but it should work.

Hell, she thought. *They might just settle for sealing off the bottleneck and keeping us separate from our allies. Or even using the bottleneck as bait in a trap.*

She took a long breath, carefully putting together a plan. "Signal Commodore Valentine," she ordered. "I want him and his squadron, what's left of it, to travel to Point Delta and link up with us there. In the meantime, we want to make them think we're not going anywhere *near* Terminus.

Have the tactical staff put together a plan for raiding away from Terminus, one that offers them a chance to intercept the fleet but lets us drop off the threadlines before they can bring their first fleet to us."

"Aye, Admiral," Olson said.

"And then deploy scouts along the route to Terminus," Naomi added. "I want them to either find a transmitter to signal Point Delta or simply set off to alert us, when the enemy fleet comes into view."

"They may cloak," Olson pointed out.

"It'll be difficult to cloak a *Crossroads*-class ship," Naomi said. Pashtali cloaking technology was good...was it *that* good? She didn't know. They'd have realised the problem, if she was any judge, and started trying to do something about it. If they'd succeeded..."They'll have problems hiding their presence."

She smiled, suddenly. "And they will want to show off their power to their rivals," she added, after a moment. "It's one thing to threaten a defenceless star nation, with warships so dispersed they can be picked off one by one, but quite another to challenge a fleet that's armed to the teeth and ready to press matters. They need to defeat the alliance as quickly as possible."

Olson scowled. "Admiral, it might be a trap."

"I know." Naomi had already considered the possibility. "But if it is a trap, we can make it work for us."

She grinned. "And I want you to prepare the units assigned to Operation Booby Prize," she added. "I think, with a little careful work, we can turn the ambush back on them."

"Aye, Admiral," Olson said.

• • •

"Are you sure the enemy fleet is heading to Terminus?" Nancy leaned forward. It was difficult to guess at the motives and intentions of her fellow humans and the Pashtali were very *far* from human. Admiral Yagami seemed to think she could read alien minds. "Really?"

"There's no way to be *entirely* sure," Naomi told her, calmly. "We *should* have some warning as they make their way to Terminus—they'll have to pass through two narrow threadlines and we'll have them both under observation before the fleet can arrive—but they may have something else in mind. However, their best bet for winning the war outright is either taking Terminus or destroying our fleet. They can attempt both by heading directly to Terminus."

"I see," Nancy said. She didn't. "And you want me to pass on the warning?"

"Yes," Naomi said. "Under the circumstances, we need to prepare our allies for the coming storm."

"They seemed certain they can hold the system," Nancy protested. "Did that change?"

"I think a lot of their tactical assessments were based on the assumption the enemy would have to come through the bottleneck," Naomi said. "They didn't spend time thinking about an enemy who could open a crossroads into their rear, because opening one into Terminus was supposed to be difficult."

Nancy nodded. "And now that might have bitten them. Hard."

"Yes," Naomi said, flatly. "Alert them, please. Let them tighten their defences. If we're wrong, we're wrong. If we're right...we need to be ready, we need to make the enemy dance to our tune."

"I'll inform them," Nancy said. "And Earth?"

"No details," Naomi said. "In fact, send the first message via courier. They know we saw their fleet—probably—but they may not realise we got the alert. We'll try and keep them in the dark. Use code phrases for Earth and refrain from including anything beyond the basics."

"I'll do my best," Nancy said. "Earth won't be happy."

"If the message is decrypted, they could set up a trap—an additional trap—themselves," Naomi told her. "We dare not let them pin us down, Ambassador, not until the time is right."

"Understood," Nancy said. "And I hope you know what you're doing."

Naomi nodded. "So do I."

CHAPTER THIRTY-TWO

ESS *Dauntless*, P-42

"ADMIRAL," OLSON REPORTED. "We have completed transit. The enemy platforms are powering up their weapons, preparing to engage."

"Fire at will," Naomi ordered. "Clear the crossroads!"

She leaned forward as the enemy platforms opened fire. The Pashtali had mined the crossroads and placed weapons platforms in position to cover the minefield, but the crossroads was just too big to mine effectively. She'd thrown a salvo of decoys through the crossroads to clear the way, then taken the fleet through in a mass transit. It was risky—standard tactics called for a slow and steady approach to clearing a minefield—but it had ensured she entered the system before the platforms were ready to meet her fleet. Her lips twitched in cold amusement. The automated defences had clearly been caught by surprise.

"Incoming missiles," Olson reported. "Point defence engaging...*now*."

Naomi nodded. The Pashtali hadn't sealed off the crossroads—they couldn't—and she wasn't sure what they thought they were doing. The tactical deck suggested they were trying to force invaders to expend their weapons before they encountered the enemy fleet, but the minefield wasn't large enough to do it. She mulled the question over in her mind, considering several different possibilities. The Pashtali might just be trying to make life difficult for the other powers, as well as her. They could claim it was an accident if an alien fleet just *happened* to pop through a crossroads—without clearance—and ran straight into an automated minefield.

And they might get away with it too, under normal circumstances, she mused. *But now?*

She shrugged as the last of the enemy missiles crashed into her point defence and were blown into dust. There just hadn't been enough modern missiles to get through her point defence and hit her fleet, which suggested...what? She made a mental note to send a signal announcing they'd cleared the shipping lanes through the system, something that would be sure to draw in the other powers *and* get under the enemy's skin. It wouldn't change things in a hurry, if at all, but it would present them with another problem they'd have to solve.

"Deploy recon drones," she ordered. "If there is a major enemy presence within the system, I want to know about it."

"Aye, Admiral," Olson said.

Naomi forced herself to relax as the fleet formed up and moved away from the crossroads. P-42 was an odd system, one that would have been a great deal more valuable if it hadn't been impossible to defend. There were seven crossroads within the system, the smallest still far too large to count as a bottleneck, ensuring that a major enemy fleet—like hers—could gain entry and control of the outer system very quickly. The Pashtali had established heavy defences around the rocky planets, and the gas giants, but they were irrelevant so long as she stayed clear of their engagement range. Her drones were already spreading out, pulsing space with active sensors. If there was a cloaked fleet lurking near the crossroads, she'd know about it shortly.

But it isn't too likely, she thought. *Our best estimates place Force One several threadlines from here.*

She scowled as she studied the starchart. There was no hard data on where the enemy fleet was lurking. The Pashtali were filling the FTL transmitter network with disinformation, spreading rumours that ranged from the plausible to the completely insane. Naomi's intelligence staffers were sifting through the data, trying to sort the grains of truth from the mountain of lies, but she suspected they were wasting their time. The rumours suggested the Pashtali fleet was either far larger than they thought, or it was in several different star systems at the same time. Naomi thought they were being conned. If the Pashtali had had *that* many ships under their command, Earth and Terminus would both have been taken by now and the war would be over.

"Admiral, long-range sensors are picking up a handful of freighters leaving the planet," Olson said. "They'll be through the nearest crossroads before we can catch them."

"Noted," Naomi said. There was no point in worrying about it. "Do we have any hard IDs?"

"No, Admiral," Olson said. "I think they're Pashtali designs, but at this distance it's impossible to be sure."

"Keep an eye on them," Naomi said. "And detach the strike squads now."

"Aye, Admiral," Olson said. "They'll be on their targets in twenty hours."

Naomi nodded, hiding her doubts. The system might be impossible to defend—and impossible to turn into a second trap, unless the Pashtali really *did* have thousands of ships within striking distance—but it was quite possible she'd have to increase speed and leave the system in a hurry. If that happened...she tried not to think about the men she'd be leaving behind. There were contingency plans, but still...she shook her head. She hated the idea of leaving *anyone* behind.

And they have to see us as a viable threat, she thought. There was no doubt the enemy already knew where she was. The planet would already be screaming for help unless they had absolute faith in their fixed defences. *We can't make them think we're the real threat unless we take some risks.*

She gritted her teeth. Twenty hours...how long would it take, really, for the Pashtali to react? Would they send their fleet into P-42, in hopes of running her down, or would they try to ambush her when she slipped through the crossroads? She thought they'd try to run her down—it was their only real hope of catching her, unless they got very lucky—but she dared not assume they'd do what she *wanted* them to do. They might have a surprise or two up their sleeves.

Her lips twitched. *Do they even wear sleeves?*

She leaned back in her chair, forcing herself to relax. It would take quite some time before the shooting started and she needed to be alert, ready to react, when the enemy fleet arrived. Her eyes lingered on the display, noting the multitude of places the enemy could open a crossroads and charge out of multispace…she had contingency plans for that too, if she was wrong about the enemy fleet not having a *Crossroads* of its own, but she knew too many things could go wrong. What would happen, she asked herself, if they came out of multispace too close to her fleet for comfort?

They can't, she told herself. *They'd need realtime data on our position they couldn't get from the planet.*

But, even though she knew it was unlikely, the thought still worried her.

• • •

"Wake up."

Wesley jerked awake, feeling a brief moment of disorientation before training asserted itself. He was in a shuttlecraft, waking up from a semi-hypnotic sleep…his mind revolted, unable to accept—as always—that it had been effectively switched off for nearly twenty hours. He concentrated on calming himself, checking the suit to ensure there was no immediate threat. The communications network was buzzing with the typical complaints of men who'd been yanked out of induced sleep. It was restful—Wesley had to admit it—but waking up was always unpleasant. He'd have preferred to wake up naturally.

"We'll be in the drop zone in ten minutes," the jumpmaster said. He kept his voice low. "If anyone has any problems, I want to hear about them now."

"Yes, sir," Private Milligan said. "I have a terrible problem. When I close my eyes, I can't see!"

Wesley smiled and tried not to snicker. "If you're making terrible jokes, you're clearly fine," he said, although he'd seen wounded men crack jokes in a bid to hide from the pain. "Does anyone have any *real* problems?"

"I haven't seen my boyfriend and girlfriend in months, sir," Private Hoskins said. "They might be having fun without me."

"Use your hand, you stupid bastard," someone said. Wesley carefully *didn't* check to see who it was. "Or go into a VR sim and have fun and..."

"All right, all right," Wesley said. "If no one has any *real* problems, get ready for the drop."

He closed his eyes and centred himself, then ran through the rest of the checks. The armoured combat suit was ready and raring to go, even though half of its systems and all of its weapons were locked down until they landed. A timer appeared in his HUD, counting down the minutes to launch. Wesley took a long breath, silently cursing himself for volunteering. The Marines hadn't had much to do, save for assisting with damage control efforts, but still...

"Five minutes," the jumpmaster said. "Get ready."

Wesley nodded, feeling oddly alone. The suit gave him the impression of being completely isolated from the universe, even though he *knew* it wasn't true. A dull rumble echoed through the shuttle, tractor fields picking up the suited people and preparing them for launch. Wesley allowed himself another sigh of relief. He knew his squadmates wouldn't back out—they'd had ample time to get used to the idea of being aimed at an enemy target—but a technical failure now would be disastrous. If they had to pull someone out of the line at very short notice...

He closed his eyes as an invisible force propelled them through the hatch and out into open space. The enemy target—a moon, only slightly smaller than Luna—seemed to glow in front of him, reflecting the light of the primary star. His lips twitched—the term *dark side of the moon* might be poetic, but it wasn't accurate—as the moon grew in size, expanding rapidly until it dominated his sight. It was easy to believe, on a planet, that a moon was nothing more than a tiny piece of rock, yet spacers knew better. Luna—and the alien world in front of him—was a large object in its own right.

At least on a human scale, he thought. *Luna is tiny compared to Jupiter, or Sol.*

He put the thought aside as he plummeted to the ground, the antigravs kicking in a few short seconds before he landed. His perspective shifted violently; he squeezed his eyes shut, even though it meant he'd be blind for a few short seconds. He landed gently and knelt, bringing up his plasma rifle as he opened his eyes. There was no sign of anything threatening—if the enemy had seen them coming, they'd have blown the shuttle out of space a *long* time before it could deploy its human cargo—but he swept the horizon anyway. They had to be careful they weren't spotted until it was too late. He'd spent time on Luna. There were so many prospectors crawling over the airless surface that there was a very real risk a team of infiltrators would be noticed and a report called in to the military command. The Pashtali might easily have their own people swarming over the surface, ready to report the team's presence if they got a good look at it...

They'll know something is wrong the moment they see us, he told himself, as he used hand signals to direct the team to follow him. *We're humanoid. They are not.*

His lips twitched as they began their march, picking their way through the dusty landscape and carefully moving around the remnants of long-ago asteroid impacts. The Pashtali hadn't settled the moon as extensively as he'd expected, if the intelligence reports and long-range sensor probes were accurate, but they'd established planetary defence centres in position to threaten any ships nearing the moon. Wesley was mildly surprised they'd put so much effort into it, although he supposed they had a point. Better to have the base, one of the system's prime targets, well away from civilian populations. A near miss with a nuclear-tipped missile would be utterly disastrous if it struck a city instead.

They slowed as they came closer to the enemy position and took cover in an asteroid crater, peering towards the base. The Pashtali had dug deep into a mountain, relying on layers upon layers of rock to protect the base from enemy attack, but there were limits. The giant missile batteries, plasma cannons and railguns couldn't be buried, nor could the sensor arrays and shuttle hangars surrounding the base. He couldn't help thinking, as he sketched out a quick plan of attack, that the base looked surprisingly akin to its human counterparts.

But we never saw them land commando forces behind enemy lines, he thought. *Either they never thought of it or they're simply not very good at it.*

He held up his hand, counting down the seconds, then led his squad towards the sensor arrays as the rest of the team prepared to lay down covering fire. The enemy showed no reaction until they crossed a tripwire, his HUD flashing up a series of alerts as enemy weapons and sensors came online. His imagination filled in alarms howling through the enemy base as he neared the sensor array, adjusting his cutter to burn right through the armoured hull. The atmosphere streamed out, carrying everything that wasn't nailed down with it. His lips twisted as he saw a lone alien flash past him, legs waving helplessly as the outflow carried him out of the base and dropped him on the airless ground. Normally, he'd have been more careful about maintaining the base's integrity—the suits were too large to manoeuvre through human-sized corridors—but he didn't have to worry about it here. The alien corridors were large enough to take the team without slowing them down.

"Get the hacker node in place," he snapped. The briefing team hadn't been sure they'd be *able* to hack the enemy network—the Pashtali *knew* they'd lost a handful of ships and would presumably have hardened their network against human hackers—but it was worth a try. If it failed, they could always destroy the sensor array and run. "Anything?"

"Not yet," Private Jones reported. "The node is having problems getting into the alien system."

Wesley cursed under his breath as a warning flickered up on his HUD. The enemy were already responding, armoured spiders darting out of the underground fortress and making their way towards the sensor array. He recalled the aliens tunnelling *under* the humans before and shuddered, keeping a wary eye on the ground. The sensor array *had* to be connected to the rest of the base through an underground tunnel, unless the Pashtali *wanted* to suit up all the time. He cursed under his breath as another update blinked up. The enemy were scrambling troops from a distant base. They'd be on the humans in ten minutes at most.

"Prep the nuke," he ordered, curtly. The hacker node was still trying, but it looked as if the base had already been cut out of the enemy network. Smart of them. He'd hoped they'd be able to upload viruses, perhaps even crash the whole system, but it looked as if that wasn't going to happen. The best they could do was damage the local network and that wasn't going to have any real effect on anything outside the alien base. "We need to move."

"Aye, sir." Jones unslung his backpack and shoved the nuke into position, then started fiddling with the controls. "Five minutes?"

Wesley nodded. Five minutes would be cutting it very fine, but they were running out of time. Once the enemy aircars took up firing position, the humans would be trapped, unable to retreat. He understood he might die, if the mission went to hell, but...

"Do it."

Jones finished keying in the authorisation codes, then half-concealed the nuke under a pile of debris. The Pashtali might guess what they were doing and start looking for it...Wesley took one last look at the alien compartment, then turned and led the way out of the base. A full-scale battle had broken out, with the Pashtali trying to overwhelm the sensor array and the humans keeping them back. Wesley kicked his suit into high gear, running at breakneck speed away from the base. Jones followed, keeping his head low. The remainder of the squad broke off a moment later, firing a handful of shots to force the enemy to stay back as they fled. Wesley felt sweat trickling down his back as he reached a crater he'd noted earlier and took cover, bracing himself as the timer ticked down to zero. The ground shook violently as the nuke detonated, blowing the sensor array and the surrounding troops to hell. Wesley scowled as pieces of rocky debris flew in all directions. The PDC would barely have been scratched, if he was any judge. The underground complex was designed to resist far nastier attacks…

But it'll be blind, a sitting duck for a long-range strike, he thought. He'd been told the fleet intended to deploy ballistic projectiles, once the team were on their way. *And then they'll be sure we intend to hit the planet itself.*

His radio bleeped. "The shuttle will land in five minutes," the jump-master informed them, curtly. "There's no time to hang about. Be ready."

Wesley nodded. The enemy would be confused, of course, but they'd recover fast and then come after the landing party. Their aircars might be able to catch the shuttle, even follow it into space. He didn't know if they were armed or not, but it didn't matter. A single suicide runner would be enough to take out the shuttle and the entire squad.

"Signal the fleet," he ordered, as the shuttle came into view. Its rear guns were already firing, spraying railgun pellets at the enemy positions. He hoped they'd keep their heads down for a few seconds more. "Mission accomplished."

CHAPTER THIRTY-THREE

ESS DAUNTLESS, P-42

"THE LANDING PARTIES ARE RETURNING to the fleet," Olson reported. "Not all of them were successful."

Naomi nodded. She'd never heard of a major race using daring commando raids when long-range missile bombardments would do—the Pashtali had never actually landed commandos on Earth, during the invasion—but it stood to reason they'd take at least *some* precautions to prevent someone from doing it to them. The Marines had killed a handful of PDCs and cloudscoops, weakening both the enemy defences *and* the system's economy, yet it wasn't enough to make it easy to browbeat the locals into surrender. They *still* had enough PDCs to keep her from seizing the high orbitals. If that had been her goal, she reflected, she wouldn't have been very pleased at all.

But instead we kept them guessing what we have in mind, she thought. *And their cries for help will become ever more urgent.*

She leaned forward, studying the display. The fleet was plunging onwards, carefully angling its course to make it hard to determine which crossroads she intended to use. She'd run the vectors very carefully to figure out when she'd have to commit herself...the enemy would have no trouble running the same calculations themselves, of course, but they wouldn't be sure. And if they got it wrong, they'd have no time to correct the mistake before her fleet swept into multispace and vanished.

They're on their way, she told herself. She was morbidly sure of it. *How long do we have until they arrive?*

"Admiral," Olson said. "The ballistic projectiles have been launched. The last of the shuttles will dock in thirty minutes."

"Continue on our current course," Naomi ordered. She knew she'd have to pick a destination soon, but she wanted the enemy fleet to appear first. She *needed* them to see her go. "Once we have our people back onboard, we'll prepare to burst into the next system."

Her heart sank. P-42 was ideal for her purposes. There were too many ways in and out of the system for the enemy to block her, or even to realise what she was doing before it was too late. But she needed the enemy fleet to arrive first...she raised her eyes to the display, feeling the seconds tick away. There was plenty of slack in her plan, but she didn't want *both* enemy fleets to start breathing down her neck. *That* would make it impossible to break contact as planned...

"Admiral," Olson snapped. "Long-range sensors are picking up enemy ships transiting Crossroads Three!"

"Noted," Naomi said. That pretty much *had* to be the fleet they'd faced earlier, unless the enemy had a *third* fleet poking around. It wasn't impossible. If she was in command of the enemy fleet, she would have pulled out from human space and concentrated on shoring up her defences against greater powers. "See if you can get solid IDs on any of the ships."

She took a breath. "And signal the fleet," she ordered. "We'll go with Delta-Three. All ships are to adjust course as planned, on my mark."

"Aye, Admiral," Olson said. His hands darted across his console. "Signal sent."

Naomi silently counted down the seconds. The enemy fleet wouldn't be able to run them down for several hours, even though she was giving them a clear shot at her, unless they had a crossroads generator. Did they?

She wished she knew. It wouldn't be easy for them, but...she shook her head. They had time to adjust their course, to let the enemy see what she wanted them to see...to fool them, unless they got very lucky. Thankfully, the enemy fleet had arrived in force. They wouldn't think there was anything *odd* in her turning her ships around and running for her life.

They'll be making jokes about brave humans bravely running away, she thought, *even if they do understand.*

She sighed inwardly—the Pashtali would make hay out of the whole affair, at least until they realised they'd been tricked—and then leaned forward, checking and rechecking the vectors. They had to give the enemy a chance, or at least the ghost of one, without letting the enemy get too close. The idiosyncrasies of multispace *should* make it impossible for them to get ships in place to ambush her fleet, as they made transit, but if Naomi was wrong...she snorted to herself. The plan would fail if they managed to ambush her fleet, yet...it wouldn't be fatal. Perhaps...

"Mark," she ordered. "Alter course."

"Aye, Admiral," Olson said.

"Curious," Observer Salix said. "The enemy will have no trouble catching up with you."

Naomi tried not to jump. She'd almost forgotten he was there. "Watch and learn," she said, calmly. Salix was right, on paper. The Pashtali ships *would* slowly catch up with their human counterparts. She'd have to push her drives to the limit to be sure of reaching the crossroads first. "If this works, it really won't matter."

• • •

Observer Salix carefully concealed the flash of naked anger that ran through him at the human's casual dismissal of his concerns. The human fleet was dawdling, practically inviting the Pashtali to catch up and blow them to hell. Salix knew the humans would give a good account of themselves, but even if they won the battle it would be costly enough to ensure the humans lost the war. They should be cramming on the speed, or altering course to head towards a nearer crossroads, not hanging around in interplanetary space. He'd wondered if the Pashtali were trying to set up a second ambush, but they hardly needed to bother. The humans really *were* offering the Pashtali a chance to close the range.

He forced himself to study the display as calmly as possible. The Pashtali ships were slightly faster in realspace than their human counterparts, even the purpose-built warships. They would overrun the human ships unless they broke off for some reason of their own. Salix couldn't think of any reason for them to abandon the chase...he tried to bury his dismay as the range steadily closed. The human admiral had a plan, didn't she? He hoped so. If she didn't, she was about to lose the war in a few short and terrible hours.

His mind churned. What did the humans have in mind? He'd thought they intended to lure the Pashtali onto a minefield, but they weren't even trying to lay one! They weren't feinting at the planet either, as if that would convince the Pashtali fleet to back off. Salix had no doubt the Pashtali would happily abandon the planet and its entire population, if it meant their fleet had a chance to bring the humans to battle. Did the humans think they could speed up in time to escape? It was their only hope and yet, as the range closed, the prospects for avoiding engagement were growing slimmer and slimmer...

"Signal the fleet," the human admiral ordered. "On my mark, all ships are to proceed with Phase Two."

"Aye, Admiral," the little human said. "The timing will be close."

"Close enough to make it look convincing," the human admiral agreed. There was a long chilling pause. "Mark!"

Salix frowned, studying the display. The humans had ramped up their ECM, fired a barrage of missiles that *would* go ballistic *long* before they reached their target, deployed decoy drones...and cloaked? What were they *doing?* Astonishment ran through him. The Pashtali were too far away to be hit. They had plenty of time to pick out the missiles, plot firing solutions and blow them to dust...he felt a sudden upswing of disgust. The

Pashtali could simply evade the missiles and continue the pursuit, without ever wasting their time on taking them out one by one. There would be a little confusion, perhaps, but it wouldn't last. How could it?

"Alter course, as planned," the human admiral ordered. "And head straight for Crossroads Five."

Salix blinked in surprise as the cloaked ships started to separate from the drones. The Pashtali…unless they got *very* lucky, the Pashtali wouldn't have noticed the drones taking the place of the cloaked starships. They'd keep following the drones, allowing the human ships a chance to break contact without being noticed. He smiled, despite himself, as he realised the drones were pushing their drives to the utmost. The Pashtali would have to redline their drives if they wanted to catch the fake fleet, making it harder for them to realise they'd been tricked. He wondered, suddenly, what his superiors would say about the drones they'd loaned the humans being used in such a manner, then decided it didn't matter. The humans needed to use the drones if they wanted to survive.

"I see, I think," he said. "You want them to think you're going to Crossroads Two, when you're actually going to Crossroads Five."

"More than that," the human said. "They won't be able to run the drones down unless they chase them into multispace, but the drones will self-destruct the moment they make transit. They'll assume the drones have flown off the beaten track"—her lips curved into something that might charitably be called a smile—"and yet, thanks to the curvature of multispace, they'll know the drones can't have gone too far from the threadlines. They'll have to conclude we're in entirely the wrong sector and go hunting for us, rather than tracking us down."

"Which gives you a chance to break contact entirely," Salix said. The human plan relied on too many moving parts, he thought, but it seemed workable. "And then what?"

"And then we surprise them by appearing where we're least expected," the human admiral said. "Now, let's see…"

• • •

Naomi watched, grimly, as the fleet and the drones parted. It was hard not to feel a twinge of discomfort, even fear. The drones were the very latest in Alphan technology—she'd been cautioned to use them only as a last resort, and *never* to let them fall into enemy hands—but if the enemy got a good look at them, they might see through the deception ahead of time. She'd fired on their ships to make them blink, to force them to defend themselves while the starships cloaked and the drones took their places, but…

They won't notice any difference, she told herself. *If we merely cloaked the fleet, they'd know they were there, but here…they still* know *where we are.*

She scowled. She was showing the enemy precisely what they knew they *should* see. And yet…her heart raced as the distance grew and grew. The Pashtali were pushing their drives to the limit, clearly hoping to either run down the fake fleet or—more likely—shadow it to its next destination. She suspected they'd want to try to bring in other fleets in hopes of herding her into a trap, as they'd done before…they might even use the threadlines to get around the fleet and catch it by surprise. They were in for a shock, if they tried. The drones couldn't do anything to defend themselves.

And they'll appear to have vanished, the moment they cross the line, she told herself. *The enemy won't have the slightest idea what happened to them.*

"Admiral," Olson said. "Long-range probes report the crossroads is clear. There are no surviving weapons platforms."

"Keep us cloaked as we make transit," Naomi ordered. The cloaks would fluctuate as they passed through the crossroads, but it would be unnoticeable unless there was someone watching on the far side. The tactical staff had crunched the numbers and decided it was unlikely. "And then set course for the RV point."

"Aye, Admiral," Olson said.

Naomi keyed her console, bringing up the system display. She hadn't dared fantasize about taking and holding the system—it was impossible, even if she'd had a bigger fleet—but she'd done quite a bit of damage. The

Pashtali would need weeks, if not months, to patch up the holes in their defences. Worse, they might have noticed the human attempt to hack their datanet. If they had, they'd need to start installing more protections to prevent the next attempt from actually working, which would make their network more fragmented and prone to disruption. If they hadn't...

Safer to assume they did notice, she thought. *And that they'll take precautions to make sure it doesn't happen again.*

She braced herself as the fleet made transit, *Dauntless* quivering slightly as she fell back into multispace. The local region seemed clear...she waited, counting down the seconds, for the sensor crew to check it truly was before the fleet set course for the RV point. She had contingency plans for being detected, if the Pashtali *had* had someone watching from a safe distance, but...she shook her head. They'd made it.

"Admiral," Olson said. "We'll reach the RV point in five days, unless we run into trouble."

We could be there sooner, if we were willing to use regular shipping lanes, Naomi thought coldly. They could be there in two days, yet they'd almost certainly be detected unless they got insanely lucky. She didn't know what would happen, if they ran into a warship from another power, but she didn't want to find out the hard way. There was no way she could fire on an alien warship unless it was blatantly hostile. Earth didn't need more enemies. *Better to take our time than risk losing everything because we moved too quickly.*

She studied the display for a long moment. She'd detached a pair of scouts to monitor events in P-42, and inform her if the drones were exposed before they crossed into multispace and self-destructed, but it would be several days before they caught up with her. If the plan had gone off perfectly, the enemy had lost track of her fleet; even if it hadn't, they'd have problems deducing where she'd gone. And yet...she keyed the starchart, silently assessing the plan. The enemy had to dance to her tune.

"We'll continue as planned," she said, finally. "The scouts should be waiting for us at the RV point. We'll check their reports, then decide if we want to proceed."

"Aye, Admiral," Olson said.

"And tell everyone to get some rest," Naomi added. "We'll be very busy indeed when we reach the RV point."

• • •

"The message was very clear," Nancy said, as she joined Admiral Yagami in her cabin. "The Pashtali have formally placed Terminus under siege."

"Interesting," Naomi said. "How many times in the past few centuries has anyone bothered to declare a siege?"

Nancy smiled. She and her staff had spent a few hours looking up the references. "Four times in the last five hundred years," she said. "There *are* protocols for declaring a siege, of course, and the Pashtali are following them, but they're rarely used. Normally, the battle is decided quickly enough for the legalities to be left behind."

"Interesting," Naomi repeated. "What do you think it means?"

"My best guess is that the Pashtali think they can't take Terminus in a hurry," Nancy said, flatly. "Either we were wrong about them being able to open a crossroads in the rear or they thought better of it. Regardless, they've made an effective show of force on their side of the crossroads and they've informed the galaxy that there's a siege, which makes it nice and legal for them to fire on anyone trying to get in or out of the system."

"They're throwing down a gauntlet," Naomi mused. "Do you think there's a prospect of the other powers intervening?"

"No," Nancy said. "It's one thing to run patrols through enemy space, and to consider biting off chunks of their territory, but trying to break a siege would be a declaration of war. They might get together as a group, given time, yet..."

"Which means it might still be a trap for us," Naomi said. "Do we have any obligations?"

"Not as far as we can determine, but there are so few precedents," Nancy said. "Legally, they cannot declare a siege unless they are both willing and able to block the crossroads and keep people from crossing the line. If we break the siege, they'll have to set it up again before they make a second declaration."

"I see." Naomi frowned. "Which means it is almost certainly a trap."

Nancy raised her eyebrows. "How can you be sure?"

"I can't," Naomi said. "But they're tying down a lot of their units to keep the system closed down. They can't afford to do it for long, unless they want to lose control of a bunch of other systems. And that means"—her lips quirked—"right now, they have to be thinking we're a *long* way away. They won't be expecting us to mount an attack in less than two weeks and that's optimistic."

"If they intended to lure you into a trap," Nancy pointed out, "they might think it's impossible now."

"They can't raise the siege, then lower it again," Naomi said. "That'll just make them look weak as well as indecisive. And if they think we can't attack their rear, they might even try to break the defences. Even if they don't, they need to keep the crossroads closed or the lesser powers will claim the siege isn't really a siege."

"An argument that won't impress the Pashtali," Nancy commented. "But it might convince the greater powers to intervene."

"Pity they don't have more trading missions running through Terminus," Naomi agreed. "It would make them more inclined to help."

"But they'd come with strings attached," Nancy said. "We may be the first power to try to deal with everyone as equals."

"And that means we have to try to raise the siege," Naomi said. "They know it too."

CHAPTER THIRTY-FOUR

ESS DAUNTLESS, RV POINT THETA

"IT FEELS GOOD TO BE ON A HUMAN SHIP AGAIN," Roger said. "The gravity is right, the lighting is right, the atmosphere is right… and I don't feel, when I stand upright, that I'm going to crack my head into the ceiling."

Admiral Yagami smiled. "I trust you and your shorthanded crew managed to cope?"

"We coped," Roger told her. He tried not to grimace. There'd been a frank exchange of views when the squadron regrouped at the RV point, before they'd received their orders to abandon their mission and rejoin the fleet. "We're pretty overworked, Admiral, but we managed to cope."

"I can imagine," Admiral Yagami agreed. "They *say* you can run a ship with a skeleton crew, but *they* have never actually tried."

Roger nodded. "My report tells the full story, Admiral," he said. "Basically, we harassed the enemy as much as possible, doing everything in our power to make them paranoid. We used their ships and codes, even after they worked out what we were doing, and hit a number of their facilities with long-range ballistic fire. My crews, however, are pretty badly spent. We really did push ourselves to the limit."

"I understand," Admiral Yagami said. "If I could afford to send them and you on shore leave, I would."

"Nowhere to go," Roger said. "Unless you think you can lift the siege of Terminus..."

Admiral Yagami tapped her console. Roger leaned forward as a holographic tactical display appeared in front of him, showing a crossroads and enemy units surrounded it. His eyes narrowed. It was rare for anyone to establish fixed defences in multispace—the tides normally pushed them back into realspace—but the Pashtali seemed to be trying their best to make it work. There were at least forty starships within sensor range and, if he was any judge, quite a few more lurking in the shadows. It was hard to believe that such a force would wind up nothing more than scattered atoms, if it charged through the crossroads. And yet, he knew the enemy would be fools to try.

"We ran a pair of covert scoutships along the threadline, with orders to turn tail and run the moment they got a good look at the enemy fleet," Admiral Yagami told him. "One of the ships didn't return, which should tell you worrying things about their alertness. The other"—she nodded to the display—"brought us some intelligence. We assume the enemy will have altered their dispositions, as they probably know the freighter escaped, but they can't have shifted them *that* much."

Roger frowned. "Those are the ships we saw earlier, aren't they?"

"Yes," Admiral Yagami said. "And to answer your next question, we don't know where they sent their *Crossroads*."

"I was wondering," Roger said, dryly. "Where *could* they have sent her?"

"The tactical staff thinks there's a good chance they're trying to open a backdoor to hit Terminus from the rear," Admiral Yagami said. "If so, we imagine they're looking for a point they can open a crossroads without excessive risk. If not...we don't know. We spotted the fleet as it made transit earlier, passing through P-27 and P-35, but their *Crossroads* was with them at the time. We don't know where it is now."

Roger frowned. "I recall a theory that one could *expand* a crossroads, or even disrupt it in some ways," he said. "It was the basis of *our* jamming theory..."

"The researchers believed any attempt to *widen* a natural crossroads would require power that was truly off the scale," Admiral Yagami said. "If they could do something like that, they wouldn't need to mess around with a siege or looking for a backdoor."

"Yes, Admiral," Roger agreed. "Still, it is a little odd."

Admiral Yagami met his eyes. "Are your crews up to one more mission, if they have a few days of semi-leave on the fleet?"

Roger said nothing for a long moment. "I think so," he said. It would be better for his crew than himself, if he was any judge. His rank made it impossible to let his hair down and have fun on deployment. There were times when he thought attaching a pleasure liner to the fleet would be a very good idea indeed. "It won't be quite the same, of course, but it will be better than nothing. What do you want us to do?"

"This is a copy of the assault plan," Admiral Yagami said. She took a datachip from a locked drawer and held it out for him. "I don't need to remind you, I hope, that this is highly classified, your eyes only. Do not attempt to access the files until you return to your ship and *don't* share anything with your crews until you're underway. We think there are no spies on the fleet, or ships watching us from a safe distance, but there's no point in taking chances."

"Aye, Admiral," Roger said. It was hard not to feel a hint of irritation at the suggestion there might be spies, but...there might. "When do you intend to begin the mission?"

"Five days from now, unless things change before then," Admiral Yagami said. "The fleet is already resupplying, one final time, before we detach the rest of our units to take up position and wait. If this"—she nodded to the display—"is a trap, we can turn it to our advantage and make them dance to our tune."

Roger lifted his eyebrows. "You think it's a trap?"

"I think their siege is a perfect win-win-win for them," Admiral Yagami said. "If they keep the siege in place, they reaffirm their control over the sector and win. If we engage them and lose, they win. If we engage them and win, we'll still take a beating and that will make it easier for them to beat us next time. They'd be foolish if they didn't consider the possibilities."

"What if we ignore the siege?" Roger sat back in his chair. "We could just claim we didn't know about it."

"They've made sure we have no deniability," Admiral Yagami said. "The entire galaxy knows about the siege by now. If we do nothing, they still win. We'd be cut off from our allies, forcing them to reconsider their alliance with us. If they back out..."

Roger nodded, curtly. Galactic alliances rarely lasted. It was too easy for one power to betray the others. If this one was to be different, the human race had to come to the aid of its allies...and if they did, the Pashtali might win. And if that happened, humanity was doomed.

"You have a few days of leave, while the engineering crews go over your ships," Admiral Yagami said. "I wish I could offer sun, sea and sand, but..."

"A starship designed for humans will be quite good enough," Roger said. VR chambers weren't anything like the real thing, but they'd suffice. "Do I have time to write a new will before I go?"

"Probably," Admiral Yagami said. "Have fun. I'll see you before we set out. Dismissed."

Roger stood. "Aye, Admiral."

• • •

"I spoke briefly to the alliance command," Nancy Middleton said, once she was shown into the admiral's office. "They insist they have confidence in their ability to withstand the siege."

"They might be right," Naomi said. "They're getting stronger with every day that goes past without a major attack."

Her lips thinned. "Did you warn them about the *Crossroads*?"

"Yes," Nancy said. "But I don't know if they took my warnings seriously."

"It will be hard to open a crossroads in their rear," Naomi agreed. "But hard isn't the same as impossible."

"I'll take your word for it," Nancy said. "As per your instructions, I didn't tell them anything about your plans."

"Good," Naomi said. "There are still Pashtali on the far side of the crossroads. If they try to get a message out..."

"You don't need to spell it out," Nancy assured her. "That said, I don't know how long we have to prove ourselves to them. On one hand, they can keep the crossroads fairly secure indefinitely, unless the enemy is prepared to soak up heavy losses or open a crossroads behind their lines. On the other, they've been cut off from the rest of the galaxy and that's going to harm their economies. They will undergo a recession, at least on a small scale, and that's going to encourage them to make peace."

"To sell out their long-term interests for short-term gain," Naomi commented. "Perhaps not even *that*, if the Pashtali aren't interested in keeping their agreements."

"It's never easy to decide the right thing to do when you're starving," Nancy countered, sourly. "The more you stare at absolute ruin, the harder it is to look at the greater good. I hope their governments will have the wit to set up an emergency aid program, but there will be limits to how much they can actually do."

Naomi frowned. "So...they may betray us or they may not?"

"Betrayal is a strong word," Nancy said. "One fundamental truth of interstellar power politics is that *everyone* puts their own self-interests first. They won't hesitate to throw us into the fire if the alternative is their own children starving to death. We'd do the same, wouldn't we? I used to think the Alphans would take care of us, but..."

"I didn't," Naomi said, quietly. "My last CO only ever took care of himself—and he wasn't even the worst of them."

"I dealt with viceroys and political representatives," Nancy said. "They could afford to be a little altruistic, but only as long as their interests weren't at stake."

Naomi leaned back in her chair. "A discussion for another time, perhaps," she said. "I have a different question for you. We'll be leaving in two days, barring incidents. Do you want to accompany the fleet?"

Nancy blinked. "Do I have a choice?"

"Yes." Naomi met her eyes, evenly. "My orders said you were to remain on the ship, unless it seemed expedient to put you elsewhere. There was some thinking, I believe, that you might have to remain on Terminus or simply get sent to one of the neighbouring powers—or even recalled to Earth. Right now, I intend to send the fleet train and a handful of other units to wait for us near our final destination. You can accompany them, if you wish, or you can ride into battle with us. If you want to leave the ship, I would understand."

"I see." Nancy took a breath. "How long do I have to decide?"

"The fleet train will leave tomorrow," Naomi said. "You have until then to decide."

Nancy said nothing for a long moment. She knew she was no coward—she'd been on the ship during the last few engagements—and yet, this one promised to be decisive. She had no idea if the enemy would do as the admiral expected, or if they'd come up with something new, but... she was torn, unsure if she wanted to put her life at risk or step aside and watch from the sidelines. It wasn't just her though, she thought. It was her staff as well...

Her mind churned. She was a diplomat and yet, what was a diplomat without a star nation that could back her up? She had no illusions. If the battle was lost and the fleet was destroyed, Earth would be lost too. They'd either become an Alphan protectorate—again—or wind up being conquered by another great power. She wondered if she'd live to see it, if Earth lost the war. It was quite possible her name would be on a list of humans to be eliminated if the Pashtali won the war.

You came this far, she told herself. *You can't back out now.*

She thought, suddenly, of Abraham Douglas. He'd been her rival, once upon a time, and now they were allies...he was back on Earth, unsure of what was happening so many hundred light years away. Would he stand on the bridge and watch the battle? Or would he bow out? And...

"I'll stay," she said, finally. "If the fleet is lost, so is the war."

"There won't be a second chance," Naomi warned. "If you change your mind, let us know by 1600 tomorrow. Check with your staff too. If they want to leave, they can."

"I will," Nancy promised. "But I think I'll see it through."

"Glad to have you with us," Naomi said. Nancy couldn't tell if the admiral was being sincere. "I'll see you on the CIC, if you don't leave tomorrow."

"I'll be fine, Admiral," Nancy said. She stood. "Good luck."

• • •

"I thank you for your offer," Observer Salix said. It was impossible to tell if the alien was offended or amused or simply uncaring, when she'd offered him the chance to disembark. "But my superiors wish me to remain on your ship."

Nancy nodded, unsure if she should be pleased or deeply worried. The Alphans understood the risks—they *had* to know the human fleet would take losses, and the flagship might be one of those losses—but it would still be a diplomatic nightmare if their observer was blown to dust. She wanted to think the Alphans would use it as an excuse to declare war on the Pashtali...she shook her head. It wasn't going to happen. She had no idea how much the Alphans had debated sending ships to Earth, to cover the homeworld as the human navy struck deep into enemy space, but—reading between the lines—she suspected the debate had been intense. They'd come very close to simply saying no.

"I understand," she said. "It'll be good to have you on the command deck."

The alien seemed to take her remark at face value. Naomi reminded herself she couldn't be sure. The Alphans had known humans for a long time and she was *sure* Observer Salix was one of the few who'd studied humans carefully. Human humour and sarcasm meant very little to them—they thought pre-space science-fiction movies were meant to be comedies—but this one might be different. And yet...

"I thank you, both for your offer and for your willingness to accept me." Observer Salix stood and bowed. "With your permission, I will include dispatches to my people in the reports you'll be sending with the fleet train."

"Granted," Naomi said. "If you change your mind, let us know before the fleet train departs."

The alien bowed again, then glided out of the compartment. Naomi watched the door hissing closed behind him, before looking down at the latest reports. The fleet was as close to ready as it would ever be, with all the damages patched up and new missiles transferred from the supply ship. Her gaze lingered on the light codes representing the alien squadrons, their flag officers the only ones outside her tactical staff to know the plan. She'd sooner have kept it to a tiny circle, just in case, but the ambassador had warned her to make sure the aliens were kept fully briefed. The last thing she needed was for their commanders to decide the war was lost and take their squadrons home.

Which isn't possible right now, she told herself. *There's a bloody great enemy fleet in the way.*

Her lips twitched, then thinned as she studied the starchart. The Pashtali should have *no* idea her fleet was so close to Terminus. They had to think—worst-case—she was still ten days from lifting the siege. Unless they hadn't been fooled at all. She didn't want to consider the possibility, but it was inescapable. They might have realise she was trying to con them, deduced what she'd really done and taken steps. And yet, they would want to believe what they'd seen. The essence of a good con job, she'd been told, was to make sure the mark was told what he wanted to hear, so he'd be less inclined to question it. Would the Pashtali see what they wanted to see?

She stared down at her hands. The gambit might work. It would give the enemy a bloody nose, at the very least, and perhaps even raise the siege. If the second part worked...she gritted her teeth. The Pashtali could keep fighting, even as the cost of suppressing the human race reached astronomical levels, if they considered the consequences of continuing the fight to be better than giving up and agreeing to a truce. How long could she continue to wage war if they refused to come to terms? She didn't have to look at the reports to know that her fleet was already running critically short of everything from missiles to spare parts.

Admiral Glass must have felt the same way, she thought, numbly. She wanted to see her old mentor, to speak to him one final time. *He was the only man who could lose the war in a single battle.*

She wished, as the loneliness of command fell around her like a shroud, that she had someone she could talk to, someone who would see her as a person, not as an admiral or a naval officer or even a representative of her race. A lover, perhaps, or even a sibling. But there was no one. Janet was the closest thing she had to a friend on the ship and *she* was Naomi's subordinate. There were limits to how much she could share with her...

Her eyes drifted over the starchart, before she clicked it off. She'd get some rest before the fleet departed, heading straight for Terminus. Again. And then...

Win or lose, she promised herself, *those bastards will know they've been in a fight.*

CHAPTER THIRTY-FIVE

TERMINUS CROSSROADS (MULTISPACE)

"CAPTAIN," MARQUEZ SAID. "I have hard locks on a dozen enemy warships and soft locks on at least twenty more."

"Show me." Roger leaned forward, studying the display. "They do seem determined to keep people from leaving, don't they?"

"Yes, Captain," Marquez agreed. "Anything that pops through the crossroads is dead."

Roger nodded, curtly. The Pashtali had deployed in a classic siege formation, with smaller ships in position to engage anything making transit and larger warships held in reserve to back them up if they encountered something they couldn't handle. The sheer volume of minelaying was impressive and he was fairly sure the mines were actually cheap and expendable, intended more to warn the besiegers of a sally than stop an offensive on their own. The more he looked at it, the more he had to admit he was impressed. It seemed clear the enemy had no intention of mounting an offensive of their own.

Which makes a great deal of sense, he told himself. *Why bother throwing away a guaranteed win when you can just keep the cork in the bottle and wait?*

His eyes narrowed as he studied the display. The folds of reality within multispace were dangerously close to the crossroads, providing all the cover a major fleet could want. The scouts had yet to find the missing enemy vessels and there were no reports of them breaking into Terminus from the rear, suggesting the enemy was up to something. He had a nasty feeling the remaining ships were lurking nearby, waiting for the humans—or someone—to stumble into their trap. It was impossible to be sure—multispace made it difficult to trust one's own sensors, no matter how advanced—but it made sense. The Pashtali were giant spiders. It stood to reason they'd weave a web and wait for their enemies to blunder into it.

And yet, they still think our fleet is light-years away, he thought. He reminded himself, sharply, not to take it for granted. There were enough clearly visible enemy warships to give Admiral Yagami a very hard time, if she took her fleet into range. *Even if they don't know we're close, they're still ready and waiting for someone to fly into their trap.*

He glanced at Lieutenant Hawke. "Are the slave links up and running?"

"Aye, sir," Hawke said. "The squadron is ready for anything, as long as *anything* isn't a target that can shoot back."

Roger nodded. He'd spent two days on leave—or as close to it as the fleet could manage—and the third reorganising his ships and crew. Half his personnel had been reassigned to the fleet train—they were too important to risk any further—and the remainder had been assigned to his ship, leaving the rest of the squadron slaved to the flagship. It was the kind of arrangement, he'd noted at the time, that would give a responsible commanding officer a fit of the vapours—the slave datalinks could be broken at any moment, cutting the flagship off from the rest of the squadron—but it cut the manpower requirements down to the bare minimum. He simply hadn't seen any other way to do it. There was no way in hell the squadron was going to fly away from the crossroads, not unless the enemy were both incompetent and asleep. It was going to be hard enough preserving what few crewmen he'd kept on his ship.

"Keep us moving," he said. "Load the final set of IFF codes into the transmitter and prepare to transmit."

"Aye, sir," Hawke said. "Do you think they'll buy it?"

Roger shrugged. The Pashtali had seen his ships. They *knew* the vessels were in human hands. He'd done what he could to fiddle with the drive signatures—and no one was going to get a clear look at their hulls in multispace—but he doubted the trick would last for long. The IFF codes might win them a few seconds—multispace would distort the signal, providing a convincing explanation for the code not matching any in the enemy database—but he doubted it would be anything more than a minute at most. The moment they charged the enemy position, they'd be fired upon. The Pashtali weren't the only ones who used suicide tactics. And his fleet *was* completely expendable.

He keyed his terminal. "All crew on the beta list, proceed to the shuttle," he ordered. "I say again, all beta crewers proceed to the shuttle."

"We should be trying to fly this ship from the shuttle," Marquez commented. "We could run datalinks through the ship and into the shuttle..."

"There wasn't time." Roger had made a note for the next time, if there *was* a next time. "There's nothing to be gained by worrying about it now."

He took a breath, bracing himself. They'd run hundreds of simulations and few, very few, ended with them getting out alive. The enemy were alert, their sensors probing the energy storms and sensor distortions of multispace like a man peering into a driving rainstorm. He wondered, idly, if they'd fire on a sensor ghost and ask questions later. He'd been on military bases where the guards had had orders to shoot first and not bother with the questions. They'd never struck him as particularly safe.

But then, anyone who enters a restricted zone does so at the risk of his life, he reminded himself, wryly. *And the Pashtali have already told the entire galaxy that they've placed the system under siege.*

Marquez looked up. "Captain, we're entering detection range now."

"Hold us steady," Roger said. The display showed two lines, indicating the point when they *could* be detected and the point where detection was inevitable. There was no way to be sure *when* they'd be detected...he shook his head. It didn't matter. They weren't trying to sneak around the enemy position. "Remember, we're a nicely innocent squadron that's just been recalled to reinforce the besiegers."

Hawke snickered. "It might be too late to convince them."

"Perhaps," Roger agreed. The deception might have worked in the early days—technically, it *had*—but now, the Pashtali would have recalled and redeployed every ship they could. They might need to keep their homeworlds protected, ensuring there were hard limits on how many vessels they could point at Terminus or Earth, yet...he put the thought out of his head. "We'll maintain the pretence as long as they're not shooting at us."

Marquez scowled at her console. "They just swept an active sensor beam over us," she said, grimly. "I'm not sure they detected us..."

Her console bleeped, warningly. "They *did*," she corrected herself. "We're being pinged."

"Shoot them the distorted IFFs," Roger ordered. "And then signal the drones."

"Aye, sir," Hawke said.

Roger gritted his teeth as the display sharpened, dozens of enemy ships coming into view. He'd been right, he noted, although he took no pleasure in it. The enemy *did* have an entire fleet lurking near the crossroads, enough ships to stop the admiral dead in her tracks. He wondered if the enemy hadn't been fooled at all, or if they expected the other interstellar powers to intervene and raise the siege. It wasn't impossible. The Galactics might come up with an argument that justified conquering the crossroads in the name of liberating it. His teeth clenched in disgust. The more he saw the truth behind the honeyed words, the more he hated it.

"They're transmitting a set of questions," Hawke said. "I think they're unconvinced."

"And they're locking weapons on our hulls," Marquez said. "We've been rumbled."

Roger keyed his console. There was no longer any time to delay. Locking weapons on an incoming ship's hull was a clear warning, a threat of lethal force if the ship didn't come about and run for its life. The Pashtali either knew they were faking or they were simply being cautious. It didn't matter. There was no way they could reverse course or even come to a stop. It was time to go.

"All hands, report to the shuttle," he ordered, standing. "I say again, all hands report to the shuttle."

He looked at Marquez. "Prime the attack pattern, then trigger it to activate in one minute."

"Aye, sir," Marquez said. Hawke was already on his feet, heading for the hatch. "Done."

"Go," Roger snapped.

Marquez stood and hurried to the airlock. Roger looked around the bridge—his first real command, even though she was a captured alien warship—and felt a twinge of regret. He'd never expected to keep her, he'd never expected she'd survive the war, but...he shook his head and headed for the hatch himself, trying to keep his feelings under control. He'd heard stories of grown men, experienced commanding officers, weeping as they left their commands for the final time. He hadn't understood it until now. He felt as if he was about to lose something important.

He stepped through the hatch and hurried down the corridor to the airlock, scrambling into the shuttle. The hatch banged closed behind him as a low vibration ran through the ship, the drives powering up for the final time. The cruiser was picking up speed, charging right into the teeth of enemy fire; the remainder of the squadron, slaved to the flagship, would follow suit. Their missile launchers were already coming online. They'd be lucky if they got close enough to ram—the moment they opened fire, the enemy would return it—but they'd give the enemy a fright. And the decoy drones behind them were already powering up...

Let them commit themselves, he thought. *And then they'll have to give chase.*

A series of jerks ran through the shuttle, followed by a quiver as she undocked from the starship and floated into multispace. Roger took his seat—there was no point in issuing orders, not now—and keyed his console, bringing up the live feed from outside the hull. The enemy were opening fire, their missiles lancing towards his ships...he grinned, savagely, as the automated point defence started to blast missiles into dust. They'd be beaten down quickly, but...his smile grew wider as the drones came online. It looked, very much, like a full-scale attack. The nearer warships were lashing out in all directions, the further ones gliding forward in what looked like a simple pincer movement. They didn't know they were being conned, not yet. Roger thought they probably had their suspicions, but...

They can't take the chance, he told himself. *They'd be risking us defeating the nearer units first, then either backing off or trying to take on the further units.*

He put the thought aside as his squadron staggered under enemy fire. The ships were taking a beating, steaming oxygen and plasma as they closed on the enemy ships. He'd considered depressurising the slaved vessels before they'd departed, but it would have been far too revealing if the enemy blew holes in the hull. In hindsight...he shrugged, enjoying the sight of an enemy vessel taking hits from an automated cruiser. The firing pattern wasn't as intuitive as an organic brain—the Galactics had never developed true AI—but at such close range it hardly mattered. Three of his vessels exploded into balls of expanding plasma, a fourth overloaded its engines and rammed an enemy warship, destroying both ships. His ship kept going, aiming itself straight at a battleship. The Pashtali poured fire into her hull, but it was too late. The two ships collided and exploded.

"Bet they wish they hadn't built the ships so well," Hawke commented, from the other side of the shuttlecraft. "Their designers did a very good job."

Roger snorted, watching the brief engagement unfold. There was nothing else he could do as the shuttle fled towards the human fleet. The enemy ships were completing their pincer, discovering—too late—that their jaws had closed on empty space. Their fleet seemed to be swarming around like angry hornets—*or spiders*, his thoughts added—who'd just had their nest kicked by a sadistic child. His eyes narrowed as he saw the other vessels, lurking in the distance. The Pashtali had kept their *Crossroads* in reserve.

Odd choice, he thought. *But at least we know where it is now.*

The intercom bleeped. "This is your captain speaking," the pilot said. "I'm afraid we're going to be experiencing some turbulence on our flight, so please enjoy the company of the stewardesses and relax."

Roger snorted, without taking his eyes off the live feed. The enemy fleet had seen the human fleet now—the *real* fleet, lurking behind the drones—and, if he was any judge, the enemy commanders were trying to decide what to do. If they thought they were being tricked—again—they might go back to their original positions, rather than taking the bait Admiral Yagami was offering. Roger had no idea which way they'd jump. A person who'd been tricked once might hesitate to risk it again, even though there wasn't a second trick. And then...

Marquez caught his eye. "Sir, what do we do now?"

"Nothing," Roger said. Their fate was no longer in their hands. The shuttle pilot could get them to *Dauntless*, and Admiral Yagami could get them to their next destination, but *he* could do nothing. His ship was gone. His crew were either fleeing beside him or already on their way home. "We watch and wait."

His eyes narrowed as the enemy fleet consolidated itself. They seemed unsure of what to do. He wondered, idly, if the kamikaze attack had taken out the enemy flagship. It seemed unlikely—the Solar Navy had a chain of command that ran from the highest admiral to the lowest midshipman, with a clear procedure for determining who was in command at any given point—but possible. Command might have devolved on someone unprepared to handle it, afraid of fucking up and getting someone killed...he shook his head, reminding himself—again—of the dangers of assigning human motivations to aliens. The Pashtali were definitely not human. Their reasoning might be so out of left field that the human race would find it incomprehensible.

They may simply be playing it safe, he thought. *We tricked them with drones and as long as our fleet doesn't open fire, they may assume the ships are nothing more than drones too.*

His lips twitched. The Pashtali had to be annoyed at themselves. The attack had not only cost them a number of ships—damaged or destroyed—but also revealed how many other ships were lurking near the crossroads. He was surprised they weren't throwing missiles at the unarmed shuttlecraft. If they managed to reach a starship, or an FTL transmitter, the entire galaxy would know about the enemy fleet. And this time they couldn't reposition themselves, not without lifting the siege.

And if the fleet is here, it can't be somewhere else, he thought. Even if the enemy *did* change their position, it wouldn't be hard to calculate how far it could travel. *How much mischief could their enemies do if they knew the Pashtali couldn't react in a hurry?*

Admiral Yagami was clearly thinking along the same lines. Her fleet closed slowly but surely—entering missile range without getting too close—and then opened fire. Roger winced, feeling a stab of sympathy for the Pashtali as a barrage of missiles flashed towards them. It was normally difficult to get accurate targeting data in multispace, certainly at extreme range, but the admiral had solved *that* problem by drawing targeting information from the shuttle. The Pashtali would be kicking themselves, when they worked it out. They really *should* have fired on the shuttle. Sure, it was against Galactic Law, but when had they ever given a damn about that?

Perhaps it's a good sign, he thought. In his experience, people paid more attention to the rules if they thought they'd be caught and punished for breaking them. *If they're paying attention to the legalities, they're clearly feeling vulnerable.*

He watched, grimly, as the fleet reversed course, without even *trying* to fire a second barrage before retreating. Admiral Yagami's crews had spent *days* bolting missile pods to the hulls, and attaching others to tethers, to ensure their first punch was as powerful as possible. There were so many missiles that the enemy fleet would be wise to break off, yet… he smiled, grimly, as the enemy point defence opened fire. They'd kill hundreds, perhaps thousands, of missiles, but there would be hundreds more ready to blow their targets to atoms. The enemy couldn't be in any doubt any longer. They really *were* facing the human fleet.

And Admiral Yagami is already out of range, he thought. *They wasted their one chance to return fire.*

The intercom bleeped, again. "We'll be docking with *Dauntless* shortly," the pilot said. He sounded absurdly cheerful for a man who'd just flown a lumbering shuttle through a cloud of missiles. "And then you can disembark. Thank you for flying with Apocalypse Spacelanes and we hope you enjoy the rest of your holiday. Don't forget to tip the stewardesses. They've put up with enough from you."

Roger rolled his eyes, then concentrated on the display. The enemy were launching decoys, their position dissolving into a haze of distortion as the ECM drones drew missiles onto them instead of their targets. It was impossible to tell, as missiles started to detonate, how many of them had reached their targets, let alone destroyed them. The tactical analysts might be able to work out how much damage the humans had done, but the admiral would have to assume they'd done no damage without hard data. And that meant...

Come on, you bastards, he thought. Would the Pashtali take the bait? There'd never have a better chance to win the war. *We had our chance to cut off your head. Don't you want the chance to cut off ours?*

CHAPTER THIRTY-SIX

ESS DAUNTLESS, TERMINUS CROSSROADS (MULTISPACE)

"ADMIRAL," OLSON SAID. "The shuttle has docked safety."

Naomi nodded, never taking her eyes off the display. The enemy fleet seemed unsure of itself. She'd caught them with their pants down and hit them hard, harder than they could have expected, but she'd also given them a chance to run her down. The live feed from the shuttle told her the enemy had a *Crossroads*, giving them a chance to get ahead of her...if they reacted in time. If they refused to take the bait...

We'll have hurt them, she thought, *but not enough to stop them.*

She sighed inwardly, feeling the seconds tick away. A *conventional* attempt to raise the siege would have been, ideally, paired with an attack from the far side. The Pashtali had clearly expected it, judging by how quickly they'd moved their fleet, and yet...one hadn't materialised. Did they think the attackers had screwed up the timing? Or... she forced herself to wait, hoping and praying the Pashtali took the bait. They'd never have a better chance to bring her fleet to battle on favourable terms.

"Admiral," Olson said. "The enemy fleet is raising the siege and coming after us."

"Not all the siege," Naomi commented. "The minefields will still be in place."

She took a breath as the display updated. The Pashtali had clearly taken a few minutes to reorganise their fleet. She'd had a chance to hammer them into submission, but not the ships and firepower to take advantage of it. And now...the enemy ships were picking up speed rapidly, coming after the human ships. Her instincts told her to run. It was unfortunate, in a way, that her plans insisted they be allowed to chase her along a very predictable course.

"Signal the fleet," she ordered. "Set course for Antigen, as planned."

"Aye, Admiral," Olson said. The display updated, again. "The fleet is underway."

Naomi keyed her terminal, bringing up the starchart although she knew it by heart. It was hard to be sure—she knew there was at least one other enemy fleet in the region and there might be others—but unless the Pashtali got very lucky they wouldn't be able to ambush her short of Antigen itself. The threadlines wouldn't let them get ahead of her until then, even though they had a *Crossroads*. They weren't the only race that had surveyed the sector, in both realspace and multi-space. If there were threadlines that would let them outrun her, she'd know about them.

Unless everyone decided to keep them a secret, she thought. *But what are the odds of that?*

She put the thought aside. The enemy fleet was *tough*. She'd hurt it—the analysts were still arguing over how *badly*- but it was still powerful enough to smash *her* fleet if she gave it a chance. And there was the other fleet...she gritted her teeth. Her most pessimistic calculations insisted the other fleet couldn't get into position to block them, not unless they'd run a decoy campaign akin to the one she'd pulled. It wasn't a reassuring thought. If the enemy worked out what she'd done—and they would, because they knew where her fleet was now—they might steal the idea for themselves. Why not? She'd certainly stolen some of their ideas.

"Admiral," Olson said. "We'll be leaving the threadline in two days and making transit in realspace to another crossroads, then proceeding through two more to Antigen."

Naomi nodded. "We don't want to get too far ahead," she said. There were shorter routes to their destination, but they ran the risk of being intercepted ahead of time. "We don't want them to give up and reverse course."

Her mind churned. What would the enemy do? She'd tempted them with the prospect of destroying her entire fleet and, in return, they'd effectively lifted the siege. The Terminus powers would have no trouble blowing away the minefield, and the handful of ships backing it up, and securing the far side of the crossroads...the Pashtali would have to choose between running her fleet down, which would knock the human race out of the war, or reversing course and going back to re-establish the siege. *That* wouldn't be easy. The best they could hope for, if they did, was locking the crossroads down again. And they'd still look weak in front of the entire galaxy.

The vultures are really starting to gather now, she thought. The news reports were all too clear. *They need a victory or they're toast.*

"They'll be chasing us for a week or so," Olson said. "Do you think they'll give up?"

"They can't," Naomi said, although she wasn't sure that was true. The Pashtali could break contact anytime they liked. Hell, they might assume *she* intended to break contact and simply abandon the pursuit before she had a chance. "They need a victory."

She smiled, inwardly. The aliens might be very alien, but their thinking couldn't be *that* alien. The iron law of galactic politics was that the strong did what they liked, as the Athenians had argued thousands of years ago, and the weak suffered what they must...if they weren't accidentally wiped out. It stood to reason that the Pashtali would do everything in their power to avoid looking vulnerable, with so many other powers eying their territory with hungry eyes. If they broke contact, even if they re-established the siege, they'd look weak and weakness invited attack. No, they'd come after her...

Unless they decide to abandon large chunks of their empire and defend their core worlds while building up their forces to resume the war, she thought. *But that would bring powerful enemy forces far too close to their homeworld for comfort.*

"Keep the range close, but not too close," she reminded him. Her mother had told her once, years ago, that the secret to catching a guy's heart was to run...but not too fast. The principle was the same. As long as the enemy thought they could catch her, as long as they thought they could still win, they wouldn't give up and go home. "And signal the fleet. If anyone has any problems, I want to know about them."

"Aye, Admiral," Olson said.

"And make sure the alpha crews get some rest," Naomi added. They were going to be keeping their distance for a week, rather than skirmishing with the enemy. There was no need to wear her people out. "You, too."

"Aye, Admiral," Olson said. "And you."

Naomi nodded. "Alert me if anything changes," she ordered. Perversely, the best thing she could do for her crew was to make a show of going to her cabin to sleep. The fact that the cabin was right next to the CIC, and she could get from one to the other in less than a minute, was immaterial. She had to make a show of calm confidence. "And transfer command to the beta crews at the end of your shift."

"Aye, Admiral."

• • •

It was customary, Observer Salix reflected, for hostile encounters in space to be decided very quickly. Or at least it had been. Observer Salix had grown up in a universe where *his* race's warcruisers were the finest instruments of destruction in the known galaxy, armed with burners that could chop through armour like a knife through butter and protected by armour that could stand off anything less. It had been galling for his people to lose so many fine ships to a primitive race—his heart clenched every time he thought about it—but even those engagements had been decided quickly.

The idea of a long, drawn-out battle was alien to him.

And yet, this battle...

He was uneasily aware of the minutes turning into hours and the hours turning into days as he moved between the CIC and his cabin, snatching a few hours of sleep before returning to his lonely vigil. The human fleet was moving as fast as it could, yet there was no way it could escape unless it lost itself somewhere in multispace. Observer Salix knew the humans *wanted* to be chased and yet, as time wore on, he found himself wondering if the humans had made a deadly mistake. Their course wasn't as random as it looked. There was no reason the Pashtali couldn't bring their second fleet into position to intercept and trap the humans as they made transit through the next crossroads.

They're taking an immense risk, he mused, slowly. *For what?*

It was hard to decide, he conceded to himself, if the humans were doing the right thing. The plan looked good on paper. The Pashtali would lose—even if they won, they lost—but it could cost the humans everything too. His thoughts ran in circles as he studied the unchanging display, his eyes lingering on the tidal wave of red icons shadowing the human fleet. The last update had made it clear the siege had been broken, once and for all. The Pashtali *needed* to win, or the rest of the galaxy would turn on them. They no longer even had the option of backing off and conceding human independence.

He wasn't sure himself what he wanted to happen. His people wanted the Pashtali to lose, ideally so badly they couldn't capitalise on their technological breakthroughs. They'd backed the humans in a bid to make sure of it and yet...he couldn't help wondering what would happen if the humans won the war. Would they remain friends and allies to their former masters, or would they seek revenge? Or...would they just grow distant and ignore any future pleas for help, if the Alphans needed it? He scowled. Even a decade ago, the idea of his people needing help would have seemed absurd. Now, it had happened.

We are looking for ways to put together a peace treaty, he thought. The last update had made that clear, although it was also clear the message had been sent before the besiegers had been attacked and their fleet had given chase. *But will that mean exchanging one enemy for another?*

He wished, not for the first time, that he wasn't so alone. There were no other Alphans on the fleet, no one he could talk to…no one who could confirm his fears or tell him he was being silly and worrying over nothing. He'd been cautioned of the risks of travelling alone, of falling into a trap laid by his own thoughts, but…he knew his fears were valid. What would happen, many years from now, if Earth and Alphan Prime had a disagreement? The humans might be primitive, and foolish enough not to capitalise on their own technology before the invasion fleet arrived, but they were also dangerous. The Lupines, and the Vulteks, and now the Pashtali had found that out. Would his own people make the same discovery, at some later date?

And there's no one to talk to, he thought. He couldn't talk to a human. He'd been discouraged from forming friendships, let alone…no, he couldn't talk to them about *this*. It would bring on the crisis he feared. What would the humans do, if they knew he saw them as a potential threat? *What do I do?*

He considered, briefly, trying to ensure both sides lost. But how? No answer came to mind. His people wouldn't thank him if he broke his neutrality. Nor could he do anything, even if he was prepared to throw his life away. *Dauntless* was a human ship, not one that had been begged, borrowed or stolen. The most he could do was kill a handful of humans before being killed himself, leaving his people with a diplomatic crisis at the worst possible time. They wanted the humans to win, but…

You might be jumping at shadows, he told himself. It would be years before the humans finished digesting their conquests, if they somehow pulled off a complete victory…and they wouldn't. *There's no reason to assume there'll be a future crisis between Earth and Alphan Prime.*

But he knew, as he continued his lonely watch, that history argued otherwise.

• • •

"We got the latest set of updates from Antigen," Nancy Middleton said. "Apparently, there are now warships from seventeen different races patrolling the outer system."

"Witnesses," Naomi commented. She studied the message thoughtfully. The Galactics wouldn't have any trouble deducing her fleet was heading straight for Antigen. They just needed to look at a starchart and draw a line. "Is there any risk they'll try to stop us?"

"I don't think so," Nancy said. She sounded confident, but she was trained to project such an air at all times. "They don't want the Pashtali to win."

"The enemy of my enemy is my enemy's enemy," Naomi quoted. "No more, no less."

She keyed the terminal, bringing up the starchart. *James Bond* had done yeoman work, forwarding intelligence through the FTL network... the odds were good, she thought, that the Pashtali would uncover them shortly. She hoped the crew had the sense to keep their heads as low as possible, perhaps even undock and head for safety before the aliens caught up with them. And yet, she needed the intelligence. If the Galactics tried to take control of the crossroads, it could bring more and more powers into the war.

And not on the right side, she thought. The intelligence briefings claimed that certain powers were running convoys to Terminus and beyond, even setting up bases in enemy space, but she didn't know for sure. *If they turn against us, instead...*

"They aren't interested in starting a war with us," Nancy commented. "They certainly don't want to side with the Pashtali."

"Just because we have enemies in common doesn't mean we're friends," Naomi said. Human history had dozens of examples of allies becoming enemies, after winning the war and trying to come to terms with the post-war universe. The British and Americans had allied with the Soviet Union to defeat Nazi Germany, only to wind up in a cold war with the Russians after the Germans were defeated. It was sheer luck that the human race hadn't fallen into civil war, after the Alphans had withdrawn. "Can we rely on them to keep their distance?"

"I think so," Nancy said. Her lips twisted in distaste. "There's nothing to gain from taking sides against us."

Naomi smiled. "Except for eternal gratitude from the Pashtali?"

Nancy smiled back. "Like I said, nothing."

"Hah." Naomi studied the display for a long cold moment. "As long as they look strong, the vultures won't dare to close on them."

She scowled. The fleet was two days from Antigen, with the enemy fleet in hot pursuit. It was hard to be sure, but it looked as if they'd shed a handful of ships...including the *Crossroads*. And that meant...she was sure the enemy had signalled ahead, trying to organise an ambush. They were herding her in the right direction...the direction she *wanted* to be herded. If she was in command of the enemy fleet, she would have wondered at an enemy who was doing precisely what she wanted her to do.

There aren't many other choices, she thought. *We gave up our best chance to break contact when we passed through the last crossroads. Right now, no matter how they work the problem, the only real hope of escape is flying through Antigen and hoping the neutral powers prevent the Pashtali from chasing us.*

"They're on thin ice," Nancy assured her, calmly. It took Naomi a moment to remember what the ambassador had been saying. "The Alphans are trying to put together a proper peace conference. The Galactics are preparing to grab what they can, so they get a seat at the table. They've already lost their control over the Terminus bottleneck, Admiral, and one more defeat will ruin them. They know it too."

"And one more victory will give them a breathing space," Naomi said. She shook her head in frustration. She could kill five enemy warships for every ship they killed, an exchange rate so lopsided it was completely absurd, and they'd still have enough ships to protect their core worlds from the rest of the galaxy. "Why didn't they just try to grab the Occupied Zone, then stop and force us to accept it?"

"They'd never have a better chance to place bases on the edge of the Alphan Empire," Nancy said. "They knew the Alphans wouldn't intervene, not at first. And then they could decide if they wanted to use the Alphans as a buffer, or a target, at leisure."

"Madness," Naomi said. "It would be one hell of a gamble."

"Less of a risk than you might think," Nancy said. "If the Alphans let them get away with it, the Pashtali have bases; if they don't, the Alphans are unlikely to drive them all the way back to their homeworld. Either way, their losses are minimised."

The intercom bleeped. "Admiral," Olson's voice said. "We just got a solid look at the enemy fleet. I can confirm the *Crossroads* is not accompanying the warships."

Naomi nodded. "Good," she said. It wasn't *entirely* good news, but it suggested the enemy would hesitate to close the range before Antigen. They'd want to keep her heading in the right direction. Her lips twisted. Someone was flying into a trap, but she wasn't sure who. Who was the trapper, and who was going to be trapped? "Expand our recon shell. We don't want them sneaking up on us."

And if our timing is messed up, this will go horribly wrong, she thought. They'd have a brief chance to break off and run, if they were warned in time, but...the odds wouldn't be in their favour. *We could lose the battle, and the war, in a few short hours.*

CHAPTER THIRTY-SEVEN

ANTIGEN

"THEY SHOULD BE HERE BY NOW," Sarah said. "Do you think…?"

Thomas said nothing. The entire system had been buzzing for days, ever since it had become clear the human fleet was heading directly towards Antigen…and that a powerful enemy force was on its tail, snapping at its heels. The neutral warships had assembled to 'protect' the planet, and—purely coincidentally—make it difficult for the planet's defenders to take up position on the crossroads, while reporters and observers had flooded in from all the neighbouring systems. Thomas suspected they were in for one hell of a show. The Pashtali couldn't afford to let the fleet escape, not now. Antigen was too open a system.

"There was never a precise arrival time," he reminded her, finally. He'd been a trader long enough to know that trying to keep a precise timetable was asking for trouble. There was no way to guarantee a starship would arrive on the right date, at the right time, and anyone who claimed otherwise was lying. "We only ever had a rough ETA."

Sarah shot him a sharp look. *James Bond* was undocked, heading away from the planet on a course that would—eventually—take her to a crossroads that would lead her into neutral space. He hadn't been given contingency orders for when the fleet arrived—what orders he had been given were vague—but he intended to record the engagement, then ensure the recordings reached Earth even if the fleet didn't. And yet…he eyed the timer balefully. They might have messed up the timing. They'd had to leave the high orbitals before they were locked down, as they would be when the fleet arrived, but they couldn't dawdle too long before someone started asking questions. He had a nasty feeling their cover wasn't as tight as he wished. The Pashtali had had plenty of opportunities to notice *James Bond* wasn't quite what she seemed.

"We'll have to pass through the crossroads in four hours," she said, tartly. "And then…"

She broke off as her console bleeped an alert. "They're here!"

Thomas leaned forward, watching as the human fleet spilled out of the crossroads. There were a *lot* of ships, ranging from purpose-built warships to converted freighters and the massive crossroads generator. It was huge and yet, he could see gaps in the formations that suggested the fleet had been in a battle and hadn't had time to reorganise. He wondered, idly, if the watching Galactics believed what they were seeing. The fleet had been running for over a week. They'd had plenty of time to reorganise and reform before reaching Antigen.

"They look ready for anything, don't they?" Sarah never took her eyes off her console. "But the Pashtali won't be impressed."

"No," Thomas agreed. The converted freighters weren't proper warships and never would be, no matter how many weapons and defences were crammed into their hulls. The best they could do, once they'd fired off their missiles, was serve as point defence platforms to cover the *real* warships. Or soak up missiles that would otherwise be aimed at them. "They have to win here, don't they?"

He felt his heart turn to ice. It hadn't been easy to monitor the ever-shifting patterns of galactic opinion—there were so many rumours it was hard to tell which ones were even remotely true—but it was clear opinion was turning against the Pashtali. They'd made too many enemies in the past decade and now those enemies were scenting weakness, readying themselves to take advantage. They might not be friendly to humanity—they'd snatch human territory too, if they thought they could get away with it—but their selfishness would work in humanity's favour. The coming battle would decide the war, he reflected numbly. If the Pashtali won, they'd buy time; if they lost...

"The fleet is taking up position," Sarah said. "The enemy ships can't be far behind."

"No," Thomas agreed. He scowled as he saw the starships jockeying for a better view, too close to the coming battle for comfort. If they were unlucky, they'd be blown away by a passing missile...he wondered, sourly, if they were being sent to the battlefield to provide an excuse for their superiors to join the war. Or if they were just foolish. He'd yet to meet a reporter with a working brain. "It's going to be one hell of a show."

• • •

"Transit complete, Admiral," Olson reported. "No enemy ships within attack range."

Naomi allowed herself a moment of relief. Antigen *was* Pashtali territory, at least in theory, and with so many alien warships within the system it had been quite likely the enemy would dispatch their fleet to remind everyone it was *theirs*. Or that their second fleet had headed for the system directly, instead of linking up with the first. The reports had suggested the fleet hadn't arrived, but there was no way to be sure. The Pashtali had every right to sneak a fleet through their own system.

"Deploy crossroads defences," she ordered. The crossroads was too large for a classic defence—she didn't have anything like enough mines to blunt an enemy offensive—but she could give them a black eye when they started to come through the crossroads. "And order the fleet to reposition itself as planned."

"Aye, Admiral," Olson said.

"And signal *Crossroads*," Naomi added. "She is to stand ready."

"Aye, Admiral," Olson said, again. "The carrier commanders are requesting permission to launch their starfighters."

"Hold them in reserve," Naomi said. There was no need to launch her pilots into space just yet. The enemy hadn't arrived. "We'll deploy shortly."

She forced herself to wait, eying the display warily. There were a *lot* of alien ships in the system, from powerful battle squadrons to hundreds of civilian craft nosing disturbingly close to the crossroads. It was going to be a diplomatic headache if one or more of the civilian craft were mistaken for warships and destroyed or, worse, if the Pashtali used them as cover for a sneak attack. There weren't many warships assigned to the system itself—nothing heavier than a frigate, according to *James Bond*—but they could still pose a threat. Or...

The timer bleeped. "Admiral," Olson said. "The attack could come at any moment."

Naomi nodded. She'd assumed the enemy fleet would keep coming, pushing its drives to the limit, as it neared the crossroads. If so...they were on the other side of the crossroads now, preparing to attack. Would they come crashing through, weapons blazing, or would they suspect an ambush? If so...she looked away from the crossroads. She'd given them the perfect opportunity, if they had the nerve...

A red icon appeared on the display, followed by two more. "Admiral," Olson said, as more icons flashed into existence. "They're probing the crossroads."

"Clear the alpha platforms to open fire," Naomi ordered. The Pashtali had had enough time to take a good look at her fleet, standing guard on the crossroads. "Drive them away."

"Aye, Admiral," Olson said. "Platforms going live...now."

Naomi braced herself as two enemy icons vanished. They'd gone to alert their commanders on the far side. Good thinking on their part, she supposed. There was no way they could get updates from Antigen as long as they were in multispace, which meant they needed to send ships through and...she smiled, briefly, as the remaining ships writhed under her fire. They didn't have a chance to return fire themselves before they were destroyed.

"Admiral," Olson said. "All targets destroyed."

"That was a probe, nothing more," Naomi said. "The next attack will be a great deal more serious."

She studied the display thoughtfully, counting the seconds. What would the enemy do? Her fleet was dangerously close to the crossroads, tempting them into launching a major attack, but it would be costly. They'd be far better off waiting, yet...could they? They might prefer to try to keep her pinned down, ensuring she couldn't leave the crossroads. The tactical handbooks insisted the most dangerous moment of a crossroads defence was when the defenders were trying to break off and Naomi was inclined to agree. And yet, the crossroads was impossible to defend for long...

"Move the scouts into position," she ordered. "And prepare the missile pods to back them up."

"Aye, Admiral," Olson said.

Naomi gritted her teeth as a handful of enemy ships materialised on the crossroads and opened fire, spitting missiles in all directions. Their targeting wasn't great, part of her mind noted thoughtfully, but they weren't shooting at random. She guessed they'd downloaded targeting data from the first wave, then used it to program the launch...not bad thinking, she supposed, if one had missiles to burn. They didn't have to waste time orienting themselves after the jump. They just had to fire off the missiles and rely on the uploaded data to guide them to their targets.

And they do want us pinned down, she thought. She felt uneasy, even though she'd planned it that way. It felt as if she'd undressed in front of a man she intended to kill, baring herself to lull him into a false sense of security. *They wouldn't be wasting so many missiles if they didn't want to keep our eyes on the crossroads.*

"Return fire, but only with the alpha platforms," she ordered, making a mental bet with herself that the enemy ships would jump back as soon as they'd finished launching missile salvos at her. There was nothing to gain, and everything to lose, by sticking around to be killed. "And order the scouts to jump with the enemy ships."

"Aye, Admiral," Olson said. The display updated, red icons vanishing again. "They're jumping now."

"Order the missile pods to jump as soon as they get targeting data," Naomi said. The enemy would probably be moving their fleet randomly, making it harder for her to fire on their positions. "And activate the first web of decoy beacons."

"Aye, Admiral."

"You have no way to know if your missiles will hit their targets," Observer Salix said, calmly. "How can you be sure you'll hit anything?"

"I can't," Naomi said. There was a decent chance of hitting *something*, as the enemy would have very little time to adjust their positions before the missile pods arrived and opened fire, but Salix was right. There was no way to *know*. "But we just want to keep them thinking we're pinned here."

Observer Salix gave her an unreadable look. "You *are* pinned here."

"Matter of opinion," Naomi said. "One of us has caught a tiger by the tail. We just don't know who."

She returned her attention to the display as the battle spluttered on, both sides shooting missiles at each other rather than trying to punch their way through the crossroads and close the range to zero. More proof, if she'd needed it, that the enemy were trying to stall until their *real* attack began. She suspected they were trying to wear her fleet out, although her fleet was big enough for her to make sure some of her crewmen were resting while others manned their stations. The wear and tear on her equipment was a far greater concern, but even that wasn't as bad as it could be. She had enough ships on station to keep some powered down, giving her crews a chance to make repairs before they were needed once again. And yet, she knew the longer the battle raged on, the greater the chance of something going wrong…

• • •

A tiger by the tail, Observer Salix thought.

It was a human expression. He'd heard it before, during a visit to the zoological planet where his people preserved plants and animals from all over the known galaxy. Tigers struck him as dangerous and savage and he had no idea why humans thought it was a good idea to grab their tails. Perhaps that was why the poor creatures had been hunted into extinction. The humans grabbed their tails, the tigers understandably lashed out... and got killed by watching humans. It was...

He leaned forward, wondering why the Pashtali didn't press the offensive. They weren't flying straight into a bottleneck. They had all the time they needed to assemble their forces, and all the space they needed to make sure their arrival coordinates weren't predictable, and then push the offensive as hard as possible. The human ships were far too close to the crossroads—some of them were even *on* the crossroads—for anyone's peace of mind. The Pashtali might get lucky, when they sent the next flight through the crossroads, and take out a warship through interpenetration.

Odd, he mused. *What are they doing?*

It made no sense. The eyes of the universe were on them. Antigen was a *connected* world with several FTL transmitters, including two in neutral hands. The Great Powers were receiving realtime updates, the battle being broadcast even as it took place. *That* was unprecedented, at least in recent years. The Pashtali were making themselves look like fools who couldn't push through a simple crossroads, while the humans...

They're stalling, he thought, coldly. The Pashtali were biding their time, deliberately making themselves look weak. *Why?*

"The enemy launched another flight through the crossroads," the little human reported. "Our scouts are ready to take advantage."

"Send them through," the human admiral ordered. She didn't seem to care that the scouts were unlikely to return. The Pashtali were alert, ready to spot the intruders and blow them away before they could cycle their drives and jump back into realspace. "And ready the next flight of missile pods."

Observer Salix shook his head. The humans weren't precisely firing blind, but...close enough. Their targeting data was imprecise at best and the enemy were evading constantly—and probably also deploying decoys of their own. There was no way to get around the simple fact they were expending a great many missiles for very little return. No, it was worse. They might have scored an improbable number of hits, killing a dozen enemy targets, and for what? They'd never know what they'd done.

His eyes turned to the distant ships, watching the engagement. The humans hadn't been very clear on what they intended to do...did they *want* to make the Pashtali look like fools? Or...or what? And if that were so, why were the Pashtali cooperating? They were a self-spacefaring race! They *knew* they were in trouble, they *knew* the rest of the galaxy was eying their territory...why were they taking the risk of allowing the humans to make them look like fools? The watching ships were reporting home, right now! The Pashtali might be jumped at any moment.

The display flickered again, a set of missile-heavy enemy ships materialising on the crossroads. They fired a set of heavy broadsides, then vanished ahead of a tidal wave of return fire. Observer Salix tried not to wince as the human missiles powered down, becoming *de facto* mines... they'd be a petty nuisance, he was sure, but hardly anything bad enough to slow down the main offensive. What were they doing?

He looked at the human admiral. "They're playing themselves for fools."

"Perhaps," the human agreed. Her face twitched into a wry smile. "Or perhaps they're crazy like a fox."

"What is a fox?" Observer Salix shook his head. "What are they doing?"

"They are trying to keep us pinned down," the human admiral told him. She sounded confident, insanely so. "And we're letting them think they're succeeding."

Observer Salix turned away in disbelief. There was no question about it. The Pashtali *had* succeeded. The humans had left it too late to retreat, to put some distance between themselves and the crossroads before the Pashtali crashed through and opened fire. They were stuck now, desperately needing to retreat and yet unable to break contact and run. And then…they couldn't stay where they were, not indefinitely. The Pashtali could afford to fight—and win—a long drawn-out war of attrition. The humans could not.

Insane, he thought. *What are they doing?*

• • •

"No one seems to be sure what's happening," Thomas commented. "The chatter is decidedly confused."

Sarah frowned. "Do we know what's happening?"

"No." Thomas had been listening to the communications chatter, from starship officers who knew what they were talking about to media talking heads who clearly didn't. Human and alien—there were an astonishing number of aliens in the system—arguing…none of them understood what was happening. The speculation was intense, with sensible arguments being drowned under tidal waves of nonsense and outright trolling, but there was no consensus. "I don't have the slightest idea."

He scowled. Everyone had expected a quick engagement. Instead, it was puttering on like a bout between a pair of very battered boxers, neither of whom wanted to risk closing for the kill for fear they might lose. They were just staggering around the ring…or the crossroads…jabbing at each other. It looked as if it would go on forever and yet it couldn't. Sooner or later, one side would run out of missiles and retreat.

Except we can't retreat, he thought. Admiral Yagami might have outsmarted herself. She couldn't abandon the crossroads without getting knifed in the rear. *What do we do if…*

The display updated, red lights flashing an alert. "Gravity waves," Sarah snapped. A low shudder ran through the ship, something normally impossible in realspace. "*Lots* of gravity waves!

Thomas saw it, too late. "Shit," he said. The epicentre was far too close to the fleet for comfort. No *wonder* the Pashtali had been content to play a waiting game. They'd been waiting for their fleet to get into position. "They're opening a fucking crossroads!"

CHAPTER THIRTY-EIGHT

ANTIGEN

GOTCHA, NAOMI THOUGHT.

She'd done everything in her power to offer the enemy incentive to open a crossroads behind her and yet, she'd feared it wouldn't be enough. The Pashtali no longer *needed* to keep their technology a secret—the entire galaxy knew what they'd done—and showing off their power *might* keep the vultures away for a little longer, but they might easily try to force the real crossroads rather than use the artificial one. It had been all too easy, in the long, lonely nights when she'd been unable to sleep, to think the Pashtali would spot the trap, or simply miss the golden opportunity she was giving them. They liked being clever, they liked elaborate plans, and yet...

"Admiral," Olson said. "The gravity waves are building to a crescendo."

Naomi nodded, feeling the starship quiver as if she were a wet-navy vessel bobbling on the waves. It was rare to feel anything of the sort in realspace...she pushed the thought out of her head and studied the display. The crossroads was taking shape rapidly, the fabric of space-time warping and twisting as something forced its way out of multispace and into realspace. She had to admit it was an impressive piece of technology, even though the Alphans did it better. If she hadn't known the enemy could do that, they might have caught her by surprise.

"Signal *Crossroads*," she ordered. The timing was tight, but...better to err on the side of caution. "They are to begin counter-gravity transmissions at once."

"Aye, Admiral," Olson said.

Naomi took a breath. She'd gambled everything on the enemy choosing to bypass the crossroads and attacking her rear. If they failed—if the enemy poured through the artificial crossroads or even attacked through the natural one—she would be trapped between two enemy fleets, unable to defeat them in open battle or even retreat. She glanced at the live feed from the drones, popping through the crossroads and then back again. The enemy fleet was guarding the crossroads, blocking even *that* line of retreat. Her lips twisted. If the plan failed, she might have to rush the crossroads anyway, absorbing the losses in a desperate bid to get *some* of her ships out before it was too late. And the enemy knew it. No *wonder* they were readying themselves to meet a charge.

They did the timing very well, she conceded ruefully. *But they gave us an opportunity to win the battle in a single blow.*

• • •

"Crude, compared to Alphan tech," Sarah commented. The enemy crossroads was growing bigger and bigger, gravity waves spinning out in all directions. It would be visible right across the system. "How's the chatter?"

"Lots of stunned shouting," Thomas said, glancing at the communications console. The pundits seemed to be having a collective orgasm, while the talking heads were babbling nonsense...he scowled, wondering when a matter of life and death became a stage show for Galactics who had nothing at stake, who could afford to sit back and eat popcorn as if the engagement was nothing more than a movie or holovision series. "The general consensus seems to be that the bad guys have won."

"At least they recognise they're bad guys," Sarah said. "Can we get out if the fleet can't?"

"I think so," Thomas said, although he wasn't sure. The Pashtali wouldn't pick a fight with the rest of the galaxy, but if they won the battle they'd be in a good position to re-establish control over the system and search every commercial vessel passing through the crossroads. "But we'll linger as long as possible."

His heart sank as the crossroads deepened, a gateway opening into multispace. They'd planned it well. The crossroads was too close to the human fleet for the humans to run before the enemy fleet arrived, too far for the human ships to take up position and fire on anything coming out of the crossroads. It looked more like a vortex than a natural crossroads, allowing the enemy ships to come screaming out of multispace, firing as they came. He scowled as he saw communications beacons coming online, broadcasting messages towards the new crossroads. He didn't need to decrypt the signals to know they were providing targeting data to the newcomers. What else would they be?

"They still think the bad guys have won," he said, after a moment. The pundits were growing even more excited, damn them. He felt a surge of hatred. This was war, not a sporting event. There'd be no handshakes after the match, no showers in the changing room and no nights on the town, just destroyed starships and vaporised lives. He wanted to pick up the pundits and shake them, one by one. They were gambling on his people's future. "We might need to run."

Sarah glanced at him. "That bad?"

Thomas nodded. The Pashtali looked weak—*had* looked weak—but that might be about to change. The Galactics who'd been hovering like vultures, swarming around vulnerable star systems as if they were starving animals on the verge of becoming carrion, would back off hastily if they thought snatching the systems would lead to a real war. They'd sooner kiss the enemy rear than get into a war that could end badly, even if they won. He scowled, bitterly. The realities of interstellar power politics were a fact of life, but that didn't make them any easier to take.

"Yeah," he said. They might have pushed their luck too far. "Get ready to run."

"Aye, sir."

• • •

"Gravity generator online," Marquez said. "We are ready to begin."

Roger nodded, gritting his teeth. He hadn't expected the transfer to *Crossroads* after they'd abandoned their old ship, although he supposed it made a certain kind of sense. The techs who'd manned the giant ship, doing what they could to repair the generators after the last battle, were too important to be simply thrown away. They were not expendable, by any reasonable definition of the word. Marquez and the rest of his team were much easier to replace.

And besides, one way or the other, this ship isn't going to be heading home again, he thought. *She'll be for the scrapyard even if we win the battle.*

"Activate the gravity generators," he ordered. It was time. Everything rested on them now. "And shut that crossroads down!"

He braced himself as a low hum echoed through the ship, the sound disconcerting in a manner he couldn't put into words. The admiral wanted the enemy fleet caught in the gravity flux and crushed, but Roger wasn't sure it was possible. They'd be lucky if they trapped and destroyed more than a handful of ships, although the gravity waves boiling through multispace would give the Pashtali a very hard time indeed. His imagination hinted at enemy starships picked up and thrown right across the galaxy—there were stories of starships being caught in storms and finding themselves so far from explored space it took years to get home—but he had to admit it was unlikely. The majority of the stories had grown in the telling.

The display lit up as the focused gravity waves crashed into the crossroads. He leaned forward, his heart starting to race. No one had *ever* tried to shut down a crossroads before and no one was sure what would happen if they did. The simulations were little more than guesswork. Some insisted the crossroads would simply come apart, unable to abide even a hint of interference; others, more practically, thought the outcome would be determined by a tug of war between the two generators. Roger himself wasn't sure. It was a great deal easier to disrupt a crossroads, rather than open it up and then *keep* it open, but the gradient of multispace would assist the intruder in slipping through into realspace. Multispace didn't *like* material objects passing through its realm, he'd been told, and it tried to kick them out. The very first crossroads had been discovered when something had been thrown out of multispace in a shower of radiation...

Which begs the question of just who was flying through multispace before the Alphans, he thought, with a flicker of irrelevant humour. *They always insisted they were the very first race to discover how to use the crossroads to travel faster than light.*

Crossroads shivered, a low whine growing stronger as her generators struggled for supremacy. Roger kept his expression calm, even as he saw the first enemy ships start to glide through the crossroads. There was nothing he could do now, but watch. He was just a spectator on his own bridge...

"Generator Two is threatening to destabilise," Marquez reported. Her display flickered, showing power curves rapidly climbing to infinity. "Generator Three is losing power."

"Divert everything to the generators and the command network," Roger ordered. How long did they have to keep going? Alerts flashed up in front of him, power surges threatening to overload the conduits and trigger explosions. His lips twitched. Exploding consoles were the stuff of holovision shows, not reality, but here...it might happen. He'd thought *Crossroads* had been over-designed to the point of absurdity, yet now he was starting to think the designers hadn't gone far enough. "We have to keep up the pressure."

Crossroads shook, as though the ship had been slapped by an angry god.

Roger gritted his teeth, watching as gravity waves crashed across the system and slammed into the watching starships. They rocked under the blow, a handful hastily coming around and fleeing for their lives. The gravity pulses were growing stronger…Roger wondered, suddenly, if they'd do long-term damage to the system itself. How many orbiting stations would start to drift out of orbit? How many wandering comets and meteors would have their trajectories subtly altered? How many of them would strike planets or plunge into the star? How many…he shook his head. There was no point in worrying about it now. The battle was still in the balance.

"We're going to lose Generator Two," Marquez said. "I think…"

The ship rocked, violently. "She exploded," Marquez added. She bit off a curse as the ship rocked again. "Generator Three is on the verge of going too."

"Keep it up as long as possible," Roger said. The enemy was rushing ships through the crossroads, enough warships to pin Admiral Yagami against the other crossroads and crush her before she could reposition her fleet. "We need to…"

Crossroads shook, again. The display blanked, then rebooted. Roger sucked in his breath as the energy readings went off the scale. Waves of raw power—the raw stuff of multispace itself—blasted into real space, tongues of lightning sweeping through space and wiping out everything they touched. Roger had seen burners carve ships into pieces, but this…a bolt of lightning struck a battleship and vaporised the ship effortlessly. Others followed…he realised, to his horror, that the energy was drawn to starship drive fields. His heart twisted—his ship rang like a gong—as the crossroads started to collapse, folds of space-time falling in on themselves. He thought he saw a starship vanish in the nightmare, either trapped within a multidimensional bubble or crushed to atoms and less than atoms. It was hard not to feel guilty, even though he knew there'd been little choice. The enemy spacers would be lucky if they were just dead…

"Generator Three is gone," Marquez said, quietly.

"I don't think it matters," Roger said. The display was updating rapidly—it looked as if there *had* been internal explosions, scattered throughout the ship—but it wasn't a problem any longer. He barely noticed the gravity field flicker and die. "I think we did it."

He leaned forward, drinking in the sight as the enemy crossroads shattered, releasing a final torrent of energy before vanishing. Space boiled like superheated water, then returned to normal. Roger felt sick as he realised only a couple of enemy starships had survived the transit and both were heavily damaged. A third looked almost *melted*...

Crossroads shuddered, once again. "That was Generator One," Marquez said, as alarms howled through the ship. "Your orders?"

"We did all we could," Roger said. He keyed his communicator, silently blessing his foresight in insisting his crew carried proper communicators, instead of relying on the ship's datanet. "All hands, head to the shuttles. I say again, head to the shuttles. It's time to abandon ship."

Marquez giggled. "They'll be saying we're jinxes before too long," she said. "This is the second ship we've had to abandon."

Roger shrugged. It might be a problem later—spacers tended to be very superstitious—but right now it didn't matter. The real problem was getting off the oversized vessel before she lost power completely or exploded. The internal power distribution network was still surging, raw power crashing through the net and overloading nodes he'd thought could handle the strain. His lips curved into a cold smile as they hurried to the shuttles. The designers really *had* underestimated the problem. He was tempted to send a formal complaint.

Better not, he thought, wryly. The Pashtali would be churning out more ships as soon as possible. There was nothing to be gained from helping them. *They can find out their mistakes on their own.*

• • •

The CIC was silent.

Observer Salix found himself, for once, at a complete loss for words.

The enemy crossroads had been disconcerting enough—it was still hard to wrap his head around the concept of someone else being able to open crossroads—but the humans using their own generator to shut down the crossroads and crush the enemy fleet was terrifying. They'd unleashed so much power...he shuddered, unable to comprehend what he'd seen. He'd grown up in a universe where nothing could vaporise a warcruiser instantly unless the crew did something insanely stupid like flying straight into a star. Now...

"Signal the enemy." Admiral Yagami's voice broke the silence. "Inform them that we will accept their surrender."

"Aye, Admiral," the little human said.

Observer Salix said nothing. He couldn't tell—he couldn't even *guess*—how many ships had been wiped out in a handful of hellish seconds. The display insisted that forty starships had died...how many more, he asked himself, had been on the wrong side of the crossroads when it collapsed? He had no way to know what had happened to them...or, for that matter, what had happened to the enemy crossroads generator. Had it been destroyed too? Or was it powering up for another try?

"No response," the little human said.

"There aren't enough ships in realspace to surrender," Observer Salix said. He wasn't meant to offer advice so openly, but he was too stunned to care. Besides, it was obvious. The humans would work it out shortly, if they hadn't already. "They'll have to take your message to the ships in multispace."

"True," Admiral Yagami agreed. She looked at her subordinate. "Have the signal relayed to a drone, then order it through the crossroads."

"Aye, Admiral."

"And then signal the planet, wide beam," Admiral Yagami added. There was an ugly note in her voice. "Inform them we want their surrender."

Observer Salix felt a flicker of admiration, mingled with concern. There were warships from at least fifteen different major powers within the system, none of which would want Antigen to become a human possession.

But they'd have bare moments to act...if they took control of the system now, asserting the Pashtali no longer held it, they'd stave off a shift to human control. And yet, if they did, they'd be effectively declaring war. The act would force them to take more and more territory, triggering off a large-scale feeding frenzy. The Pashtali would be in deep trouble...

No, he told himself. *The war would be over, and they would have lost, before the fighting had a chance to begin.*

"Admiral," the little human said. "The planet has been declared a protectorate. Galactic forces are taking possession of the high orbitals now, and readying themselves to land troops on the surface. There's been no comment from the planetary government, not yet, but they don't have the forces to resist a hostile takeover."

"Good," Admiral Yagami said. She turned her attention to the display. "And the enemy fleet?"

"The drone just popped back from multispace," her aide said. "The enemy fleet is retreating. It's over."

No, Observer Salix thought. *It's only just begun.*

• • •

Naomi studied the display, not daring to speak as the drone downloaded its sensor records into the command network. She knew her forces had taken a beating. She'd feared the Pashtali would try to rush the crossroads, in a final desperate attempt to win the engagement—or at least make sure they took the human race down with them. Instead...she felt hope blossom in her heart. The battle was over and she'd won, in all senses of the word. It was irritating to be robbed of the fruits of her victory—technically, Antigen was hers now—but the planet would be a poisoned chalice to whoever wound up in charge. And there was no way the new owners could blame her for it.

"Signal Earth," she ordered. "Inform them..."

She paused, unsure what to say. *We have met the enemy and he is ours? We won, so there?*

"Inform them we won the battle," she said. They might just have won the war. The Galactics were already starting to occupy enemy territory. The Pashtali weren't insane. They were on the brink of total defeat. They'd know they needed to put an end to the war as quickly as possible, even if it meant conceding human independence and that of their allies. "And now they have to win the peace."

"Aye, Admiral."

CHAPTER THIRTY-NINE

SOLAR CITY, EARTH

"WELCOME," AMBASSADOR YASUKE SAID. He kept his voice calm and even, although it was the oddest peace conference he'd ever attended, let alone mediated. The Pashtali dominated one side of the chamber—five giant spider-like beings, so implacably hostile Yasuke was *sure* they were already planning a war of revenge—while the other was split between the humans and their allies. Individually, none of them were a great power; collectively, they could give any major power a run for its money. "We are gathered here to discuss a permanent settlement that will end the war."

He let the words hang in the air for a long, cold moment. It had taken nearly three months to organise the conference, three months during which the galactic balance of power had shifted rapidly. The Pashtali had abandoned large swathes of space, pulling their forces back to defend their homeworlds, but that had led to fighting amongst the gathered vultures. Under the circumstances, Yasuke thought the humans and their allies had behaved with remarkable restraint. They'd secured shipping lanes to ensure they could move goods from one system to another, but otherwise they'd refrained from taking territory for themselves. It spoke well of them,

Yasuke thought, and galactic opinion generally agreed. The humans had more friends, now, than they'd expected. It wouldn't last, but—for the moment—they could bask in the warmth and relax.

"The terms have been proposed," he said. Both parties had fired off position papers—the humans surprisingly reasonable, the Pashtali unsurprisingly unreasonable—before the conference had started. "Now, we must discuss how to turn those proposals into something everyone can accept."

He braced himself, then motioned for the Pashtali to speak. They *were* the senior race...although, perhaps, not for much longer. They were still powerful, but their ability to project military power had been sharply curtailed. Yasuke had seen intelligence assessments suggesting it would be at least a decade before the Pashtali could start retaking their lost territory, let alone resuming the invasion of human space. They needed peace and yet, if they refused to make concessions, the war might go on. And then...

We are pushing for a permanent peace, he told himself, as the aliens began. *And if we address most of the issues here and now, we can put an end to the fighting for good.*

But he knew, as the Pashtali speaker droned on, that that might be insanely optimistic.

• • •

It was a great honour, Abraham had been told, for the peace talks to be held on Earth. The Pashtali had conceded the point without a fight, something that suggested—to the diplomats—that they wanted the war over as much as their erstwhile enemies. Personally, Abraham suspected they simply didn't care. They'd spent most of a month haggling over minor details, a stalling tactic that had won them time to stabilise their lines and rebuild their forces. The hell of it was that they could have stalled even longer. The human race needed time to rebuild, too.

He stood in his office, staring out at the darkening city. The human race had celebrated, when they'd heard the news, but now reality was starting to bite. The Pashtali had lost the battle, and they now had too many other enemies taking bites out of their territory, yet they'd stubbornly refused to concede peace. Abraham had made an offer, shortly after the battle, that would have settled everything, but the Pashtali had said nothing. He feared that portended ill for the future. If they decided to bide their time and wait…

His heart sank. He wished he'd been able to take part in the discussions himself, but he'd been told—gently, but firmly—that his presence would be unhelpful. The ambassadors would speak for their governments, of course, yet they'd also take the fall if the talks went off the rails or failed completely. It had never struck him as *fair* to blame an ambassador for following government policy and making the poor bastard the scapegoat if the policy turned out to be a bad idea, but it was part of their jobs. Their government would blame the disaster on the ambassador and everyone else would pretend to believe them. He just hoped the ambassadors were rewarded for their role in the affair.

The intercom bleeped. "Sir," Rachel said. "Ambassador Middleton has arrived."

"Send her in, and bring some coffee and sandwiches," Abraham said. If he was any judge, the ambassador would need refreshment. The Pashtali had declined to allow food to be served during the talks. He had no idea if that was out of a desire to make the talks go quicker or if it was just petty spite. "And then hold all my calls."

"Yes, sir," Rachel said.

Abraham turned as Nancy Middleton was shown into the chamber. She looked as if she'd been in the wars; tired, drained, keeping herself going through sheer force of will. Abraham had no idea if the Pashtali had more endurance than their human counterparts, but it hardly mattered. He reminded himself it had only been a few days since the talks began. By galactic standards, that was unbelievably fast.

"Nancy," he said. "Take a seat."

"Thank you." Nancy sounded tired, too. "The talks are moving quickly, for better or worse."

"The sooner we have an agreement, the better," Abraham said, although he knew the Pashtali might well break their agreements once they recovered from the war. "How did it go?"

"Surprisingly well, once we got through all the posturing," Nancy told him. She accepted a cup of coffee from Rachel, then leaned back in her chair. "They've accepted our independence and that of our allies. They've conceded our control of the Occupied Zone—charming—and shipping rights through the crossroads and threadlines linking us to the allied stars. They have also agreed to drop complaints about us using their ships and IFF codes in combat, largely—I think—because they weren't getting any traction."

Abraham frowned. "What's the bad news?"

Nancy sipped her coffee. "They're refusing to concede that they started the war, through undermining our control of the Occupied Zone, and they have flatly refused to pay us any reparations. They did offer to assist us in regaining control, but my general feeling is that we'd be fools to accept. Letting them have any sort of legal presence within the zone will let them resume the war at a later date."

"Or even simply undermine our control," Abraham agreed. "We'd be blamed for everything they did."

"Yes." Nancy picked up a sandwich and nibbled it thoughtfully. "In short, sir, there are limits to how far we can press them."

Abraham sipped his own coffee. "Do you think we could get anything more from them, if we push the issue?"

"It's hard to say," Nancy said, "but I doubt it. They are not...shall we say...inclined to make any concessions they don't have to. The ones they have offered are concessions that cost them very little. Demanding reparations in addition to everything else will probably prolong the war, as well as making us look greedy."

"They did a hell of a lot of damage to our world," Abraham said, coldly.

"Yes, and they will argue we did a lot of damage in return," Nancy countered. "Right now, sir, we have the edge. Their fleet took heavy losses and they're losing territory to a multitude of races. Galactic opinion is on our side. But that will change, given time. Not everyone likes us, sir, and not everyone is inclined to see us as any better than our enemies. We have a window of opportunity to secure a favourable peace, if we don't push it too hard."

"Point taken," Abraham said. "How do our allies feel?"

"They're willing to go along with it, for the moment," Nancy said. "The Pashtali have conceded the independence of the Terminus powers, as well as shipping lanes through the surrounding systems. It's the best they could have expected when they allied with us."

"I'll have to see what the cabinet thinks," Abraham said. "They won't be happy if I make the final call alone."

He turned back to the window, his mind churning. The darkness hid the damage—the ruined buildings, the shattered lives—left behind by the invasion, but he knew it was there. No amount of wishful thinking could repair the scars the enemy had left on humanity's homeworld. He wanted to turn the screws as much as possible, to hurt the enemy...to make them *pay* for what they'd done. But, no matter how he looked at it, there was no way to force the Pashtali to concede much more. If anything...prolonging the talks might give them time to rebalance and resume the war.

We'll never be able to let our guard down, he thought. *And we'll never dare look weak.*

He sighed. There were still immense challenges, from regaining control of the Occupied Zone to rebuilding the fleet and repairing the damage to Earth. It was going to be a bloody nightmare...no, it already *was*. The public might cheer his name right now, as if he'd led the fleet in combat and won the war singlehandedly, but that would change the moment the recession began to bite. God knew how *that* would work out. He was powerful—and war had given him more personal authority than any previous First Speaker—yet he couldn't fix the planet's problems with a wave of his hand. The credit for the victory would be replaced by blame for the economic crisis.

"I'll speak to them tomorrow morning, then you can put together the final proposal," he said, turning back to her. "Do you think they'll accept?"

"I think they want to get the war over as quickly as possible," Nancy reminded him. "The fighting hurt them, too."

"They have more slack in their system," Abraham grumbled. "Are they trying to come to terms with the rest of their enemies?"

"Probably." Nancy shrugged. "They'll find it harder to talk to the Great Powers. There aren't so many concessions they can offer, not without weakening themselves quite badly."

"True," Abraham agreed. He shook his head. "You did well, out there."

"Thank you," Nancy said. If she was surprised by the sudden change in subject, she hid it well. "But after this, I'm going to retire."

"Me too, perhaps," Abraham said. They shared tired smiles. "We'll see."

• • •

Nancy wondered, as she took her seat at the table, if the Pashtali found humans as disconcerting as humans found them. The five ambassadors were huddled so close together that it was hard to tell them apart...hell, it was hard to even *look* at them. She saw flashes of eyes and claws and spidery legs that looked profoundly unnatural, even to an experienced diplomat and galactic traveller. She supposed the humans looked just as odd to their eyes. They had to think humans were constantly on the verge of falling over as they walked from place to place.

She put the thought aside as Ambassador Yasuke called the meeting to order. The talks had progressed with astonishing speed, in stark contrast to the talks held after the Battle of Earth, but she feared they hadn't proceeded fast enough. The political situation kept changing, to the point she suspected there might come a time—sooner rather than later—when the Pashtali would feel confident enough to resume the war. And if that happened...who knew? The human race might lose the war and, in doing so, lose everything.

"I have put together a set of proposals," she said, as if she'd done the work herself. Her staff had worked overnight, drawing together the preliminary outline and then discussing them with their allies before forwarding them to her. "We believe these address all the issues raised in the last few days. If you accept them, we can proceed to signing and implementing the agreement."

She pushed a sheet of paper across the table. It was almost painfully short by Galactic standards—normally, a peace treaty would be hundreds of pages and consist largely of flowery phrases and verbiage that hardly anyone would ever read—but there was no need to waste time. The Pashtali wanted peace as much as their human enemies. She tried to ignore the way her skin crawled as the alien picked up the paper, his eyes seeming to bulge as he ran his eyes down the sheet. It wouldn't be the final copy, of course—she expected the Pashtali to insist on a handful of minor and pointless changes—but still…

"We accept, in principle," the spokesman said. Nancy blinked in surprise. *That* quickly? A nasty suspicion ran through her mind. Were they being conned in some way? Or did the Pashtali want to sign quickly before their position worsened? Nancy had checked the datanet during breakfast and discovered there were an astonishing number of humans who wanted to make the Pashtali *scream*. "We will consult with our government, then sign tomorrow."

Nancy sat back in her chair as the aliens withdrew, unsure if she should be relieved or deeply worried. The Pashtali wouldn't risk breaking the treaty in a hurry, would they? The peace talks *had* been sponsored by the Alphans, after all, and they wouldn't take kindly to anyone messing them about. There were perfectly legal ways to stall…

Take what you can get, she told herself. She'd seen the economic projections. The war could *not* be allowed to go on, or the entire planet would collapse. *And hope they're not lulling you to sleep while they prepare to put a knife in your back.*

• • •

There was no point, many would argue, in holding a signing ceremony when the *real* agreement had been made over the FTL network, between several governments hundreds of light years apart. Ambassador Yasuke disagreed with such assertions, at least in part because a formal ceremony made it clear that talks had been completed and the matter was now closed. And besides, they made for good theatre.

He wondered, as he watched the representatives take their places—and the media take positions behind them—if they understood what was *really* happening. His government had expected, from what he'd been told, that the human-led alliance would fall apart within days of the final battle. It was rare for an alliance to last very long, not when the various parties stood to gain more from betraying their former allies, but here... the humans were treating their partners as equals, rather than selling them out. Yasuke had watched with interest as new defence and trade agreements were signed, the alliance even recruiting new members from amongst the lesser powers. It was hard to believe it would last, but...

A rustle ran through the chamber as the representatives read the paper one final time—as if there'd be any changes, after endless haggling over the communications network—and then started to sign their names. Yasuke watched calmly—even the reporters were quiet—as more and more names were added to the sheet, before putting his own at the end as a witness and facilitator. The room seemed to explode with life as the paper was placed on display, humans and aliens cheering loudly even though the war had technically ended hours ago. He hid his amusement as the Pashtali stood, bowed stiffly, and retreated from the chamber. Yasuke felt a stab of sympathy, despite everything. The ambassadors were probably going to be blamed for the treaty.

But it's better than they had any right to expect, Yasuke thought. Personally, he'd suspected that the humans and their allies would demand more. His staff was undecided as to whether the humans had made a wise move. On one hand, they'd limited their own commitments and avoided giving their enemies a ready-made excuse to resume the war; on the other, the Pashtali still had a powerful fleet and a solid core of fixed defences. *They might feel strong enough to resume the war sooner than the humans think.*

He stood up—with the departure of the alien ambassadors, the formal aspect of the meeting was over—and made his way back to his aircar. The humans wanted to dance and sing and do whatever else humans did, to cheer the end of a war, but he simply wanted to return to the embassy. His government would want a report, as soon as possible, and he wanted… he sighed inwardly. Reading between the lines, he suspected his time on Earth was about to come to an end. Too many people back home thought he'd gone native.

And the humans are more important now, he reflected, as he took the elevator to the aircar pad on the roof. *There'll be many more volunteers for the job.*

He stepped onto the roof and stopped, surprised. Observer Salix stood there, hands bent into the posture of respect. Yasuke frowned. They weren't friends or even acquaintances. And yet, they had *something* in common. They were both Alphans.

"My Lord Viceroy," Observer Salix said. "Might I beg a moment of your time?"

Yasuke paused. Technically, he had the right to be addressed as *viceroy*. It was the highest rank he'd ever held. Practically, he'd let that fall by the wayside. The Viceregal Government no longer existed. To use the title on Earth would cause considerable offense…

"You may," he said, finally. The younger man wanted something, something important. He would have made an appointment otherwise. Meeting Yasuke like *this* was a major breach in protocol. He wondered, idly, how the observer had even reached the aircar pad. The guards should have stopped him before he reached the roof. "If you would care to fly with me…?"

"It would be my pleasure," Observer Salix said. "We have much to discuss."

CHAPTER FORTY

SOLAR CITY, EARTH

"ADMIRAL," FIRST SPEAKER DOUGLAS SAID. "I'm sorry I didn't have a chance to speak with you earlier."

"I understand," Naomi said. She'd brought the majority of the fleet home a month after the Battle of Antigen, passing through the former Occupied Zone to show the flag and remind the inhabitants Earth would be reasserting its authority shortly. The remainder of her ships had remained to patrol the shipping lanes and monitor the Pashtali from a safe distance. "We both had other duties."

"You need some leave," Douglas said. "And I suggest you take some now."

Naomi frowned. "Two-thirds of my crew are already on leave," she said. She'd had to draw lots to determine who'd remain with the ships for a week before they had their own chance to take a break. "I'll go on leave with the rest of them."

"Make sure you do," Douglas said. "You did well, out there."

"Thanks." Naomi knew she was being curt, but it was hard to care. She'd been working herself too hard for too long. "Do you think Admiral Glass would approve?"

"You won a battle that ended the war," Douglas said. "It didn't end the threat completely—they're still out there, nursing their wounds and plotting revenge—but you bought us time to repair the damage and expand the fleet. You did very well indeed."

"We can't rest on our laurels," Naomi cautioned him. "The Galactics didn't give us very good odds of surviving, when the Pashtali decided we'd make a suitable target. They saw a ragtag fleet of outdated warships and converted freighters, built around a hard core of home-made battleships. They thought we'd lose. Instead, we convinced them they had to take us seriously."

"Good," Douglas said. "It'll take some time for someone else to work up the nerve to confront us."

"Not as long as you might think," Naomi said. "We used to look like a minor power, barely able to police its own home systems. Now, we look powerful and dangerous...and, perhaps, capable of building our own crossroads generators."

Douglas leaned forward. "Can we?"

"In theory." Naomi had discussed the matter extensively with Commodore Valentine, before he and his remaining crew had returned to the Pournelle Shipyards. "In practice, it might be a little harder than we want to admit. We really need to build up our hard core of warships first."

"We will," Douglas said. "You won us time, Admiral. And the planet is grateful."

"We also got lucky," Naomi said. "We must always bear that in mind."

Douglas nodded. "I read your reports very carefully," he said. "But is there anything you want to bring to my attention? Anything in particular?"

Naomi considered it. "The fleet is weaker than it seems, sir," she said. "We need to be careful not to get into any more fights, if possible. And..."

She took a breath. "We also need to refrain from cheating our allies," she added. "If we can keep the alliance together, we will be punching well above our weight."

"As long as everyone marches in unison," Douglas said. "We'll see what we can do, but the future is always uncertain."

"Yes, sir," Naomi said. "And one other thing, something I left out of my reports."

Douglas's eyes narrowed. "You thought it might be intercepted?"

"Yes, sir," Naomi said. "During the campaign, I worked closely with Observer Salix. My original fears were ill-founded. He wasn't—isn't—a blowhard, nor was he consumed with racial superiority or arrogance or anything else that might blind him to the truth. It was a little awkward working with him, but...it was better than my old CO."

She smiled, humourlessly. "I know how to read Alphans, sir, and even the smartest of them aren't always capable of hiding their feelings. I had the impression, towards the end of the campaign, that something was bothering him. If he were human, I'd say he was brooding over something. And I don't know what."

"A romantic interest?" Douglas looked as if he wasn't sure what to make of it. "Or...the prospect of us losing the war?"

"I don't know," Naomi said. "They...don't tend to get crazy-obsessed with relationships, unlike us. I've never known one to be particularly bothered at the thought of being apart from his partner—I don't think they even *have* permanent partners. I think it was something more political."

"But you don't know what," Douglas said. "Any thoughts?"

"Nothing concrete," Naomi said. "But our former masters may not be too pleased if we become *too* powerful too quickly."

"I'll discuss it with my staff," Douglas said. "You might be jumping at shadows, though."

"Yes." Naomi had wondered, more than once, if she was imagining it. "It's just something I thought I should bring to your attention."

Douglas nodded, glancing at his terminal. "Thank you," he said. "Go get some rest. I'll speak to you later, once all the hubbub"—he waved at the window and the cheering crowds beyond—"is over, and reality starts to bite again."

"Yes, sir," Naomi said.

She stood, saluted, and made her way back to the shuttle. The noise from the streets below was growing louder, the entire planet forgetting its woes long enough to celebrate the victory. Her lips twitched. Her crewmen were down there, getting thoroughly drunk or laid or both...she was tempted to join them, even though she knew she had to get back to orbit. There were just too many things that needed her personal attention.

But at least we can catch our breath, she thought. They *had* won a victory and they *had* won some time...time enough, she hoped, to build up the fleet to the point no one, not even the Great Powers, would challenge them. *And if the alliance lasts long enough, we can change galactic politics once and for all.*

• • •

"I apologise for meeting you like this," Observer Salix said, once the automated aircar was on its way. "I wanted to speak with you well away from prying eyes and ears."

"My office would have been quite suitable," Yasuke said, not bothering to conceal his irritation. The youngster had not only intercepted him but insisted on sweeping the aircar for bugs before exchanging more than light pleasantries. "You could easily have arranged an appointment."

"Perhaps, but not without raising eyebrows," Observer Salix said.

Yasuke felt his patience snap. "Perhaps you should get to the point," he said. "I am, as hard as it may be to believe, a very busy man. Drop the formalities and come to the point."

Observer Salix nodded, curtly. "As you know, My Lord Viceroy, I had the pleasure of accompanying the human fleet as it engaged the enemy. I stood on their command deck and watched how they fought, making careful note for the future. The humans fought well."

"I am aware," Yasuke said.

"They are also a potential threat," Observer Salix said, bluntly. "And one that might become a very *real* threat all too soon."

Yasuke's eyes narrowed. "A potential threat?"

"Yes, My Lord Viceroy." Observer Salix didn't look away. "We must start taking precautions. Now."

"Indeed?" Yasuke leaned forward, hardening his voice. "I *suggest* you explain. Now."

Observer Salix didn't wince at the unspoken rebuke. "It is easy to underestimate the humans. They made no attempt to settle their home system before we invaded and brought them into the empire. Their tech level was higher than typical, for a planet-bound race, but no match for us. We made use of them in expanding our empire. It seemed safe."

"You tell me nothing I don't already know," Yasuke said.

"We underestimated their ability to study our technology and reverse-engineer it," Observer Salix said. "We also underestimated their ability to adapt technology from a dozen different races and blend it together. There are no *other* races that could have taken captured ships and used them so effectively, not even us. And, perhaps most importantly of all, the humans have a knack for making friends. We assumed their alliances wouldn't last beyond the victory and peace talks. Instead, it has lasted—and it is an alliance of equals."

"The humans do not have the firepower to dominate the alliance," Yasuke pointed out. "And they understand the value of cooperation."

"Not yet," Observer Salix said. "They have already duplicated our burners, although as one-shot weapons. They have also had plenty of time to study the captured crossroads generator and work out how to duplicate, perhaps make the jump from the Pashtali designs to ours. Their drives are inferior, again, but they'll crack those problems soon. They know it can be done. In short, it is only a matter of time before they reach our level and surpass us."

He pressed on before Yasuke could object. "The humans also have other advantages," he said. "Their production rate is actually higher than ours, although that's concealed by our significantly greater industrial base. Their starships are lighter than ours, but they can be repaired or replaced quicker; their troops aren't as well-equipped, but they are tough and capable and, again, replaceable. And, most importantly of all, there are millions of humans scattered through the empire. The official figures are worryingly high. The *real* figure might be much greater."

Yasuke scowled. "Are you suggesting the humans will go to war against us?"

"I think, sooner or later, there will be a clash," Observer Salix said. "We may have traded one threat for another."

"And you think they'll risk war with us?" Yasuke shook his head. "It doesn't seem likely."

"The humans are incredibly adaptive," Observer Salix said. "Like I said, it is just a matter of time before they match or exceed our technology."

"That doesn't mean they will turn into a threat," Yasuke insisted.

"Galactic history says otherwise," Observer Salix pointed out. "We dominated the known galaxy for centuries. We codified Galactic Law and enforced it. Everyone took us into account. Everyone. It wasn't until the Lupines challenged us, nearly *beat* us, that galactic politics started to shift. Everything is changing now, My Lord Viceroy, and the humans will find themselves forced to play an ever-greater role. And what will happen if they choose to challenge us?"

"We are still powerful," Yasuke said.

"Yes," Observer Salix agreed. "And so were the Pashtali."

Yasuke took a breath. "I have lived and worked on Earth for much of my professional career," he said. "I know humans. They are...not bad people. They want to climb to the top, and they resented it when we held them down, but...they don't have any reason, now, to go to war against us."

"They want to rise to the top," Observer Salix echoed. "And how can they do that, except by surpassing us?"

"I think there is no cause for alarm," Yasuke said. "The humans have good reason to be grateful to us."

"Gratitude never lasts," Observer Salix said, flatly. "I'm due to return home on the warcruiser flagship, when it departs a week from now. I intend to press for...*precautions*."

Yasuke scowled. "What *sort* of precautions?"

"Whatever seems appropriate," Observer Salix said. The aircar touched down neatly on the embassy shuttlepad. "I bear the humans no ill will, My Lord Viceroy, but our people come first."

"I think you're wrong," Yasuke said, flatly.

"I hope you're right," Observer Salix agreed. "But, in truth, the galaxy is changing. And we can no longer afford to be complacent about our future."

• • •

THE END (FOR NOW)

If you want more...

Please let me know.

AFTERWORD

Longstreet pointed to the map on the wall. "Suppose we win an overwhelming victory in this war, which God grant. Can we hope to overrun and conquer the United States?"

Jackson didn't need to look at the map. "Of course not, sir."

"Good." The president of the CSA nodded approval. "There you have the first point: any success we win must of necessity be limited in scope. After it, we still face a United States larger and stronger than ourselves."

—HARRY TURTLEDOVE, *How Few Remain*

THE PROBLEM WITH FIGHTING A WAR, as a general rule, is that it takes one party to start a war and two to end it. If there is a clear aggressor, the aggressor must either win the war outright or the defender must give the aggressor enough of a bloody nose to make him rethink fighting the war. This is easier said than done, for all sorts of reasons. An aggressor has never gone to war on the assumption he'd lose—he *is* the aggressor for a reason—and discovering the hard way all his calculations are in error may force him to rethink or, perhaps worse, to double down. The defender, who has been attacked without due cause, will want both revenge and certain guarantees it won't be refighting the war ten years in the future, when the aggressor has learnt from its mistakes and prepared for a rematch. Ideally, from the defender's point of view, overrunning and occupying the aggressor would be the best possible outcome, at least in the short run.

This is, however, not always possible, nor desirable. The Falklands War pitted Argentina (aggressor) against Britain (defender), but at no point was Britain ever able to invade and occupy Argentina. The war ended with a clear British victory, through the liberation of the Falklands and the effective destruction of Argentina's ability to continue the war, yet there were limits to how much the British could demand in recompense for the invasion and military struggle. Argentina was down, but not out. By contrast, the American conflict with Saddam Hussein ended with the invasion of Iraq and the destruction of Saddam's government, but this was very much a mixed blessing. American found itself responsible for running Iraq afterwards, which was a very difficult task at the best of times, and—perversely—executing Saddam actually helped the insurgents as they could no longer be accused of fighting to bring back a known and loathed tyrant.

There is, of course, a more modern version of this issue. Putin's invasion of Ukraine surprised me for two reasons. First, I assumed Putin—who I saw as cold, calculating and not given to rash moves—would refrain from an invasion that would be, even in the best possible case, one hell of a gamble. Second, that the invasion was so poorly planned and carried out. Putin appears to have gambled on an Operation Iraqi Freedom-style blitzkrieg, something that might have worked on paper, if one overlooked the monumental disparity between the US and Iraqi forces, the latter weakened by over a decade of poor maintenance and terrible leadership, the former with far better technology, training and air superiority. Instead, Russia's forces have run into a meatgrinder and international sanctions have taken a severe (if hotly debated) toll on Russia's economy and, as of writing, Ukraine has gone on the offensive.

This is not the first time Russia has launched an unprovoked invasion and discovered, too late, that it might have made a mistake. Stalin's invasion of Finland was expected to be a short victorious war—a term coined, ironically, by a Russian statesman shortly before the Russo-Japanese War—with the Finns quickly crushed, the Red Army established as a powerful force that could not be ignored in a very dangerous world and Russia in a stronger position for the inevitable clash with Hitler and Nazi Germany. Instead, it turned into a disaster. The Russians took immense losses, the Finns maintained at least some of their independence and the Red Army looked toothless, which encouraged Hitler to invade Russia in 1941. And yet, a case can be made that the Russians still won the war. The Finns certainly could not march all the way to Moscow and crush the communist beast in its lair...

And that meant Russia had time to recover, adapt, and win the war.

This leads to a curious and thorny diplomatic problem. On one hand, Russia is the aggressor and she must pay a price for her aggression. On the other, there are limits to how far Ukraine (with or without outside support) can push the Russians. An offensive into Russian Crimea could be easily used to raise the ghosts of the Great Patriotic War to drum up support for Putin, a problem that would grow worse if the offensive is carried into Russia proper. Russia also has considerable economic muscle, which it can use to push Europe into abandoning Ukraine (at the price of underlining how foolish Europe was to let Putin get that influence and start building nuclear power plants in vast numbers), and—at worst—it has nuclear weapons. Faced with a flat choice between watching Russia collapse and taking everyone else down with him, Putin might lash out at Europe and America. We are therefore faced with the need to give Putin a way out of the conflict that won't hurt him—and Russia—too badly, while this is very much the *last* thing we want to do.

On one hand, Putin—and by extension—deserves punishment; on the other, administrating the punishment without convincing Putin—or worse, his replacement after he gets overthrown and murdered—that he has nothing to lose and he might as well burn the world is an extremely tricky task.

I did not expect Russia to invade when I started outlining the plot for *Cast Adrift* and its two sequels. But it does uncannily match the problem facing the human race, when the Pashtali invaded…

And now you've read this far, I have a request to make.

It's growing harder to make a living through self-published writing these days. If you liked this book, please leave a review where you found it, share the link, let your friends know (etc, etc). Every little helps (particularly reviews).

Thank you.
Christopher G. Nuttall
Edinburgh, 2022

PS—I'd also like to draw your attention to *Chrishangers*—my collection of short stories and novellas, published to mark my first decade as a writer. Search for it online now!

HOW TO FOLLOW

Basic Mailing List—http://orion.crucis.net/mailman/listinfo/chrishanger-list
Nothing, but announcements of new books.

Newsletter—https://gmail.us1.list-manage.com/subscribe?u=c8f9f7391e5bfa369a9b1e76c&id=55fc83a213
New books releases, new audio releases, maybe a handful of other things of interest.

Blog—https://chrishanger.wordpress.com/
Everything from new books to reviews, commentary on things that interest me, etc.

Facebook Fan Page—https://www.facebook.com/ChristopherGNuttall
New books releases, new audio releases, maybe a handful of other things of interest.

Website—http://chrishanger.net/
New books releases, new audio releases, free samples (plus some older books free to anyone who wants a quick read)

Forums—https://authornuttall.com
Book discussions—new, but I hope to expand.

Amazon Author Page—https://www.amazon.com/ Christopher-G-Nuttall/e/B008L9Q4ES
My books on Amazon.

Books2Read—https://books2read.com/author/christopher-g-nuttall/ subscribe/19723/
Notifications of new books (normally on Amazon too, but not included in B2R notifications.

Twitter—@chrisgnuttall
New books releases, new audio releases—definitely nothing beyond (no politics or culture war stuff).

IF YOU LIKED THIS...

You Might Like...*Swords of Rasna*, by Gustavo Bondoni.

The Etruscan nation is about to be wiped from the face of the Earth by the advancing Roman armies.

A master tactician and the only man who knows how to effectively apply Etruscan black magic on the battlefield, General Velthur Leinie is the only man standing between his people and subjugation.

But the Romans are implacable and Velthur retreats, abandoning city after agonizing city.

His only choice is to ask the Etruscan lords of the underworld, Manus and Mania, for their help.

Velthur won't know the price until after they've agreed to help... but surrender is unthinkable.

CHAPTER 1

Aulus Fabius Ambustus tried, by sheer force of will, to see through the choking dust. He knew there was a pocket of enemy soldiers in there somewhere, but the charge of his own troops had stirred the earth enough to make it impossible to tell exactly where.

The right side of the maniple was still visible some distance away, but, like Aulus's own command, it had lost cohesion. It was a good thing that there were no senior officers present, because it would have gone badly for both centurions—it was unacceptable to lose formation that way in a lopsided, easy battle. It was a sign of low discipline.

But discipline was difficult to maintain when a unit smelled blood, and that was what was happening now. His velites and his hastati—troops accustomed to bearing the brunt of much more desperate charges—had plunged through the front ranks of Etruscan defenders with hardly any losses. They'd howled into the town as though the very hosts of the Underworld were behind them. Even the principes, who should have known better, had broken ranks and rushed into the unprotected houses.

He turned to Gaius Curius, a grizzled and respected triarius. "I think the men will be on half-rations for the next ten days."

The older man nodded. "They will probably consider it a fine bargain. After all, a bit of hunger is a small price to pay for even a little Etruscan gold. How often do they find themselves surrounded by unguarded wealth with no officers in sight?"

Aulus smiled. "Itching to join them?"

"Not really. But fifteen years ago, I would have been the first to break ranks. Now? I guess I've learned that these border towns never have much wealth lying around. I'd rather avoid the punishment."

"That sounds wise. But I believe they've had more than enough time to do their looting. We'd better get in there before they make the civilian population hate us forever. We want to be able to control this area, after all." Aulus's first order of business had been to subdue any Etruscan resistance that the village might have harbored. He'd been instructed to be firm but cautious, as other small towns outside of Veii had held vicious elite units just waiting to catch Roman maniples unawares.

His instructions were also very clear about civilian casualties. A certain amount of pillaging was acceptable—and impossible to police—but atrocities on a grand scale were strictly forbidden. They wanted the people of Veii and the outlying towns to bend willingly to Roman rule, and making the population hate them would not help Rome achieve that goal. This village, though small, would become a valuable asset. It controlled a fertile valley of the kind that, correctly managed, could feed an army.

*

Aulus barked orders, and his triarri responded. He was satisfied to see that the more experienced unit showed little sign of breaking apart. "Head towards the sound of the fighting. Let's mop up and then get our troops back in order."

They advanced into the wall of dust.

For the first ten seconds he saw nothing. But soon, the silhouette of a makeshift barricade—nothing more formidable than some stacked furniture and a burning hay bale—became visible. The fighting had moved beyond it, and they advanced through the gap his men had created in the precarious defenses.

A small cluster of Etruscans had chosen a defensive position behind a low stone wall. Triarii from the right side of the maniple—troops not under Aulus's command—had stationed themselves in front and were advancing towards them. It didn't take a trained military mind to know that the mob of defenders would take only moments to fall to the disciplined Roman formation.

"Reinforce them. Get in on the left side." Aulus knew there was little risk of the Etruscans mounting a flanking maneuver, but he didn't want to have to face his counterparts if his command wasn't involved in the final defeat of the enemy.

He admired the Etruscans' determination. They'd chosen a position that, though only marginally defensible, was impossible to retreat from. The only thing awaiting the men if they stood firm was a slightly slower death. Even as his own troops reached the wall—barely waist-high—Aulus watched the right side of the Roman forces begin to overrun it.

He commanded his troops to vault the barrier and execute a quick pincer, and they jogged towards the Etruscans.

Suddenly, a wide-eyed Roman soldier ran screaming at them, escaping the battle as fast as his legs could carry him; he was joined almost immediately by a second, and then a third. The advance of the right flank had been halted. It looked as though the small group of ragged Etruscans were managing to push back a much larger force of Romans.

Incredibly, the right side of the maniple broke, and Roman troops scattered. Aulus smiled as he realized his opportunity.

"Forward! Victory will be ours today!"

Ignoring all protocol and training, he led his triarii himself—advancing at a dead run, knowing that they would scythe through the few remaining defenders like so much wheat. It took him four strides to reach the first rank, and he thrust his hasta—the long spear of the true Roman soldier—into the nearest man's chest. He was satisfied to see that the point emerged from the Etruscan's back—a worthy blow. Aulus looked into the other's eyes, wanting the man to know that he died at the hands of a foe who respected his valor.

But the other man's eyes were grey, glassy pools. There was no life in them, not even rapidly escaping life. It seemed as though he'd been dead for days, not seconds.

Aulus hesitated. His foe did not. Ignoring the haft of the spear that buried itself ever further into his chest, the Etruscan took the two steps needed to close the gap between them and plunged his short sword deep into Aulus's gut.

As the Roman's blood poured onto the dust at his feet, he could hear the screams of his own men, and, dying, looked into the eyes of a foe for whom retreat had long since ceased to be a valid option.

CHAPTER 2

Numesi Leinie smiled grimly as the Romans fell back in disarray and wished he had some sort of power to keep his wights in position. But they'd tasted enemy blood, and there was nothing he could do other than watch his most fearsome troops abandon the defensive position and pursue the panicked legions. Sadly, the chase always ended the same way: eventually Roman discipline would reassert itself, or some soldier with more courage than intelligence would discover that hacking the undead troops to bits destroyed them as an effective fighting force.

Had they deployed the wights too soon? Perhaps. But the truth was that they had little choice in the matter. Veii, the Rasna city nearest Rome, was doomed to fall in the short term no matter what the army did. But it was imperative that they buy some time for the Council to organize an evacuation of the important citizens. If the League could call in its alliances, if they could fortify the more distant towns...then perhaps there was hope for his people.

"What do we have left?" he asked.

A man he didn't recognize, wearing a bloodstained bandage around his head, approached. "Just a single group of chariots. Everyone else has been ordered to fall back towards Veii," the man reported. His accent was strong, the harsh tones of Tarchna hammering Numesi's ears. He decided not to ask where his own officers—loyal men of Veii—were. He knew the answer to that.

"And our undead? The Swords of the Rasna?"

"Hacked to pieces, for the most part. The rest are chasing Romans through the countryside. They'll likely be back by nightfall." The man left the rest unsaid. By nightfall, the valley would be in enemy hands. It was true that they'd fought off a few cohorts and made the southerners pay in blood for every league they conquered, but the rest of the legion was still intact. His scouts informed him that the enemy were advancing and had closed to a point just over the nearest line of hills. They would arrive to investigate the failure of their lost cohorts long before nightfall. By his count, the legion should still be more than two thousand men strong… even if none of the soldiers who'd already fought in the valley returned for a second helping.

Numesi had fewer than fifty charioteers to pit against that army. He sighed. "All right. Set the chariots at the top of that hill. Order them to make a run at the Roman scouts as they arrive, and then at the vanguard. When the main force appears, tell them to retreat to Veii."

"Our orders are to fight to the last man."

"The chariot archers will be more useful from behind the walls of the city. The rest of us can hold this position and delay them as long as possible."

The man looked dubious. "It won't help much."

"Every second counts. And besides, we've held this little village for two days. If the Council really expected us to do more for them, then they deserve to lose the war." The other man nodded and began to marshal the few remaining men—mostly the injured who would have held back the retreat and those who, for whatever reason, refused to abandon their posts—around the wall, facing the oncoming death. He spotted a boy among them—a child who couldn't have been more than ten or eleven years old—clutching a spear with white knuckles.

Numesi called him over. "What's your name, soldier?" he asked the child.

"Vulna, your highness."

Numesi smiled at the honorific. The boy was obviously from Veii, the only place where a mere military commander from another city might be saddled with such a term. "I have a mission for you."

"I will do whatever you need." The boy's eyes showed a fatalism and acceptance well beyond his short years—a life in which the struggle against the growing ambitions of Rome were constant, and one in which death was a familiar companion. There was no childhood in a war zone.

"Good. I have an urgent message for my brother in Veii. I need you to deliver it."

"You want me to go to Veii?" Despite the boy's discipline, Numesi was certain that he could detect a small spark of hope in his eyes. Or perhaps he just wanted it to be there.

"Yes. I need my brother to know that the dead man they are taking him is a Roman Centurion. He needs to deliver the corpse to my mother, and she will know what to do with it. Do you know who my brother is?"

"Of course, your highness. He is Velthur the Conqueror."

Numesi smiled. Another exaggeration. His younger brother had, it was true, managed to demolish and drive back legions in a well-planned ambush, but he was still an inexperienced soldier almost too young to grow a decent beard. Nevertheless, he didn't begrudge his sibling the glory: in the face of an implacable Roman advance, the Rasna needed heroes wherever they might be found.

"Good. Find him and give him my message."

"Is that all?"

The boy seemed disappointed. "No. Of course not. You need to warn him that the legion approaching us from the south will be at his walls tomorrow at mid-morning. We'll keep them here as long as we can, but there is no hope of driving them back. I need Velthur to know. Do you think you can make it to the city before them?"

If the boy had suspected that Numesi was trying to keep him out of harm's way, that challenge was all it took to drive away any suspicion. The lad straightened. "Of course. I'll run all the way and be there before nightfall."

"Are you sure? It's a long way."

"I've done it before. And this time, I won't be carrying live chickens for my father, either."

"All right, then. Go now. Every moment you save will allow my brother a little extra time to prepare. It might make the difference between saving Veii and losing the city."

The child took off at a run, and Numesi sent a prayer behind him. Only luck would keep him out of the hands of scouting parties who wouldn't care that he should have been playing sticks with his friends. They'd assume—correctly, as it happened—that any male old enough to hold a spear would have been made a part of the effort to resist their advances. He would be tortured for any information he might have, and then put to the sword. Emotion would play no part in it.

Vulna disappeared behind a stand of trees, and Numesi smiled again. At the speed he was moving, it was more likely that the boy would kill himself by sprinting all the way than die through any efforts of the Romans.

Speaking of Romans, Numesi saw a cloud of dust approaching from the south. It dwarfed the ones that had announced the cohorts over the past two days. He mouthed a small prayer to Mantus, husband to Mania and lord of the underworld. He asked the deity to welcome him when he arrived.

And he warned the god to expect him for the evening meal.

CHAPTER 3

Velthur dismissed the boy and looked around at his surroundings. The society, the splendor, would not last. In the next few days—or tens of days, at most—the brightly painted walls around him, this beautiful noble house of Veii, would lie in ruins. Roman emissaries had announced that they would allow conquered cities—at least those who didn't oppose their rule—a certain amount of autonomy. But he knew that no conqueror would let a symbol of past power stand. The Romans might be a young, upstart nation attacking their cultural ancestors, but they were wise to the realities of the world.

The people in the room, likewise, had two choices: to flee or to die. Seated around him were the surviving members of the Council of Veii, as well as representatives from four or five of the other cities in the League, all seemingly hanging on Velthur's every word. None of them would be welcomed by the new government of their vanquished city.

Had the situation not been quite so serious, the irony would have been sweet. The people hanging on his every word were the same men and women who, mere months earlier—when it seemed that the Roman advance had stalled—had voted to keep him off the Council, right here in his adopted city. It would never have happened in Volsinii, of course. If they'd tried leaving a member of the Leinie clan out of any sort of public function there, they knew they would have to answer to his mother. No one wanted to answer to his mother.

As usual, Sethra—impatient, dark-eyed Sethra—was the first to speak. "What news?" she asked.

"None of note," Velthur responded. He left unsaid the fact that the small boy was his brother's final message to him. A message which said: I will sacrifice myself, but there is no need for this boy to die. "The situation is the same as it was before the boy arrived. We are stuck inside a city which we have no hope of holding against even a single legion. And they won't send just one." He looked at each of them in turn. "The only difference is that we now know that the best military mind the Rasna had available to them will be dead before nightfall."

Unwittingly, every head turned to look between the columns of the meeting room, out towards the west. They all saw what Velthur already knew: the sun was kissing the mountains. Numesi was, most likely, already dead at some Roman's feet, just another forgotten body. They probably didn't even know the extent of the damage they'd done to the Rasna, the importance of the man they'd killed in that tiny village.

"It seems that you disapprove of our decision," the delegate from Pupluna said.

"I think that throwing away our best military commander to buy an extra few hours for a doomed city might not have been the best decision. But we've been over this already, and it's not something we can fix." He gave the man a hard glare. "We need to start thinking ahead, moving forward."

"Are you saying we need to abandon Veii?" the head of the council—the matronly patriarch of one of Veii's noble houses, a woman with more than a little Tarchna blood—demanded.

"I will leave that decision to the exalted Council. I don't plan to be here to suffer the consequences of what you will inevitably decree. I'm leaving tonight."

Shouts of "What?" and "Treason!" filled the room. But no one dared move towards him. All present were well aware that if it came down to it, every soldier in Etruria would obey Velthur the Conqueror without hesitation. Besides, though many of the men in the room wore the traditional short swords, none would be foolhardy enough to challenge him.

He waited for the commotion to die down. "As a military commander, it is my opinion that the city is lost." The murmurs rose again, and he patiently awaited their end. Only now did he allow any passion to reach his voice. "Listen to me. You, all of you, whether you're from Veii or from one of the other cities, needs to stop thinking of the cities first and of everyone else later. Right now, we're fighting for the survival of the Rasna. Our people face a choice: to fight for our precious towns and be enslaved individually, or to join together as we never have and resist as one. The second choice is the only hope for a Rasna homeland to continue existing in half a year." He looked over the cowed faces, silently measuring each. "That decision is yours, but I've made mine already. My troops and I are leaving."

This wasn't a crippling blow if the city decided to stand and fight. Velthur had less than a hundred men under his command. A single Roman first cohort was a larger force. But the message it would send to the remaining soldiers would be clear.

"What will you do?"

"Do? We'll hold our city, of course," the matron said. The rest of the council echoed her words, while the representatives of the other cities remained silent. This wasn't their fight.

The motion passed without opposition and Velthur turned to leave. "You are fools. Brave fools, but fools all the same." He turned to go.

"Wait." He turned to see Sethra walking towards him. "Where are you going?"

"Back to Volsinii, to confer with my family. They will help me decide what happens next."

"I want to go with you. Can you arrange safe passage to Volsinii for my household?"

"If you can get them packed before midnight, I will wait."

He expected excuses and pleading. She surprised him. "They are already packed. We can leave whenever you want." The surprise must have shown on his face. "You may not like our decisions, Velthur, but all of us listen when you speak, and all of us respect your opinion on military matters. I would never vote against the wishes of the council on something of this magnitude, but my personal affairs are my own concern. And in this case, I have decided that the advice of the military is the wisdom I should be following." She turned back to the rest of them. "Keep our city strong. If you prevail, I will return to thank you." She paused. "And if you don't, I will keep our memory alive."

She crossed in front of Velthur, and he got a close look at her face. He was certain that of all those present, he was the only one who saw her tears.

• • •

Preparations to march his men out of the city were well underway when he reached the barracks. The horses were saddled or in their traces, the men were lined up for inspection. Slaves were still loading the final bundles onto the wagons—still some time away from finishing the task, but that wasn't because they were moving slowly. Quite the contrary: the normally lethargic porters were moving at a decent clip. It seemed that the prospect of being killed by Roman spears made them slightly more enthusiastic about their hard work.

Sepu approached. "What's the mood? Will they let us out?"

"If it were up to the council, they'd mount our heads on spikes and feed our entrails to the carrion-fowl. But I think the soldiers will let us through, and if you can't deal with the civilians...then you're the wrong man for your job."

"Do you think it will come to that? Killing our own?"

"No, I don't. I suspect that half the garrison will try to come with us."

"Desert their posts, you mean?"

"Yes."

"And you will allow it? You'd allow deserters to fight with us?"

He gave his friend and right-hand man a long look. Then he sighed. "Right now, the Rasna need any man willing to fight. With or without honor. Dead or alive."

Mention of the wights, the so-called Swords of the Rasna, ended the discussion. Sepu hated them with a passion that he couldn't disguise. The main difference between the two men on that point was that Velthur was more than willing to accept anything that might give him an advantage. Any advantage.

"Is the boy here?" Velthur asked his lieutenant.

"The one Numesi sent? What about him?"

"Give him a spear and a uniform and tell him he's a soldier now."

Sepu gave him a look that spoke volumes. His lieutenant knew exactly what Velthur was doing—knew that taking a green boy, barely out of swaddling, into an elite unit was just his way of getting the boy out of the city before the Romans arrived. But the other man said nothing. He also knew Velthur well enough to save his breath and not start arguments he wouldn't win. "There's also some woman here," he said instead. "Says you agreed to give her safe passage to Volsinii. By the look of her, I assumed she was telling the truth. And if she wasn't, I'll give her safe passage myself." Sepu leered at him.

Velthur ignored the jibe. "Is her household ready for the march, or will they slow us down?"

"They looked readier than we are. Everything packed, a couple of ceremonial guards keeping the rabble off, and even the children tucked into wagons. They'll be alright."

It confirmed what Velthur had suspected. Sethra Zalthu—a leading light of Veii society with few friends anywhere else—had long since decided to abandon her only power base and attempt to survive through whatever gold she could bring with her and whatever charity she might receive elsewhere. Or perhaps she was betting on those big black eyes and the curves which her robes failed to conceal. She seemed just the kind of girl to appeal to one of the Tarchna lords...but there were few of those in Volsinii, and they had few friends anywhere else. The League of Twelve Cities still blamed Tarchna for invading Roman territory and rekindling the war.

And if she was aiming for a Volsinii lord...Velthur decided not to think about that. With the death of his brother, he was the next in line to his mother's position. Perhaps this girl, alone among the Veii nobles, was able to truly think strategically about her position and act decisively to improve her position. He suspected he might soon find out just how decisively.

He shook his head to clear it of unwelcome visions of darkened rooms and dark eyes in the throes of finely calculated passion. He had a war to fight against an implacable enemy with more men, better training, and better equipment than his. He didn't have time to be distracted with trivialities.

That didn't stop him from taking a long, speculative look at Sethra as they left the city, however.

Printed in Great Britain
by Amazon

22873466R00225